ATONED

The Wardens: Book 1

Steve J. McHugh

Hidden Realms Publishing.

Copyright © 2023 Steve McHugh

This is a work of fiction. Names, characters, organizations, places, events, and incidents are either products of the author's imagination or are used fictitiously. Any resemblance to actual persons, living or dead, or actual events is purely coincidental. Text copyright © 2023 by Steve McHugh

All rights reserved.

No part of this book may be reproduced, or stored in a retrieval system, or transmitted in any form or by any means, electronic, mechanical, photocopying, recording, or otherwise, without express written permission of the publisher.

For avoidance of doubt, Author reserves the rights, and no publisher or platform has the rights to reproduce and/or otherwise use the Work in any manner for purposes of training artificial intelligence technologies to generate text, including without limitation, technologies that are capable of generating works in the same style or genre as the Work, unless the Author's specific and express permission to do so.

Published by Hidden Realms Publishing

Cover illustration by Jamie Noble Frier

For My Dad

CONTENTS

Title Page
Copyright
Dedication
List of Characters 3
Chapter One 7
Chapter Two 17
Chapter Three 31
Chapter Four 46
Chapter Five 59
Chapter Six 71
Chapter Seven 84
Chapter Eight 95
Chapter Nine 103
Chapter Ten 118
Chapter Eleven 129
Chapter Twelve 136
Chapter Thirteen 147
Chapter Fourteen 158
Chapter Fifteen 171
Chapter Sixteen 186
Chapter Seventeen 197

Chapter Eighteen	208
Chapter Nineteen	217
Chapter Twenty	227
Chapter Twenty-One	240
Chapter Twenty-Two	251
Chapter Twenty-Three	263
Chapter Twenty-Four	271
Chapter Twenty-Five	281
Chapter Twenty-Six	292
Chapter Twenty-Seven	305
Chapter Twenty-Eight	317
Chapter Twenty-Nine	331
Chapter Thirty	340
Chapter Thirty-One	356
Chapter Thirty-Two	369
Chapter Thirty-Three	379
Chapter Thirty-Four	391
Acknowledgements	395
About The Author	397

Also By Steve McHugh

The Hellequin Chronicles

Crimes Against Magic
Born of Hatred
With Silent Screams
Prison of Hope
Lies Ripped Open
Promise of Wrath
Scorched Shadows
Infamous Reign
Frozen Rage

The Avalon Chronicles

A Glimmer of Hope
A Flicker of Steel
A Thunder of War
Hunted

The Rebellion Chronicles

Sorcery Reborn
Death Unleashed
Horsemen's War

Riftborn

The Last Raven
Blessed Odds
A Talon's Wrath

As Steve J. McHugh

Blackcoat

LIST OF CHARACTERS

The Wardens

Felix Drake: Human. Sage. Warden team leader.
Celine Moro: Human. Warden Commander.
Dai'ix: Oreaf. Warden team member.
Luca Ridge: Human. Warden team member. Brother to Rollos.
Rollos Ridge. Human. Warden team member. Brother to Luca.
Tuck: Half-human, half sarcian. Warden team member.
Rosie: Human. Warden team member.
Sateri: Sarcian. Warden team member.

Trackers

Jaysa Benezta: Sarcian. Captain of *Tracked Retribution*.
Etamus: Dreic. Second-in-Command on *Tracked Retribution*.
Yanton: Sarcian. Doctor on *Tracked Retribution*.
Kayos: Human. Pilot on *Tracked Retribution*

Royal Family

Jubei: Human. Sage. King of Stars.
Miyako Wynn: Human. Sage. Queen.
Hideo Wynn: Human. Sage. Prince.
Kimi Wynn: Human. Sage. Princess.
Norio Kong: Human. Sage. Prince.
Ren Summers: Human. Sage. Princess.
Ryota Kong: Human. Sage. Prince.
Takumi Summers: Human. Sage. Prince.

The Union Empire

Helice Tranton: Human. Sage. Daughter of Union Councillor.
Septimus Mowatt: Human. Son of Union Councillor.
Gret: Sarcian. Suns Watch Officer.
Whesker: Human. Guard.

Others

Alastia Sark: Human. Sage. Unknown Allegiance.
Bokk: Seventh-generation security synth. Owned by Felix Drake.
Ramin Gossard: Human. Crime Boss. Father to Sabas.
Sabas Gossard: Human. Criminal. Son to Ramin.
Radnar Puley: Human. Lawyer. Works for Ramin Gossard.
Xendo: Prototype Synth. Owned by Union Council.

The worst thing you can do to someone who excels at killing, is give them a reason to never stop.

Unknown Atoned master

CHAPTER ONE

Sabas Gossard

Two-dozen large dorsal fins broke the water as fourteen people in military-spec combat armour stood on the bank of the lake tossing bodies in, the strong current immediately carrying them toward deeper waters where the sharks waited for their next meal.

Sabas Gossard watched the gruesome display from atop a stone bridge, a hundred feet above the lake itself. He continued to watch as the bodies were thrown into the lake. It was horrific and terrifying, but Sabas couldn't turn away. He watched as the town of Onnab's dead became food for those monstrous creatures beneath the darkness of the water.

A forest nestled beside the lake, and the barren tundra to the south stretched for hundreds of kilometres. Onnab had been built to allow the population to mine the nearby mountains, and they'd done a good job. Being so far from anything close to civilisation also meant they were in an excellent place to be manipulated into doing exactly what Sabas' partners needed them to do.

Onnab had been home to a little over four thousand

people. One of the few towns on the planet of Ocrion, the majority of which were all there to mine the vast mountain reaches. Men, women, and children living in a thriving mining community in a quiet part of Union space.

All dead.

When Sabas had been informed of the deaths, he'd assumed something a lot more dramatic than the empty streets he'd walked though upon arriving. He'd wondered why there were no corpses. No blood. No scent of death. Although there was a sharp, pungent odour he couldn't quite place.

Doors to homes were open, food on tables that had been left to rot explained the caustic scent. Visi-screens showed nothing but static as the satellite system for the city of Onnab had been destroyed. No one had been able to get a message out about what had happened, and the vast distances and general distrust between towns meant people minded their own business. A saving grace.

It had been eerily quiet.

Sabas had the sudden need to be off the bridge but this was where he was told to meet her, and he was not about to become the first living meal for those monsters in the lake.

He was still a little unsure exactly *what* had happened to the town. He'd heard that everyone had died, and been told to come to the planet quickly, but no one had explained what he would be walking into. They'd said it was safe, but that was the extent of their imparted knowledge.

While Sabas had arrived on-planet with his three bodyguards, he'd left them back at the small space port. Two ships had been moored there, both squire corvette's—sleek, red and chrome ships with seats for four—and both with extensive plasma burns around the engines and wings. Neither would fly again.

He was a little sad about that. The ships had done nothing wrong, and both looked like something he would have enjoyed flying. He cared little about the human or alien population of Onnab, but destroying expensive property for no reason just seemed... wasteful. If there was one lesson he'd actually learned from his father—other than shoot first—it was to not be wasteful.

It was a fifteen-minute walk from the port to the meeting point. Onnab was a warm city on a mostly warm planet, and the walk was almost entirely up a gentle incline. Sabas was not a small man. Prison had given him time to do little else but train his muscles, his mind, and devise ways he was going to kill everyone who had put in him in his cell. He stood six-and-a-half-feet tall, and weighed nearly three hundred pounds of almost solid, albeit surgically-enhanced muscle.

Sabas removed his navy jacket, and rolled up the sleeves on his white shirt, the latter of which was probably a size too small. Colourful tattoos covered both arms, depicting mythological creatures of a time when stories told of heroes testing themselves against such things. He'd always wanted to prove himself against the best. He'd done just that for several years before his arrest, although the vast majority of people he'd encountered hadn't lived up to expectations.

The sun was high in the cloudless blue sky, and it was as hot as it was going to get. Sabas wanted to be done by nightfall, when the temperature plunged and the creatures that lived in the nearby forest came out to hunt. He ran a large, tanned hand over his bald head, and wished that his contact would hurry up. Although, he would *never* tell her to do such a thing.

Then Sabas spotted his contact, and her own bodyguards. Alastia Sark was about as close to a monster as Sabas had ever actually met. She was probably the only person who genuinely scared him.

The woman was slight of build, with pale skin, and wore dark ion-armour—a lightweight plating useful against projectiles, but almost pointless against bladed weapons—with several buckles across her chest and stomach. The colour was a stark contrast to her white-blonde hair, which cascaded over her shoulders. A sheathed sword hung from her hip, and she wore two magnus bracers.

Sabas stared at the dark-brown, leather-fibre bracers covered in metal rivets – they gave an imposing look. About halfway up each bracer sat a gemstone roughly three inches in circumference; both were currently dark as there was no power being used.

He had not met Alastia in person for the entirety of his five years in prison, but he'd never forgotten she was a Sage – powerful beings, capable of using aether. This inherent power gave them a connection to The Aperture, a dimension of pure energy that sat alongside their own. The magnus bracer allowed Sage to control their aether. Without the bracer, the aether would be wild and unpredictable, dangerous to its user and everyone around them.

The gem in a magnus bracer was dark until the Sage activated their aether. Once that happened, the gem glowed a different colour—the same as their eyes—depending on the type of aether used.

There was a time when sage meant someone who had obtained wisdom. Sabas was certain not all Sage could be considered such things, but he did know that every single Sage was dangerous.

"See something interesting?" Alastia asked, her tone conversational with a hint of amusement at Sabas' obvious discomfort.

"The people of Onnab?" Sobas asked, glancing at her trio of bodyguards. They wore predator-armour, specialised helmeted suits designed to protect the wearer from all but the most powerful of ordinance. They were all black, with three warm-grey slashes across their helmets and chests, as if a large creature had attacked them. The armour was heavy, and slowed the wearer, but it was quite literally designed to take a beating and hit you back harder than you could imagine.

All carried coil rifles, each one capable of firing a dozen incendiary projectiles within seconds. They were the weapon of choice for the Union military; reliable, accurate, and used to great effect throughout the worlds that made up the Union Empire.

The three bodyguards looked over at Sabas, the red lenses on their helmets flashing as they stared. They made

Sabas uncomfortable, not just because they were taller by at least a foot, and heavily outweighed him. Not because he didn't have anything on him that could do little more than scratch them. And not even because they neither spoke nor removed their helmets so he could see their faces. What made Sabas uncomfortable was that no one should be able to get predator-armour except the highest ranks of the Union Empire. Even then it was kept to the military. How did someone like Alastia get hold of high-grade military tech? It was a question Sabas had asked himself often over the years.

"Had to get rid of them somehow," Alastia said, leaning against the bridge parapet to watch the feeding. "The sharks here are voracious. I don't actually know their type. I assume big shark is probably not their name."

"Was this necessary?" Sabas asked, motioning to the town of Onnab. "Lots of dead."

"Do you know why we work with you and your people?" Alastia asked.

"Because I'm rich, I have connections, and I don't ask..." Sabas nodded. "Yes, fine, but on this occasion, you called *me* here."

"A fair point," Alastia agreed. "Walk with me." She looked over to her guards. "Stay here."

All three nodded once.

It took every ounce of self-control for Sabas not to stare at them as he walked by.

"You were in jail a long time," Alastia said from where she walked at his side along the lengthy bridge. "Five years for killing a Warden is much shorter than I'd expected."

"I was innocent," Sabas said in a tone of someone who had repeated it so often he'd actually started to believe it. "They found the guilty party. They'd left an authenticated suicide note when the guilt finally got to them."

"Your father pulled strings then," Alastia said with a slight chuckle.

"My *father*," Sabas said, his patience tested. "Did fuck all to get me out of prison. Do you plan on answering my questions, or is this some kind of therapy session?" The words left his mouth with more force than he'd meant, and fear rippled through him.

Alastia stopped walking, turned to Sabas and laughed. "If I didn't find you so entertaining, I'd have killed you by now. Anyway, you're right, I asked you to come here. Explanations are in order."

"And the sharks?" Sabas asked.

Alastia's smile made Sabas' skin crawl. "I wanted to ensure you understand the order of things. Why am I here?"

The question caught Sabas by surprise, and he stayed confused for several seconds. "Isn't that what I just asked?"

Alastia sighed. "A decade ago, we entered into an agreement. We both wanted the same thing, neither of us asked why the other wanted it, but that's not the point. We needed muscle. We needed power. Onnab was chosen partly because of its relative size and population density, partly because the mayor here is a corrupt piece of horseshit, and partly because… well, because of what these idiots found."

Sabas couldn't help himself. "You're talking about the catacombs?"

"I am," Alastia said. "We have been taking people from this city for a decade. People who were *officially* stated as having died in the mountains, or from sickness. We took those the mayor said were drafted by the Union. Others without families who came here to work and earn a living, who wanted to escape Union eyes. We spiked their water, their food, we conducted experiments on this city unknown to a single inhabitant. We took the animals from their forests and did unspeakable things to them. The city of Onnab treated us well without ever really knowing it. We made them better humans, gave them enhancements that made them sleep less, eat less, work harder. We pumped hundreds of millions of credits into this little place. And the whole time we had no idea they were sat on something so… important."

"I assume you're not going to tell me more than I already know," Sabas said.

Alastia looked over at him. "I could tell you, if you'd like, but then you'd have to go for a swim."

Sabas glanced down at the fins again and decided quickly. "I'm good."

Alastia looked slightly disappointed. "Smart man. I called you here to inform you that our deal is done. We have a gift for you, and it will be sent to your ship on your agreement. Other than that, we have concluded our involvement. We will remove all traces of your company, Expedited Systems, from this planet."

"That's it?" Sabas asked, struggling to stop his irritation despite how unwise it was. "I gave you vast amounts of money to make a weapon for me."

"Which we have done," Alastia said, her voice calm. "We gave you the preliminary findings years ago. You went to prison, and we continued in earnest to work on the project. We have made great strides in that time. The weapon, and all of the research we conducted on it, are yours. You will never come to this planet again. You will never mention this planet, or my name, or anything about our agreement. To anyone. Ever."

Sabas knew Alastia was unarmed with conventional weaponry, but he also knew that she could kill him with a click of her fingers. He looked back at the trio of bodyguards, who were staring at them both. Sabas had been brought halfway across the Union Empire to be told his services and his money were no longer needed. Alastia had done this to show him exactly where he stood in the pecking order, and exactly who was in charge of this operation. She'd threatened his way of life. He hated and admired her for it.

"How'd you kill everyone?" Sabas asked. "Idle curiosity."

"They killed themselves," she said. "One of the strains we'd gotten into their system was designed to kill them should we need. Combined with a toxin we created and pumped into the atmosphere, we killed everything in that town in about three minutes. We took those we wanted out first, of course. The mayor for example. Those we felt could advance our work. Everyone else was expendable."

"It's been a pleasure," Sabas said, unsure what else to say, and offered his hand.

Alastia stepped forward and shook his hand firmly. "If you ever speak of what was done here, I will personally hunt you down and make you watch as I kill your entire family."

Sabas stared at Alastia's smiling expression and tried to pull his hand away, but she kept a tight hold.

"And when I'm done," she continued. "I will give you to our greatest scientific minds and they can flay you alive while you undergo every conceivable surgery to see what happens."

"I understand," Sabas said, no longer sweating just because of the heat.

Alastia's smile widened, and she released his hand, stepping away. "Good. We'll sort all of this out. There won't be a trace, I assure you. Thank you for your assistance over the years, please do enjoy our gifts."

Sabas couldn't have gotten off that planet quicker.

CHAPTER TWO

Felix Drake

Drake heard the shouting as he exited the elevator and began the short walk along the hallway of the two-hundred-and-thirty-seventh floor of the skyblock he called home. There were four other apartments on his floor, one occupied by an elderly married couple—Estana and Kamri—who in Drake's estimation, were pleasant enough to talk to in short bursts. The second was a forty-something single businessman whose name Drake couldn't even remember. The third were a young family with their year-old baby, and Drake was grateful the walls between apartments were sound proofed.

The charcoal-coloured metal door to their apartment opened as Drake walked by it, and the two women inside waved to him the moment they caught his eye. He waved back, as one of them—the shorter of the two, with long, pink hair—motioned for him to stop. He did, and knew exactly what they wanted to talk to him about.

"Can you hear that?" she asked.

"Sele," the second woman called out. "We've called the authorities."

"So?" Sele asked without turning back to her wife. "Drake is a Blackcoat, Rhina. He can help."

"I'm not a Blackcoat," Drake said. "Never have been."

Sele looked slightly taken aback. "You still investigate crimes."

Drake reluctantly nodded; Sele was correct about that much. "I'm still not a Blackcoat," he said. "Although, maybe I can help."

"If they want to go at it all day, just keep their door shut. It's not hard." Sele sounded exasperated, and Drake sympathised. Not just because of the noise, which no soundproofing could stop when people argued with their door wide open.

Drake wondered if anyone in the nine inhabited floors above floor two-thirty-seven, could hear the racket the inhabitants of apartment number four made. "I'll have a word," he promised. "Either way, call the Watch and they'll send someone over to have a second word."

Sele smiled, and Rhina silently mouthed thank you as she rocked the baby boy on her hip.

Their door closed and Drake sighed. Did he have time to take the bag he was carrying home before dealing with the fourth and final apartment on his floor? He decided that if he went home, he'd just not want to leave again. He dropped his bag off in front of his own apartment door and continued around the corner of the hallway to the sounds of cursing coming from the open apartment door.

Drake didn't know the names of the man and woman who lived there, he'd never bothered to learn them. To him, they were Noise One and Noise Two. He hoped this didn't get out of control, as domestics were wont to do. Especially when someone in a position of authority arrived to try and calm the situation. He stood in front of the open door and watched the man and woman shout at one another. The man was maybe thirty, with short dark hair, and pale skin. He was muscular and clean-shaven, and from what Drake had witnessed, always walked around with an expression of perpetual anger.

The woman was about his height, with long brown and green hair that was plaited down her back. There was a small neural interface on her temple, which meant she'd probably had some kind of augmentation for allowing her to access computer systems.

"You can't help yourself, can you?" the man shouted. "Flirting with everything that moves."

"You're the one who can't keep his dick out of other women," the woman shouted back.

Drake sighed and cleared his throat.

Both spun toward him. "What do you want?" the man asked.

"If you're going to fight, you could close the door," Drake suggested.

"Oh, could I?" the man said. "Maybe I don't want to. Maybe I want everyone here to know what a cheating little whore I married." He turned to his wife. "That's right, I know. I know it all. I have pictures."

"That you probably jerk off to," the woman snapped back.

"Seriously, close the door," Drake interjected.

The man stormed over. He was a good few inches taller than Drake's own six-feet-one, and probably outweighed him by a considerable amount, but Drake wasn't worried. He moved his long, black jacket aside slightly, showing the badge clipped to his belt, along with the G71s viper-class energy pistol sat in the quick-release holster against his hip. When the man refused to look, Drake pointed down.

The man's gaze dropped, slowly, his eyes widening in fright. Drake knew it wasn't the gun, and that the man was unable to see the energy dagger that sat against his other hip. He was never going to draw his weapons on two people being loud. And he was pretty sure he could take them both without the need to fire a shot. No, Drake knew that it was the badge that had drawn the fear in the man's eyes.

The star shimmered different amounts of red and orange depending on how the light struck it. Drake's name sat at the bottom of the badge in black, standing out against the vibrant colour.

"You're a Warden?" the man managed to get out, licking his lips and clearly wishing he was somewhere else.

"Want to keep your door closed when you fight?" Drake kept his tone neutral.

The man nodded.

"You going all wimp on me?" his wife called out. "Why haven't you hit him?"

The man turned around, allowing his wife to see the badge for the first time. Her complexion suddenly paled. "We're sorry," she said a second later. "We didn't know one of your... station was living on this floor."

"Just try to keep the noise down," Drake said.

Both occupants nodded furiously, and Drake walked away, the door quickly closing behind him. He walked back to his apartment, gathered his synthetic paper bag before placing his palm on the door reader. The door moved aside, allowing Drake entry.

The apartment was spacious but felt much larger considering he still hadn't unpacked from arriving on the planet of Atharoth—the capital city of the Union Empire—six months earlier. Croleni was the largest city on the planet, and a place Drake now called home. He hadn't been happy to move to Atharoth, far from it, but he was here now. Unfortunately, his apathy of having to move a quarter way across the galaxy to his new home hadn't quite yet left him.

Drake glanced at the metal-fibre crates piled up in the corner of the hallway just beyond the door. He'd get round to unpacking when he had time. Next to the crates was a synth recharging point, although BOKK, the synth in question, was nowhere to be seen.

Beyond the hallway was a large open room with floor-to-ceiling tinted windows along one side, showcasing incredible views of a city that never slept. Nor paused for breath. A variety of vehicles flew along the marked lanes between the skyblocks, hovering illuminated signs showing directions. The lanes were the same as any roads for any vehicles on the ground, and Drake took a short while to watch the ballet of vehicles as they continued their never-ending movement. Like bees in a hive.

Inside the room, Drake had a comfortable sofa, an old armchair that had once belonged to his mother, and a large visi-screen on the wall. A faux-wood table sat in the middle of the room, with several boxes of unfinished model ships piled up in the corner, awaiting the time that Drake never seemed to have.

There were two doors inside the living room, one to the left contained the small, but well-stocked kitchen, and to the right was a second hallway leading to two bedrooms and a good-sized bathroom.

"Evening, Bokk," Drake called out as he placed the white bag on the kitchen counter, removing the meat and vegetables and putting them in the fridge for later.

He walked back into the living room and removed all of his weapons, placing the dagger and pistol on the counter beside him. The G24 viper class was standard Warden issue. Drake used a modified version usually reserved for high impact special operation units; the G71s. A quick-draw weapon with incredible stopping power. Unlike the standard G24, that had to have its heat-core ejected after twenty-six shots before overheating, the G71s only managed fourteen shots. Still, Drake had never met anything that needed more than fourteen shots to put down, and if something did need that kind of firepower, the snub-nose blast pistol in his shoulder holster would do the job.

After showering, and getting changed in his bedroom—that at the moment contained a bed, and enough storage for his clothes, but nothing to suggest he actually lived there—Drake headed back into the living room. It was the only room in the house he'd spent time decorating, mostly so he didn't come home from a long day to anything dreary.

Drake switched on the large visi-screen and flicked through the channels to find a film to watch, eventually settling on something with a plot so flimsy he barely had to pay attention to follow.

"Do I need to activate myself these days?" The voice was synthetic, although it still managed to convey emotion. Something it had taken Drake a long time to get used to.

Bokk walked out of the hallway, and sat on a chair opposite Drake. It was a seventh-generation security synth, and had been a present from Drake's father thirty-five years ago, probably the last thing ever given him. Well, apart from a need to keep his father's identity secret. He didn't need the hassle of the inevitable whispers and glares that would occur if his true parentage were discovered. That was the gift that just never got old, and the reason he told as few people as possible about who he was.

The synth stood five and a half feet tall, painted dark green with yellow and brown patches, which made him look like he'd been painted for camouflage purposes. The small lights that signified his eyes glowed burnt-orange. Like all seventh-generation security synths, Bokk was a stocky model and capable of defending both itself and its owners without pause. Drake had made a few modifications to it over the years, although most would have been legally considered a grey area. Unfortunately for some, all seventh-generation security synths had a tendency to develop personalities. It was why they'd been replaced so quickly, and were now cheap to buy. Drake had never once considered changing Bokk; doing so wasn't an upgrade in his eyes.

Bokk stood and turned around, and Drake's gaze fell to the serial number—B1-04-KK117—printed on the back of their left shoulder. They straightened one of the framed photos on the wall that changed picture every few seconds. It had been a farewell gift. Drake wasn't certain his old commander hadn't thrown a party when he'd finally left.

"You know, you could just let me decorate," Bokk said. "At least it would give me something to do."

Bokk had given the impression he'd like to decorate for the

last few months, and so far, Drake had managed to avoid it. It wasn't that Bokk couldn't be trusted, but seventh-generation security droids were not meant to be able to decorate an apartment. Drake might not have a lot of friends but if anyone did come over, they might wonder when he'd had the time to decorate considering he was always at work.

"I'm taking a week off in a month," Drake said. "Then we'll do the whole place."

If Bokk had a mouth instead of a line of dotted lights, they would have smiled, Drake was certain of it.

"It's been a long day." Drake rubbed his eyes with the heel of his palms.

"You're back several hours earlier than usual," Bokk said.

"I meant emotionally," Drake said. "Since coming back here, my job seems to consist of having to put up with a lot more Council nonsense than ever before. I know my job means I have to deal with Council members and their families, but politics isn't exactly my idea of a good time. On top of that, it's been a month since Sabas Gossard was released from prison, and he hasn't actually committed any crimes I'm aware of. I'm wondering if he's just biding his time."

"Ah," Bokk said. "Did you go see him?"

"I'm officially not allowed anywhere near him," Drake reminded the synth.

Bokk made a noise that might have been agreement. "You broke several of his bones according to the report."

Drake stared at Bokk for several seconds. "You shouldn't be snooping around secure reports."

"Let's pretend I didn't then," Bokk eventually said. "So, his release upsets you?"

"He murdered at least one Warden. He's getting out because he has friends in high places, or people who are easily threatened or bribed." Drake sighed. "It hasn't been the best day."

Bokk made an affirmative noise, which sounded like the jingle of a little bell. "From the large number of movies I've been able to watch, it appears that people in your job should have some sort of vice. Maybe that would help."

"No, Bokk, that wouldn't help. Besides, I have a vice." Drake motioned toward the several large spaceship models that sat on a nearby counter.

Bokk didn't turn to look. "I think most vices, by their very definition, are more destructive than model ship building."

"And now do you see why I do ship building instead?" Drake headed into the kitchen, where he prepared a meal for himself. After eating, he spent the rest of the evening watching bad movies on the visi-screen before going to bed, and immediately falling asleep.

When his comm-unit went off three hours later, resounding throughout the apartment, he woke groggy and managed to answer it before the noise drilled too far into his brain. The turquoise-coloured numbers of his wall clock read 2:42 am. "I actually got an early night," he said as he slotted the earpiece in place.

"Sorry, Drake, but you're needed." The voice belonged to his boss, Celine Moro.

She had been a Blackcoat on a factory planet by the name of Estra, and had almost single-handedly brought down its corrupt government. While it had nearly gotten her killed, it had also gotten her a job with the Wardens, where her reputation for taking no shit from anyone had seen her rise quickly through the ranks.

The Blackcoats were investigators of the highest calibre and were meant to be untouchable. Celine's time on Estra had shown that to not be the case, and Drake knew she found trusting people difficult. He also knew she trusted him, and it was something he felt he had to live up to.

Celine was a fair boss; she listened and was keen to create a good working atmosphere.

"Can you tell me exactly what happened?" Drake asked as he swung his legs out of bed, feet resting on the cold, faux-wooden floor.

"I'll explain when you get here. I've sent the details to your comm. Don't bring your synth." The line went dead, and Drake dropped the earpiece onto the charging dock next to his bed. Dread filled his chest; had Sabas or one of his gangster friends done something?

It took him five minutes to get dressed in a black suit and white shirt, grabbing hold of his long, dark-grey jacket before he left the apartment. It took another two for the elevator to take him down to the ground floor of the building. True to Celine's word, she'd sent the address to his comm unit. He tapped the screen, and it automatically gave him directions. It would be an hour's walk, so he took a grav-cab – the automated hover vehicle provided a smooth ride to his destination, despite his never-wavering anxiety.

A crowd had gathered outside of the older building. The place was only a dozen-storeys high, and in a neighbourhood where the local Blackcoats usually took their time in attending calls. Rumours of investment had meant it was an almost-slum, with increasingly expensive housing. A bad combination.

As the grav-cab lowered itself to the road, Drake spotted Celine at the bottom of a set of stairs leading up to the front door. When he left the cab, the opening salvo of raindrops hit his cheek. He sighed, and pushed his way past the civilians, flashing his badge to the Blackcoats who were given the unenviable duty of crowd control.

"So, what happened?" Drake asked.

"Come inside," Celine told him.

She was slightly shorter than Drake, with pale skin, an athletic build, and dark brown hair that fell over her shoulders. Celine was sixty, although looked to be forty, at most. Considering the number of genetic, medical, and biological treatments humans could go through, their lifespan was generally put at about two hundred years, and the richer you were the higher that number rose.

The elegant dark blue shirt and black trousers Celine wore

had metal fibre sown into the garments. Drake knew they could stop a blast-gun at close range. Drake's jacket was made of the same substance.

"Three dead," Celine said, as she stood with Drake in the empty foyer while the rain outside increased in ferocity. "And at least one of them is a Council member, or from one of their families."

The job of a Warden was to investigate and deal with crimes committed by, and against, members of the ruling Council, or their families. Their jurisdiction also included the King of Stars and his royal family, something that had often caused contention over the years. They were given almost complete power to go anywhere they wished on the planet of Atharoth – the centre of power for the entire Union. On one occasion even arresting a member of the royal household, although nothing like that had happened in decades.

"Do we have any ideas on who might have done this?" Drake asked.

"No," Celine told him. "But then, we don't know who the victims are."

Drake was confused. "You don't know? How is that possible?"

"There's no ID," Celine said.

Drake turned to see Rollos Ridge and his younger brother Luca walk into the foyer. Both had been on his team for several years, and he was glad to see them. Rollos was the larger of the two, although they were both six and a half feet tall, and muscular enough to make anyone think twice about picking a fight. Rollos had dark skin and a baldhead, with a beard that he'd taken to platting. His dark blue suit strained at the seams, and his badge and viper pistol sat against one hip, with an energy dagger on the other.

Luca was clean-shaven, and appeared unassuming in a black shirt and dark-grey trousers. However, Luca carried two plasma knives on the back of his belt, along with a viper-class pistol. Drake had seen Luca use those same knives on people who had deserved it.

Good to see you, Drake. Luca's voice infiltrated Drake's head.

Luca was genetically enhanced. At some point he had been taken into military custody and experimented on, giving him the ability to speak telepathically, and enhancing various parts of his physiology. Luca was one of the few gen-en around; most had been killed or vanished without a trace when the military's experiments had come to light a decade earlier.

"You too," Drake said.

"I honestly thought we were going to have a quiet night," Rollos said, his voice a deep baritone that echoed around the foyer.

"So, anyone want to tell me why we can't ID these people?" Drake asked. "No ID is something I haven't come across in years. These people still have blood, so do a test and see who comes up."

"Thanks for the explanation," Celine said dryly. "We can't do that, because there's no way *to* do that."

Drake couldn't believe what he'd heard. "What?"

"They were injected with something various criminal minds are calling 'chameleon'. The drug makes a trace through normal means impossible. It gives false reads of blood types, molecule and acid readings, everything."

Drake had heard something about the drug since arriving back in Croleni but hadn't actually come across it himself. "So, we have zero idea who the victims are?"

"That's right," Rollos said.

"So, what's the plan?" Drake asked Celine.

She smiled. "You're going up there with Rollos and Luca to look around. I'll be accompanying you."

Drake raised an eyebrow in question. It was an odd thing to suggest. Normally, his team would all go into the room. "Why? And where's the rest of the team?"

"I only contacted Rollos," Celine admitted. "As for why, this could be an important case, and I want to see your first impression of it all."

Drake shrugged. "Let's get it over with then."

They took one of the elevators up to the twelfth floor, where they were met by several uniformed Watch officers who were busy interviewing neighbours and checking the hallway for clues.

"This is an all-hands-on-deck situation," Drake said. "Why not bring in the rest of the team?"

"You'll see," Celine told him, her tone making it clear the conversation was officially over.

Drake, Rollos, and Luca followed Celine down the hallway; nodding to several Watch officers they passed, until they found themselves in a large apartment.

"Drake, look around and tell me what you see," Celine said from the edge of the room.

He was beginning to think that something really was up with Celine, but he couldn't quite figure out what it might be. Was she evaluating him for something?

He pushed the thought aside and removed two small metal bracelets from his pockets, placing them on his wrists and tapping each in turn. A thin layer of medi-skin slid over his hands. It was essentially the same as using gloves, but they were translucent. Each bracelet held enough of the compound to last for several months without needing to be replenished.

The apartment consisted of a living area—with dining, living room, and kitchen in one—a single bedroom, and one bathroom according to the data Celine had sent over on his comm. Drake walked around the main living area and found nothing of note. No pictures, no data-pads, nothing to suggest the identities of the victims. The kitchen and dining area were the same. Like the main living area, they were pokey, designed for the minimal number of people possible.

He walked down the hallway, saying hello to those Watch officers he knew by face, if not by name, and entered the bathroom. The two officers inside left him alone with the body in the bathtub. The tub had been white, or cream at some point, although now it was covered in so much blood it was hard to tell.

The man in the tub was human, Caucasian, with tattoos adorning his blood-covered torso. There were dozens of deep lacerations across his chest and arms, and at some point, his attackers had partially scalped him. His fingertips were missing, although Drake had no way of telling at that moment if they were taken post-mortem or not.

Two bullet holes sat above the victim's heart, along with a third in his forehead, directly between his eyes. The burn marks surroundings the holes were in keeping with an energy weapon, possibly something similar to the viper Drake used.

"What did you find?" Celine asked from the bathroom entrance.

Drake looked between Celine and the dead body. "He was tortured in the bathtub. There are needle marks on his arms. He was injected with something, presumably this chameleon drug you told me about. Then he was killed. Where are the other two?"

Celine stepped aside. "In the bedroom."

Drake made his way to the bedroom. It was the first room that had pictures on the wall, and it reminded him a little of his own sparse apartment. He felt the need to unpack as soon as possible.

Two victims sat in one corner. Each on a wooden chair —although Drake doubted that the owner of this place could afford real wood—with their arms tied around their backs. Beige hoods sat over their head, and blood had seeped into them from the gunshot hole in each. He knew he didn't want to go over there and remove them. Didn't want to see the victims as they really were. It wasn't like he had a choice though.

He crossed the floor, aware of several Blackcoats in the room watching him do so, aware of Celine stood in the doorway. Drake tore the hood off the closest victim. He dropped the hood, his mouth agape with horror, and quickly removed the second victim's hood, the shock and dismay at what he saw trembling through him.

Drake knew them. Both of them. It was a long time ago, but the memories of a time when he had enjoyed their company flooded back to him. A bunch of young kids thinking they knew everything before his world crashed around him. Before their worlds did the same.

"You know these people?" Celine asked.

Drake nodded. "His name is Septimus, and hers is Helice. Is this why I needed to come here? Because I know them?"

"No," Celine asked. "I needed to see your reaction to their deaths. I needed to see for myself."

It took a moment for Drake to remember where he was and calm his tone. "Why? You think I did this?"

Celine's expression was cold. "I had to be certain you weren't involved."

"Why would you think I was?" Drake fought the rage that bubbled up inside him.

Celine's features softened somewhat. "Because the last person Helice tried to contact before she died was you."

The emptiness inside him grew, and he needed air. "That doesn't mean I killed her."

"No," Celine agreed. "Helice wrote two messages. One, we assume while she was tied up. It just said, *please help me*. It was sent to your email two hours ago."

Drake shook his head with disbelief. "I was asleep. I didn't... and the other?"

Celine stared at Drake for a moment, before passing him a data-pad. "She never sent the message, saved it under drafts."

Drake read the message, gut churning as he did.

I'm so sorry for everything that happened, Drake. I know you must hate me. I only hope you can learn to forgive. And if not, I will forfeit my life if that's what it takes to prove to you that I'm not that person anymore.

Drake looked back at Helice, and noticed the balcony door behind her. He walked over, opened it, and stepped outside onto the dark balcony and into the rain.

CHAPTER THREE

Felix Drake

"**D**o you plan on staying out here all night?" Celine asked as she opened the balcony door.

"It's only been five minutes," Drake told her without looking her way. "If that."

Celine looked up at the sky and back to Drake. "You're a bit wet."

"I'll manage," Drake said without emotion.

"You're annoyed I told you we didn't know who they were," Celine said.

"A little," Drake admitted.

Celine nodded as if she understood, but she didn't apologise. "So, you want to tell me how you know those two in there?"

Drake's initial anger had subsided a little, but he could still feel it in the pit of his stomach. "You had Rollos come here in case I was involved. You knew he'd get me to stop whatever it was I would do and hand myself in. That's why the rest of the team weren't involved. You know they might help me escape. Doesn't explain Luca."

Celine sighed. "He wasn't meant to be here. Are we really doing this out here? It's raining."

"It's not heavy," Drake said. "And my clothes are still dry underneath. Just my hair that's wet."

Celine stared at Drake for several seconds. "Yes, I got Rollos here because I knew he'd stop you. Luca was never meant to come. He's too loyal to you."

Drake forced a smile. "All of my people are loyal to me. Rollos included."

Celine nodded. "Yes, but Rollos will do the right thing. Luca will do the right thing too, but the right thing in *his* mind. He places loyalty to a person above loyalty to the job. You can't deny it."

Drake continued to stare out across the city lights. He'd been told countless times that they were peaceful. He could see across Lake Orisonto, and make out the lights under it that turned it a light shade of blue, even at night, but he found the whole thing too artificial.

"How do you know those two victims?" Celine asked again.

It was Drake's turn to sigh, he knew he was going to have to tell her the truth, he just didn't want to. "I grew up here. In this city. Left when I was sixteen. Helice and Septimus were friends of mine, part of the group I hung around with. There were nine of us."

Celine nodded as if she understood, but it was clear she still had more questions. "You were friends with the children of councillors? Were your parents Council members?"

Drake shook his head. "My mum was the daughter of a councillor. My father was… something else. It caused a stir when they married, or so I hear."

"And you chose to be a lowly member of the Wardens?" Celine asked. "Shouldn't you be living the life of luxury?"

Drake looked over at his boss for the first time since she'd joined him. "No."

Celine took the less than subtle hint that the conversation about his family was done. "Okay, so you knew these two victims. When did you last see them?"

Drake thought back. "Septimus was the last time I was on this planet. Twenty-something years ago." He took a breath. He knew exactly when he'd last been on Atharoth, he just didn't want to have that conversation. "Helice was a principle in a Warden protection case about five years ago. Spoke to her for five minutes, she wasn't happy to see me."

"Why?" Celine asked.

Drake had been expecting the question, and wasn't sure how much he wanted to open that particular memory. "Old resentments on her part that I left the planet without a word. She had a lot of issues, and I was a sounding board for them. I want this case, is that a problem?"

Celine shook her head. "You're going to need to talk to the other members of your old friendship circle."

Something else Drake didn't want to do. "I know," he said softly.

"Any members that I need to know about in advance?"

"Hideo Wynn," Drake told her. "His sister Kimi too."

Celine's response was immediate, "Hideo and Kimi? The prince and princess? One of which is quite possibly going to become the next King of Stars?"

Drake nodded. "There are about ten or eleven candidates for the job, and I'm not sure which one of them is more likely. So, yes, that's them."

"Well, aren't you full of surprises," Celine said with a loud exhale.

Drake chuckled. "I haven't seen or heard from either of them since the day I left this place. Hopefully, they're still vaguely the people I remember. Some of the other members of that family were less than pleasant."

Celine remained silent for several seconds. "The body in the bathtub, you know him?"

Drake shook his head. "Sorry. His tattoos might help identify him, but if its someone I've met before, I don't remember them. We need to find out who the third victim was as a matter of urgency. That could help."

"I've contacted the rest of your team," Celine told him. "They'll meet you at The Descent. I figured you'd want to be a little away from this area when you saw them. A bar seemed appropriate."

"And you don't want the media taking pictures of a whole squad of Warden running around," Drake said.

The slight smile on Celine's lips, told him he was correct in his thinking.

"I've also forwarded you all everything I have on the murders, and victims," Celine told him. "I'm going to assume you're right on the identities, but you never can be sure, so we'll do a full test once we've managed to get any drugs out of their systems. If we even can."

"We both know it's definitely them," Drake said. "I could have saved them. If I'd been up, and seen that email."

"Time of death was about five minutes after that message was sent," Celine said, sadly. "You'd have gotten here to find three bodies and probably a lot of very bad people. You might have been killed. Whoever did this were professionals. This isn't some random drug deal gone wrong. Any idea what they were into? Two rich kids all the way out here?"

Drake shook his head. He didn't bother correcting the 'kids' terminology. To Celine, anyone under fifty was still a kid. "I'll go speak to some people, see their families, that kind of thing."

"Looks like you being back here was a fortunate piece of business," Celine said.

"Yeah, doesn't it just," Drake replied, using as much sarcasm as he dared.

Celine stared at Drake for a moment. "You think someone arranged for you to return to this planet because your friends might get killed?"

Drake shook his head. "No, but I think someone wanted me back here for a reason. My whole team was transferred to Atharoth with me, and that's more than a little unusual. Whoever that is, they have a lot of pull."

"One of your old friends?"

Drake shrugged. He had an idea who was behind it but

didn't want to start pulling on that thread until he was ready. "I guess I'll find out." He looked back into the room. "Shit. This wasn't how I envisaged seeing old friends again."

"The message she saved," Celine said. "What did it mean?"

Drake looked away from the room, and over to his boss. "Do I have to tell you, or is this just a friendly chat?"

"I'm not going to force you, Drake," Celine said. "I'd like to think the trust goes both ways, though."

"You brought me here because you weren't sure if I was a murderer," Drake reminded her.

"I brought you here to eliminate you from the investigation. Because it's my job," Celine corrected.

Drake knew he should offer her something about the message, but it was deeply personal, and the experience it referenced was not something he wished to re-visit. Even so, he had to give her something. "There used to be a girl in our group," he said. "Her name was Novia. She was my girlfriend. In as much as a teenage kid can have a girlfriend. A few years after I left, she died. I blamed several of the old group for her death. Maybe unfairly. Maybe not."

"Another councillor's kid?" Celine asked.

Drake nodded slowly. He wasn't willing to divulge further in case he made things awkward for Celine. She didn't need to know her family still blamed Drake for her death despite the fact that he wasn't even on-planet at the time.

He opened the balcony door and stepped inside, the quick-dry of his coat activating and removing any residual moisture.

"You need to be careful on this one, Drake," Celine said as she entered the room a few seconds later. "Whoever did this isn't someone to go blindly stumbling around into."

Drake nodded as Rollos and Luca appeared in the doorway. Rollos glanced over at Celine, his face a mask of anger.

"Yell later," Drake said. "We need to meet the rest of the team."

The trio left the apartment, and were soon standing

outside the building. The crowds had grown since Drake had gone inside, although the police were still heavily present.

"She lied to me," Rollos said, his irritation clear. "Didn't say anything about you being a suspect. Didn't say a damned thing to me."

Let it go, Luca said in the heads of both Rollos and Drake. *She was doing her job. Just like we're about to.*

Rollos made a non-committal sound, and crossed his arms over his chest until the grav-cab arrived, taking the three to The Descent. The bar was frequented by several branches of the military, and was well known as a place you didn't start trouble. Or at least only started trouble the once.

The grav-cab pulled up outside of the green metal door, allowing the three to exit the vehicle. "I've got this," Drake called after Luca and Rollos, allowing his comm device to automatically make the payment the second he stepped out into the increasingly heavy rain.

Once inside, they nodded to the two women tending bar. Drake had been to The Descent several times since he'd arrived back on Croleni, and had found it to be an affordable and, more importantly, peaceful place to while away the hours after a long shift.

Several of the tables were already occupied by patrons, both in uniform and not. A few looked up and nodded an acknowledgement but most continued to chat amongst their group. Drake found a table at the far end of the bar, up a set of steps. It was quiet, even with the pool table, and Luca had soon placed his thumb on the table activation screen, the holographic hard-light balls all appearing on the green felt of the table a moment later.

Rollos tapped the activation screen a few times, changing the type of game to be played. "Blackball?" he asked as seven red and seven yellow balls appeared at the far end of the table with the black eight ball nestled in the middle. A white ball appeared at the other end, with two hard-light cues resting against the table.

Luca shrugged off his jacket, laying it on the back of the table. *I'm up for that. Usual rules?* Drake knew he was included just to get a laugh out of the conversation that followed.

Rollos frowned. "No, because your augs mean you always cheat."

It's not cheating if it's natural selection.

Rollos' expression didn't change. "It's cheating if you can use your augs to figure out the best path to the pocket."

Drake removed his coat and placed it on the nearby coatrack. "I'll get drinks." He left the two brothers to argue about the finer aspects of the cheating, knowing full-well they'd never be finished by the time he returned. He caught the attention of the bartender – a twenty-something looking human with brown skin and big hazel eyes. Her dark blue hair shimmered green as she walked.

"Long day?" she asked.

Drake quickly read the woman's nametag that had been clipped to the plain-black top. "It's not been the best day ever, Pia, no."

The woman gave a sympathetic nod. "So, what would you like?"

"Two beers, something cold. I really doubt they care on the make. And whisky. Best you've got." A lot had changed about the world since Drake's ancestors had first settled the system over ten-thousand-years ago, but the names of alcoholic drinks had changed very little.

"Felix Drake, right?" she asked as she put his order into the five inch-screen of the data-pad she'd picked up.

Drake nodded and removed his comm unit. He tapped the accept button that had appeared on the screen, paying for his drinks.

"Why not just have a hard-light table?" he asked Pia when she returned with two glasses of perfectly poured beer, light-blue in colour with only a small amount of foam on each. His whisky was deep brown, and he was looking forward to tasting it.

"People prefer a real table," a voice from behind Drake said.

"What she said," Pia agreed, nodding in the direction of the newcomer.

"Sateri, you want a drink?" Drake asked without turning around to see his second-in-command.

Sateri ordered a red wine from the list and stood beside Drake. "Miss me?" she asked with a grin. "Heard the commander thought you might be a murderer."

Drake couldn't help but smile. "You *heard,* did you?"

Sateri's grin increased in size. "Okay, Luca told me when I walked in."

"How are you two doing?" Drake asked.

"You mean because we're having sex?" Sateri said, her last word an exaggerated whisper.

"Yes," Drake said with a roll of his eyes.

"We're keeping it to ourselves at the moment. We might start telling people, or jump straight into some kind of marriage. Be nice to see people's expressions. Or we could start going at it on a table, that could let people know." Sateri winked at Pia who shook her head and walked off.

"I think she thought you were coming on to her," Drake said.

"Not my type," Sateri said. "I like my humans to have all the augs they can manage. And I mean all of them."

Drake laughed. "Thanks for that particular mental image."

Sateri winked again as her wine was brought to her. "Anything I can do to make the day more pleasant." She picked up one of the two beers and walked over to the Ridge brothers, who were still arguing about playing pool. She passed one of the drinks to Luca and kissed him gently on the lips.

"Get a room," Rollos said.

"This is a room," Sateri pointed out, making Rollos smile.

Sateri had an ability to make friends with anyone, something Drake envied. She was sarcian, and like most of her species, had skin the colour of emerald and deep-black hair, Sateri's was held back with a colourful tie. Like all of her species, her hair changed colour when she was hot or cold. On her home-world, tying her hair back would have been frowned upon, which, Drake was pretty certain, was why she did it.

He'd noticed that some sarcian women who obeyed the homeward rules give Sateri odd looks, but she always seemed to ignore them. On one occasion, a sarcian female had called Sateri a name Drake hadn't quite heard, but it had been enough for several of the team to have to stop Sateri from beating the woman within an inch of her life for the transgression.

Sateri had lived on Benoran for twenty-two years, and had celebrated her ninth year of 'freedom' only a few months earlier. Even so, some of the old customs still rankled her. Drake had tried to talk to her about it, but she made it very clear that talking wasn't something she was interested in.

"So, while you two complain and bicker, can I just play a game?" Sateri asked. "I assume whatever this case is, we're not getting more info on it until the rest of the team arrive."

As she stepped up to the table, the door opened. "Dai'ix is here," she said.

Drake turned to find the oreaf stood in the doorway, leaving no space except for a small piece on either side of Dai'ix's massive head. The crest that adorned the ridge of his forehead was dark purple, indicating that he was male. Gender in oreaf wasn't set until they made a conscious decision. Feathers covered his bare arms and upper body, creating a mixture of blues, greens, and yellows. Oreafs didn't wear upper body armour, as they considered it an affront to their honour. Besides, the feathers hid a skin that Drake had personally seen stop a coil-rifle round with little damage to Dai'ix. The man who had fired it had very much wished he hadn't a few minutes later, though.

Dai'ix ignored any glances as he walked through the room, stopping to order a drink. After a few seconds, he accepted the metal cup in one of his claw-like hands. Each oreaf wrist housed a sheathed talon coated in venom that was designed to paralyse. He carried his drink over to the rest of the group and placed it on a nearby table. Oreaf weren't even considered the apex predators on their planet; they were just the ones that went off-world first. The idea of some of the other creatures on the oreaf home world of Flayison ever leaving the confines of the planet was not a pleasant thought for most people who'd been there.

"First beer in a month," Dai'ix said, his voice gruff and deep. He took a swig of the liquid, making a contented sound, before taking a seat.

"I hope that's reinforced," a young woman said as she walked over to Dai'ix and sat beside him.

"Rosie," Dai'ix said with a slight nod. "If it isn't, I'll sit on the floor."

Rosie smiled before drinking the water she'd purchased. Drake hadn't even seen her enter the building, let alone go to the bar.

She was twenty-nine, and human. Her eyes—a mixture of red, blue, and green—betrayed the augs she'd had installed as a child. Her purple and black hair was braided, and both ears held several piercings. Rosie was the tech member of the team, although Drake knew she was more than capable of handling herself in a fight if needs arose.

"Tuck," Rollos said with a smile as the final member of the team sat next to Drake. "Glad you could make it."

Tuck made a hand-gesture that was, at best, considered to be rude, and at worst, highly offensive, but Rollos laughed it off.

Tuck was half-human, half sarcian. Short and wiry, his eyes darted from one person to the next, taking in everything around him. Drake knew little about his childhood except he had been born on a battleship and lived most of his early life running around its hallways. By the time he'd been taken to a planet, he already had a working knowledge of most weapon systems, and was in high demand by people who liked to pay a lot of money for someone to acquire things in a less than legal manner. Like Luca, Tuck had been recruited from prison—although in Luca's case it had been a military one—but Drake didn't mind such things. He only cared about loyalty to one another, and whether they could carry their share of the work.

"So, we're all here," Rosie said. "We all got the info from Celine. Want to tell us what's actually going on?"

"You all seem a bit too jovial considering three people are dead," Tuck said.

"Not jovial," Rollos said, his voice measured. "Just blowing off steam."

Tuck gave a slight shrug in response.

"Three victims," Drake said. "I know two of them. Or knew. Septimus Mowatt and Helice Tranton."

"Mowatt and Tranton?" Rosie said with a slight shake of her head. "Two councillor families. This is going to become a mess."

"It gets worse," Drake began. "Helice was a Sage. She wasn't wearing her magnus bracer."

"There were no signs of aether being used," Rollos said. "We'd have seen that."

Drake checked that no one else in the bar could see them, before placing his comm unit on the table. He tapped the screen and a holographic view of the crime scene hovered a foot above the table. "Helice used storm aether. If she'd fought back, we'd have seen a hole where half of the apartment used to be."

Sateri rubbed her chin with her fingertips. "So, she was either subdued before she could, or didn't wear it. Sage can use their aether without the bracer."

"True, but there are a few problems with that," Tuck said. "Without the bracer means a lot of concentration and control to use their aether with any real effect. It's also dangerous."

"Yes, I know all of those things, thanks, Tuck," Sateri said with as much sarcasm as she could muster.

Drake spoke quickly, before Tuck could begin arguing.

"When I last saw Helice, she wasn't the kind of person who'd practise without her bracer. Most Sage don't bother; the bracer is all they need to let them wield and control their power."

"So, someone removed it from her," Rollos said.

"Or she removed it to ensure she didn't stand out," Rosie added.

"We didn't find it," Drake said. "And I'm unsure why her killer would want it. Rosie, Tuck, and Rollos, I want you all to go see the two families. Rosie, you're in charge." Drake looked at both Rollos and Tuck to see if either of them would argue, but they both remained quiet. Drake knew Rosie wouldn't put up with their bickering.

"Will they have been informed?" Tuck asked.

"No, unfortunately you'll have to do it," Drake said, unhappy that his people had to carry out such unpleasantness. "You also need to check where they both lived. I'm guessing we'll get the details from Celine."

"Speaking of which," Rosie said as she removed the comm unit from her pocket. She took a small clip from the rear of the unit and placed it in the aug port behind her ear. Her eyes closed for a few seconds, and when she opened them again, she placed the clip back into the comm unit. "Good news, bad news. The bathtub victim had enough drugs in his system to launch a battleship; I'm surprised his heart didn't explode from them all. He was tortured for several hours. His name was Trinas Brong. Had previous for assault, drug dealing, and a few other crimes that aren't really conducive with the awful way he died. Most people don't get their fingertips cut off because they punched a navy guy in the face at a bar."

"That the bad news?" Sateri asked.

"No," Rosie said. "The bad news is that he has no record of address. He's human though, no aether in his blood. And that isn't the good news either. The good news is that neither Septimus Mowatt nor Helice Tranton had any drugs in their system. None. Septimus took some sort of highly potent pain meds about four months ago, but Helice is six months of clean records. Not even headache meds. Nothing. She was cleaner than I am."

"So, they weren't there to get a fix," Tuck said. "Buying for someone else?"

Drake wished he knew. "I plan on finding out. Thanks for the info, Rosie. Okay this changes nothing. Sateri and Luca, you're with me. We're going to pay someone a visit. Rosie, how long would it take you to hack Helice and Septimus' records? Full access?"

Rosie whistled softly. "It's under Council encryption, so a few hours maybe? You want to know why they were in the same room as a known piece of crap like Trinas?"

"I want to know if they owed anyone money, if their banking records are strange, if they gambled," Drake said. "*Anything*. Check with the family first. Last I remember, the Mowatt's were pretty open about their records. Tranton was a new family when we all last saw one another, so I'm not familiar with how they might have changed. Get them to help, too, if you can. If you can't, hack it. I want to know everything about those three."

"And do we know if Sabas is involved?" Rosie asked. "I'm just asking the question before anyone else does. He's been awfully quiet for the last month, and now two prominent people turn up dead."

"Sabas is only to be investigated if we get something linking him," Drake said, finding it difficult not to just tell everyone to get the man. "Until then, Sabas is left as far alone as he can possibly be."

"We'll get him eventually," Rollos said. "He's too stupid to stay out of trouble."

"Or stay alive," Tuck said with a smile.

"What about me?" Dai'ix asked, taking the conversation away from Sabas. "What am I meant to be doing?"

"I need you to look into Trinas," Drake said. "I need you to do what you do best."

Dai'ix's smile was wide and concerning. "Hit people?"

Drake smiled. "If it comes to that, but in the meantime, I want people to know the Wardens are looking into his murder. I want to know who he worked for, and how concerned they are about us. Be big, be obvious, go to the usual places. On second thought, have Tuck go with you; Rollos and Rosie can deal with the families. Once you're done there, get hacking on their bank records. I'm sure Tuck wouldn't mind *asking* questions."

Tuck grinned. "I wouldn't mind at all."

"There's something you need to know about this chameleon stuff," Rosie said, looking up from her comm unit. "If you inject someone with enough of it, they go into a frenzied rage. If Trinas hadn't been shot to death, he would have started trying to tear his attackers into pieces. It's incredibly dangerous stuff. You remember those riots on Leturn?"

Leturn was the second largest of Atharoth's four moons. It's used as a huge port hub for most cargo ships bringing items to and from the surface of Atharoth. They'd had some civil unrest regarding safety protocols, and when a peaceful march turned violent, the Watch went in. The results had been bad.

"Thirty-six dead," Tuck said. "I remember seeing it. Fourteen Watch, the rest the scum who protested."

"They were peaceful," Rosie said, a hardness in her voice. "Right up until the point a canister of gas was thrown into the crowd. The gas came back negative for pretty much everything." She tapped on her screen before turning it around for Drake to see, showing him the results of the blood tests from the protestors, and that from Trinas.

"They're the same," Rollos said.

Rosie nodded. "I helped with the investigation. It was the first time chameleon came up. I saw what those people did after they were infected, I saw what it took to put them down. Those not infected were fighting for their lives up there, no matter what the news told you. This wasn't a violent protest where both sides tried to kill each other. It was a peaceful protest hi-jacked by a madman. If this shit gets out there into the public and someone takes too much, we're going to have homicidal people on our hands."

Drake stood and removed the comm unit from the table, replacing it in his pocket. "Then we need to make sure that doesn't happen. Did you ever find footage of who threw the canister?"

Rosie shook her head. "I only helped identify the bodies and try and figure out what the stuff inside them was. I didn't touch the investigation itself."

"Any chance you can get the footage?" Drake asked. "Find out who threw the canister? They might be a link who whoever used this stuff today."

"I can find out," Rosie said. "I have a friend on Leturn. She owes me a few things."

"Get on that once you've seen the families."

Rosie nodded.

And us? Luca asked.

"We're going to go see an old friend," Drake told him.

"You have old friends?" Sateri asked with a smile.

"Well, take the word friend and replace it with bottom-feeding piece of dried-up shit," Drake said.

"So, he's going to be hostile?" Sateri asked.

Drake shook his head. "Not if he knows what's good for him."

CHAPTER FOUR

Felix Drake

"So, do you feel like telling us who this person is?" Sateri asked after the grav-cab had been heading toward their destination for several minutes.

Drake knew that by law grav-cabs weren't allowed to have any kind of recording equipment hidden within, but he still removed his comm device and opened software that blocked anything that might be listening in. "His name is Metan Glornv. He was one of the group of people I used to be friends with, which included Helice and Septimus." He told Luca and Sateri exactly what he'd told Celine, leaving nothing out. You couldn't hope to keep secrets about a case from your teammates if you wanted to all go home safe at the end of the night.

"So, when did you ask where this Metan guy lives?" Sateri asked. "I only ask because you clearly don't know where your other friends live, so was he some sort of special case?"

Drake nodded. "Yes. A very special case. He was the one person in the group I wanted to make sure was still behaving himself."

Luca looked out of the tinted window. *This is a wealthy neighbourhood. I'd say he did well for himself, even if it turns out he didn't behave.*

"He's involved with some very... questionable people,"

Drake continued. "Possibly the kinds of people that the now dead Trinas associated with."

"You think Metan is involved?" Sateri asked.

"I don't know," Drake admitted. "He was close to Helice. Really close when I last knew them. I just wonder whether or not he kept tabs on her. Maybe they were still in a relationship. I don't know. What I do know, is that he's the type of person to keep an eye on those who might owe him favours down the line."

"And what kind of favours would Helice owe Metan?" Sateri asked as the grav-cab came to a stop.

"The kind that get people killed," Drake said as he stepped out.

Metan Glornv owned a large three-bedroom property that sat atop a hill overlooking the River of Stars. The water there eventually reached Lake Orisonto. When Drake had been a child, his mother had brought him to the river and explained how it was named after the King of Stars due to the constant twinkling of crystals beneath the clear water.

"Metan did well for himself," Sateri said.

She made a good point. His home sat on one level, with a perfectly manicured front lawn. It looked identical to the other ten properties on the street. The house was painted white, and had a large picture window in the front of the house. Drake touched the screen beside the door, allowing the occupants to know that someone was here.

"Who is it?" Metan asked, his face coming on the screen. The half of his head that wasn't shaved had long black hair that cascaded over his face.

"Did I wake you?" Drake asked.

Metan pushed the hair out of his eyes, and stared at Drake for several seconds. "You here to kill me?"

Drake held up his badge. "Talk. Not kill."

Metan nodded and the screen went blank, the door opening a second later.

You wanted to kill him? Luca asked as they stepped into

Metan's house.

"Still might," Drake said as light flooded the area, revealing a sparsely decorated room. There were two couches and a chair next to a large window overlooking the rear of the property, which held a swimming pool and barbecue pit.

"It's real," Metan said. "The pit. It uses wood, not anything synthetic. Cost a fortune, but worth it for the smell alone."

Drake turned and surveyed the man he'd once called friend. Metan was nearly seven feet tall, and probably weighed more than twice what Drake did. He was shirtless, his muscular body almost gleaming in the light. His long, black trousers reached his bare feet.

"Augs?" Drake asked.

Metan smiled. "A few. Needed a change after all of those years looking up to those who already have everything. Besides, in my line of work, you need to be able to take care of yourself."

"And what line of work is that?" Sateri asked.

Metan looked both Sateri and Luca up and down, stopping at the badges on their hips. "More Wardens? It's a regular party here, you should have called, and I'd have gotten food and dip." He walked back into the room he'd left, and re-emerged a few seconds later wearing a silken red top that did little to hide his torso.

"You going to answer the question?" Sateri asked.

"I'm in information," Metan said. "I help people acquire information they need for a modest price."

"Modest?" Drake asked, motioning to the house around him. "There's nothing here you could say makes it looked lived in."

"I like to be able to drop and move at a moment's notice." Metan kept eye contact with Drake. "You know what that's like, yes?"

"We need to talk," Drake said, ignoring his irritation.

"Alone?" Metan asked.

Drake nodded. "You two stay here, we'll go out to the rear

of the property. If you see me trying to drown him, come tell me to stop... or don't."

"That's not funny," Metan said as the pair walked away. "There was a time we were friends." He opened the door to the garden, the purple glow from the lights in the pool, illuminating all around them.

As Drake stepped out into the garden, he removed his comm-unit and activated the same software he'd used in the grav-cab.

"You don't trust me?" Metan mocked, taking a seat on a nearby chair.

"Let's get something straight, Metan," Drake said, remaining standing. "I want answers, and I know you can give them."

"I'll tell you what, Drake. We'll play a game. Truth for truth. I'm unlikely to get a chance to do this again."

"I'm not here to play games," Drake snapped. "If I want the information, I could have Luca tear it from your skull."

Metan glanced back toward his house. "He's the quiet one, yes? What's his deal?"

Drake sighed.

"Oh, come on, Drake," Metan exclaimed. "You can torture me, but we both know you won't. You're not that person. If you like, you can have your mute friend do whatever it is he does."

"You have no idea who I am, Metan," Drake said, trying to keep his anger in check. He hadn't expected to feel anything close to it, but seeing Metan brought back unpleasant memories. "None. However, in the interest of our past, I'll answer your questions. I find you lied to me; I'll make you suffer. I don't care if I have to hunt you down across a dozen systems, I *will* find you."

"I'm surprised you found me here," Metan said. "Nothing is in my name."

Drake smiled, although it wasn't pleasant. "This place is in your mother's name. You still miss her, I assume."

"She was an awful human being, Drake, and a dreadful

mother, as well you know," Metan said. "So, obviously I have issues with our relationship. Odd how you care about those who hurt you the most, isn't it?"

"Luca's a telepath," Drake explained. "No aether involved. Human telepath."

Metan exhaled a breath. "The military managed it? That's astonishing. That's why he's mute, isn't it?"

Drake nodded. "They cut out his tongue so the telepathy could work better. He tried to have an artificial one, but it gives him headaches, and he'd rather have the power than the speech."

"Thanks for telling me," Metan said, sounding something close to being genuine. "Your turn to ask."

"You asked two," Drake pointed out.

Metan rolled his eyes. "*Fine*, you get two."

"Who killed Helice and Septimus?" Drake asked immediately.

The shock on Metan's face was easy to read. "Helice is dead? *What?* This is about Helice? I had no idea she was dead. When? How?"

Drake stared at Metan until the larger man become physically uncomfortable, before telling him about the deaths of the two friends.

"Honestly, I don't know who did it," Metan said. "Haven't heard anything. Where were they found?"

Drake told him where their once-friends had died, how they'd died, and about Trinas.

"Shit," Metan said through clenched teeth. "Trinas, I know. If he's dead, this planet is better off."

"How'd you know him?"

"He did bad things for bad people," Metan said. "Got caught dealing drugs and a few other things, but they never managed to get him with the murders or anything else too serious. He was a bad guy, Drake. He hurt people for fun. Why would Helice and Septimus be mixed up with him?"

"That's why I'm here," Drake said. "You once dated Helice."

Metan laughed. "When we were sixteen, yes. That was twenty-seven years ago. I know you've been gone a long time, but a lot has changed in twenty-seven years."

"You did time for her, Metan," Drake said. "That's the kind of thing you don't forget. That's the kind of person you'd keep an eye on just in case you ever needed a favour. Daughter of a councillor? Big favour to keep the truth secret."

For the first time since Drake had arrived, Metan looked angry. "Fuck you, Drake. Bastard."

Drake sighed. "Going to stop calling me names and give me an answer?"

"I was seventeen when we got busted," Metan snapped. "I didn't even know about the drugs. Helice had bought them. So, yes, I was in love with her and I was an idiot and took the fall. I got a year for it. When I got out, I'd made contacts and Helice wanted some extra fun. So, I got her some more drugs, and told her that from that moment on if I ever needed a favour, she'd do it. No questions. She'd moved on, could you believe it? I did time for her, and she'd moved on."

"What drugs were they?" Drake kept his tone level for fear of saying something he shouldn't.

Metan slammed his fist onto the table between them. "You know damn well what drugs they were."

"The same ones that Novia used," Drake said, already knowing the answer.

"I didn't kill Novia," Metan snapped, getting to his feet, and walking away before turning around to face Drake. "She was my friend. You'd left by the time I was released from prison. Gone off to wherever they sent you. She started to party a little too hard, started to take a little too much stuff." Metan paused and looked away. "I didn't kill her."

"I know," Drake said, his voice soft yet without emotion. His control total, lest he give something away. "The drug Novia took was called 'explosion'. She took too much of it, and in the middle of a high, leapt off one of the skyblocks. Nine-hundred-and-thirty-seven-feet from the leap to her death."

Metan was silent for several seconds before he asked, "How do you know that?"

"I know everything about her death," Drake told him. "I know the name of the man who supplied her the drugs. I know it wasn't you; you'd already walked away from the group. However, I also know that you would have kept an eye on them. Did you ever call in the favour?"

"No," Metan said, sounding deflated. "If you knew it wasn't me, why hate me?"

"I killed the man who gave her the drugs," Drake said. "I ensured he'd never hurt another. And while I knew her death wasn't your fault, that it wasn't your hand on the drugs she took, I still hated you for giving her drugs to begin with. She took them of her own free will, and it took me a long time to come to terms with that."

Metan stared at Drake for a heartbeat. "So what's your problem with me?"

"I don't like you," Drake said. "Before I left, you changed. Always too eager to do whatever it took to make the others like you. You were always so keen to make them your friends, but it became obvious you were looking for future help."

Metan stared at Drake for several more seconds before bursting out laughing. "So, for all these years I thought you blamed me for her death, it was just a simple dislike?"

"Essentially, yes," Drake said with a nod. "I don't trust you, Metan. Don't trust your friends or associates. And I know the kinds of people you call friends. So, answer the question. You kept an eye on Helice, yes?"

Metan nodded. "Like you said, it was a favour that was too good to just waste."

"Why not ask for it sooner?"

"Didn't need anything," Metan said, making it sound simple. "Didn't want to ruin her life for nothing. I'm a career criminal now, haven't you heard? That first drug bust sent me on a spiral I never recovered from."

Drake shook his head slightly. "Bullshit."

Metan laughed. "Haven't heard that swear in a while. Haven't seen a bull in years, not one outside of a zoo anyway. Not a lot of farms on this planet. Everyone's too busy building industry and trying to make the biggest skyblock."

"If you're a career criminal, it's because you wanted it that way," Drake said.

"Too many riches to be acquired by people who have a lot of them and not a lot of morals," Metan replied. "This is true. I'm rich now. Richer than any of the rest of the group, except maybe Hideo. The prince. I was never that sure about your financial background either. Anyway, you get the point. I have a question for you, actually. Where did you go?"

Drake saw no reason to lie, but also no reason to give the whole truth. "Military."

"Bullshit," Metan said, and his smile widened. "I checked military records for you. Novia asked me to. Couldn't find anything, and I was damn good even back then. About ten years ago, I checked again. I figured I'd find something I missed. You never joined the military. Not under the name Felix Drake. You were on this planet one minute and you vanished the next. No one had even heard of you until you joined the Wardens. Years of your life missing from official records."

Drake wanted to tell Metan to stop talking, but that would have only made things much worse. "No one should be able to hack those records."

"It took me a long time, Drake," Metan said. "And a lot of effort, but there was nothing there to read. You want to tell me where you really went? There were a lot of rumours at the time. Military Shadow Ops was a prevailing bet."

"I just went away," Drake said. "No secrets or interesting stories to tell."

Metan laughed again. "You're a terrible liar considering your job."

"Was Helice into anything illegal or illicit?" Drake asked, wanting to change the conversation topic. "After she stopped taking drugs, I mean."

"Not that I ever saw," Metan said with a shrug. "I liked to make sure that she was okay. I didn't have feelings for her, they disappeared a long time ago, but it was wise to make sure she didn't do anything stupid. I could have cashed in my favour if I saw her behaviour would jeopardise her standing within the people she called friends. No drugs, nothing illegal… not even anything immoral. She did a lot of activist stuff for the forests to the east of here, using her privilege for good."

The fact that Helice had tried to do good in the world made Drake wish he'd contacted her before it was too late. "What activist stuff?"

Metan pointed off in a vague direction into the darkness beyond. "Oh, some of the corporations want to chop down part of the Jagged Forest. Apparently, it's just ripe for making more soulless skyblocks so that people can look down one their common man from up high."

Drake chuckled. "You live in a house that cost more than a street of slums."

"Yes, but I actually also get to care about the environment. Those two things aren't mutually exclusive."

Drake felt the conversation moving away again. "So, why did Helice care about the forest?"

"Several million square miles of forest, along with everything that lives there," Metan said. "It's one of the few unspoilt areas on this planet. Apparently, the corporate overlords had tried to get a law passed allowing them to tear a part of it down, but the Council threw it out. Helice helped make it known that her father wouldn't approve such a law. Some were less than impressed that she cost them money."

"You think a councillor had her killed?" Drake asked. "What about Septimus?"

"Didn't you know? They were lovers. Where one went, Septimus followed." Metan's tone suggested he was less than happy about it.

"You didn't approve?" Drake already knew the answer, but

he wanted to hear it from Metan.

"He was a wet blanket of a man," Metan snapped. "She'd have been better off having a synth follow her around."

Someone doth protest too much. "So, ignoring your obvious disdain, why would people want to kill Helice just for her environmental protest?"

"Don't know," Metan said with a dismissive wave of his hand. "For what feels like the millionth time, I didn't kill her. I do know that she'd been putting out feelers to try and find information on the corporations and who was backing the move to... de-clutter a forest."

"What's the corporation's name?"

"Expedited Systems," Metan told him.

"Never heard of them."

"Most people haven't," Metan said with a dismissive wave of his hand. "They have their fingers in a lot of other little ventures. You might know them by their original name: Shield Welders."

The name took a few seconds for Drake to recognise. "One of the gangs on the moon of Leturn. They have that much power?"

"There used to be eight gangs on that moon," Metan said. "Right up until Ramin Gossard got his grubby little mitts on the Welders. Now, there are four. Not saying he had anything to do with their acquisition, but well... actually, that's exactly what I'm saying. He wants to be *the man* on Leturn, and also be respected as a businessman here, on Atharoth. Word has it he's got some friends in the Council. Another word has it that he was pretty angry about losing out to Helice's little plan."

"Ramin Gossard?" Drake asked with more than a little trepidation. "Seriously? Sabas' father?"

"I heard Sabas got out of prison," Metan said. "Heard what he did to get put in there in the first place, and how his father never once fought to get him released."

"Ignoring Sabas for a second," Drake said. "You can't possibly think that Ramin was angry enough to kill Helice?

He's a gangster, but he's not the murder-the-children-of-councillors type. He's not psychotic."

"Not sure," Metan said. "Honestly, I never thought someone would even try to kill her. She's connected, and with more than just her family. When Hideo finds out... well, would you want to be the person to feel his wrath?"

"The last time I saw Hideo, he was a sweet fifteen year old with very little interest in vengeance," Drake said, fully aware of just how much had changed for him in twenty-seven years.

"And now he's a forty-two-year-old man, and heir to the throne, who had more than once made it very clear what he thinks of the gangs on Leturn."

"Now you're telling me it's a conspiracy against the royal family?" Drake chuckled, barely believing how insane the theory was. "No one would be in so much of a hurry to have themselves killed."

Metan shrugged. "That's probably true, but someone killed Helice and Septimus, and it wasn't for nothing."

"Even if Ramin is involved, none of it explains what Helice and Septimus were doing where they were found, and what they were doing with a known criminal like Trinas."

"Maybe they were spicing up their relationship?" Metan said and chuckled to himself.

"That really your suggestion?" Drake almost snapped.

Metan shook his head. "I can't believe she's gone. When I was younger, I really loved her. Even after I came out of prison and found her with someone else, I still loved her. Broke my heart to have her cast me away like that. I wished a lot of awful things on her over the years, but I never thought someone would kill her. I haven't seen her in years. Just kept tabs on her via my terminal. I know you don't like me, Drake, but I want you to find out who did this."

"I will," Drake said. "You really think Ramin is a suspect?"

"I think if someone cost you a few million credits, wouldn't you be a suspect when they were murdered soon after?"

"If Ramin did it, that means Helice was the target, and that means Septimus was just in the wrong place at the wrong time."

"It also means there are members of the Council involved," Metan said, a slight grin on his face. "More than one of them works with Ramin. And if that was ever made public, it wouldn't be good for their image. Might lose them their seat. Councillors are meant to be above reproach, meant to be incorruptible."

Drake laughed. "We both know that's not true."

"We do," Metan admitted. "We also know that a public scandal linking a Leturn crime boss and some councillors to develop on Atharoth land... well, that would be something the news would jump all over. Not even the King of Stars himself could keep that from the masses."

Drake looked out across the darkness of the floodplains. "Did Trinas work for Ramin?"

Metan rubbed one hand over his jaw as if in thought. "Possibly. He worked for whomever had the credits and willingness to look the other way. Ramin has both those things."

Drake looked back at Metan. "I thought you dealt in information."

"The kind of information I deal with is to know what people such as Trinas are like, so I can stay away from them. I do background checks for wealthy clients."

"Doesn't sound as illegal as I'm guessing it is," Drake said, wondering just how deep Metan was in criminal activity.

"I do very *thorough* background checks. Sometimes I need to access information that would be considered... secure."

Illegal. Drake thought to himself. "I guess I assumed most people in your line of work were more synth than human these days."

Metan looked down at his hands. "Bio-synth. That's what they call themselves. People like me because I don't have any synth running through my head, and I'm still just as good as they are. They needed the synth parts to catch up to me. And people don't employ full synths to do my job, too many inconsistencies in their ability to think on the fly."

Drake tapped the screen of his comm-unit. "I've sent you my details. If you think of anything let me know."

"You should be careful of Ramin," Metan called after Drake.

Drake stopped and turned back. "Yeah, we've met."

"So, you know that if it is him, he won't go easily," Metan continued. "He surrounds himself with people almost as unpleasant as him. I worked for him once. Never again. And we both know his son hasn't fallen far from that particular tree."

Drake left the garden, finding Luca and Sateri in the foyer, before the three headed back toward the waiting grav-cab, and where he told them everything Metan had said.

"You find it odd that Metan gives up Sabas' father as a possible suspect a month after his son is released from prison?" Sateri asked.

You think it's a set up? Luca replied.

"Yes," Drake said. "I just haven't figured out exactly who is being set up."

CHAPTER FIVE

Jaysa Benezta

Jaysa was less than impressed with her current circumstances. She and her five-strong crew had landed at the largest port in Leturn, leaving the other four crewmembers on board the Tracked Retribution – the corsair-class battlecruiser that doubled as her home. Jaysa had contacted Votix, a man she trusted only slightly less than she liked. Which, considering she found him to be an odious little worm, wasn't exactly high in her estimation. However, he was the main contact for the job she'd agreed to undertake, and while he wasn't her employer as such, he'd been given special dispensation to act as their go-between.

Votix had told her to go to a bar in a part of town where the word rough was used to describe almost everything and everyone that lived there. On the plus side, very few people who did live there ever paid much attention to anyone else. It was a quick way to end up with a plasma round in the back of your skull.

Jaysa stood at the mouth of a dark alley across an empty street from the bar in question. It was called The Hive, and if she was perfectly honest, she didn't want to know why. She had taken a contract to find a vile little cretin by the name of Trinas Brong, who was mean, cruel, and worked for whomever or whatever offered him the most credits to do the worst things they could imagine. Recently, he'd been working security on Ocrion, a wasteland of a planet in the middle of the Zetya system. They latter of which had the sole claim to fame that another planet in the same system once tore itself apart because some idiot ruptured an aether drive inside the planet's gravity.

Jaysa had gone to the city of Onnab on Ocrion, and found that apart from a large number of security working for Expedited Systems, there was nothing of interest. She'd asked around, gotten nowhere, and been told that she'd be better off looking into Trinas on Atharoth. Quite why the little weasel had gone to the Union's capital planet, no one could, or more likely would, say. Two weeks later, she was on Leturn wanting to know what was going on, and why no one had mentioned to her that her target was nowhere to be found. The whole job was beginning to stink.

"You know, boss, you could have sent one of us up here to go do this for you," Etamus said into the earpiece that had been implanted deep inside Jaysa's ear. It only lasted for a few weeks before dissolving, but Jaysa wouldn't have done the job without contact with her ship and crew.

"Yes, but I'm the captain," she pointed out.

"Sort of making my point for me there," Etamus said.

"I need to show everyone that I'm still capable of doing stuff like this." *And our employer specifically asked for me to do it,* she thought to herself. Another tick in the 'we're being set up' column.

"We all know you're capable, boss," Etamus said. "You just like to show everyone what a badass you are."

Jaysa stifled a chuckle. "I don't feel very badass at this moment. This blasted moon has its own artificial weather, and someone appears to have set it to continuous rain. It's not exactly a fun place to be at the moment." Jaysa wore a combat-armour jacket – black and grey and thin enough that it wasn't bulky or restrictive, but could still stop a blast-gun shot from being lethal. Her tan trousers were wet, and her black boots covered in mud. She was ready for trouble if it happened her way, she just hoped it wouldn't happen at all.

A brown, leather-fibre holster hung from her hip, and she found the weight of her disrupter revolver a comfort. Larger than a pistol, but not as cumbersome as a rifle, it was the perfect weapon to draw in a hurry. It was also one of the few things from her home world of Benoran that actually held any value for her. Jaysa would rather have not used the disrupter at all; she had a reputation to uphold as someone who didn't cause a lot of trouble when acquiring her targets, a reputation built over several years of hard graft. She wasn't about to throw it all away for one gang member with a well-used trigger finger, but if she needed to, she'd kill anyone else who got in her way. And if her mysterious employer didn't like that, well… she'd have to deal with that later.

"You'll figure something out," Etamus said. "See you soon."

Etamus disconnected the transmission, and Jaysa glanced up and down the street at the thinning crowds. Although as she was in a part of the moon with only a few thousand residents, the crowds were never that big to begin with. Besides, pistol blasts were a regular occurrence, so Jaysa wasn't concerned about someone hearing a few more.

She crossed the empty road and pushed open the door to The Hive. Inside, there were three occupied tables. Jaysa dismissed the first two as being no threat; one had two men who were very interested in their weak looking ale. The second was in the corner of the bar, where a woman smoked a vapour-stick, the smoke cascading down over the tables' surface, changing colour as it moved. The third table had four men sat around it, one of which was Votix.

He was a male sarcian with deep-blue skin and long dark hair that flowed over his shoulders. He was shorter than Jaysa by several inches, and appeared to be scrawny, although she imagined that under his expensive dark suit, he was probably muscular and more than capable of taking care of himself. You didn't get to work with of any of the gangs on Leturn without being able to get your hands bloody.

Jaysa walked over to the bartender and ordered an ale. Several of her five-person crew had told her that Leturn produced some amazing variations of the drink, and Jaysa figured she probably had time to try a few. Her sarcian physiology would burn the alcohol off within a few minutes. Sarcians were rarely capable of getting drunk on anything that wasn't sarcian made.

The bartender placed a dark glass bottle in front of her. "Ten Ruby credits," he told her.

"Ten? Is this made from the urine of the King of Stars or something? I think the word you were looking for there, was emerald." Credits came in four types: Emerald, Ruby, Sapphire, and Diamond. Ten ruby credits was the equivalent to a hundred emerald, more than any bottle of ale on Leturn could possibly cost.

The bartender opened his mouth to argue and noticed the holstered disrupter at Jaysa's hip. He changed his mind. "Sorry, been a long day. Ten emerald is what I meant."

Jaysa placed a ten emerald credit chip on the bar "Thought so."

"Don't get many of your kind here," a male voice said from behind her.

Jaysa turned and forced a smile at Votix. "Exactly what about me don't you get around here often? You told me to come, and here I am."

"You're sarcian, we don't see many of them," the human male beside Votix told her. "You look different to the last few I met."

Jaysa's skin was a slightly lighter green than many of her species, and her irises were orange, a fairly unusual colour considering most were yellow. She knew what the man meant – her hair. "I'm what you humans would call an albino," Jaysa said, tucking her shoulder length silver hair behind her ears.

"Does it still change?" one of the other men asked. He

wore combat armour, albeit very old combat armour, with dark marks on it that suggested he had seen one too many battles. A coil-rifle was strapped across his back. He'd grown a moustache to cover a scar on his lip, but it hadn't worked and instead appeared as if part of his lip were bald. "I once had me a sarcian whore, her hair changed when she got excited."

"I assume it went blue," Jaysa said.

The man looked furious and stood, his expression only increasing in rage as his companions laughed, but when Votix placed a hand absentmindedly on his companions arm, he sat back down.

"You feel like telling me what's going on?" Jaysa asked.

"Your contract has been terminated," Votix said, placing a small pouch on the table in front of him. "These men are here to ensure you take the news well."

"Why has my contract been terminated?" Jaysa asked.

"Trinas is dead," Votix told her. "The Wardens are investigating it, so as you can see, your services will not be required."

Jaysa picked up the pouch and opened it. "This is half my fee. You cancel, you pay the whole fee. That was the deal."

"A deal I'm changing," Votix said with a smug grin. "You're more than welcome to argue with me."

"I was hoping this meeting was going to be nice and dull," Jaysa told him.

"Well, I'm right here to make things more exciting for you," another of Votix's friends, a grey-skinned kiretan said and laughed at whatever he considered was being witty.

The kiretan was Jaysa's main concern. He was nearly seven feet tall and could have broken her in half with one hand. He was bare-chested; there was nothing that could have covered the three four-inch spikes that sat on each of his shoulders. Hardened bone, purple in colour, ran around the top of his large skull, giving him another weapon that Jaysa had seen used on the soft flesh of other species to devastating effect.

"I'd offer to have you stop for a drink, but we're just leaving," Votix said and stood. His friends followed suit, although the angry human kept his eyes firmly planted on Jaysa. Votix removed a card from his pocket and passed it to Jaysa. "That's where I'll be this evening, there's a party there, why don't you come along? If you are capable of *pleasing* me, I'll see to it that your fee is included in full."

Jaysa smiled, and tried hard not to reach across the table and break the little bastard in half. She was outnumbered and outgunned. If she wanted to get out of here with her full payment, she needed to be smart about it. "If I've got nothing else on, I might see you there."

There was a sparkle behind Votix's eyes, one which Jaysa had to force herself not to feel sick over. She placed her drink beside her and pocketed the card as Votix and his entourage exited the bar. She needed to splash water on her face, needed to be out of the stank of Votix's presence. Jaysa told the bartender she'd be back shortly and then she followed the signs to the restroom at the rear of the bar.

She stood in the blue room, in front of one of three large mirrors and pressed the button for the water to activate. Murky liquid cascaded from a slit in the wall, into the sink. Jaysa splashed it on her face, the coolness taking away some of the anger she felt at not putting a round in the heads of each of the bastards who'd spoken down to her.

The door to the restroom was around the corner from Jaysa, so she heard it bang open but didn't see anyone until two of Votix's bodyguards came into view.

"Wrong room," Jaysa said.

"I don't think it is," the man she'd angered said. "I think this is exactly where I'm meant to be."

Jaysa let out a long sigh. "I don't think your boss will like it very much if you attack me, do you?"

"Oh, I don't think that'll be a problem," the second man said. He was shorter than his angry friend, with greasy dark hair and an eye that glowed red. *Cybernetic implant.* She wondered what else they had augmented into their bodies.

The angry man drew a knife from his belt. When he turned the six-inch blade to the side, it shimmered red as the light touched it.

Jaysa considered the disrupter. It was set onto its third of six settings, so it would hurt. A lot. Probably not kill, though. It was at least the fourth setting before any blasts from it would actually pierce the skin. Jaysa discarded the idea. She had some aggression to work out.

"Well, I haven't got all day," she said.

The angry man darted forward, his movements silky smooth. Jaysa batted his arm aside, head-butting him on the nose, which exploded from the force. A kick to his gut sent him flying back to the ground. The second man flanked her, grabbing her wrist, but Jaysa clamped her free hand over his, twisted her arm, forcing the man forward and down as his elbow turned in the most painful way possible. She put a bit more pressure on it until she felt the bone crunch, and his screams of agony started. Jaysa brought her boot down across his temple, and he was quiet.

"I expected more of a challenge," Jaysa said as the door to the restroom was torn free and thrown at her. She dodged aside—drawing her disrupter in the process—but the kiretan had covered the distance between them, and batted it out of her hand before punching her in the face. She took the blow, wiping away the blood from her nose on the back of her hand.

"I heard kiretans were badasses," Jaysa said, registering that her disrupter had landed just under the sink at the far end of the rest room. Too far for her to make it before the kiretan got hold of her. "Let's see."

The kiretan stepped over his injured comrade, and fainted with an elbow, which Jaysa avoided, but his follow up punch was fast and deadly. Jaysa only just moved aside in time for the massive fist to catch her on the shoulder, causing her arm to go numb for a moment.

Shit, he's fast.

The kiretan kicked out at Jaysa; she grabbed the limb and twisted, lifting him into the air and dumping him down on his head. The floor splintered from the impact, but he rolled away to ensure she couldn't follow up. The kiretan slowly got to his knees, the hate in his eyes easy to spot as his gaze never wavered from Jaysa. He was now between her and her gun, not exactly an ideal situation. She took a step beyond the man whose arm she'd broken and when he moved, she swiftly kicked him in the side of the head, ensuring he didn't involve himself in the fight. The angry man was somewhere behind her, but before she could look, he grabbed her leg.

"Now," he screeched at his ally.

Jaysa twisted and brought her boot down onto the angry man's face with a loud crunch. His grip went slack, and she grabbed him by the scruff of his jacket as the kiretan charged toward her with unstoppable power. The kiretan raised his head back, preparing to head-butt Jaysa, but she hauled the angry man off the floor and the kiretan's head connected with Angry Man's sternum, crushing the bone, and sending both him and Jaysa flying back to the far wall.

She shoved the seriously injured man off her and rolled away as the kiretan kicked out at her. Jaysa tried to catch him in the knee with a kick, but he grabbed her leg and threw her aside. She hit the floor with enough force to knock the wind out of her, and slid across the smooth ground, impacting with the far wall. The kiretan turned to her, murder in his eyes. He slowly made his way toward her, each step done with purpose.

Jaysa removed her hand from behind her back. It held the disrupter. She'd been trying to use the few seconds to turn up the level to make it a lethal blast, but wasn't entirely sure what level she'd managed.

She fired.

The round hit the kiretan in the chest, and the big man crumpled to the ground, making an almighty crack as his head struck the floor. Jaysa checked the level readout on the side of the disrupter. Four lights were lit up. She removed her finger from the trigger and tapped one of two buttons on the guard, engaging the fifth light.

Blood flowed from the wound on the kiretan's chest, pooling under him. The blast hadn't gone all the way through his thick skin. She was glad he didn't wear armour; under the circumstances, she wasn't sure she could have pulled off a headshot first time. Jaysa considered killing the kiretan, but he wasn't getting up again for a while. Besides, she hadn't been paid to kill him, so didn't want to waste time when Votix would be waiting for his friends. She kicked the kiretan in the groin though, just to make a point.

She left the rest room and found Votix stood in the middle of the bar, holding an elderly looking human man against him, an energy blade up against his throat.

"I figured they'd be enough to take you out," Votix said.

Jaysa shrugged. "Should have sent more men. Or better men. Not too many of the latter here though." She took a small step forward. "Why betray me? Did the person I'm working for order it?"

"Figured I'd just get the credits back," Votix said. "And someone on your crew paid us more to make sure you didn't come back."

That was information Jaysa hadn't expected, although she didn't let her surprise show. "Okay, you tell me who betrayed me and I'll let you go. We never have to cross paths again."

Votix pulled the man's head back, exposing more of his throat. "I'll kill him if you're lying."

"Don't care about you now." Jaysa holstered her disrupter. "Only care about who betrayed me. Their name. Now."

"Ortros."

"Shit," Jaysa whispered. Ortros was a man she'd helped escape debt from a gang of mercenaries. They were going to kill him, and Jaysa had given him a second chance. She liked him.

"So, you're going to leave now?" Votix asked. "This wasn't

meant to cost me so much. Meant to have been an easy pay."

"Yep, I'm done here." She walked toward Votix and he moved aside, dragging the man with him.

She reached the exit and paused. "Most of your men are alive, I think. I didn't bother checking."

He turned to glance over at the restroom and Jaysa drew her disruptor and pulled the trigger in one smooth movement. The blast went through his wrist, and into his chest, he dropped the knife and screamed out in pain. The elderly man hurried away, and Jaysa kept the disrupter steady.

"I'll pay you," Votix begged as he fell to his knees.

"They all say that. No one ever has enough though. Besides, this time it's not about money." She shot Votix through the eye, killing him instantly. Jaysa tapped her ear. "Votix is dead. Get down here. Make sure Ortros is outside the ship when you land. I need to talk to him."

"Be there in ten, boss," Etamus said. "You okay, just don't sound right."

"Just get here." She glanced over at the elderly man, who appeared to be okay.

"You could have hit the old man," the bartender said.

Jaysa looked back at the bartender. "I didn't." She pulled her badge from her pocket. It identified her as a Tracker.

When the Watch finally showed up, it ended any criticism anyone might have had. No one second-guessed a Tracker; they had the backing of the Union, and worked alongside the kind of people the vast majority of the populous hoped never to meet.

The Watch said they'd arrange for the bodies to be dealt with. Jaysa thanked them and took a grav-cab to the spaceport at the far end of the city.

She'd clipped her badge to her trousers, ensuring no one tried to stop her as she walked through the port toward the drop-ship Etamus would have used to make land. And it was Etamus who was the first to greet her, smile fading when she saw Jaysa's expression.

"Where's Ortros?" Jaysa asked.

"Just coming down the shuttle ramp."

"The job didn't go as expected. I'll need to talk to our employer." Jaysa walked around the shuttle – a six-man craft used only to travel short distances from orbit to a planet's surface. No one wanted to try to land a battleship if they didn't have to.

Ortros was smoking a vapour-stick. "Hey, boss."

"Shouldn't have betrayed me," Jaysa said and raised her disrupter.

Ortros dropped the vapour-stick. "Mercs wanted you dead. They said they'd remove the bounty from my head if I arranged it. Figured that Votix was the man for the job."

Jaysa's disruptor didn't waver an inch. "I gave you a second chance."

"I wanted out, couldn't do it without old debts being paid." His human face became indignant. "Anyone with half a brain would have done the same thing."

She shot him in the head twice, the blast echoing around the spaceport as Ortros crumpled to the ground, accompanied with the sound of clapping.

Jaysa aimed the disrupter at the woman walking toward her, who looked no older than early forties but was probably at least twice that as the dark-grey magnus bracer on each hand suggested she was a Sage. The Sage lived longer lives than those who had no connection to the aether.

Jaysa wasn't sure a Sage could even use two magnus bracers, making the wearing of them look slightly odd in her eyes. Maybe it was some sort of fashion statement that went on with her kind on Leturn.

The woman's hair was almost black, and fell past her shoulders. Of Asian descent, she had on a burgundy lipstick, and her dress ended just above her bare feet. It shimmered different shades of red as she moved. The woman stopped clapping and smiled.

"And you are?" Jaysa asked.

"You don't recognise me?" the woman asked. "That's actually a little disappointing."

"Should I?" Jaysa asked.

"My name is Ren Summers," she said, as if that explained it all. "Daughter to the King of Stars."

Jaysa lowered the disrupter. Aiming one at a member of the royal family was probably a bad idea. "And what do you want?"

"Well, I'm the person who hired you to find Trinas, so I was hoping to keep your employ for a while longer," Ren told her. "I asked Votix and his people to bring you to me so that we could talk about what you'd discovered. Unfortunately, I hadn't expected them to go into business for themselves. I guess I should be grateful, as I assume I would become a target for them to clean up once they were done with you. That is, unless you'd prefer to leave with what I surmise is a lot less than I wanted to pay?"

"You have transport of your own?" Jaysa asked.

Ren nodded. "Obviously, but I thought I'd ride to my estate with you. I have questions about what you saw on Onnab."

Jaysa shook her head. "I didn't see anything."

Ren stopped just beside Jaysa, and smiled. "Now, dear Jaysa, we both know that's not true. The only question is, exactly how much of what you saw is something I can use?"

CHAPTER SIX

Felix Drake

"So, do you trust your friend?" Sateri asked after a few minutes in the grav-cab.

Drake didn't bother to correct her use of the word. "He was surprised when I told him about Helice. He could have faked it, but I think it was genuine."

"Do we go knock on a crime lord's door?" Sateri asked. "Because even if he's on this planet, he'll have immunity."

The Wardens' jurisdiction had once spread across the planet of Atharoth and its three moons. A few decades earlier, the Council had made it so inhabitants of the moon of Leturn were out of the Wardens' grasp, unless they were given special permission to go after someone. Permission only given by a group of councillors who Drake believed were more interested in serving themselves than the people.

It unfortunately meant that anyone from Leturn who was on Atharoth for work came under the normal law enforcement jurisdiction, which meant no Wardens allowed. And Drake had little hope they'd be able to get the Watch, or even the Blackcoats, to help without the possibility they worked for one of the gangs on the side.

"We might not be able to arrest anyone, but we can still go talk to them," Drake said. "I just want to see how they deal with us getting in their business a little."

Just a little? Luca asked with a smirk on his soundless lips.

"For now," Drake replied with a smile of his own as the grav-cab pulled up beside them.

"You're going to need to tell Celine," Sateri said. "She is not going to be happy."

The three of them climbed inside and Sateri gave the destination as the Wardens' precinct. The grav-cab moved away just as Drake's comm-unit beeped, signalling an incoming message. He removed the unit from his pocket and after checking that Sateri had her jamming software activated, pressed the screen where a picture of Dai'ix sprang to life.

"What have you found?" Drake asked.

"Asked a few people, yelled at a few people," Dai'ix said proudly. "Might know who Trinas works for."

"Ramin, by chance?" Sateri asked.

Dai'ix huffed. "Ah, you got the same info. Well, it looks like Trinas did some pretty nasty stuff for the crime lord. He worked security on Ocrion for a while, and word has it he was put there so he could stay low for a while. Nothing official, but people are scared to talk about him."

"More scared than they are of you?" Drake asked.

"I'm a big kitten," Dai'ix said with a smile that made his face look even more aggressive than usual.

"Where's Tuck?" Drake asked.

Dai'ix looked behind him as if he wanted to make sure he was alone. "Sent him over to Rollos and Rosie, sometimes his natural charm means people don't like to talk to him."

"He was being a dick, I assume," Sateri said.

Dai'ix waved away Sateri's words. "Not quite, but he knew some of the people in the bar I went to, and we didn't want them to think his being there was to do with previous transgressions."

"He owed someone money?" Drake asked.

"He knocked someone out who was there a few months ago," Dai'ix said. "The man in question has been looking for retribution since."

Drake nodded, but wasn't thrilled about that piece of information. "We were going to the precinct, so meet us there. We'll go to Ramin as a group."

"See you there." Dai'ix disconnected the call and Drake immediately contacted Celine, dreading the conversation that was about to follow.

"How badly have you messed up?" Celine said as her image came into view.

"Not a lot yet," Drake told her. "Although, it's early, so you need to build up to these things."

Celine almost suppressed a smile. "What do you want, Drake? I've got enough to deal with. There was a shoot-out on Leturn."

"There are always shoot-outs on Leturn," Drake pointed out.

"This one involved a Tracker who was then taken by Ren Summers to her compound on Atharoth," Celine said. "Obviously, a member of the royal family leaving Atharoth without Wardens is a bit of a political juggling act I'd have rather not been involved with. And the fact that Ren is with a Tracker gives me no end of headaches. Thankfully, you're not involved to make things worse."

Drake smiled. "You're not going to like what I have to say then."

"You found out Sabas is involved?" Celine said, "Because I would not like that."

"How about I just don't tell you?" Drake asked.

"Just get it done," Celine told him.

"Possibly Sabas, possibly his father," Drake said. "At least according to info."

"Ramin?" Celine rubbed her temples. "The same Ramin who, when we arrested his son, told us to throw everything we had at him? The same one that you're... unofficially friendly with?"

"That would be the one," Drake said.

"You know him best, Drake," Celine said, sitting back

in her chair. "You think he could have two Council family members murdered?"

Drake thought for a moment. "He has both the money, the know-how, and the contacts to, yes."

"And?" Celine asked.

"He's not an idiot," Drake finished. "Sabas on the other hand."

Celine rubbed her eyes with the backs of her palms. "Damn it all. Go say hi, kick over whatever wasp's nest Sabas is living in. Let's see what happens."

Drake smiled; he knew he could count on Celine. "You going to be okay from higher ups?"

"The Council will have to suck it up and deal with their disappointment that is me ordering my people to do their jobs," Celine told him. "I don't care how many powerful friends that prick has, you have my permission to go be you."

"Thank you," Drake said, ending the call before contacting Rollos, Rosie, and Tuck, the former of which answered.

"How's it going your end?" Drake asked.

"Good news, bad news," Rollos said. "Good news, Septimus Mowatt's family will do whatever it takes to ensure that those responsible are brought to justice. They seem to think that his relationship with Helice is responsible for his death. They do not like her at all. They let us look around his apartment in the family complex, but there's nothing there of note. We'll get a team over to scrub the place clean through."

"And Helice's family?" Sateri asked.

"Fine to begin with," Rosie said. "Although, it didn't take long for their representatives to turn up and tell them not to say anything."

Damn lawyers, Luca said.

"Well, that's not great," Drake said. "Why would the lawyers not want them to say anything?"

"Not sure, but the parents were both being quite open about Helice before they arrived," Rollos said. "Apparently, Helice was pretty big in her activism. She managed to stop a forest being destroyed, might have made a few councillors pretty angry."

Drake nodded. "We heard the same thing."

"Doesn't explain the thug in the bathtub," Tuck said. "Trinas wasn't really the kind of person Helice and her high-and-mighty allies would be happy to befriend."

Drake ignored the slight anger in Tuck's voice. The man had always had a problem with the councillors and the way their children became more powerful just because of who they were. It made him excellent at not over-looking information regarding those people who happened to have powerful friends and family, but it also gave him a chip on his shoulder. One that he'd never bothered to try and shake off.

"Okay, Dai'ix is going back to the precinct, so we'll meet you there," Drake told his team. "We're all going to go say hello to Ramin and see what he knows."

"He's on the planet?" Tuck asked. "Surely, he'd have gone back to Leturn now?"

I've been checking, Luca said. *He's here doing some meetings with various people who I'm sure don't work for councillors at all.*

"Do you know where he's staying?" Drake asked.

Luca showed Drake the screen on his comm-unit.

"He's staying at The Spire," Drake told everyone.

"Excellent, so we're going to walk into the most heavily defended building in the city?" Tuck asked. "That's the hotel used by everyone with even an ounce of power. They're not going to let us just stroll in there."

"We're Wardens, they can't stop us," Rollos pointed out.

"They can with a disrupter rifle," Tuck shot back.

"We're not storming the building," Drake interrupted. "We're going to go see if Ramin is willing to talk to us."

"He'd be stupid to," Tuck said.

"Tuck, Ramin is a lot of things, but he's not an idiot," Drake began. "If he's involved, he'll know that we know, and he'll want to see exactly *what* we know. He'll meet us, don't you worry about that."

"We're all going together?" Rosie asked. "I'm still waiting on the footage, by the way. My friend said it might take a while to get it to me covertly."

"Covertly?" Sateri asked.

"Some of the people she works with might be on the payroll of a few less than pleasant gang members," Rosie explained. "I'd rather she didn't get a bat wrapped around her head for helping us."

"Let me know if you get anything," Drake said. "As for your first question, we might as well. I don't want anything left to chance. We'll get a vehicle from the precinct and use that. Oh and Tuck, could you please make a list of everyone you've angered in the last few months so I have a good idea about where I can and can't send you?"

Tuck at least had the decency to look ashamed. "You spoke to Dai'ix. Look, I can explain."

"I don't care what any of you do outside of work," Drake said, irritated that he had to say anything at all. "So long as it doesn't interfere with your work, do what you like. You either sort it with this guy, or I will."

"Yes, boss," Tuck said, and ended the call.

Drake glanced out of the window, staring down at the ground dozens of feet beneath them. There were plenty of vehicles around, but as soon as the sun came up, that would change into hundreds, if not thousands, of transport and personal-use vehicles dotting the sky and ground.

Drake tapped the panel inside the grav-cab, bringing up the times for sunrise across the planet. He found the correct city, and checked how long they had. "Only an hour until sunrise, we'll get to Ramin just as he's getting up."

"And what if they've fled the planet?" Sateri asked.

"We get a jurisdiction increase from a judge," Drake said, feeling less than hopeful about that. "And if I can't find one to do it, I'm sure Celine knows one or two."

The conversation finished soon after, with Drake wondering if several members of his team were second-guessing his plan. Even so, he went to the precinct—a three-storey building set outside of the city, and some distance from any of the residential buildings in the district—and met up with the rest of the team. The precinct was inhabited by several teams of Wardens working on a rotating shift-pattern, so there were always a few others hanging around and working. One of those there when Drake arrived—a large human with a cybernetic arm—told him to take whichever vehicle he wanted, before going back to the game of cards he was having with two of his comrades.

Drake headed up to the roof and found half-a-dozen sky-skimmers. They were small, four-person vehicles used exclusively for travelling within the atmosphere of a planet. They were the most commonly used vehicles on the Atharoth, and the Wardens liked them because of their adaptability. They were easily modified for speed or combat, and the ones used by the Wardens had more than their fair share of changes in armour and weaponry that most owners of a sky-skimmer would have never even dreamed of.

Drake climbed into the nearest skimmer—a red and green new model—and ignited the on-board computer, which immediately tried to identify him. Drake pushed down a button on the side of the central terminal in the skimmer, and tapped the correct sequence of symbols that appeared on the control panel that sat beside the driver's wheel, allowing the computer to register him as a new user.

"Welcome to the sky-skimmer," the computer said, in a pleasant, if slightly high-pitched voice. "Please take a moment to log in your details for your new ship."

Drake sighed and held down a few of the keys on the console. "I really don't have time for that." He turned to the rest of the group. "Three of you with me, the rest of you take one of the other skimmers."

"Registry has been postponed," the sky-skimmer said. "Please state your desired destination for auto pilot."

"Manual controls," Drake said and the lights behind the

steering wheel came to life.

"Warning, manual controls are more dangerous than the autopilot," the sky-skimmer chastised.

"Tell me again why we use these things?" Drake asked Rosie, Dai'ix, and Rollos as they climbed into the sky-skimmer, with Dai'ix almost entirely filling the rear of the vehicle, Rosie squashed in behind Rollos.

"I could stay, if you like," Dai'ix said, sounding sorry about his considerable bulk.

"It's fine," Rosie said. "I get the front seat coming back."

Dai'ix laughed as Drake pushed the start button and the small but powerful engine came to life. Drake then eased the throttle as the ship rose slightly from the roof. A few seconds later, they were flying toward The Spire and the very real possibility of meeting the murderer of Helice and Septimus.

The Spire wasn't in the city of Croleni, but in Yivas, the fifth largest city on the planet. It was where a lot of business deals were conducted, away from the rush and bustle of Croleni. Most of the buildings in Yivas were at least two hundred stories high, and owned by at least one of the larger corporations who worked on the planet. There was little room for anyone in that city that wasn't incredibly rich, or helping to make someone richer.

The two sky-skimmers flew over several smaller towns until they reached the outskirts of the wealthy homes an hour later. Each home had several miles of land attached to it, with their nearest neighbour being a short drive away. Most of the wealthy on the planet wanted to live as high as possible, but those who lived in the outskirts of Yivas wanted their anonymity, and they wanted to be able to touch the land. Despite the incredible wealth of the homeowners, it wasn't even the most expensive place on the planet to live.

More than once Drake wished he could open a breach to The Aperture to make the journey considerably quicker. As anyone who went to school knew, opening a breach inside a planet's atmosphere essentially tore the planet apart. It's why ships with aperture-drives had to be deactivated before they entered orbit. This was despite the fact that modern aperture-drives were impossible to activate if they detected any kind of atmosphere close by – it was just too dangerous to risk otherwise.

Drake flew through designated flight paths so that he didn't go over any of the rich people's houses. Someone would have notified the local Watch, and that was trouble he didn't need. Instead, he continued on into Yivas, the traffic increasing exponentially. Yivas was a few hours behind Croleni, and the inhabitants of the massive skyblocks were beginning to take their own sky-skimmers or similar vehicles to work. Drake avoided the worst of the traffic, and flew up to the top of The Spire, parking the ship on the private dock that was easily big enough to house a battlecruiser.

Drake exited the sky-skimmer, but not before wrapping the lower half of his face in cloth and putting on some goggles to stop the wind from stinging his eyes. The barriers around the dock stopped the worst of the wind, and sound-dampeners allowed people to talk without having to shout over the howls this high up, but short of putting a dome on top of the building, there was never going to be a complete escape from the elements.

Drake admired the view as he waited for the rest of his team to join him. The Spire was the highest point in the city, and while it still had another twenty stories above the dock, he couldn't imagine the views becoming any more spectacular. The rich and powerful that lived in their massive mansions Drake had ensured not to fly over, were tiny specs in the distance. He wondered how happy they'd be knowing that no matter how much wealth you spent, there was always someone who had spent more. Anyone living on top of The Spire had certainly spent a considerable amount of credits.

He looked around at the dozen other ships on the dock, some of which were big enough to seat a few dozen people, but he ignored the two guards stood in front of the entrance to the building. Both had been inside when they'd arrived. They couldn't stop the Wardens, but they could notify their employees in the building the Wardens had arrived. A fact Drake wasn't overly concerned about.

A second sky-skimmer landed a few seconds later, and the rest of the team exited onto the dock.

"So, do you have a plan?" Tuck asked, sounding exactly like he knew Drake didn't.

"Tuck, Rollos, Dai'ix, you stay out here. I don't want anyone screwing around with our rides home, and I don't want to make anyone nervous." He glanced at Dai'ix. "Well, more nervous. If Luca says to come running, I want you all in there. You can take it from me that you're going to want to be armed."

"Got it," Rollos said with a smile.

"Rosie, you're with me, Sateri, and Luca. Rollos, you're in charge out here." Tuck didn't look pleased, but if he'd left Dai'ix in charge and Tuck and Rollos had started to argue, the oreaf might have decided to interject himself on a more physical basis. And putting Tuck in charge of anything more than himself was a recipe for disaster. Tuck was a good man, and a good Warden, but there were some people for whom the idea of having a small measure of authority turned them into a totalitarian ass of massive proportions.

"Rollos, if anything happens that we don't like, Luca will let you know. Just be careful, okay?"

Drake and Rosie headed toward the entrance to the Spire. "So, why am I coming again?" Rosie asked.

"You're a valuable member of the team, and I need you with me," Drake pointed out.

Rosie nodded. "Yeah, but I'm a technology person, not a people person. People make me feel... a little unhappy."

Drake rested a hand on Rosie's shoulder. "I know, and I'm not asking you to interact with people. So, don't worry."

Rosie nodded once, but it was obvious she wasn't sold. "So, what am I doing?"

Drake motioned to one of the guards, who stepped aside

to allow the four of them into The Spire. "Ramin. What level is he on?"

The guards shared a glance. "Top floor. There's an elevator that's for the top floor only. It only goes between here and there."

"And how do we get to use it?" Sateri asked.

The guard looked genuinely nervous. "We would need to notify Mister Gossard... Ramin, and he gets to decide who can and can't ascend."

Drake counted to five in his head. "You want to go do that now?"

The guard nodded enthusiastically and rushed off to talk to Ramin, leaving Drake and three of his team with one guard, who slinked off after his friend a few seconds later. "So, do you feel like sharing?" Rosie asked when they were alone. "Why am I coming with you?"

"I need you to sit outside of whatever room we're put in and play on your comm unit," Drake whispered. "I need you to find out where Hideo Wynn is and where he'll be in a few hours."

"You want me to hack Hideo Wynn's encrypted calendar?" She spoke between gritted teeth. "Are you insane? I can't do that with a portable comm-unit. I'd need something considerably more impressive."

"You don't need to hack anything," Drake assured her. "Just call him and tell him that Felix Drake wants to talk. I just need you to make it look like it's a big deal. Like you're getting lots of interesting information from him."

"You want me to make Ramin think that Hideo has all kinds of interesting things to tell us?" Rosie clarified.

"Pretty much," Drake said. "As soon as we go in, make it look like they're contacting you, not the other way around. Can you do that?"

"I can call and make their phone contact me straight back, yes," Rosie said. "That's easy. It's going to be a bit harder to explain to the person on the other end why I called and why they're calling me back."

"Drake," he said.

Rosie looked confused. "Yes, I know your name."

"No," Drake said with a chuckle. "Just tell them that Drake wants to see Hideo."

Rosie stared at Drake for a moment. "Do you want to see him?"

Drake paused for a fraction of a second. He wanted to say no. "Unfortunately, yes. I think he's going to be able to help us here."

"To get to Ramin?" Rosie asked. "Or Sabas?"

"Not exactly," Drake said. "If either Ramin or Sabas are responsible, you'll probably see them run the second we finish here. Especially if they know Hideo is involved. Hideo can help us get a judge to agree to extend our jurisdiction. Hopefully."

"You're basing a lot of this on guess work," Rosie pointed out.

"Hideo and Helice were friends," Drake said. "They were really close. Same as Hideo and me. I'm banking on that closeness still meaning something to him."

"He's meant to be a good man," Rosie said.

"He used to be," Drake said, hoping it was still the case.

The guard returned, looking considerably prouder with himself. "Mister Gossard says to go on up. The elevator is down the hall to the left, it has golden doors."

"Because of course it does," Sateri said as she opened the door and the four of them walked into hallway beyond.

"You used to be friends with rich people, yes?" Sateri asked as they reached the golden elevator doors. "Are they all this proud of themselves, or is this the rich man equivalent of penis measuring?"

"Golden elevator doors?" Drake asked. "Yeah, this is new to me. I was sixteen when I last saw anyone I was friends with. There weren't a lot of golden elevator doors in our life."

"So, you didn't all drive expensive vehicles and live in big houses?" Rosie asked.

"None of us drove anywhere, we were sixteen," Drake said. "We weren't even allowed to fly a sky-skimmer without an adult there too. We mostly did what every group of teenagers does."

The elevator doors opened and the four of them got in, with Luca pressing the up button on the panel beside the doors.

"Which was?" Sateri asked as the elevator began to rise toward its destination.

Drake's mind flashed back to the kinds of things he did as a teenager. The life he'd already lead, the fact that not one of them would have been his friend if they'd known who he really was. "Nothing of note."

The elevator stopped soon after, the doors opening to reveal two armed thugs, their plasma rifles slung over their shoulders. They were both taller than anyone in the lift and considerably more muscular than even Luca. They looked similar enough to have been brothers, or maybe they'd just had too many surgeries to *improve* parts of them that they now couldn't be told apart.

They don't look friendly, Luca said. *You want me to make them friendly?*

Drake wondered if his friend could take both of them out, and decided that actually he probably could. Luca was not a man Drake would want to get into a fight with. Not without cheating a whole lot. He glanced over at Luca who smiled, and winked, making Drake grin before the group were asked to take a seat and wait.

CHAPTER SEVEN

Felix Drake

Luca, Sateri, Rosie and Drake sat together on the comfortable chairs, remaining quiet for close to an hour. The only noise was Rosie's tapping on her comm unit, and occasional muttering under her breath as if irritated.

Two guards stood watch the whole time; their pistols remained holstered, even if they appeared incredibly twitchy.

"The boss would like to speak to you alone," the closest of the two neckless pieces of muscle said after someone spoke to him through the earpiece both guards wore.

"Not a chance," Sateri interrupted. "Luca and I will be going with Drake."

"They can remain seated out here on the chairs," the second thug said. "Mister Gossard won't be happy if we let you all in."

"It's okay," Drake said. "Ramin isn't going to try and hurt a member of the Wardens, that would null and void his immunity while on this planet. That would mean I could kill him, do a little dance, and then go home and have some food."

The two guards glanced at one another.

"Keep Rosie company," Drake said. "She's got a call coming in from Hideo Wynn at some point."

The expression of concern on the guard's faces told Drake that they both heard what he said.

"Shall we?" Drake asked as Sateri returned to her seat, obviously unhappy about the situation. He followed the two thugs out of the small room they'd been placed in, and down the golden hallway, through the set of red double-doors.

The room inside was decorated in the same reds and golds of everything else Drake had seen, although the desk was a deep brown, and presumably made of real wood. The windows stretched down one side of the room, allowing in a lot of bright light, showing off the impressive art collection on the opposite wall. There was a red and silver rug on the floor between Drake and the desk, and he noticed that the thugs walked around it as they made their way over to a third thug stood behind the desk. Drake walked straight onto it, standing in the middle of the rug while he waited for someone to talk to him.

The two thugs left the room via a door at the far end, behind the third thug who just stood and stared at him. "You want to speak to Mister Gossard?" he asked after several seconds of silence.

"Yes, I'm pretty sure that's been established," Drake said.

"You are not to accuse him of any illegal activities," the man said. "He is here of his own volition, and wishes to aid in whatever matter you have a problem with. Do you understand?"

Drake looked at the thug for a heartbeat. He was bald, had pale skin, and beard that dropped to his chest. His dark glasses presumably hid whatever his eyes had been augmented with. Or maybe he just had a bad hangover, and was waiting for meds to kick in. Drake decided it was more likely to be the first. The thug wore an expensive dark-blue suit, and despite his obvious musculature, didn't strike Drake as the kind of thug a person like Ramin would usually employ. At least not for anything that needed a... hands-on approach to dealing with his inevitable issues.

"Do we have an agreement?" the man asked.

"What's your name?" Drake replied.

"Radner Puley. I'm Mister Gossard's legal representative."

Drake nodded slightly. "You didn't look like the two who escorted me here, I figured you had a more impressive job title. Didn't expect a lawyer to be here though, I'm not planning on arresting anyone."

"Sabas is also here," Radner said, and Drake knew for a fact that he was there more for Sabas than Ramin. "You will not attempt to engage Sabas in conversation about alleged criminal activity."

"I honestly hadn't thought about engaging in conversation with Sabas in any way, shape, or form," Drake told him.

"Glad to hear," Radner said, either not hearing or not caring about the sarcasm in Drake's voice. "I found it pays to be prepared where questions are concerned. Now, before we begin, do you have any questions about what we've discussed?"

Drake knew a question that might piss off the lawyer, but he figured he'd ask anyway. "You know anything about the murder of Helice and Septimus?"

"I'm not here to answer your questions, Mister Drake," Radner said smoothly. "And you will not directly suggest either Mister Gossards are involved in their murders. You can ask your questions, but I won't hear accusations thrown their way."

"Had to give it a shot," Drake said with a shrug. "You understand?"

Radner's slight nod told Drake that in fact the man understood, but wasn't keen on being questioned. Before Drake could ask anything else, the door opened and a huge man walked in. He wasn't huge like the first two thugs—all muscle and augments—Ramin was just a tall and wide man. There was a lot of muscle there, a man like Ramin was never going to let himself get out of shape, but he was never going to be muscle-bound like his thuggish employees.

Behind him was Sabas, who was a few inches taller than Drake, and outweighed him by maybe fifty pounds. His arms bulged with surgically-enhanced muscle, his shirt struggling to take the strain of them. Drake seethed at his appearance, and noticed that the smug expression on the man's face hadn't changed since he'd been arrested. Even when he'd been sent to prison for murdering a Warden, he was still smug. Like it didn't faze him at all.

Ramin sat in the huge leather chair behind the desk, placing his hands on the wood and linking his fingers. A smile fixed on his weathered face.

Sabas stood behind his father, his arms crossed, a permanent smile on his face as Drake took a seat. Each of Sabas' huge hands were capable of enveloping the top of a person's head, and Drake wondered if those same hands had been around Trinas Brong's head before he died. Or if they'd helped kill Helice and Septimus. Drake pushed the thought aside. The anger it created wouldn't do him any good. It took a lot of effort for Drake not to launch over the desk where Sabas was concerned, he didn't need more ammunition.

"The Wardens don't pay me a lot of visits," Ramin said. His voice was a deep baritone. He rubbed his hand across his chin, stroking several days of stumble on his bronze skin.

"Probably worried your boy will murder one of them," Drake said before he could stop himself.

"I was exonerated," Sabas said. "All charges dropped."

"I never suggested otherwise," Drake said. "I just said that people will remember you were charged and found guilty of the murder of a Warden, and that might make those same people slightly more nervous about being in a room with you."

"The man who did it killed himself from the guilt," Sabas said with what Drake assumed the man considered an approximation of sadness. "I hear he murdered another Warden some time before the crime I was wrongly convicted of. And after that he hunted down three Suns Watch too. To kill three members of the very people who protect our valued royal family is just... horrific. Three men and two women in all, I believe. All gunned down in cold blood. Ambushed, if I heard correctly. I heard the murders of the other Warden had been an open case for several years."

"Always good to get some closure," Drake assured him.

Sabas' eyes narrowed in anger. "Must be hard for you, knowing that those who aided him could still out there."

"Are you two done?" Radner asked. "Drake is not here to discuss on-going Warden cases outside of the remit for this meeting." Radner turned to Drake. "Please continue."

"A few hours ago Septimus Mowatt and Helice Tranton were found murdered in an apartment, along with someone you might know – Trinas Brong," Drake said.

"I heard about Helice and Septimus," Ramin said. "I was informed of their deaths earlier. I'm very sorry to hear of it. You think I'm involved?"

"Your name came up as someone who may have had issues with Helice," Drake said.

"You don't *really* think I'm involved, do you?" Ramin asked.

"We have to look at all avenues of investigation," Drake told him. "I just want to ask you a few questions."

"Radner and Sabas can wait outside," Ramin said.

"That's a terrible idea," Radner said.

"Yeah, why would you do that?" Sabas demanded, his temper threatening to bubble over.

"Because I need our Warden friend here to understand that I am innocent," Ramin said. "Besides, I have questions that he may not want to answer in front of you both. Also, I have nothing to hide."

Neither Radner nor Sabas argued twice, and they left the room without comment. Drake looked around the office, taking in the artwork on the walls, the real pale-wood cabinet opposite the large window which overlooked the city. Ramin was a gangster, and had fought every inch of the way from his impoverished childhood to the leader of one of the most powerful gangs on Leturn. Despite his rich living, cordial temperament, and friends in high places, he was still a gangster. Drake had to sometimes remind himself of that.

Ramin got up from his desk, walked around, and pulled Drake up into a hug. "How are you, my friend?" He asked, motioning for Drake to take a seat.

"Good, you?" Drake asked him, as he sat.

"Tired," Ramin said. "I have worked for the Wardens as an informant for many years now. I got my own son arrested, but he has friends in high places. He is… a monster, Drake. I'd hoped to get him somewhere they could help him."

"I'm sorry," Drake said, meaning it. He liked Ramin. Yes, the man was a gangster, and a criminal, but he didn't hurt innocent people, and he sure as hell didn't hurt councillors or their families. "You knew Helice and Septimus."

Ramin nodded sadly. "I did, yes. Someone told you I killed them?"

"They suggested it," Drake said. "Told me you were angry with Helice for ensuring your plans to develop on Atharoth were stopped. Said that it cost you a lot of credits."

Ramin smiled and nodded. "Yes, she cost me a great deal. Doesn't mean I killed her. If I killed everyone who ever stopped me making deals, Leturn would be a smoking ruin at the moment. Honestly, I'm impressed you even knew about it, those talks were confidential. Even to Wardens."

"We all have our ways," Drake said with a smile of his own. "Something to do with de-forestation?

Ramin looked confused. "That was a long time ago. It never even left a Council preliminary investment meeting."

Drake's mind began to put pieces together. "You know Metan Glornv?"

Ramin nodded. "A weasel."

"A nice way of putting it," Drake said and nodded in agreement. "He told me about the deforestation."

"I have no idea what he's talking about," Ramin said, and was quiet for a moment before he continued. "Thank you for not killing my son." He looked up at Drake and sadness lined every inch of his face.

"You asked me not to," Drake said. "You helped us bring

closure to the family of a Warden. Sabas didn't make it easy though. The man does not know when to quit."

"Gets that from me," Ramin said with a hint of pride. "I just wish he didn't get so much else."

"As much as I enjoy our conversations," Drake said. "We don't have time."

Ramin nodded. "You're right. I have no idea who would want either of those two dead. Helice was… an opinionated pain in my ass, but I respected her. Septimus was a wet cloth. His death would be utterly pointless."

"What about Sabas?" Drake asked, wishing he didn't have to.

"I can look into it," Ramin said. "He's been complaining about cashflow problems, and he keeps his cards close to his chest. I think he's trying to get enough power and money together to remove me as head of the family. A little surprised he hasn't tried already. I do not wish to go to war with my own son, Felix. No father should have to do that."

"He never mentioned them then?"

"Not once," Ramin said, getting to his feet. "I'll let you know what I find out."

Drake nodded slightly. "Thank you."

"You ready to recommence normal function?" Ramin asked with a smile.

Drake returned the smile with one of his own. "Yeah, let's get this done."

Ramin opened the doors to his office and called Sabas and his lawyer back into the room, before retaking his seat behind his desk.

Sabas entered, saw that Drake was now on the sofa, and leaned up against the far wall instead as Radner stood in the doorway after closing the doors.

"So, did you find out anything you needed?" Radner asked.

"Someone is accusing me of murdering two children of councillors," Ramin said. "I won't divulge the name of the person who told Drake, but I assured him it was not me. I gave him my alibi."

"And you didn't want us to hear it?" Sabas asked, irritated.

"No, I didn't," Ramin said quietly. "Drake will confirm it, and I will be exonerated, but there are some things neither my son nor my lawyer need to know."

Apparently, that was enough for the pair of them.

Sabas glared at Drake. "You were on Vanesta, yes? Not during the war, obviously, I mean recently."

Drake's eyes narrowed as he wondered where Sabas could have gotten his information. "Yes."

Sabas laughed. "The Wardens having to look after a bunch of jumped-up brats on an extended vacation. You know the history of that planet, I assume."

Over thirty-five years ago, Vanesta had been home to a battle between the Rebel fleet, who were trying to overthrow the Union, and the Union itself. After the battle was done, the planet was mostly nothing but a ruined husk, although an influx of credits had turned it into a playground for the rich and powerful. The battle and destruction forgotten for bright lights and loud music.

"I'm aware, yes," Drake said.

Sabas' smile was predatory. "The Rebels spent a decade defeating the Union at every turn, laying waste to planets who refused to bend the knee to them. For spoilt, rich brats to go to a planet that was the scene of such an horrific battle and turn it into a hedonistic retreat, must be difficult for someone who works for the Union."

"The Rebellion ended over thirty years ago, I think people move on," Drake said softly. "I'd like to believe that anyway."

"Even so, it must have been a nightmare to people like yourself who are trained to protect," Sabas continued. "All of those people, all of those drugs and parties. I think being here must be a more pleasant experience."

"Everywhere has its good and bad points," Drake said. "I'm wondering what yours is."

"I just wanted to let you know that we can all look into

people's pasts," Sabas said with a shrug. "We can all learn about one another. I think that's important, don't you? To learn about one another? To understand where each of us come from?"

Drake knew what was coming next.

Sabas smiled as he spoke. "Your mother was murdered, and you got to live the life of luxury in the palace. I wonder why that is. I mean, your mother was well known as someone who *befriended* one of the councillors."

"The same one who murdered her," Drake's tone was flat, emotionless. He couldn't risk anything else. "I'm aware."

"It was a good job the King of Stars and his family took pity on you then," Sabas continued.

Drake said nothing.

"I think sometimes it's best for things to remain buried," Sabas said. "For information to just stay placed away with no need to tell the wider world what you know. Don't you agree?"

"I find that any secret that big gets out sooner or later," Drake said, noting the confusion on both Ramin and Radner's face.

"It doesn't have to," Sabas said without any hint of the tension he was creating in the room. "Sometimes who our parents were will mean that people judge us by their actions. Your mother was a woman who married a councillor while she was already with a young child... you. Such an awful childhood. Raised on a battleship, I assume, before your mother met the councillor in question."

Drake balled one of his hands in to a fist, immediately regretting the action as showing how much the sack of shit was getting to him. "We could all look into things, Sabas."

"Mister Gossard," he corrected.

"Yeah, we're past that, Sabas," Drake said. "We were past that when I went to arrest you for the murder of a Warden. We were past that when you tried to attack me, and I broke three of your ribs, and your left arm. If you're involved in these murders in any way, I'm going to come back here, and I'm going to drag you back to prison." He looked over at Radner. "And you're not going to be able to stop me. Nice magnus bracer by the way."

Radner adjusted the sleeve of his jacket, to cover more of the bracer.

"*Drake*, I would think very long and hard about what you think you're going to do here." Ramin's tone was now one of all business. Drake knew that Ramin was his ally, but he also knew Ramin was not a man to allow a fight to break out in his office. The emphasis on the Drake was as much of a threat as any Drake had ever received.

"Why did you change your name?" Sabas asked, walking across the room to stand behind his father. "I heard from a friend that when you arrived here, your name was Drake Varlus. That's unfortunate considering who that name once belonged to. Any relation?"

Drake walked to the desk and placed his hands on it. "You know who my father is, don't you?"

Sabas nodded, a smile back on his lips. "And I assure you, soon everyone else will too. Felix Drake and Drake Varlus are one and the same. The son of Evan Varlus. Is that why you left last time? When you first came here, you were an innocent child, but it didn't take long for people to start to suggest you were your father's son. A man not to be trusted, a man who would have destroyed the Union if he'd been given the chance."

"My father went to war against the Union because of what he believed in," Drake said before he could stop himself. "He went to war against his friends and family just because he thought it was the right thing to do. People who knew him used to say we were very similar, so *Mister Gossard*, exactly what do you think I'd do to someone I despise? Because I know I'd go to war against those who crossed me. And trust me, you don't want that."

Sabas' hand went to the pistol holstered under his open jacket, and Radner had to motion for him not to do anything to make things worse.

Drake looked up at Sabas, and noticed the smile had gone for the first time. Drake's iris turned purple, and he lifted his hands off the table as the smell of burning wood reached his nostrils. He followed Ramin's gaze to the two burned handprints on the wood.

"Sage," Sabas almost whispered.

"You're not wearing a bracer," Radner said, sounding more than a little shocked and concerned.

Drake remained staring at Sabas. "The last time you crossed me, I left you with only broken bones. You draw your weapon on me, and I'll end you. If I find out that you were involved with the murders of Council family members, I'm going to bury you so deep that not even your powerful friends will be able to help." Without another word, Drake turned and walked out of the office.

CHAPTER EIGHT

Bokk

Bokk had been left alone for several hours by the time the sunlight streamed through the automatically darkening windows, bathing Drake's collection of model ships in a beautiful morning glow. They weren't sure why they found the morning sunlight to be so lovely, why they enjoyed the feeling of warmth on the receptors on their metallic frame. Bokk wasn't sure about a lot of things, like feelings and emotions, except that they had a feeling they weren't meant to have any. They were a synth, and while they knew they'd developed a personality—many synths of their generation did the same—Bokk was different. Drake certainly saw it, although Bokk was grateful their friend had never decided to root out the cause.

Friend. It was something Bokk had taken several weeks to come to terms with. They'd researched the word, and tried to decipher whether or not the information was what they felt. After some deliberation, they'd decided it was. An odd thing for a synth to be able to admit. And based on Drake's vocal patterns on the few occasions they discussed it, Bokk knew Drake felt the same way.

Most synths considered their owners to be just that – an owner, or a master, but a… friend? That was different. Bokk knew there was a reason for it, but how they knew such a thing, they couldn't say. They felt like there was something hidden, just beyond their reach. A memory shrouded in fog; something they could occasionally catch a glimpse of but never truly see.

Bokk had been a gift. Maybe the only one that still gave Drake any link to his father. Memories of being owned by Drake's father had been wiped clean before they'd been placed in Drake's care. Bokk neither knew what Drake's father looked like, or was like as a person. Didn't even know Drake's father's name even though they felt like they should.

While Drake was out working, Bokk often cleaned the apartment and got things ready for Drake's return. They would occasionally cook, although their inability to taste food meant they often added too much seasoning or not enough. And on one memorable occasion, used enough salt that Drake would have been violently ill after only a few mouthfuls. Bokk knew Drake enjoyed cooking – it was one of his ways of relaxing, so apart from cleaning and organising the kitchen, they left the preparation of food to those with taste buds.

Bokk's main role was to keep Drake safe, and while that might have been pertinent when he was a child, Drake was now an incredibly competent member of the Wardens. However, those old protocols remained in place. They'd long-since hacked into the Warden communication devices, having their chatter on in the background of their day. Occasionally, Bokk would hear something to do with Drake and they would wonder whether or not to leave and rush to help him, but since arriving back on Atharoth, Bokk had managed to contain their need to protect their friend.

Apart from the security on Drake's front door, there were also several private guards who patrolled the entire building, making sure to keep those deemed undesirable away. Drake had often told Bokk of their dislike of the guards, of the way they create a 'them' and 'us' culture. As far as Bokk was concerned, the guards added an extra piece of security for a man who would need it should the identity of their father ever become public knowledge. Bokk might not know the name of Drake's father, but they knew that it was a big deal.

Bokk paused from their thoughts when they heard someone try the door to the apartment. They walked over to their recharge point and plugged themself back in, but refused to power down. Instead, they remained still and watched as the door swung open and two men entered, closing the door behind them.

Both men wore black clothes with black and silver masks covering their faces, along with gloves instead of a medi-skin variant that would allow them to leave no biological evidence behind. Bokk wondered why that was, and then they saw the yellow pulse of light on the back of one of the gloves – bone smashers.

Bone smashers weren't their official name, but it was what everyone called them. They were designed to absorb the kinetic energy of a punch and increase its power ten-fold, unleashing it upon impact. They were also ten years out of date, as there were problems with the power supply that meant sometimes that power would re-direct back into the person's hands, causing them to shatter. Drake had mentioned they were a popular street-fighting weapon, but had fallen out of favour as they couldn't hold up against a Sage, and really only worked on flesh.

Apart from the gloves, each man had an energy dagger, but no ranged weapon. That would make things easier.

"How long do we have to wait?" the first thug asked.

"Until Drake gets home," the second replied. "He's got to come home sometime, and then we do what we need to do."

The first thug chuckled. "I'm looking forward to it. Wardens always look down on us."

The second thug nodded their agreement, but kept silent.

Both men were well over six-feet tall, with muscular arms and chests. Thug One walked over to the control panel on the wall and disabled the security features in the apartment. "Drake doesn't have any cameras in the apartment. Just that synth over there."

The second thug walked over to Bokk, standing in front of them. "Why keep such an old relic like this?"

"People get attached to stupid stuff, you know that," Thug One said. "Anyway, where do you want to wait for him?"

"Bedroom," the second thug said, moving away from Bokk. "We'll wait until Drake's in, he'll get nice and comfortable, and then we'll make sure he has a really bad day."

"How much are we getting paid for this?" Thug One asked.

"Enough," Thug Two told him. "Just take some enjoyment in your work. How many times have you been turned down to work with these people?"

There were several seconds of silence before Thug One said, "Seven."

Thug Two whistled. "That's seven times worth of hate you've got in you. Drake's face is going to take a lot of beating for that."

Thug One laughed, and the pair walked away together.

As much as Bokk wanted to send a message to Drake and tell him that people were in his apartment, they would need to get to the control system to do so. That might mean the two interlopers in the apartment would notice him.

Bokk disconnected themself from the recharge point, and followed the two men's footsteps, stopping short of entering the spare bedroom. There was nowhere to hide in the room, it was almost completely empty save for a few pieces of equipment Drake used to work out.

Bokk's sensors picked up the men's whispers before heading back toward the apartment door. They tapped on the control pad, which made a slight *ping* sound, and selected the message centre. Tapping to create a new message, Bokk paused and looked over at the two men.

"And who are you?" Thug One asked.

"The synth must have woken up," Thug Two decided. "Looks like they want to send their master a message."

Bokk looked back at the screen, lowering their arm to

their side. The message could wait, but they doubted the two thugs would let them have the time to send one.

"Why not just use a comm unit?" Thug One asked.

"Synths are weird sometimes," Thug Two said.

"The comm unit isn't encrypted," Bokk explained. "The messaging system built into this apartment has alpha encryption. No one alive can hack it without several weeks and enough processing power to fit inside a warehouse. It's the safest way for me to contact Drake in an emergency."

There was a slight hum as the two thugs activated their gloves.

"I'm a security synth," Bokk explained. "Those gloves won't do a lot of good against my kind. They're made to break bones, and I don't have any of those."

"These have been enhanced," Thug One said. "We'll do okay."

Bokk took a step toward the two men. "Why are you after Drake? If you tell me, I will go easy on you." Bokk paused while the two men laughed. "Or not."

Bokk moved quickly toward Thug One, dodging a clumsy punch, pushing the man's arm down, and back in one smooth motion. They held onto the limb, breaking it at the joint, before throwing him to the floor, where he hit his head hard enough to remain where he fell.

The second thug used the plight of their friend to close the distance, landing a punch to Bokk's chest that forced the synth back several feet.

Bokk's internal sensors showed the damage caused by the bone smashers; the outer-skin of their torso was cracked, and several components inside had received significant impact.

"What did we say?" Thug Two asked with a smile.

Bokk remained silent as the man cautiously moved toward him, the hum of the gloves constantly reminding them just what was in store should the glove connect with their body again.

A cruel smile spread across the lips of the thug. "Your

master is going to come home and find you in pieces, and then I'm going to make him wish he hadn't gotten up today."

Bokk remained silent, unmoving as they continued to watch. The thug moved like an experienced fighter. A man not to be underestimated.

Thug Two threw a weak punch at Bokk's head, just testing distance and Bokk's ability to block. They knew the man would be more cautious than his still-unconscious partner.

Another punch, this one quicker, with more purpose, once again aimed at Bokk's head. They swayed back, unwilling to block the blow, to get close to those gloves, unless they were certain they could end the fight.

Thug Two moved forward again, testing with a third punch, and following up with a powerful blow that was meant to land on their torso. Bokk moved away in time, punching the man in the face with a blow of their own, knocking him aside. Thug Two tried to re-balance himself, but Bokk was already on the offensive, landing another blow to his stomach, and a third to the thug's chest that lifted him off the ground and sent him flying back into the wall.

The man picked himself up just as Bokk grabbed their arm, tearing the glove off one hand, before doing the same to the other. They switched the gloves off, and tossed them onto the floor.

"I have questions," Bokk said, his tone never anything more than cordial.

Thug Two kicked them away, the synth surprised by the force in the blow. The thug took a swing at Bokk, who caught the fist in their open palm, using their power to crush the man's hand, causing him to scream out in pain.

"First question," Bokk continued. "Who sent you?"

The man dropped to his knees and Bokk increased the pressure on their ruined hand.

"Who sent you?" they asked in the same neutral tone.

The man swiped up with a dagger in their free hand, forcing Bokk to block the energy blade and punch the thug in the jaw. The man fell back to the floor, and Bokk placed a foot on their spine, pushing down with a small amount of the force at their disposal.

"Let's try this one," Bokk said conversationally. "Who are you?"

"I'm a Blackcoat," Thug Two cried out.

Bokk removed the man's mask, using their built-in software to take a picture. "Who sent you?"

"Sabas," the man managed to stammer.

"Thank you," Bokk said, and punched the man in the head hard enough to knock him out.

Bokk left the prone man on the floor and returned to the apartment messaging system. They placed their hand on the glass panel, and their fingertips opened, allowing him to link their software with the system. They took the photo of Thug Two and began their search. Bokk knew that as a Warden, Drake had access to the databases of all the authorities on the planet, so it didn't take long to discover the identity of the unconscious man on the floor behind them.

"Bennos," Bokk said, glancing back over at the man in question. "Blackcoat second class. Not very high up the rankings considering you worked there for twenty years. Lots of complaints about you." Bokk accessed the confidential material that only Wardens would have been able to see.

"You've been bad," Bokk continued. "Lots of investigations into your involvement with Sabas. Nothing found. Nothing proven, anyway. It appears you made anyone who might testify against your boss, disappear. Drake often mentioned that Sabas must have had inside help. I guess we know who it was."

Bokk moved toward Thug One, and removed their mask. Blood leaked from his eyes and ears. They were dead. Bokk took their photo and checked, discovering that they, too, were a Blackcoat second class. Bokk returned to Bennos, who was beginning to stir.

"Why were you sent here to hurt Drake?" Bokk asked.

"Shouldn't have angered the wrong man," Bennos told him.

"Nor the wrong synth." Bokk grabbed hold of Bennos' head and broke their neck in one quick movement, allowing the dead Blackcoat to drop back to the ground with a thud.

Bokk returned to the control panel and accessed the apartment system once more. "Emergency protocol one-six," they said.

The system was designed to locate the owner of the apartment should an emergency happen. Protocols for emergencies were pre-installed, and one-six stood for a break-in, armed assailants, which Bokk felt summed up the current situation quite well.

The computer gave Drake's current whereabouts as The Spire.

Bokk looked around the room; they would have to explain about the two dead Blackcoats, but their first priority was to protect Drake. They'd have to get transport, which went without saying, but they were certain they could steal a sky-skimmer should the need arise. Bokk went to Drake's bedroom and pressed the small button just beside where the visi-screen sat on the wall.

Part of the wall slid away, revealing dozens of weapons for both close-quarters and ranged-combat. Bokk ran another systems check, discovering that the damage done by the bone smasher was enough that it would need attending to sooner rather than later. They selected a coil-rifle; while it was intended to be used from distance, it had a semi-automatic fire option they knew would come in useful to clear out any rooms where enemies might be waiting.

Bokk placed the rifle in a bag, along with a plasma knife and several ammunition pouches, and slung the bag over their shoulder. They left the apartment without looking at either of the dead interlopers. There would be more where they came from if Drake was harmed. Bokk would make sure of it.

CHAPTER NINE

Felix Drake

Drake, Rosie, Luca and Sateri left The Spire penthouse behind. Neither Sabas nor the lawyer Radner had appeared to be happy with Drake's little display of power. The Wardens met up with the rest of the team on the landing port.

Drake had managed to calm down by the time the cold air rushed across the port. "Any problems?" he asked the other members of the team.

"Not one," Rollos said. "They left us alone, and we didn't have to throw anyone off this rooftop. Wins all around, I think. Judging from your expression, your time with Ramin and Sabas was less than pleasant."

Drake flashed back to Sabas threatening to tell the world who Drake's father was, to the man's smug expression. He considered telling his team that Ramin was working as an informant, and had been for some time, but decided that it was information better kept to himself for now. "It wasn't a fun time, no."

"I couldn't get hold of Hideo," Rosie admitted. "I tried, but their encryption is better than I thought. Couldn't even get through to their phones so that it forced them to call me. I do know where he is though."

Drake tried not to outwardly give any indication that he

was uncomfortable about involving Hideo in anything. "Give me the address, we'll go pay a visit."

"You okay, boss?" Dai'ix asked.

Drake shook his head. "After I've spoken to Hideo, we need to get together, I have some things I need to tell you all. Things I'd rather you heard from me than anyone else."

"You leaving?" Rollos asked with a smile that quickly vanished when he saw Drake's expression.

"I'm not planning on it," Drake assured everyone. "Even so, you need to know a few things." He glanced over at the sky-skimmer he'd arrived in. "I'm taking that one to Hideo."

"We need to look into Sabas a bit more," Sateri said. "I think something is going on with that man."

Drake nodded. "Check into Metan too. Either way, it feels like Sabas knows something. It's entirely possible that either he had them killed himself, or someone did it for him."

"We'll find out," Sateri said. "You think Hideo can help?"

Drake nodded. "I think Hideo can arrange a jurisdiction increase. I'm hoping he still has a soft spot for old friends. It's not a play I wanted to make, but it's the quickest way."

"Not through Celine and her bosses?" Rollos asked.

"I know, that's the normal route for one," Drake said. "It could take too long. I'd have to present the case for it, and it would have to be signed off by Celine's superiors. It could take a day or two to sort out. Hideo can grant it in an hour."

"That it?" Rollos asked.

"I think having Hideo in our corner will help," Drake said. "He has a lot of power, and if Sabas is working with councillors, he'll be able to tell us which ones."

You know this roof is probably bugged, right? Luca said.

"I'm counting on it," Drake said with a slight smile. "I need some of you to go to Hideo's mansion. I don't want to miss him if he isn't where Rosie thinks he'll be."

"I guess I better come along just in case you can't read directions," Rosie said sarcastically. "What with me possibly being wrong and all that."

"You know that's not what I meant," Drake said.

"I know," Rosie said with a warm smile. "I just like to mock you any chance I get."

I'm coming with you, Luca informed Drake.

"Me too," Rollos said. "My little brother gets in trouble when I'm not there."

"I'll go back with Sateri," Dai'ix said. "It's all going to turn to shit at some point, I might as well make sure I'm prepared when it happens."

"I'm with them," Tuck said. "There's a lot we don't know, and they could probably use the extra set of eyes and ears."

The team split in two again, with Drake, Luca, Rollos and Rosie climbing into one of the sky-skimmers and lifting off the port.

"This is going to get worse before it's over, isn't it?" Rosie asked.

"I imagine so, yes," Drake answered.

It was a short journey to Hideo's tower across town, and after they'd landed on the tower's dock, Drake asked the other members of his team to stay in the sky-skimmer. "I just don't want four Wardens spooking anyone. Not yet anyway."

Drake left the ship and watched the tower guard walk toward him. "Are you here to see someone, sir?" the guard asked. They wore a dark grey uniform with a picture of a white sun on each arm.

"Hideo Wynn," Drake told him.

There was a pause before the guard continued to speak. "Is Prince Wynn expecting you?"

Drake moved his jacket slightly, showing his Warden badge and holstered pistol. "It's on official business."

The guards eyes narrowed. "Wardens are meant to make appointments."

Drake had expected such a reaction. "Well, on this occasion it was an urgent thing. Didn't have time."

"You're going to have to wait until Prince Wynn is done," the guard said.

Drake didn't want to wait hours. "I'd be appreciative if you could just tell him Drake is here to see him."

The guard nodded and tapped his chest. "I've got a Drake here to see Prince Wynn."

There was a moment's silence before the guard continued. "Prince Wynn has no appointment to meet anyone by that name, sir," the guard told Drake, his hand dropping slightly to the disruptor on his hip.

"I know that. I've just got here. Can you just let Hideo know that Drake Varlus is here to see him. Also, do you really want to threaten a member of the Wardens?"

The guard remained steadfast. "I am not allowed to speak to Prince Wynn directly; it would be a gross over-step of my boundaries as one of his guard. The second your name was not on the list of approved visitors, it notified the Suns Watch of your arrival. I doubt very much they will be as relaxed as I am. Now, please, leave."

As if on cue, the lift doors behind the guard opened and two officers of the Suns Watch exited. They each wore a burgundy magnus bracer and carried sheathed swords that Drake already knew would be made of obsidian-fibre. They were encased in blood-red and burnt-orange predator-armour. This was not how it was meant to go. Drake turned back to his team and motioned for them to stay.

He turned to the two Suns Watch officers and the guard. The Suns Watch were the elite guards to the Council, and by law they had to be Sage. They weren't well known for their understanding and tolerance of people, and Drake doubted they'd suddenly find some for his case. There had been more than one documented occasion when the Suns Watch had tried to stop the Wardens from arresting or even interviewing their councillor. Drake didn't want today to become another such incident.

"Look, my name is Felix Drake," he said, desperate to avoid anyone getting hurt.

"You told me it was Drake Varlus," the guard said, his eyes

showing distrust.

"That's the name Hideo will know me by," Drake said. "My name is *now* Felix Drake. I'm with the Wardens. I'm not going to arrest Hideo, but I need to talk to him. It's urgent. Please tell him I'm here."

"I already know," a voice shouted from the lift.

Drake's attention had been on the two Suns Watch officers, he'd completely ignored the lift still being in use. The man who walked toward him was a head taller than Drake and about as broad shouldered. The black and dark blue outfit looked good on him, which it should for the amount of money he would have paid for it. The tunic alone probably cost more than the sky-skimmer Drake had used.

Hideo was flanked by two more Suns Watch officers, both female, both carrying their helmets under their arms. Neither of whom looked that happy to see Drake.

"I heard you wanted to see me," Hideo said, his voice tight. "But you can't be Drake. He wouldn't be foolish enough to come here after so many years away. Not without so much as a hello since you arrived back on the planet several months ago."

"I wasn't sure how to start," Drake admitted. "I wasn't sure how I'd be received."

Hideo took several steps toward Drake and hugged him tightly. "You're home," he whispered and released Drake.

"You knew I was back on Atharoth?" Drake asked. "You knew I'd changed my name."

"I have good Intel," Hideo said. "Also, you kept the name Drake, it wasn't exactly hard to put together."

Drake's emotions swirled inside of him. "It was the only thing my parents gave me that I still had, I didn't want to lose it."

Hideo hugged him again. "It's so good to see you. My father was convinced you were alive somewhere in the cosmos, but more than a few thought you dead."

"You still think me foolish for coming here?" Drake asked.

"Stupid is a more appropriate word." Hideo turned to

the Suns Watch officers that had accompanied him from the building. "Prepare to leave at once, I wish to travel back to my home so that I can talk to my brother."

"He's your brother?" Rollos asked, clearly surprised. He'd left the sky-skimmer along with Luca and Rosie, overhearing the tail end of the conversation.

"We were like brothers growing up," Hideo said. "I told people he was my older brother."

Drake noticed that the guard who had given him a hard time had dropped to his knees, his helmet removed and beside him, while his forehead touched the ground.

"Get up," Drake told him. "You look stupid."

"I beg your forgiveness, Your Majesty," the guard said to Hideo, ignoring Drake.

"You need not ask for any," Hideo told him. "You were only doing your job. And frankly, Drake couldn't look more like a vagabond if he tried."

Drake rubbed his hand over his beard growth, a smile appearing on his lips.

The guard didn't look up. "Thank you, Your Majesty."

"You can leave now," Hideo said. The guard was quickly on his feet, jogging away toward the guard station in the centre of the dock.

"I heard you were one of the named successors," Drake said. "I assume congratulations are in order."

One of the Suns Watch who'd gone off to arrange transport, returned. "We're ready to depart, sir," she said, with only a slight glance in Drake's direction.

"Your friends can take the sky-skimmer to my residence," Hideo said. "Drake, please come with me. It has been so long, I need to catch up."

Drake looked back at his team.

Will you be okay? Luca asked.

Drake nodded. "I'll see you at his mansion."

"You're not wearing your magnus bracer," Hideo said as he walked with Drake to his ship – a sky-skimmer that was roughly three times the size of the two Drake had used. Hideo raised his wrist to show his own magnus bracer.

"Long story short, haven't used my aether with a bracer in a very long time," Drake said.

Hideo stared at his brother as if he'd grown a second head. "Why would you do that?"

Drake didn't really want to get into it. "Like I said, long story."

Hideo stared at Drake for a few seconds before saying, "Well, you can tell me all about it soon enough."

Drake walked up the ramp and into the cabin where a smartly dressed grey-haired man, who Drake assumed was a servant, offered him a seat. Drake sat while the Suns Watch appeared to try very hard not to glare at him.

Once everyone was seated, the ship's engine ignited, and they were off.

"It's a short journey," Hideo said. "Only a few minutes, but Father won't let me take anything else to work and back. This is more armoured than a tank."

"So, what is it you do?" Drake asked. "When I last saw you, you were sixteen. A lot appears to have changed."

"Not as much as you might think," Hideo said with a tone of being somewhat unhappy about it. "I run several defence contracts. There's a lot of checking with the moons and other planets, making sure to get things done. It's all very tedious, but apparently necessary."

The sky-skimmer began its descent. "Already?" Drake asked, "We were barely in the air."

Hideo rolled his eyes. "I live close, and I'm not allowed to take my own vehicle. I have this lovely entourage everywhere I go."

"That doesn't sound like much fun," Drake pointed out.

"You'd hate every second of it," Hideo said with a smile.

Drake kept quiet as the ship landed on a private airfield behind a row of exclusive mansions a few miles away from the nearest skyblock. The engines were switched off, the ramp descended, and a few seconds later the door opened. Drake left the sky-skimmer and walked down to the airfield, staring off at the open fields in front of him. He was happy to see Hideo, genuinely happy, but it wasn't a personal visit. Drake needed something and Hideo was the man he hoped would allow him to have it. There wasn't really a plan 'B' in his head.

"Amazing, isn't it?" Hideo said as he stood beside Drake and stared across the fields.

Drake nodded, enjoying the feel of the cool wind on his face. "You prefer to be on the ground?"

"I like that I'm so close to the planet," Hideo said. "Being up there, in the air, is all good, but it's not where we're meant to be. We created a set of circumstances where we need to live and work high above us. I know I'm lucky enough to be able to afford to live on the ground, to live on this planet at all, and if I could, I'd never go back to the towers or to any of the major cities. This is as close to perfect as I can imagine."

"I never saw you for a romantic," Drake said with a chuckle.

Hideo smiled. "My husband would say the same thing."

Drake paused. "You're married? Who drew that straw?"

Hideo walked away, moving around to the front of the sky-skimmer and across the airfield to a guard patrol in front of a large gate. He waited for Drake to catch him up and then had the two armed guards open the gate and let them both through.

"What about your Suns Watch?" Drake asked as he spotted the rest of his team outside of the mansion, keeping a healthy distance from any of Hideo's people.

Hideo placed a hand on Drake's shoulder. "They'll join us shortly; I like to have a few minutes alone while they check the perimeter. I assume those Wardens there are your team."

You okay, Drake? Luca asked.

Yeah, you guys stay here. I want to talk to Hideo for a few minutes. I'll be back out shortly. Drake turned to Hideo. "They'll wait here. I need to talk to you."

Hideo nodded. "So be it." The pair stopped by several guards next to a guard post, and Hideo told them to make Drake's team welcome and get them any food or drink they might require.

"You'll regret that once Dai'ix turns up," Drake told Hideo. "Oreafs don't exactly have a small appetite."

Hideo's laugh was full of warmth. "I have enough to spare, even for an oreaf."

The pair walked through an ornate garden, passing by flowers and trees that were not native to the planet, and obscured the rear of the mansion. Once past them, the massive building could be seen in all its glory.

"How many bedrooms does that thing have?" Drake asked, genuinely impressed with the architecture.

"Fourteen," Hideo said. "Two kitchens and enough other rooms that I don't think I've been in them all. I have servants, and my guards. Both of whom live on site, so I need to be able to provide for them."

"Hideo," a man called out as he left the double doors at the rear of the mansion and walked over to him.

The newcomer was slightly shorter than Hideo, although about the same size otherwise. His blue hair was tied back, and his white tunic was splattered with various paint colours, as were his trousers, along with his bare arms and hands.

"Caleus," Hideo said with a smile and embraced his husband. "You remember Drake, yes?"

Caleus' smile dissolved from his face the second he laid eyes on Drake. "You're not dead," he said with venom.

"That's what they tell me," Drake said. "Nice to see you too, Caleus."

"How has your day been?" Hideo asked, and Drake noticed the nervousness in his manner.

"I've been working," Caleus told him.

"Caleus is an accomplished painter," Hideo said, his voice full of pride. "He's had pieces sold over seventeen systems."

"Wow, that many?" Drake said, trying very hard to ensure

he didn't sound dismissive.

"Why are you here, Drake?" Caleus snapped.

"I'm here to see Hideo," Drake told him. "I need to ask him for some help."

"You're here to cause trouble," Caleus snapped. "Which is exactly what you've always done. Cause trouble and get people hurt. You should leave before whatever curse follows you around infects anyone else." Caleus turned and walked off.

"I'm sorry for that," Hideo said, sounding as if he genuinely meant it.

"You don't need to be," Drake told him. "Your husband's hatred of me was well documented when I was last on this planet."

The friends walked toward the mansion without another word and Hideo led Drake through the maze of hallways to a massive room at the front of the mansion. Drake looked out of the floor to ceiling windows that allowed light to bathe the entire room, and looked at the towers in the distance.

"The closest tower is eight miles away," Hideo said. "Close enough that I can see them, but far away that they look tiny in comparison when you're right next to one."

"And your father was okay with you living here?" Drake asked.

"Not everyone who grew up in the palace needs to rebel against him," Caleus said as he entered the room.

"Caleus, please," Hideo said softly. "I haven't seen Drake in years. No one had any idea what had happened to him. I'd like to be able to talk to him without having to field an argument between the two of you."

"You're too soft when it comes to him." Caleus gesticulated wildly toward Drake. "Just because he was nice to you back then, you allow him too much. I'm sure he was just as nice to my sister before he led her into a life of drugs and mayhem. A life that killed her."

Hideo's expression would have stopped a snow boar in its tracks.

Drake hoped that the ground might actually swallow him up. Caleus' sister was Novia, the same Novia who had once loved Drake, and who he had once loved in return. The same girl who had taken a huge dose of drugs and launched herself from the top of a skyblock. The same girl who Drake had avenged by murdering the man who had given her the drugs. Her parents had always hated Drake, and despite him being off world when she'd died, blamed him for her death. He'd learned of a bounty they'd taken out at one point, but no one knew where he was, so thankfully none had tried to collect.

Drake stopped listening to the argument that was before him, until Hideo stood. "Enough," he snapped. "Your own hatred of Drake, hatred that is misplaced, has clouded your judgment, and affected your behaviour. Please, leave me to talk."

Caleus' mouth dropped open shock, but it didn't stay that way for long. "Right, you come find me when you get rid of your murderous friend. Until then, I'll be wondering exactly how angry I am with the way you just spoke to me. Just make sure you keep him in this room, I don't want him wandering the house." He turned and marched off.

"I am not going to have a quiet day, am I?" Hideo said and rubbed his temples as he sat back down. "Why did you come to see me, Drake?"

Drake had been nervous about asking for help, and after the way Hideo's husband had reacted, that nervousness had only increased. "Helice and Septimus were murdered last night. I think Sabas Gossard is involved, but I need a jurisdiction increase to be able to officially question him."

Hideo sat down on a nearby chair. "Helice and Septimus? Are you sure?"

Drake nodded. "Unfortunately, yes. There was a gangster who was murdered alongside them who was injected with something called chameleon, it's a drug—"

"Designed to change the recordable DNA of whoever is injected with it." Hideo nodded. "We've had some people found with it in their system before. It's not new, but it is scary, especially when used in large doses. No idea who makes it, and trust me, we've looked. Why would someone kill Helice or Septimus?"

Drake explained how Helice had stopped Ramin from winning approval to clear massive amounts of forest for building, but how he believed that Ramin wouldn't murder anyone connected to the Council, while Sabas would be quite happy to. Especially if riches were involved.

Hideo sat and listened without interruption. "So, it all comes down to credits, as per usual." He sighed. "I know you want to go after those responsible and bring them to justice, but is that all there is to it?"

"I want to kill everyone involved," Drake admitted. "Slowly. Painfully. I want to look at them and make them know why they died so hard. I'll settle for getting the names of the councillors Sabas worked with."

Hideo appeared shocked for a moment. "You never used to speak like that."

Sadness settled like a weight in Drake's soul. "Things change. I'm not the boy I was when I left. I came to you because I trust you, Hideo. Can you help me?"

Hideo nodded. "On one condition. You have to see my father."

Drake shook his head. "That's a bad idea. Sabas knows who *my* father is. It won't take long for him to leak that information to those people in the Council he calls allies."

"So, you're just going to run again?" Hideo's tone was hard for the first time.

Drake shook his head. "I don't honestly know what I'm going to do."

"This isn't a negotiation," Hideo told him. "Take it or leave it."

A comm unit on the wall beeped and Hideo stood up, activating it. "Sir, you have two visitors here," a deep voice said.

Hideo sighed. "Tell them I'm busy."

"Ummm, sir, they're here to see your visitor. They're Wardens, and they say their names are Sateri and Luca, or should I say one of them says, the other doesn't appear to have a tongue, sir." The words were said without revulsion, just a guard doing his duty.

"Have them escorted in," Hideo said and turned to Drake. "Team members?"

"I told them to wait a few minutes," Drake explained. "I figured they'd come in and make sure I was okay when I ended up here longer than that."

Hideo laughed. "Do they know who you are?"

"No," Drake said, but knew he needed to say more. "I want to tell them before this goes further. Luca is a mute. Experimented on by our loving Union military, he only communicates by telepathy. Sateri is sarcian. I'm pretty sure they'll be okay with knowing the truth. Maybe."

"I think it's time to be honest," Hideo said, and before Drake could reply both Luca and Sateri walked into the room, accompanied by a guard, who left a moment later.

"Nice to meet you both," Hideo said to them, offering them both a seat. "I hear your names are Sateri and Luca. Thank you for putting up with Drake."

Drake inwardly groaned.

"I think you should tell them the truth, Drake," Hideo said. "I think they need that."

"I wanted to tell them all at once," Drake said.

"What truth?" Sateri asked. "What's going on here?"

"It's a long story," Drake began. "It's about what I was going to tell you all later, I think the whole team needs to hear this." He stood to use the comm unit on the wall beside him, activating it just as Hideo screamed something unintelligible and dove toward him.

Drake was knocked aside as the glass shattered and Hideo was thrown back with incredible force. He landed against the far wall with a horrifying thud and dropped to the floor, motionless. A second round smashed into the floor just beside

Drake, tearing the wooden boards apart. Drake rolled to the side, out of the view of the windows. "Everyone stay down," he yelled and punched his hand against the emergency situation button on the wall beside him. Thick, metallic shutters dropped across the broken windows, turning the entire room dark.

"What the hell happened in here?" Caleus asked as the lights came on. He saw Hideo and cried out, rushing to his side. He pointed a finger at Drake. "This is your doing."

"Blame later, survival now," Sateri said. "Move, let me see him." She pushed Caleus gently aside and knelt beside Hideo. Blood saturated the front of his tunic. "He's been hit with a big round, no idea what kind though. I need to stabilize him. I need to stop the bleeding."

The Suns Watch rushed into the room and quickly piled over to Hideo, while Sateri tried to explain what was happening.

"The shooter was from one of the towers," Drake said.

"That's impossible," one of the Suns Watch replied.

"Tell that to Hideo," Drake snapped. "Keep him alive. Luca you want to go find a gunman?"

"I can't let you leave," a large sarcian female Suns Watch officer said.

Drake's irritation threatened to boil over. "You let me leave, or I go through you. Keep Hideo alive, or come with me. Which one?"

"Go," a second female Suns Watch officer shouted as a something impacted with the outside of the metal shutters. A second impact a moment later caused the metal to warp slightly.

"Thank you," Drake said. "Will those shutters hold?"

"We'll deal with that," the Suns Watch officer said. "Just find who did this, and bring them back here. Dead or alive, I don't care."

"You got a fast ship?" Drake asked the Suns Watch officer, who smiled in response. "Excellent," Drake said. "Let's go hunting."

CHAPTER TEN

Felix Drake

"So, do you have a plan?" the female sarcian Suns Watch asked as she left the mansion, placing her helmet over her head. Drake and Luca followed her, and the three checked that there were no accomplices to the shooter before exiting the house.

The guards were already tense, scanning the surroundings and communicating through their comms units asking for back-up. Drake hoped that the knowledge of Hideo's injury wouldn't make the Suns Watch try and take control of the situation, making things worse. At least long enough for Drake to find those responsible before the rest of the guard and Suns Watch arrived.

"I'm going to find this guy," Drake said softly. "And then I'm going to ask him many questions." He paused and held a finger up for silence. "You hear that?"

The other two guards stopped walking and listened as they reached the edge of the mansion's property. There was a whistling noise in the air, which got louder until the sky-skimmer Drake had arrived in, exploded in a fireball. The shockwave knocked several of the guards to the ground, along with Drake and Luca. The Suns Watch officer dropped low and rolled into a nearby guard station, as another whistling noise slammed into the remains of the skimmer, sending an even bigger fireball into the sky.

A shock-wing—a four-man orbital fighter—streaked past and unleashed its twin chain-cannons that sat at the front of the ship, tearing through another sky-skimmer as if it were paper, before roaring up and vanishing into the distance.

They really want you dead, Luca said inside Drake's head.

"I appear to be very popular," Drake agreed, as he scrambled back to his feet. "Everyone okay?"

Lots of people all spoke up at once, giving Drake hope that any injuries were minor.

"They'll be back soon," Drake said to anyone who was listening. "We need to get in the air. And we need something that can counter those bastards in their shock-wing."

"We have our own shock-wing," the Suns Watch officer told him.

"Excellent, where is it?" Drake asked, unable to spot it.

The Suns Watch officer lifted a glass shield on the side of the guard's station and punched the red button. Parts of the airfield moved slightly as three automated anti-air batteries lifted from their hidden home.

"Okay, that could help," Drake said.

"All three are equipped with two plasma cannons and several particle missiles," the Suns Watch officer said. "It should keep our friends away for a while."

Drake knew first-hand the damage a particle missile could do. Designed to follow a ship's heat signature, overtake it, and then explode in its path, it bathed the ship in thousands of tiny particles, which completely screwed up the ship's electrical systems. Drake had always been thankful that particle missiles had two disadvantages, they don't work in space, and they don't work when it's wet. He'd seen people lose control of their ship after being hit by one, unable to escape, unable to do anything but wait for the inevitable crash.

Luca tapped Drake on the arm and pointed across the airfield as a ship rose out of the ground.

"That's not like any shock-wing I've ever seen," Drake said.

Like a normal shock-wing, the ship was sleek and designed for speed and manoeuvrability, with twin chain-cannons under the pointed front end. Unlike the one or two-man fighter ships, a shock-wing could take some damage too. The armour was heavy enough to withstand a fair bit of punishment, and most were fitted with shields. The cockpit sat just before the middle of the jet, giving a great view.

"It's bigger," Drake said as they ran over to it. "And what's with the wings?" Normally folded away, each were fixed and tipped with what Drake realised were missiles.

"It's a combat-ready, fourth-generation special-operations model," the Suns Watch officer told him as the ramp lowered and they made their way into the ship. "Triple thrusters instead of twin, and enough firepower to give anyone who tangles with it some serious issues." She turned to a nearby guard. "Rear guns."

The guard moved to the back of the cockpit without another word.

"I'll take the defensive systems," the Suns Watch officer said. "The pilot has the forward cannons."

"What are your names?" Drake asked the guard and Suns Watch officer as Luca sat in the pilot's seat. "If we're going to fight together, we should know that."

"Whesker," the guard said as the engines roared to life.

"Gret," the Suns Watch officer replied. "We know who you are, Felix Drake. The arrival of the Wardens isn't something we take lightly. We'll have words when this is over about you arriving without letting us know."

"Well, you might get me dead instead, wouldn't that be nice," Drake said sarcastically, and lent over to Luca. "You do know how to fly this, yes?"

Luca responded by pulling back on the throttle, taking the ship vertically into the air at incredible speed, which threw Drake back into his seat. He wisely buckled up as the ship sped toward the towers in the distance.

"You really think the shooter is still there?" Gret asked.

"Probably not," Drake replied. "Hopefully we can track them. What does this panel here actually do before I start pressing buttons?"

"Allows you to monitor and take control over everything else on the ship," Whesker said, sounding very concerned about how much control Drake now had.

Drake tapped a few panels and brought up the ship's sensors as something impacted the hull. "What was that?"

"We're being shot at," Gret said. "Looks like it came from the tower there." She tapped a few keys on the panel beside him. "Whatever they're using, it's powerful enough to make our shields really dislike it. I'm not sure we can take too many more shorts when we get close."

"Take us up, Luca," Drake said as he used the panel to try and pinpoint exactly where the shot was fired.

The shock-wing lifted up, and Luca fired the throttle once again.

"We've got two, no, three shock-wings inbound," Gret said. "I really hope you know what you're doing."

"I can't get a lock on where that shot came from," Drake said. "You need to get closer to the towers, preferably close enough for them to take another shot."

"Have you lost your mind?" Gret shouted.

On it, Luca told Drake, and the ship suddenly accelerated, flying through the clouds above them.

"Contact," Whesker shouted, and Drake felt the massive plasma cannons on the rear of the ship kicking wildly as they fired.

I can't get close to the building while dodging shock-wings. Which one do you want more?

"Get rid of them," Drake said.

The shock-wing dropped like a stone without warning as Luca changed the direction of the thrusters. They plummeted through the cloud at high speed, skimming between two walkways that connected two different towers. Drake watched on one panel as dozens of people ran across the walkway to the far tower. A panel next to him monitored the enemy shock-wings and he watched as the three tried a similar manoeuvre. They managed it, but were much slower in doing so.

"They're either not as fast or just more cautious," Drake said.

"They're not as fast," Gret said. "Although I doubt they'd want to do what we just did unless forced to."

Let's see what they will do.

Luca cut the shock-wing's engines, causing the heavier rear of the ship to drift around to the side.

"We've got all three almost on us," Gret said, her fear obvious for everyone to hear. "Ten seconds until missile lock."

The ship's shield's flickered as the enemy shock-wing opened fire. Whesker returned fire, and one of the ships on the screen vanished.

"Got one," he said.

"Good, now get the others," Drake told him.

"Five seconds," Gret said.

The rear of the ship had now drifted around 180 degrees, and was pointing at a slight angle toward the ground. Luca put the throttle in max and the ship roared forward at incredible speed, narrowly missing the remains of one of the enemy shock-wings and causing the other two to fly off in an attempt to avoid the chain-cannons.

In seconds, the shock-wing had flown back between the walkways and toward the nearest tower. A second later, another shot hit the shields, causing an alarm to ring out across the cockpit.

"Found the bastard who shot Hideo," Drake said. "Let's move, Luca."

Luca pulled up on the stick, punching the shock-wing through the cloud once more.

"I need to get onto that tower," Drake said, pointing. "Any chance you can get me there without making me a sitting duck?"

I don't think I can do both. If I stop this ship and those shock-

wings appear, we're going to have some issues.

"I've analysed what hit us," Gret said. "Someone in that tower is using a fusion rifle."

That explained how it was able to keep the power to punch through a security glass window over eight miles away and still hit Hideo with the power it had.

Fusion rifles were smaller versions of the fusion cannon found on battleship. They were capable of sending a projectile at huge speed for massive distances, inflicting an enormous amount of concentrated damage on its target. Drake was grateful for the shields that surrounded the ship.

Luca flew as close to walkways and towers as he safely could, in an effort to make their enemy lose their nerve, while he circled back toward the target tower. The ship suddenly barrel rolled and accelerated down slightly and then quickly up as one of shock-wings passed under it. Luca fired the plasma cannons, which tore into the shield of the enemy ship but didn't bring it down.

"Shields are down on that ship," Gret said as the ship in question turned and came back at them. "They're insane; they can't hope to survive this."

"We've got contact back here too," Whesker said. The rear guns began to fire as Luca weaved the ship through a barrage of cannon fire.

"They have missile lock," Gret said. "Launched."

Luca accelerated toward the shieldless ship, firing his cannons. The shells tore into one of the wings, clipping the fuel cells. The explosion threw the ship toward the tower that hid the would-be assassin. He moved as if to ram the critical ship, and then pushed down at the last second. The explosion as the missile hit its ally caused a shockwave that destroyed most of the glass within several floors of the tower. Shortly after, the remains of the ship impacted the building in a fireball.

What floor is our rifle enthusiast on? Luca asked.

Drake tapped a few buttons on his terminal. "Seven-nineteen."

Luca slowed the ship, turning it away from the glass that was close enough that Drake could have reached out and touched it. Luca turned the engines to max and destroyed the glass directly behind the ship.

Does this help? Luca asked.

"Thanks," Drake said, and pushed the button on his terminal to open the ramp on the ship.

"You're going to get out here?" Gret asked, shocked. "We're over a mile above the ground at this point."

"You got a better idea?" Drake asked, and the ship slowly reversed so that the ramp was close to the now ruined glass. "Keep safe, people."

Drake sprinted across the cockpit, down the ramp and launched himself off at the last moment. He landed inside the tower and rolled, stopping just before he collided with a wall.

Gret appeared on the ramp soon after and threw something at him, which landed close by. "It's a comm unit for use by the pilots of the ship. I'll find the frequency. Be safe."

The ramp quickly closed, and the shock-wing took off. Drake had just crouched down behind a wall when the second shock-wing flew past, in pursuit. He had no doubt that with Luca at the helm, they'd remain safe.

Drake placed the earpiece, and looked around. The floor was still under construction, with only the external glass panels and internal supports having been completed. He ran through the floor until he came to a turbo-lift. A placard next to the doors said he was on floor 866. Over a hundred floors higher than he needed to be. He pushed the button for the lift and took a few steps back, waiting for its arrival behind a stone pillar.

The turbo-lift didn't take long, and after a few seconds wait, the lift doors opened revealing it to be empty inside.

Drake stepped inside. "Floor seven-twenty-two," he said, and the doors closed. He wished he'd taken some weaponry with him, wished he'd been thinking enough to get anything, but he'd been too pre-occupied with going after whoever hurt Hideo, and was only now beginning to consider his options. Going up against someone wielding a fusion rifle was not a great plan. It would only take one shot at short range to turn him into paste.

"Pause," Drake said and the lift stopped. He tapped the screen on the side of the lift doors, which came to life showing him a variety of options, most of which were either useless or uninteresting. He found the option marked 'directory' and tapped the screen. It gave him a list of exactly what was available on each floor. He scrolled through the mass of information, but most of it simply gave a floor number with 'incomplete/unoccupied' written beside it. Even the floor with the sniper said unoccupied, which meant whoever was doing it was masking their signature somehow.

He continued to scroll down until he found what he was looking for; seven-fifteen had twenty-two people on it. He tapped the floor to see where everyone was, and discovered that they were all in one large apartment about halfway through the floor. "Seven-sixteen," Drake said, hoping that someone that floor might have a weapon he could use, or at least know where he could find one. It also occurred to him that they could be working with the sniper, which is why he picked the floor above. He couldn't imagine how anyone could have not heard the shots from the fusion rifle, but then if they were working with the sniper, he'd rather know before hand – he didn't want to get ambushed. If the sniper was masking their signature somehow, that meant others could be too.

The lift stopped a few moments later and the doors opened, showing nothing but empty space between him and the windows at the far side of the tower several hundred meters away. The apartments had at least been started on this floor, but apart from having exterior walls, there was nothing to suggest this was ever going to be anything other than a giant construction site.

"How is it going your end?" Gret asked through the

comms unit in Drake's ear.

"This skyblock is still being built," Drake said. "Where are all of the crews? Why are there no external signs of construction?"

"There were some disagreements between the Council and people who wanted this place built," Gret told him. "There's a security force present and maybe a few construction people. It's possibly a conversation for when we're not getting shot at, have you found the sniper?"

"No, I've found a floor with over twenty-people on it though, I'm going to go see if they're involved," Drake said "And hopefully find a weapon a little bit more impressive than my viper pistol. Possibly some sort of tank, or missile launcher."

"That might come in handy," Gret said.

"How goes the dogfight?" Drake asked as he pushed open the door to one of the towers stairwells and began to descend.

"This last one is a real piece of work. I think I saw your mute friend break out in a sweat a moment ago." The tension in Gret's voice still broke through her attempt at humour.

"Keep safe, I'll let you know what I find." Drake disconnected the comm just as he reached the door to floor seven-fifteen. Ordinarily, the doors would have been capable of opening as people got close to them, but as there was no power to them—much like everything else Drake had seen—they were manual operation only. Drake wondered how the Council would have coped having to do something for themselves. They probably had people for it.

He moved slowly onto the floor, and having found no one in his immediate vicinity, he made his way toward where he'd seen the group of people. The floor was fully built, showing how luxurious the living accommodation would be. There were maybe thirty apartments on either side of the central hallway, each with different coloured doors. The hallway contained various plants and a large water fountain in the centre with benches around it. The lights above absorbed natural light on the roof and then deposited it throughout the tower.

Drake knew that the people were on the left-hand side of the hallway, but didn't know which apartment, so from about halfway down he began opening doors only to find that most, while fully built and furnished, were not lived in. There was no power to any of the appliances. He pushed the fourth door, and it became stuck before he could make enough of a gap to get through. Drake put his shoulder behind it, and it budged a little bit more, enough for him to squeeze though.

The second he was in the apartment, the door slammed shut behind him and Drake realized why he'd struggled to get through. Someone was slouched behind the door. Drake moved the man's head, trying to get a pulse, but there was nothing. He shifted the dead man away from the door then began his search of the apartment. He soon found the other twenty-one people, all laid out on the floor of a spacious bedroom. He went to each and every one, and found that the majority of them were merely unconscious. During his search, Drake discovered three gas canisters. He tapped the comms unit in his ear.

"You ever heard of timoxil?" Drake asked.

"The gas?" Gret asked. "It's a military grade knock out gas. It's designed to render people unconscious in seconds, but it was withdrawn. Timoxil is still in development, but it's not used unless you don't mind the bodies."

"Let me guess," Drake said, keeping an eye out for anyone who might be hostile. "It has a tendency to kill people?"

"Pretty much," Gret said. "Anyone with a heart condition goes into cardiac arrest almost immediately."

Drake sighed. "I've found three canisters. Lots of unconscious people who, from their uniforms, I'd guess are security. One dead man who was in some nice business attire."

"They're going to be out for the better part of a day," Gret told Drake. "Apparently our attackers aren't picky if someone dies."

The comm went dead, and Drake went to searching

the unconscious victims for any weapons. He found several stun pistols, which weren't much help to him without any ammo, and a disruptor rifle which, while certainly more of a threat, was big and cumbersome and also empty of ammo. A disruptor pistol and laser revolver were similarly empty. Whoever had knocked these people out had done a fine job of making sure they couldn't be interrupted if their victims woke.

The last person to check was a kiretan. The massive male carried only a kiretan great sword, which was roughly the size of Drake, but after picking it up, it was remarkably light. He removed the harness for the blade and put it on himself, managing to make it small enough to fit him before slotting the sword so that it sat against his back. It was a quick release harness, so the second he took hold of the hilt and pulled, the sword came free.

As he left the room, he spotted a small energy dagger on the floor behind a chair. He picked it up, pressing the button on the hilt, which turned the blade midnight blue. He switched the blade off and took the sheath for that too, securing it around his waist. That made two energy daggers and a great sword to go with his viper pistol. It would have to be enough. Drake left the apartment and made his way back toward the stairwell, determined to get the answers he needed from the person who'd tried to kill him and those he cared about.

CHAPTER ELEVEN

Felix Drake

Drake jogged up the few flights of stairs until he reached the correct floor. He crouched and slowly pushed open the door. The floor itself had a few walls and supports, but little else. In the far corner, only a few hundred meters away, was a figure hunched over. They wore grey robes, obscuring themselves from Drake's view, but it didn't matter who—or what—they were, they were going to pay for what they'd done to Hideo. Drake wished he'd found the ammo for the disrupter rifle he'd left behind as he took a step toward his prey.

The figure spun on the spot and fired. Drake threw himself to the ground as the fusion-rifle round obliterated part of the door and wall behind him. He scrambled to his feet and ran for the nearest wall, and a second round tore through it just by his head. The walls hadn't been finished, and very few actually made it all the way to the windows, allowing Drake to use the gaps between the glass and walls as paper-like cover while he sprinted toward the far end of the room. Twice he had to throw himself to the ground and roll back to his feet when the sniper's round got too close for comfort. He couldn't imagine how anyone could be so accurate when walls obscured their vision and their target was moving. The sniper had to have a sensor. The thought spurred Drake to run even faster.

His only chance was to get too close for the rifle to be of use.

Instead of rounding the corner and having to run a hundred meters to the sniper, Drake sprinted through a half-built apartment and out into the hallway on the adjacent side. The robed assassin aimed the rifle at Drake, who readied himself to use his aether to avoid the incoming projectile. While under fire it wouldn't be accurate, or even safe without an appropriately-levelled magnus bracer, but it was that or die. The sniper pulled the trigger, and nothing happened.

They tossed the rifle aside, and the barrel touched the nearby glass, causing it to sizzle as it burned through to the air outside.

"You used it too much, too fast," Drake said as the sniper's hands went under his robe, re-appearing a moment later with a plasma rifle. Drake dodged to the side, grabbed the energy dagger, activating it as he flung it at the sniper in one movement. The blade buried itself into the many folds of the robes the attacker wore, where Drake knew the rib cage to be. They staggered back, and the hand holding the rifle dropped to one side.

Drake covered the ground between them as quickly as possible. Just as the sniper raised the rifle once more, Drake drew his viper pistol, pushing the barrel of the rifle aside, and fired twice at the sniper's head, but the assassin moved too quickly, and the shots only hit fabric. Drake punched the sniper in what he hoped was a jaw. They staggered, throwing the rifle at Drake's face, who had to push it aside, leaving himself open to a kick to the stomach with a synthetic foot that held three large, talon-like toes in the front and one in the back. Drake lost hold of his viper pistol as he was driven back against the nearest wall. He rubbed his stomach, grateful the armour he wore had stopped the talons from getting close to his flesh.

Red eyes blazed from inside the darkness of the robes, and Drake knew he faced a battle synth.

A synthetic hand, with only four fingers, silently pulled

away the robe and tossed it up in the air, obscuring Drake's vision.

Drake knew what was coming and moved to the side, removing the sword from his back, and waited for the attack. The synth kindly obliged and one hand tore through the robe with frightening speed and accuracy. If Drake hadn't moved, he'd have been disembowelled. Instead, Drake brought the sword down onto the synth's wrist with everything he had, cutting through the armour, as well as the cables and components that made up the tendons on the wrist.

Another hand tore through the robe and grabbed hold of the sword's blade, pulling it from Drake's grasp, and throwing it aside. Drake put some distance between himself and the synth, which tore the remains of the robe free from its body and tossed them aside as it stepped toward him.

"Not a battle synth," Drake said. "Recon. Either way, you're going to tell me who ordered you to try and kill me."

Recons were made for stealth and were less about pure power and more about speed and agility. So, on one hand it meant Drake didn't have to fight against a synth designed to fight people in full power armour. On the other, that also explained why the synth was much faster than he'd anticipated, and why it had been aware of his presence once he'd stepped off the lift. Recon synths were about the same height as Drake, but noticeably thinner, they came in a variety of colours they could change as and when they needed. Atop their human-shaped head was a silver, fist-sized dome, which gave recon synths the ability to track all movement within several hundred meters around it.

"Your death is assured," the recon synth said, its voice neutral and level. It pulled Drake's energy blade from the black and green armour plating that covered its torso, and re-activated it.

The synth darted forward, bringing the blade across in a swiping motion, down toward Drake's stomach. He dodged aside and kicked out at the back of what passed for an elbow on a synth. The synth's hand turned a hundred-eighty degrees and swiped back at Drake, cutting across his forearm.

Drake knew he couldn't beat a recon synth in a one-on-one fight, especially when the synth had an energy dagger. He dashed back, putting some distance between the two of them, forcing the synth to follow, the energy dagger held almost nonchalantly down by its side.

"You ready to talk now?" Drake asked, fully aware how pointless his words were but needing to fill the uneasy silence.

The synth answered by darting forward, swinging the knife up toward Drake's throat. Drake threw himself aside, rolling across the floor, and coming to his knees beside the glass. There was a sucking of air, and Drake noticed that a large hole had been cut from it, presumably for the rifle's barrel to be placed just outside the glass, masking the position of the first shot.

Drake drew the snub-nose blast-gun and fired point blank at the synth who'd followed his movements. The splatter of hundreds of super-heated projectiles smashed into the synth's torso, tearing apart the armour around where the heart would be on a human. The synth rolled away, avoiding the second and third blast, which tore into one of the windows, causing it to spider-web. They threw a blade at the gun, impacting with the barrel and making it useless.

Still on his knees, Drake dropped the gun, scrambled for the hilt of the nearby great-sword, and got back to his feet. He moved the sword so the blade tip rested on the floor just to the side of his foot. Then he tensed.

The synth moved forward slowly, recognising the sword as a threat but unsure how to respond. Drake assumed the synth had been programmed to kill him no matter the challenges. It would keep coming after him until one of them was dead. That included continuing to try even if it was outmatched or in danger. Recon synths weren't cheap, and Drake was certain that whoever had used one to try and kill him, would have more than enough capital to try again.

Drake rushed forward, swinging the sword up in a fast, deadly arc. It collided with the energy dagger, throwing up sparks as the blades slid against one another. The synth shoved forward with immense strength, throwing Drake back.

Keeping his feet, Drake sprinted back toward the synth, who dashed forward, allowing the sword blade to pierce its chest. The synth continued running, forcing more of the blade through its torso until it was close enough to swipe at Drake with the dagger.

Drake pushed the sword away, moving at the last possible second to evade the dagger. When the synth overreached its attack, Drake re-took the hilt and yanked the sword back out of its chest and up, attempting to sever the synth's handless arm, but it moved with tremendous speed, punching Drake in the jaw with its stump, sending him careening into the windows.

Dazed and in pain, Drake got back to his feet as the synth grabbed hold of his throat and lifted him from the ground. It smashed the back of his head into the glass. Already damaged from where the blast-gun had hit it, the window cracked further from the impact. Blood trickled down the back of Drake's neck and the synth slammed his head into the glass once more, this time shattering it. Freezing wind whipped into the tower, and Drake kicked and clawed at the synth's iron grip. He knew it could just crush his neck, but apparently taking the recon's hand had given the synth other ideas. It held on to Drake and took two steps forward, pushing him through the remains of the glass so that his feet dangled precariously over several miles of empty air.

"Your death is assured," the synth repeated and released his grip.

Drake held on to the synth's arm with everything he had, but it kicked out at him, catching him in the chest and forcing him to release. Drake fell, cursing himself for being out of practice, for losing to a synth. For losing at all. *You're a Sage.* He screamed in his head as the ground far below rushed closer and closer.

He turned in mid-air as the floors sped past him and concentrated. Using his aether without a magnus bracer was dangerous, difficult, and unpredictable, but it was that or death. He refused to go without trying. Drake had practiced without a bracer for years, making sure that if this day came, he would be able to fight.

Every thought that filled his head was of him standing next to the synth, of being on that floor again. The thoughts of death, of losing Hideo, of his murdered friends, of never getting justice… those thoughts all melted away leaving just Drake and the floor he'd been standing on seconds earlier. He closed his eyes, hoping to block out the sound of the wind as it whipped past, so couldn't see as the air around him shimmered and shifted, so he couldn't see his body grow translucent and vanish from view.

There was a scream that wasn't human, and Drake opened his eyes to find himself back in the tower block, on the correct floor. He stood next to the synth, his arm punched clean through its head.

From falling to activating his aether, Drake had been in free-fall for less than ten seconds, but it felt like a lifetime. Drake's brain took a moment to catch up with what he'd done, another side effect of not having a bracer, but once it did, he shouted in pain, dragging his hand free from the remains of the synth's head.

"Shit," Drake snapped. "I'd hoped to be able to question you." Badly cut across his hand and forearm, blood flowed freely from the wounds. He grabbed the energy blade, activating it and cutting though the synth's robe, before using it as a tourniquet. He sat next to the synth and elevated his arm by placing it up on a stack of building materials.

He wrapped another strip of cloth around his one good hand, using his teeth to help him, and then began rummaging around inside the head of the synth, all the while hoping the memory circuits hadn't been destroyed.

"You still with us?" Gret asked through the comm device

in Drake's ear.

"It'd be great if someone could come and get me," Drake suggested. "How's it going up there?"

"We got the bastard in the end," Gret said, sounding down-right enthusiastic. "We'll be right with you."

Drake resumed his search, and found the small memory capacitor. He pocketed it and pushed painfully to his feet, picking up the sword and re-attaching it to the holster. Drake gathered the energy dagger and viper pistol, re-sheathing them both. The blast-gun's barrel was warped from the impact of the dagger, and would need considerable repairs before working again. He re-holstered it anyway, and headed to the broken window to wait for his ride.

The ship didn't take long, and he was soon back inside the cockpit where the Suns Watch officer, Gret, attended to his wounds with a medical kit.

"You're lucky you didn't sever a tendon or artery," she said as she applied foam to the cuts, which quickly solidified, allowing him to wrap the whole arm in a bandage that contained a numbing agent.

"How's Hideo?" Drake asked.

"Stable is about all we know," Whesker said. "They're shipping him to the palace. I assume that's where you want to go."

Drake nodded reluctantly. As much as he really didn't want to go back to the palace, he needed secure access to see what was on the memory he'd retrieved from the synth, and the palace was the best place to find it. Besides, he wanted to check up on Hideo. "Let's get going," he said. "It's been a really long day, and I have a feeling it's not done yet."

He glanced out of the nearest window at the destruction of part of the tower.

You okay? Luca asked.

Drake nodded slightly, and looked over at the man he considered to be both his friend and teammate. *I think things just got a whole lot more complicated.*

CHAPTER TWELVE

Felix Drake

The palace of the King of Stars was as opulent as anywhere in a dozen systems. Thousands of years ago, when the position afforded the king unrivalled power and influence, the King of Stars had lived on a planet several hundred light-years from Atharoth. That was long ago, before the Sage Wars, before the universe changed. After the war, a new palace was made. A new home for a new type of King of Stars, one who needed the Council's approval to do anything, one who was no longer allowed to have the sole power and influence to dictate the Union's destiny.

Drake stepped off the shock-wing's ramp onto the almost impossibly neat and tidy grass that made up the miles of fields all around the palace.

Nice house, Luca said as he followed Drake out of the ship. *Did you grow up here?*

Drake nodded; the memories of his time here had been mostly happy ones. "Yes, I spent some time here when I was young, although I can't imagine too many people are going to be happy to see me back."

"That sounds like it's the same wherever you go," Whesker said as he left the ship.

"Let's get it over with then," Drake said and walked off toward a waiting group of Wardens who all stood outside of the palace's massive front gates, watching the three men and woman walk toward them.

Gret and Whesker were greeted by more Suns Watch and allowed to enter, while Drake and Luca were stopped. There were no threats made or even a hint that violence might be coming, but Drake knew that doing as he was asked was the best way to ensure he retained all of his limbs.

"You'll accompany us through to the palace's front entrance," one of the Suns Watch —a large female sarcian holding a blast-gun—ordered. "If you are carrying weapons, I advise you to dispose of them now."

Drake passed over his energy blade, sword, broken blast pistol, and viper. "I'm clean," Drake said. "And Luca here can't talk, but I'm not aware of any weapons on his person."

Luca responded by removing a repeater pistol and passing it to the nearest Suns Watch officer, a sheepish grin on his face. An energy blade followed soon after.

"You done?" Drake asked.

Luca nodded, and they were taken though the gates and along the path through ornate gardens filled with rare and exotic flora. Every few steps were greeted with a mixture of scents, and Drake felt himself relax.

I think the King of Stars had those plants put in on purpose, Luca said. *I think he wants people calm when they arrive.*

I imagine so, Drake said in his head. *He's not one to be above using tricks to ensure he gets an easier time of it.*

Smart man, Luca replied.

Drake didn't bother to say more as bird calls sounded from the massive trees that sat on one side of the garden.

"So, how is working for the king?" Drake asked the sarcian Suns Watch officer.

"He's a great man," she said without looking at him.

"Does he always have people walk the half mile through the gardens?" Drake asked. "Last I remember there's a port at the back of the palace."

"We had you land out front to ensure you were no danger,"

the Suns Watch officer said. "Only those welcomed here land at the back, and even then, only family or those with an appointment."

"Then I guess neither of those apply to me," Drake said. "I'm still not a threat."

"That remains to be confirmed," the sarcian told him without so much as a glance.

Drake and Luca walked the remaining distance in silence, but Drake remained vigilant, noticing the gardeners and guards who littered the area. He never felt in danger or even as if he was unwelcome, but he was eager to learn more about Hideo's condition, and he knew no one would tell him until he reached the palace. It was all he could do to not sprint the rest of the way, but that would result in him being chased and probably caught. Sometimes it's better to take the longer route so you get there in one piece.

Eventually, they reached the end of the garden and ascended the four flights of steps to the courtyard above. More guards—the Royal Swords, and the palace's elite handpicked by the King of Star and his family—milled around, trying to look as if there was nothing to be concerned about, although the amount of weaponry they carried, along with their black and blue elite armour suggested otherwise. Drake imagined Hideo's own guard would be greatly increased after what had happened.

A door at the front of the palace was opened and a woman walked out. She appeared to be in her late-forties, although she was probably a few centuries older, a by-product of the aether that coursed through her body. She wore a pair of blue trousers, a yellow top and her black hair was tied up in a bun. She was elegant and beautiful, and Drake braced himself for whatever she was about to do to him.

The Wardens moved aside as the woman walked purposefully toward Drake, until she was close enough to wrap her arms around him and bring him toward her, hugging him tightly.

"You're alive," she whispered, her voice betraying her emotion. "The king always knew you'd make it back to us somehow. He always knew."

"Miyako," Drake said softly, doing everything in his power to keep his emotions in check. "I'm so sorry for what happened today. I'm so sorry for what they did to Hideo."

Miyako moved, holding Drake's head gently between her hands as tears fell from her eyes. She made no attempt to stop them, or make herself look less emotional. She just stood there for a moment and then kissed him on his forehead. "Hideo is alive. Hideo will be fine. He's strong. Stronger than most. If he hadn't been there, you'd be dead, and then I'd be mourning your loss instead of the loss of his arm."

"He lost his arm?" Drake asked, anger bubbling up inside of him.

"Yes," Miyako said softly. "He's currently being operated on, but I've been assured he'll make a full recovery. He should be eligible for visitors tomorrow. So, today, you can speak to your king." It wasn't a suggestion.

"Where is he?"

"I'll take you," Miyako said, and turned to the rest of the Wardens. "Thank you."

The guard dispersed after a slight bow of their head, leaving only Drake and Luca.

"And this is one of your friends who helped track down my son's attacker?" Miyako asked.

"His name is Luca," Drake told her. "He's also a member of the Wardens. He can't speak."

Miyako hugged Luca, a gesture that certainly surprised the large man. "Thank you for bringing Drake home, and for going after the person who attacked my son. You have my unending gratitude for both of those actions."

A slight smile broke on Luca's lips, and he bowed his head a fraction.

"Come with me, both of you." Miyako led them into the house and through a room containing beautiful paintings and statues, some of which Drake knew were ancient, belonging to people well before the Sage Wars took place. There was no stopping to admire what the room contained as they were soon walking past several guard and out into a hallway, and then into a massive open room with forty-foot ceilings and floor to ceiling windows that allowed in an incredible amount of light. Comfortable looking furniture sat around the room, and soft music played through hidden speakers.

Luca stopped walking and closed his eyes.

"Is your friend okay?" Miyako asked.

This was one of the few pieces of music I can remember as a child, Luca explained. *It brings back warm memories for me.*

"He likes the music," Drake told Miyako. "I get the feeling he doesn't have a lot of good memories from his childhood, but this is one of them."

"Luca, you're more than welcome to sit and listen," Miyako said, motioning to one of the large, seated areas after Luca opened his eyes. "I'll have someone come and bring you food and drink in a few minutes. Please, make yourself at home."

You going to be okay? Luca asked Drake.

"He'll be fine," Miyako said. "No, I can't read your mind, but I can read your expression. You have no need to worry about Drake. He is practically family. And family I actually like which, I'm sorry to say, I don't have the same opinion of many who are actually related to us."

Family? Luca asked.

Drake walked over to Luca and placed the synths memory capacitor in his hand. "Get this to Rosie. Find out what's on it."

Luca nodded without looking down at the chip in his hand. *Anything else?*

Get Rosie to look into the Wynn house's comm network. I want to know who told people where I was.

Luca stood and walked away without a word.

"You always did inspire loyalty in your friends," Miyako said to Drake. "It's a difficult trait to manage."

"I don't try to manage anything," Drake said. "People do whatever they feel is right. Speaking of which, do you know where the rest of my team are?"

"No," Miyako told him. "You have your father's talent for making people believe in you. It's one of the reasons people from the Union Council feared you. They don't want another of your father. Your team will be with you soon enough, I'm sure."

"I'm nothing like him," Drake said without any malice or anger. "If I were, I might have been able to stop my friends from being murdered in the middle of a slum. I might have been able to stop Hideo from being hurt."

Miyako paused as she reached the doors and turned back to Drake. "My dear Drake. You can't take the burden of all that happened on your shoulders. It's not yours to carry alone. As for your team, they're currently being debriefed, I thought you'd like some time to get used to being back before you had to answer a barrage of questions."

"Thank you," Drake said and stepped outside into the rear of the palace.

While the front of the palace was full of flowers and trees, the rear was a much simpler place. A port sat off in the distance, big enough to land any non-military craft, with a security force that would have been able to take over its own planet if need be. It had been built several miles offshore, making sure that anyone who used it to arrive had to spend several minutes commute to get from the ocean to whatever the King of Stars had planned for his guests.

"Your king is on the sparing mats," Miyako said. "I'm going to go check on Hideo and Luca. Thank you for coming back here, Drake." She hugged him again. "I have missed you."

"And I you," Drake said. "If you need me, I'm sure I'll be getting a lecture of some kind."

"You're over forty years old, not a child anymore," Miyako told him. "He won't treat you like one. He missed you. You should know that."

With a nod, Drake turned and walked down the nearby stairs and across the beautifully kept lawn, the blue-green grass becoming lighter the closer Drake neared the ocean that began on the boundary of the palace property a mile away. The lawn sloped into a long, steep hill and at the bottom, near to the sandy beach that ran the length of the rear of the property, was a massive sparing mat. It could have been used as its own landing port, and Drake knew that it was regularly in use by the king and his sparing partners. And occasionally, he was told, by his father and his guests when negotiations became exceptionally tense.

Drake reached the bottom of the hill and sighed. The king was sparing with five others – two human males, two sarcian females and an oreaf, who was currently trying to get the king to back himself out of the arena. The oreaf went to sweep out the King of Stars leg's, but his target had already moved at blistering speed, catching the oreaf on the side of the head with a knee before landing on one foot and spinning around, kicking one of the two sarcians in the chest and sending her tumbling out of the ring.

"We're done," the King of Stars said when he saw Drake, and no matter what his opponents were doing, they just stopped and bowed before leaving the ring. "It appears the wayward wanderer has returned home."

The King of Stars walked over to a bowl at the far side of the ring and dunked his head, spraying freezing cold water all over himself and the floor as he brought his head out. He was six-feet tall and muscular, with long dark hair that fell over his broad shoulders. He had a neat, dark beard, and his skin was deeply tanned. He was the first King of Stars with Asian ancestry for well over two centuries, and was well liked by most, although some thought him to be too sentimental, or too forgiving… although all who had tried to go against him had discovered that wasn't the case.

"So, why are you here?" he asked.

"How do you do that?" Drake asked from behind him. He'd

walked onto the ring and been only a few steps behind the king, certain he hadn't made a sound. There were reasons the King of Stars was considered to be the most powerful of all Sage.

The king turned back with a smile on his face. "I'm the King of Stars, how else do you think I do it?"

"It's been a long time, My King," Drake said with a bow of his head.

The King of Stars picked up a towel from the floor and dried his face and chest, discarding the towel when he was done. He took the few steps over to Drake and stopped, the foot of air between them feeling like a canyon. "My King? Is that really how you're going to greet me after all these years? After you ran from everything and everyone here? After you gave no indication that you were even alive?"

Drake sighed. "It was never..." He didn't finish the sentence as the King had stepped toward him and enveloped him in a hug.

"The son of my best friend is home," the King of Stars whispered into Drake's ear. "Everything else can wait. Just please let me have this moment."

Drake and the man who his father trusted more than any other, stood silently in the ring, neither of them willing to speak first lest it ruin the moment.

Eventually, they pulled apart. "I missed you," the King of Stars said. "I missed you when you went away. I missed you when everyone told me that you were probably dead on some awful planet, and I missed you when I told them that no blood of your father's would ever be taken down by anything less than the entire Union fleet."

"I think they had better things to do than try to find me," Drake said, suppressing a chuckle.

"To find you, I'd have sent a thousand ships. It's a moot point, as we didn't even know where to start," the king said with a sad smile. "You went to see Hideo, before he was injured. I understand he will be okay. I'm glad; I didn't want to have to tear this planet apart looking for his attackers. My son is a good man."

Drake sighed. "I'd hoped you thought so, seeing how you named him in contention for your successor."

"Ah, well he was never going to actually get the job," the king explained. "He's too kind. Which isn't a knock against him; it's a knock against everyone else. He's smart and capable and is loved by everyone who meets him, but he allows himself to see the best in everyone, and he forgives too easily. I couldn't force him to become something he isn't by giving him my job."

The candid way the king spoke, surprised Drake. "If not Hideo, then who?"

The king shrugged. "I haven't decided yet. You want it?"

"I'm not in contention," Drake said. "If you named me your successor, you'd have a civil war on your hands. Again."

"That is true," the king said with a laugh. "Shame though, you have the right temperament."

"I don't mind making people angry, you mean?" Drake said with a smile.

"Something like that, yes." The sparkle of humour left his eyes as quickly as it had arrived. "I heard about Helice and Septimus, I'm sorry for your friends. I heard you believe Ramin and/or his son are involved."

"You already seem to know a lot about it."

"It's my job to know," the king replied with a shrug. "Ramin has dealings with several councillors, and I'm not exactly convinced he has the right temperament to be allowed to conduct business on this planet. Also, his son is—and I'm being frank here—a giant shit of a human."

"Ramin didn't do it," Drake admitted. "I think his son was involved though."

"I assume you want to go after him," the King of Stars said, and motioned for Drake to leave the arena with him, grabbing a tunic as they left. "Why didn't you come to me?" he asked as they made their way toward the beach.

"Politics," Drake admitted. "If I come to you, people will

know about it. I didn't want to cause you or Miyako any more trouble than my just being on this planet."

The king laughed, the sound rich and warm. "That worked out so well."

Drake didn't bother trying to hide his own chuckle. "I never said it was my best idea."

They stopped on the shore, the water lapping over golden sands just a few feet away.

"We have a lot to talk about," the king said.

"Yeah, I know." Drake let out a large sigh. "Go on then. Ask away."

"In order of how they come to my head," the king said, letting out a breath. "Why did you run? Where did you go? Why did you return to the Wardens when you must have known I'd have heard about it? Why change your last name? And last, but certainly no less important, why aren't you wearing a magnus bracer?"

"That's a lot of information."

The king looked out across the water. "Yes, it is. And I want answers to all of them, Drake. I think I deserve them."

Drake nodded; he couldn't say he disagreed with the statement from the man he considered to be something akin to an uncle. "In order of them being asked. The first question is the most difficult to answer." He looked over toward the house where Miyako walked toward them. "I assume My Queen will want the same answers."

The King of Stars nodded. "I imagine so, yes."

Drake paused for a moment. "Tell me something, why didn't you ask about why I was back here?"

The King of Stars looked back out across the water. "The truth? Because I arranged for you to come back to this planet."

Drake wasn't surprised. "You knew I was a Warden?"

"Of course. It wasn't exactly genius work on my part," the king said. "You must have known I'd have seen your name come through my database. I have to approve Warden members."

"I wasn't sure if you would, but I'd hoped," Drake said. "I figured it was the best way to let you know I was still alive."

"The best way would have been to turn up in my garden and say hello," the king said, with just a hint of sadness.

Drake hated that he'd hurt people who had been so good to him. "Yes, well, the second-best way then. You had me transferred to Atharoth, I assume."

The king nodded once.

"Why?" Drake asked.

"I could say it was because I hoped to see you again, and there's some truth in that," the king admitted. "If I'm being brutally honest, I trust you. I don't trust several members of my Council, and I hoped you'd be able to realise what they'd planned before anything awful happened."

"Like three murders?" Drake asked, the deaths of his friends still raw in his mind.

The king sighed. "Yes, like that. I couldn't contact you directly, I couldn't risk you running again. So, I sat and waited, and my plan got torn to pieces."

"Have you asked him your questions yet?" Miyako said as she joined the pair.

"Not yet, my love," the King of Stars said. "Drake thought you'd like to hear them."

"I'm going to have to repeat myself for my team too," Drake said. "Maybe I should just do this all at once."

"No," Miyako said, her voice slightly harder than usual. "We need to know, Drake. Please."

Drake looked up at the sky and exhaled. He'd been dreading this part of meeting his foster family again. "It's a really long story."

CHAPTER THIRTEEN

Jaysa Benezta

Once Jaysa and her remaining three crew had taken off from Leturn with their new passenger in the form of Ren Summers—heir to the throne of King of Stars—no one was really sure how to deal with that information. The crew themselves went about their work as if they didn't have a princess on-board, something for which Jaysa was grateful.

Ren spent most of the hour-long journey speaking with Jaysa in her cabin. Jaysa had expected to be grilled about anything and everything to do with the job she'd undertaken, but she'd soon discovered Ren was interested in anything but the job.

It wasn't until they'd landed at the private port at the rear of Ren's gigantic home that the princess mentioned the job at all. "I'm going to get changed," she told Jaysa as the two of them descended the ramp to the port. "I'll catch up with you in the main home." She walked off with her security detail, leaving Jaysa and her three crew members behind.

"She's an odd woman," Etamus said.

Jaysa's second-in-command was a dreic, whose pale green skin was much lighter than even Jaysa's. That was where the similarities ended. The brown patches on Etamus' skin gave the impression of camouflage, and her big black eyes were set close to either side of her head. Her long ears tapered to a point in line with the top of her skull. A small red diamond had been tattooed on her forehead when she was a child, and matched the same marks on her chin and cheeks.

For a race that was largely passive, they had an incredible ability to survive in pretty much any environment. Their only real weakness was that any dreic who left the confines of their planet—Trilloc—had to hook themselves up to a breathing apparatus once every month so they could absorb the nutrients they needed to live.

"Yes, yes she is," Jaysa said, wanting to talk about what had happened on the spaceport on Leturn. "How long have we worked together, now?"

"Four years," Etamus replied. "Why?"

Jaysa ignored her friend's question. "How long had Ortros worked here?"

Etamus looked like she was ready to have something sprung on her. "Little over a year. Do you plan on telling me what you're talking about?"

"He happily betrayed us all for getting his debt wiped," Jaysa said, her anger still thrumming. "I'm wondering whether he was ever really with us. I'm wondering if he was just waiting for the day he got offered a large amount to screw us all over."

"If you think about it for too long, you're going to drive yourself insane," Etamus told her. "You know that, right?"

Jaysa nodded slowly.

"He betrayed us," Yanton said from beside Jaysa as they were led through the exquisite grounds toward the main house. "You did what you had to do."

"And you, Kayos?" Jaysa asked, stopping to turn and talk to the man walking behind her.

"I'd have done the same," he said. Kayos was human, with dark skin and a bald head upon which, small lights shone under the skin. The augs he'd had installed allowed him to move and react quicker than any human without them. It made him an excellent pilot, but a weird person to talk to.

"I might not be much of a fighter," Yanton said. "My killing skills are only slightly better than that of a child, but I believe we all think that Ortros betrayed *us*. I think as head of this dysfunctional family..." He paused while a Etamus laughed at the sentence. "I think you were right to do what you did."

Jaysa was touched by Yanton's words more than she'd expected. He was a male sarcian, considerably smaller and weaker than the female, and he'd been born to a lower caste family. That gave him few rights and little say in what happened to them or their planet. Most lower caste families were second-class citizens to many minds on the planet of Benoran. They were forbidden from holding rank or a job that might elevate them, and from bettering themselves. Yanton had escaped the regime and fought for a better life. He'd joined her crew a year ago, and for some time had remained insular and afraid to speak up. She was glad to see he was becoming comfortable around the rest of the crew.

"Thank you, Doctor," Jaysa said.

Yanton beamed. Since leaving his homeland, and joining Jaysa, he'd excelled at medicine and had quickly become an indispensable member of the crew, but he still struggled to speak to Jaysa – she was, after all, female and in charge. For most male sarcians on Benoran, speaking to a female of a higher caste without being spoken to first, or being given permission, was subject to punishment.

"You're blushing," Kayos said with a smile.

"Stop teasing the only smart man between you," Etamus said with a smile of her own.

Etamus and Yanton walked off up front, allowing Kayos and Jaysa to talk.

"Is there something you wish to say?" she asked.

"It's about Yanton," Kayos said. "You know he has a... bit of a thing for you, yes?"

"It's been noted, yes," she said, wishing she hadn't noticed at all. "What's your point?"

"No point, just wanted to let you know," he said quickly.

"He's a good man, so if you do need to let him down…"

"Are you giving me romantic tips?" Jaysa said with a smirk.

Kayos shook his head violently from side to side. "No, boss. Just don't want to see someone I like to get hurt. It might do to take him to a few… establishments when we next dock. Give him a few other females to think about."

"You're going to get him drunk and laid?" Jaysa asked with a laugh.

Kayos shrugged slightly. "Not necessarily in that order, but that's the plan."

Jaysa tried with all her might not to smile. "You don't need my permission, Kayos."

"I need your help to get him off this ship," Kayos whispered. "He doesn't like going planet-side, but I think it'll do him some good. He left one prison and he's substituting it for another. I'm surprised he even left the ship to do this."

Jaysa had to admit; she had noticed that when the ship docked, Yanton rarely left. He always said he had more work, more research, more training to complete. "I'll do what I can. You can't force him to do anything he doesn't want to do, and I won't help you do that."

Kayos raised his hands placatingly. "No force, I just want him to get out for a bit, to see some of the worlds we visit."

"With alcohol and sex involved?" Jaysa asked, fully aware of what *get out for a bit* meant to Kayos.

Kayos nodded. "Well, that is usually the best part of the worlds we visit, so yes."

Jaysa laughed, despite herself. "If he's interested, go for it. You have my blessing. Don't push though, I don't want him to become more withdrawn."

"Sure thing, boss," Kayos said, walking off to catch up with the others.

All four of them were stopped outside of the glass wall of the main house that overlooked the garden. The entire wall moved aside, allowing them entry into a room that would have easily fit the *Tracked Retribution.*

"Why am I not a prince?" Kayos asked.

"Bad genes," Yanton said.

"Excuse me," a middle-aged gentleman asked from the centre of the room.

Etamus made a small wave. "And you are?"

"I am Eronokos," he told them. "I work for Princess Ren, who will be along soon. In the meantime, I've been asked to take Yanton, Etamus, and Kayos to your rooms in the block beside this one. The princess would like to talk to Jaysa alone for a moment."

"It's okay," Jaysa said when her crew looked sceptical.

"Would it be okay if I walked the grounds?" Etamus asked. "It's been a while since I was able to feel actual dirt beneath my feet."

"Actually, we have a room ready for you to undergo your meditative state," he told her.

"That would be fantastic, thank you," Etamus said, following one of the guards back the way they'd entered, with Yanton and Kayos trailing Eronokos a short while later.

Jaysa remained alone in the huge room, and looked out over the gardens. She had to admit that it was a stunning piece of architecture. The main building was single storey, but large enough that you could walk from one end to the other and probably not see all it had to offer. It was strange to know that the city of Yivas and all of its bustle was so close by, although she couldn't see it over the fifty-foot white stone walls that surrounded the property. In the distance loomed skyblocks, but she couldn't see what was directly outside of the villa. It was suddenly infuriating.

Ren entered the room from one of the eight doors. She'd changed into a long green dress, and walked barefoot over the stone floor. "You can sit," she said, motioning toward one of four sofas, each dark grey in colour and large enough to sit half a dozen people.

"It's just so..." Jaysa began.

"Grotesque?" a man asked as he walked over to them. He wore a charcoal-coloured suit, with a baby blue shirt, and a black magnus bracer on one forearm. He offered his hand to Jaysa, who shook it.

"I was going for opulent," Jaysa said.

"It looks like taste left and was replaced by someone who threw up gold," the man said with a smile. "My sister would tell you the same if she weren't trying to one-up the other members of our family."

"Thank you, Takumi," Ren said, clearly irritated.

"I'm her twin," Takumi told Jaysa as they sat opposite one another. "I think she'd keep me in the cellar with the rats if she had her way."

"I love you very much," Ren said. "Still doesn't answer the question of why are you here?"

"Because you asked me to come?" Takumi said, managing to make it sound as sarcastic as possible.

Ren sighed. "Not here in my home, here in this room."

"Oh, because I wanted to meet Jaysa," Takumi said. "You told me she was doing something important for you, and I wanted to meet the person my sister trusts enough to employ."

Ren moved to sit beside Takumi, the later of whom was clearly at ease and enjoying himself. Jaysa couldn't tell if her posture was regal because of her upbringing or if it was just exaggerated because Jaysa was here.

"You're not trying to impress anyone," Takumi said to her. "Our father doesn't care, and there are no councillors here for you to try and better."

Ren let out a long breath and her posture sagged. "Okay, fine. I don't care." She leaned back on the sofa. "Do you want to know what's the most exhausting part of being the child to the King of Stars?" she asked Jaysa.

Jaysa nodded. "Sure."

"Constantly being one-upped by peons in the Council who would love it if I wore the wrong colour because gods forbid I wear something comfortable, and not this ridiculous thing."

Ren motioned to herself.

"Go change, I'll keep her busy," Takumi said.

Ren rushed off.

"You'll have to excuse her," Takumi told Jaysa. "She's waiting for our father to name her successor, and so she feels like she has to put on a show on a regular basis."

"Must be exhausting," Jaysa said as a servant brought over a tray of drinks. Jaysa selected a tall glass of water.

Takumi waved the man away and walked over to a dark wooden cabinet, tapping a button on the side to reveal bottles of alcohol. He picked up a tumbler and bottle of whiskey and returned to Jaysa, pouring himself a healthy measure. "For her, yes," he finally said. "For me, not so much."

The politics of the Union Empire was not something Jaysa often considered. "You're not in the running to be the next King of Stars?"

Takumi laughed so much that whiskey came out of his nose. "Shit no," he managed to say. "My father wouldn't trust me with his sky-skimmer let alone the entire Union. He thinks I'm frivolous."

Ren returned wearing black trousers and a dark green tunic, but still had the dark brown magnus bracers on both forearms. She sat in her previous spot and let out a sigh. "I hate that pretentious 'you have to look the part' rubbish. Does Kimi look the part, do any of my siblings for that matter?"

"Hideo?" Takumi suggested.

"Hideo is too busy trying to save us all from our own hubris," Ren snapped. "And I have no idea what Kimi is doing from one day to the next, she's a law unto herself. No, it's just me trying to make an effort so those in the Council don't look down on me as just another princess."

"Not to hurry this along," Jaysa interjected. "However, you said you wanted to talk."

"I'm so sorry," Ren said. "Takumi has a way of making everyone lose track of whatever it is they were doing."

"It's my special power," Takumi said with a warm smile.

"That's right," Ren said, rolling her eyes. "I hired you to find Trinas Brong. Unfortunately, I used that little weasel Votix as a go between because I didn't want anyone to link me to you, no offence."

"None taken," Jaysa said with a shrug. "I'd be lying if I said I wasn't curious about *why* you asked me to find him."

"Well, Trinas is unpleasant," Ren said. "I got word that he might have been conspiring with members of the criminal element to undermine my father and the Council. I'm curious about what you discovered."

"The brief said I was to find him and bring him to Leturn," Jaysa began. "I discovered he'd vanished from Atharoth about six months before you asked me to find him. Word suggested that he was involved in the shootings of three Suns Watch."

"I saw that on the news," Ren said. "It was a big story for a few weeks."

"That's the one," Jaysa confirmed. "Anyway, Trinas was in contact with a friend of his, Sabas Gossard. Who was, at the time, in prison for murdering a Warden. And shortly after, he fled the planet and went to Onnab to work security there. He worked there for about two years, and left six months ago."

"What did you see on Onnab?" Ren asked.

Jaysa paused. "Mining equipment," she began tentatively. "They'd been digging into the mountain. Apparently, it was a good source of various precious minerals. Maybe they'd found what they were looking for, but there weren't any miners left. The town was completely deserted. It was being done by Expedited Systems – it was their equipment, although I didn't check into them further. You said, I saw something, what did you mean?"

"Trinas killed two Wardens a few years ago," Ren said. "He ran off, left the planet, took a job on Onnab, apparently. Anyway, six months ago, he came back to Atharoth. I don't know why. It was needlessly stupid. One of the Suns Watch members who had been part of my detail recognised him. They went after him. There was… a shootout, and he killed all three of them. I'd hoped that you might have found someone who knew him, someone who might be able to tell you why he came back here, risking everything in the process."

"There was nothing there," Jaysa said. "I found some old terminals in one of the buildings. Someone had wiped their memory, but one of my crew managed to hack it, they found an encrypted comms chat between Trinas and… I don't know. They were on Atharoth."

"So, you tracked him back to Atharoth?" Ren asked.

Jaysa nodded. "Yes. I didn't know where on the planet he would be. I arranged to meet Votix hoping the gangs on Leturn might be able to find something, as I didn't want to just land on Atharoth and start asking around. Turns out, criminals can't be trusted. Who knew?"

"You know that Trinas is dead?" Ren asked.

Jaysa wasn't sure what to say. "I didn't until just now, no."

Takumi shifted forward on his seat. "He was found murdered in the early hours of this morning, along with the adult children of two Councillors."

"How'd he die?" Jaysa asked.

"Hard," Takumi told her. "We believe Trinas came back here to speak to Helice and Septimus, but we don't know why. We hoped that maybe you'd be able to tell us."

"Won't the Suns Watch want to talk to me?" Jaysa asked.

"Yes," Ren said. "We thought you might have information regarding their meeting that would be awkward if it got out. I'm thinking that maybe Helice and myself were interested in Trinas for the same reasons. He killed Suns Watch people. And I think he killed them trying to get to one of the children of the King of Stars."

"Who?" Jaysa asked.

"Don't know," Ren said. "I think whoever it is, the Suns Watch found out, tracked him down, recognised who he was, and were killed for it."

"You don't want me to tell them that you hired me," Jaysa guessed.

"That's about it," Ren admitted. "The knowledge of our involvement could make matters awkward."

"I'll keep it confidential," Jaysa said. "I don't have to give up the name of my employer, it's one of the benefits of my job. I will have to inform them of my findings should they ask, though."

"That's information they can gain themselves anyway," Ren said. "You'll just be helping them get it quicker, which is probably for the best. Even so, I'd like you and your crew to stay here for a few days so that we can arrange for the Suns Watch to talk to you. I think that would be beneficial for all concerned. I'm happy to pay you your full fee for the job too. Besides, I think you could all use a few days of rest, and there's nowhere on Atharoth as secure and peaceful as this place."

"Thank you," Jaysa said. "It would be nice to stay in one place for a few days. Especially in such a beautiful home."

"It'll be like you have the whole place to yourself," Ren said. "We'll be here too, but the building is so massive, you'll barely see anyone if that's how you want to relax. We have a swimming pool, and several well-stocked bars too, so please feel free to consider this your home while you're here."

"Thank you," Jaysa repeated, as Ren and Takumi got to their feet. "I do have one question."

Ren turned to Jaysa. "Of course."

"Who did the three dead Suns Watch members work for?" Jaysa asked. "I know you were one, but who were the others? The news made it sound like Trinas hunted those members down to execute them."

"Two of the Suns Watch were protecting Kimi," Ren said. "The third one worked for me. Most of the information wasn't leaked to the media, but we were given a full briefing after their d."

"So, Kimi or you was probably the intended target?" Jaysa asked.

"Essentially," Takumi started, "we were told the guards were tortured before being murdered. It's believed Trinas was trying to gain information about Kimi's whereabouts, and apparently one of the guards said something about it before dying. We don't know why they were after Kimi, but as popular as Hideo is with the people, he does place himself as a face of the Union, so it's possible they were going to use Kimi to get to Hideo. Maybe Trinas has a grudge against us for something? Who knows why a psychopath does anything. And seeing how Trinas is dead, we'll probably never know exactly what happened."

Jaysa nodded, although she wasn't sure Takumi's suggestion was right. She said goodbye to Ren and Takumi, and they left her alone with her thoughts. Something weird was going on, and she had a feeling the royal twins knew a lot more about it than they were letting on.

CHAPTER FOURTEEN

Felix Drake

"I'd guess I'd best start at the beginning," Drake said, settling on the soft sand.

"That's usually where I find things start best," the King of Stars said.

Drake sighed. He wasn't sure if he'd ever told any one person the truth before. Pieces of the truth, certainly, but not the whole thing. "It started when I was fifteen."

"What did?" Miyako asked.

"My knowledge that I didn't need a magnus bracer to use my aether," Drake said. "Do you remember when I was fifteen and those rebels tried to grab Hideo and Kimi? You remember what happened?"

"You saved their lives," Miyako said.

Drake looked over at his aunt and smiled. "It wasn't like that. The rebels wanted revenge for having lost the civil war. They wanted you both to feel the anger they felt. I couldn't let Hideo and Kimi come to harm, so I used my aether in public for the first time. I tore those people in half. That's not an exaggeration. I was fifteen, and I killed three men. I wore a magnus bracer at the time, and the activation of my aether caused the power inside me to overwhelm my body and mind. I couldn't control it. It took all I had not to have it run amok and kill Hideo and Kimi too. Ionic aether is incredibly powerful anyway, but the fact that I manipulated gravity to tear people apart... that was like nothing I'd ever felt before. It was terrifying."

There were eight varieties of aether used by Sage. Ionic was the rarest, and potentially the most powerful. It was also the most unstable, considered to be just as dangerous to its wielder than anyone on the end of an attack, as it literally tapped into The Aperture dimension itself. If done under stress, the first time an ionic Sage tapped into their aether tended to be loud and messy.

The wielder of ionic aether could manipulate space in a variety of different ways, be it teleporting themselves, inflict distortions—such as bending or crushing—within space itself that damages anything caught inside it, replacing one part of space with another, and in some cases, constructing items from the fabric of space for use, such as weapons, or even manipulating gravity itself.

Both the king and queen knew exactly what ionic aether could do, and Drake was thankful that he saw no fear or concern in their eyes when he recounted his experience of his power awakening.

"You were only defending your friends and family," Miyako said.

"I know, but I was fifteen," Drake said, surprised at how much the memories still hurt after all this time. "Then the media discovered who my father was. Evan Varlus, the great general of the Rebellion, and a man who almost brought the Union to its knees. They started with stories about how I looked like him, but it was soon evident that wasn't enough. Stories about how I'd managed to save Hideo and Kimi began to surface, stories about the power I wielded, and whether or not that same power would allow me to continue where my father left off. They said I was the next person to try and start a civil war. That I wasn't trustworthy... that I was a monster in waiting."

"I told you they were just stories designed to make petty

people money," the King of Stars said. "I said that they'd eventually go away."

"You did, and they didn't," Drake snapped. "We both know that members of the Council and several prominent business figures around the Union were involved in those stories. Making me out to be some sort of evil curse walking the planet just so they could get back at my father. People aimed their hate at me because my father was dead. People still aim their hate at me. It's why I changed my name."

"Why not change Drake?" Miyako asked.

"My parents gave me that name," Drake said. "The human children of councillors and prominent members of society are named after people from those who ruled the Ancient empires of humans. The vast majority of people don't even know who the Ancient peoples were. It's been ten thousand years since Earth was even considered a home. I figured a Drake wasn't going to stand out all that much."

"So, that's why you left?" the King of Stars asked.

Drake nodded. "Some people were beginning to suggest that my friendship with Kimi and Hideo was going to turn them against you all. That I was just biding my time as a fifteen-year-old despot in training. So, after almost a year of being told how evil I was going to turn out to be, I left. I'm sorry I didn't tell anyone where I was going, but I felt it safer that way."

"And where did you go?" Miyako asked.

"Terentus," Drake said.

Miyako and the King of Stars shared a glance.

"The Atoned?" Miyako asked after several seconds of silence. "You went to The Atoned?" There was disbelief in her voice, and more than a little hurt. The Atoned were a people who believed that only through learning and knowledge could one become truly strong. They divided themselves into several different groups, each of which sought to achieve that philosophy in a different way. Some wanted to take a more direct involvement in Union matters, whereas others liked to learn from the shadows.

Drake nodded.

"You left all of this so you could become a... scholar?" Miyako asked.

Drake shook his head, and almost smiled at the use of the word. Most people thought of The Atoned as stuffy, almost monk-like people who spent all day reading and researching. Most people were very wrong. "No. I learned how to use my aether... without a magnus bracer. I learned how to defend myself, how to attack my enemies. I learned a lot."

"I know people who have been trained by The Atoned," the King of Stars said. Drake knew his foster uncle was aware The Atoned were more than just scholars, more than just the keepers of knowledge, but their secrets had been kept for hundreds of years, and only those who had joined the order were privy to even a handful of them. The King of Stars didn't say it, but Drake knew what he'd meant. Those who left The Atoned were dangerous. "When you were eighteen, did they have you perform the ritual? Did they have you commit murder in their name?"

So he knows that too. Everyone who joined the order had to kill someone. They said it was the only way to truly understand the gravity of taking the life of another. "I had to choose someone who was deserving of death. Someone who needed to be removed from the Union so the rest of the people could become cured from their infection. I chose the man who gave Novia the drugs that made her kill herself."

"You came back to Atharoth?" the King of Stars asked, obviously hurt by the idea that Drake had returned to the planet without informing anyone of his new life.

Drake nodded once. He closed his eyes and took a deep breath. "The man I chose to kill lived here. Look, I never meant to hurt anyone when I first ran. I was a scared sixteen-year-old who just wanted to protect those he loved, and did it in the only way he knew how. Vanishing."

The King of Stars walked over to Drake, dropping beside

him, and hugging him tight, tears in his eyes. Then he held Drake's face in his hands and spoke softly, "I am sorry you felt you had to do that. That is on me, not you. You were a child, a powerful child, but still a child. I'm sorry I didn't do more to make sure the stories told about you weren't debunked, that I didn't fight back. I thought it would all blow over and they'd get it out of their system."

Drake shook his head slightly, and the King of Stars released him, moving back beside his wife.

"Why join the Wardens?" Miyako asked.

"I thought they would let me help people," Drake said. "I spent so long with The Atoned that it felt like I was isolating myself from the rest of civilization. Like I was a part of the universe but didn't take part it in. If that makes any sense?" He shook his head. "Eventually, I figured I could join the Wardens, and be put somewhere away from this planet. They put me on a team, gave me a job, and a few years later, I was brought here."

"As I said earlier, that was my doing," the King of Stars said. "I wasn't convinced that everything was running as smoothly as my advisors tell me it is. My power is not what the position once held, and I have no absolute control over what happens on a day-to-day basis. I cannot put forward legislation without Council approval, and I can't start an investigation into Council members without enough evidence to already declare their guilt. As a member of the Wardens, you can do the latter. And I trusted you. Trust you. I didn't care where you'd gone, and I genuinely had no idea, but the discovery that you were alive and a member of the Wardens gave me hope that you were the man I knew you'd grow up to be, and I knew I needed help here."

Drake was happy to hear those words, but he also knew he wouldn't have time for a long reunion. "And then something awful happened. The Council are going to hear about what happened to Hideo, they're going to know who I really am. That might not let me hang around for much longer. They're going to hate that the son of a man who once made them fearful is now capable of arresting them."

"We'll have to deal with the Council." Miyako's tone made it clear that she had no intention of letting them treat Drake the same way it had when he was a child.

Silence lingered for several moments until the King of Stars said, "So, you don't need a magnus bracer?"

"No," Drake said, looking down at his bare forearms. "In fact, I have issues with control when I use one. It's like I can't contain the amount of power that wants to come out. A small use of power leads to a massive amount of damage."

"That's not like anything I've ever heard," Miyako said, looking at her own bracer. "Magnus bracers allow us to control the aether, without them we'd either be unable to use the aether at all, or the power would drive someone insane."

"I've heard of a few people like Drake," the King of Stars said. "There's an old tale of a man by the name of Yoshinori. You ever heard of him?"

Drake shook his head.

"My father told me about him when I was just a boy," the King said. "He was a great general from four thousand years ago. Served one of the King of Stars during the Sage Wars. No one is really sure what happened to start the war, but it tore apart planets in the hundreds of years it lasted, almost completely wiping out the Sage as a result. Yoshinori was the leader of a... I guess you could call them a Special Ops unit. They were called Venom."

Drake huffed. "That's not a name you give someone who does something good."

The King of Stars nodded. "They were monsters unleashed against the enemy of the King of Stars. They tore apart that enemy in their quest to stop the war. According to legend, none of those in the group used a magnus bracer, but all of them were Sage. The magnus bracer hasn't really changed in design in thousands of years, but for some reason there are fewer and fewer Sage able to use their aether without it now. No one knows why, but it's why a lot of Yoshinori's story is sealed. It was decided long ago that having common knowledge that a group of Sage tore through their enemies with no magnus bracers, but still managed to use incredible power, would scare people. Or it would get people to try and figure out if they could do the same."

"What happened to this Yoshinori?" Drake asked.

"He was killed by the King of Stars for betraying him," the king said. "Yoshinori decided that as he was powerful enough to lead his team, he was also powerful enough to lead what would become the Union. He lost. His team were executed, and Yoshinori became a footnote in history. The fact he was able to fight without a magnus bracer is interesting, the story goes he never even tried one on, and forbade his team from using them."

"So, it's not unheard of that people can use aether without a magnus bracer?" Drake asked, hopeful he wasn't some sort of anomaly. He'd searched for information in the library of The Atoned, but there had been precious little information on it.

"Rare, yes, and it hasn't been documented in a long time, but maybe you're a descendent of one of his team on your mother's side," the king suggested. "Your father was also incredibly powerful, so maybe that awakened some old ability to fight without a bracer. Frankly, I have no idea. I'm sure more than a few scientists would like to prod and poke you to find out though."

"In other words, keep the information to yourself," Miyako said.

"I don't think that's possible now that I've openly used my aether in public several times," Drake said.

"So, what's your plan?" the King of Stars asked.

"I'm going to find Sabas," Drake said. "I don't like coincidences, and someone tracked me back to Hideo's home. My guess is either Sabas, or one of Hideo's guards was involved. I assume they're without reproach."

"Hand-picked by Hideo himself," Miyako said. "We'll interview them all. No stone will be left unturned."

"Good," Drake said. "Anyway, I'll find Sabas and check for his involvement. And if it's not him, I'll look elsewhere. Whoever it is, I'm going to dismantle their lives. I need a jurisdiction extension for me and my team to go after Sabas, or anyone else for that matter, in case they escape the planet."

Drake looked up as Sateri walked over the dunes. "We need to talk," she shouted, before noticing who Drake was with, and paused.

The King of Stars and Miyako stood and greeted an embarrassed looking Sateri.

"I assume you work with Drake," the King of Stars said.

"Jubei, don't tease," Miyako scolded before turning to Sateri. "If you're going to kill Drake, could you make sure to bury the body far enough away so it doesn't smell."

"Actually, you might need to see this," Sateri said, her gaze never leaving Drake, who remained seated. She passed her comm unit to Miyako, who frowned.

"Damn him," she snapped, and passed the unit to her husband.

"It seems your identity is out in the open," he said, turning back to Drake. "Several councillors, who appear to want to remain unnamed, have stated that you are back on the planet. There's a news conference about it right now."

"I'll go make some calls, and see who I can shake free of the pack," the King of Stars said and walked away with Miyako.

Drake got to his feet only for Sateri to punch him in the jaw, sending him back to the sand. "You lied to me. All these years, you lied to me. You lied to the team about who you were."

Drake rubbed his jaw and nodded. "Sorry. You want the truth, or you want to hit me?"

Sateri looked down on Drake and, for a moment, wasn't sure which choice she was going to make. Sateri unclenched her fist, and sat beside Drake. "The truth. All of it."

It took Drake less time to tell her the truth than it had the king and queen.

"So, you're what, some kind of prince?" Sateri finally said.

The idea made Drake want to laugh, but the expression on Sateri's face said that would be an unwise course of action. "No, not a prince. My father was a military man, who was best friends with the king. My mother and the queen got on well too. That's it. I'm not special."

"Fucking hell," Sateri snapped. "Your father is one of the reasons we had a war."

Drake nodded.

"The King of Stars could name anyone his successor though," Sateri said. "Doesn't have to be blood. He names several people, and they're voted on by the Council. That's how it works, yes?"

Drake nodded again. "He's not going to name me successor because he was best friends with my father. A father, as you just said, started a war."

In the farther reaches of the Union systems, and beyond, people were known to pray to the King of Stars, although that was done in secret. Thinking the King of Stars was a god did not sit well with the majority of the Council. A few thousand years ago, there had been a King of Stars who considered himself a god, and several billion deaths later they swore it would never happen again.

"Why weren't you honest with us?" Sateri asked. "About who you are? Were? Whatever the correct word is in this circumstance."

"My father was an infamous traitor to the Union, and I'm a Sage who doesn't need to use a magnus bracer," Drake explained. "I can't imagine there would be a lot of trust for someone like me. There wasn't a lot of trust when I was a child, let alone an adult who had spent twelve years of his life being trained by some of the scariest and most dangerous, people in the universe."

"You were feared as a child?" Sateri asked.

Drake nodded. "It was felt that my *evil genes* would rub off on Hideo and Kimi. It was mentioned that Miyako was doing nothing to stop her children associating with the son of a monster. That I was little more than a monster in waiting myself."

"That's horrific," Sateri said sadly.

"It wasn't the best time ever, no," Drake admitted.

"So, changing topic, is Miyako the mother to all of the King of Star's children?" Sateri asked.

"No, only two of them, Hideo and his sister, Kimi," Drake said. "The rest were born from previous wives. I'm not exactly sure how it works, but from what I've been told, he meets someone he likes, they get married, have a kid, and then decide whether or not they want to stay together. Basically, they spend the first portion of their relationship trying to have a baby before they even get to know one another. Miyako has been the King of Stars wife for forty-five years. Hideo was their first child."

"You lived *here* as a child?" she asked, looking back at the mansion behind her.

Drake briefly thought back to the good times he'd spent, but they were quickly pushed aside by the bad, as if his own mind wouldn't let him have a moment to not remember who he was. "Some of it, yes."

Sateri let out a sigh. "It must have been amazing."

"The word is terrifying," Drake said. "There were older members of the royal family who hated me just for being alive, I had councillors who wanted me killed or shipped off to some mining colony somewhere. I was eight when I left my father's battleship with my mother, Ailisa, and came here. The king and queen welcomed us, despite my father being at war with them.

"I lived not far from here with my mother," Drake continued. "My father died after I'd been here for six months, and when I was ten, my mother was murdered by a man who also tried to kill me. Fortunately, I wasn't home, so he killed himself instead. The king found their bodies. He brought me to live here, and Miyako treated me as if I were one of her own. I loved being here, loved most of the people, but I just tried to avoid anyone who was important and outside of the group I trusted."

Sateri sighed. "I spent my early years pretending I didn't love my father so that my mother's friends in the senate wouldn't murder him in from of me."

Drake stared at Sateri for several seconds. "That... doesn't sound like a nice place to grow up."

"It was hell," Sateri said. "I thankfully had a mother who would allow my father and me to spend time together, she was a progressive. He was a lower caste than her by some degrees. What she did would have gotten her executed had we been caught. We managed to escape the planet because of her and people like her. My mother was arrested in the process."

"Have you been back since?"

Sateri shook her head. "Nope, never will either. Those who aided my father were executed as traitors. My mother was far too important for such punishment, but I never saw her again. I don't need to go back there to gain revenge. I do that every single day by living away from their totalitarian rule." She paused for a few heartbeats. "When we first met, do you remember what you told me you used to do?"

"Scholar," Drake said immediately.

"If you were Atoned, you were actually close to telling the truth," Sateri said with a quiet laugh. "You can't really believe there's an apocalypse coming."

"Ah, that rumour." Drake shook his head. "No, of course not, but neither did they. They told me that before the Sage Wars, Atoned ignored the signs of the impending war. They refused to ever allow that to happen again, so they train in secret."

"The Sage Wars happened a long time ago," Sateri said.

"They did," Drake agreed. "That doesn't mean they can't happen again."

"You need to talk to the rest of the team."

"I know," Drake said softly. "I assume they're waiting."

Sateri glanced back over to the mansion. "They landed a

few minutes ago. I'm sure there's going to be a lot of questions."

Drake got to his feet the moment his comm unit went off. He answered it after seeing Rollos' name, putting on loudspeaker for Sateri to hear. "I'm coming back now," Drake said. "I'll explain everything about what's happening in the news."

"Oh, yeah, that you're the son of one of the most dangerous people to ever live," Rollos said nonchalantly.

Drake had known deep down that at some point he was going to have to tell his team who he really was. "I promise I'll explain everything about who I am."

"You'd better," Rollos said. "Oh, and Rosie said she's looked into it and the last twelve hours of transmissions are gone. She said it looks like someone had taken a kinetic-hammer to the data. I assume you know what that means."

"Yes, thanks," Drake said.

Rollos hung up.

"What transmissions?" Sateri asked.

"Before Hideo was shot, I wanted all logged transmissions out of the house."

"You think one of his people arranged it?"

Drake nodded, and the two jogged back toward the dock just as his comm-unit beeped. He answered it immediately. "Hello, Celine. Good to see you."

"You won't be saying that in a minute," Celine told him. "You need to come back to your apartment."

Drake stopped as dread filled him. "What happened?"

"Two Blackcoats are dead on your floor, and your synth is missing," Celine said. "Get here. Now."

Drake turned to see Dai'ix leaving the building. "Dai'ix, do you need sleep?" Drake called out.

"Slept a few days ago, I'm good for another few," Dai'ix replied.

"Feel like accompanying me to my home? There seems to be some problems."

Dai'ix nodded.

"Anything we can help with?" Sateri asked. "You need to rest."

"That's why Dai'ix is going to fly the sky-skimmer, so I can sleep the few hours it'll take to get there," Drake told her. "As for the help, I'll be fine. Make sure everyone else gets rest. I get the feeling tomorrow isn't going to be much better than today."

CHAPTER FIFTEEN

Felix Drake

Drake managed to sleep the few hours from the palace to his skyblock, only waking when the sky-skimmer bumped gently onto the rooftop. He blinked and looked around, then blinked away the sleepiness once more.

"Have a good rest?" Dai'ix asked as they both exited the ship.

Drake yawned. "Yes, thanks, how long did it take?"

"Two hours, or there abouts. Do you want me to go down to your apartment with you?"

"You okay with staying up here?"

Dai'ix nodded. "I like being this high up at night. It's peaceful."

Drake looked across the city, at the multitude of skyblock lights. It was more peaceful than he'd imagined. Maybe he should spend more evenings sat on the roof. "I'll see you soon," he told Dai'ix and pressed the button to call the elevator.

When the elevator doors opened at his floor, two members of the local Blackcoats stood guard just outside. Drake showed his badge, and they nodded him through. None of his neighbours were out, although he imagined a few of them were using the view ports in their doors to see what was going on. Standard procedure would have been to cut the feed to the cameras operating in the public spaces, so no one could hack in.

Drake found his apartment swarming with Blackcoats who were dealing with the two holographic images of the dead bodies that had been on the floor. Removing the bodies would have been done the second their scans had been finished, leaving a workable, exact copy of the deceased. It took a few hours to complete, so he probably only just missed the actual deceased being removed, and the reason the holographics weren't used for the bodies of his friends. That, and Drake was certain Celine wanted him to see them in the flesh, so to speak, and get a true reaction from it.

"You notice anything wrong?" Celine asked Drake as she crossed the room. "Everyone out. Now. Come back in an hour to continue the investigation."

Everyone did as they were told, until it was just Drake and Celine, the latter of whom closed the apartment door. "What in the name of the gods is this?"

"My guess is someone broke in, and Bokk subdued them," Drake said.

"Your synth didn't just subdue them, Drake. It killed them." Celine walked over to the palm-sized device on a tripod in the middle of the room that created the holographic images, and pressed a few buttons. Faces appeared over each body. "Recognise anyone?"

Drake shook his head. "Should I?"

"Both are Blackcoats. Both were turned down from Wardens due to, and I'll quote your own words on this, *'Excessive levels of extreme violence'*. Must have been bad if you thought it was extreme."

"Really? You're going to complain I use violence too much?" Drake asked, slightly irritated by the suggestion.

"Actually, no, I'm not. I'm just messing with you," Celine said with a sigh. "You did turn them down though, and another reason you gave was that you believed at least one of them was working for one of the gangs on Leturn."

Drake studied at the faces and finally nodded. "I

remember them now. Both corrupt, both stunk to high heaven of being sent just so the gangs could have someone inside the Wardens. We didn't need extra people like this, we already have enough idiots."

"Not a nice summation of your colleagues," Celine said.

"I love my colleagues," Drake told her. "My colleagues are great. It's the people who pretend they're on my side while waiting to sell me out, I'm not too keen on." He looked around the room. "Where's Bokk?"

"That was my next question," Celine said. "Your synth killed two Blackcoats, and fled the scene. Why?"

Drake didn't have a good answer to that. "Bokk's a security synth, so they probably figured I was in danger and came to find me."

"You let your synth track you?" she asked, clearly surprised.

Celine knew all Wardens could be tracked via their badge. Drake didn't see the need to tell her something she already knew. "I let Bokk have access to the software that accesses my badge. In case of emergencies."

Celine looked down at the holograph bodies. "Such as two idiots coming to kill you."

"Yeah, that probably counts," Drake said. "Bokk will have gone somewhere I was when this happened. Any idea how long ago?"

"Just over seven hours," Celine said without needing to check the details on her visi-pad.

Drake thought quickly. "The Spire, or Hideo then."

"You don't seem worried," Celine said.

"If he goes to Sabas, that could be a problem, but Bokk is unlikely to kill anyone who doesn't pose a threat, and once they know I'm not there, they'll probably reactivate my sensor."

Celine considered this for a moment. "Bokk wouldn't just contact you on your comm unit?"

Drake shook his head. "Emergency protocol is also one of

silence. So, no, they won't contact me." He walked over to the panel on the wall and activated Bokk's systems, hitting the red button that said Drake was safe and Bokk should contact him. "That should solve any problems there."

"You hope," Celine said with a slight mocking edge to her tone.

"Why else did you contact me? You know I had nothing to do with these deaths, and even if I had, they came to kill *me*, so it would have been utterly within my rights to take them out. Although I'd have been a lot messier. What else is going on?"

Celine said nothing for several seconds. "How secure is this place?"

Drake activated the apartment's security protocols Rosie had designed, making it impossible for anyone to listen in. "We're good," Drake told Celine. "Not even military grade equipment can hear us."

"Someone came to your apartment about two minutes before I contacted you," Celine said. "She's currently sat in that spare bedroom."

Drake looked over at the door. "She?"

Celine nodded. "I told her not to say anything to anyone until you arrived, and I cleared out the apartment. Unfortunately, I couldn't stop the bodies from being investigated." She took a seat on the sofa, and motioned for Drake to go to the door.

When Drake opened it, he found Kimi Wynn sat on the bed inside. "Kimi?" Drake asked.

Kimi Wynn looked like her mother Miyako in almost every regard, except her hair was a forest green that certainly wasn't natural. It was also shaved on one side, with the same forest green writing tattooed on her scalp just above her ear. She wore a long silver and black dress that touched the floor, and had tattoos up both of her bare arms. Several golden bracelets sat on one wrist, and a brass-coloured magnus bracer sat on the other.

"When I last saw you, I was thirteen," Kimi told Drake,

getting up and embracing him. "I hear you got in trouble today, which proves that very little has changed since we were children."

"It's a hobby of mine," Drake said, then led her into the main room.

Kimi took a seat close to Celine, with Drake sitting opposite them. "You want a drink?"

Both shook their head.

"I'd like to know what's going on," Celine asked. "I'd *really* like to know why Princess Kimi risked coming here with no Wardens back-up, and no one even knowing she'd left the palace."

"I had to see Drake," Kimi said. "I heard about what happened to Helice and Septimus. And I heard what happened to Hideo."

"And you thought it safe to fly across the planet to come here alone?" Drake almost snapped, before reminding himself that Kimi was a grown woman now, and clearly more than capable of taking care of herself. Even so, he felt protective of her.

"I'm not someone you need to protect," Kimi said, as if reading Drake's thoughts.

Drake nodded. "Okay. I think more of an explanation is in order as to why you thought coming here was a good idea."

"I heard about the deaths and came here to find you," Kimi said. "I knew it was swarming with Blackcoats, and figured I'd be able to find Celine. I knew she could get hold of you, and from what I've heard about her, she's trustworthy."

"I'm flattered," Celine said, sounding like she was anything but. "You still shouldn't be here."

"The tattoo on your skull," Drake said. "Do you live by those word?"

Celine followed Drake's gaze to the side of Kimi's head. "They look familiar," she said.

"Once Peace Fails," Kimi said.

"It's written in ancient script," Drake said.

"And what is that meant to mean?" Celine asked.

"It's the motto of the OMC," Kimi said.

"You're Orbital Marine Corps?" Celine raised an eyebrow. "I don't think I've ever met one of you when you're not wearing your power armour."

"How long were you a part of the OMC?" Drake asked, hiding his surprise.

"Did a fifteen-year stretch," Kimi said. "Joined at twenty, left five years ago. Is that going to be a problem?"

The OMC were known for their hit them so hard the first time that there isn't a second, battle strategy. Essentially, if there was anyone left standing opposing them after the first attack, they weren't doing their jobs right. And they rarely needed to be deployed in the same place twice. On the other side of that coin, their tactics had come under question on more than one occasion, and the number of ex-members who had gone on to join criminal enterprises was high.

"That you were OMC?" Drake asked. "No, I don't think so. Although the fact that you have their motto tattooed on your skull is unexpected."

"I went through a lot as part of the OMC," Kimi said. "It's an experience that made me the person I am today."

"And that person is?" Drake asked.

"Someone who doesn't think that people like Sabas and Ramin should be walking around as free men after what they've done." The expression on Kimi's face was not one Drake had seen before. Whatever she'd gone through in the OMC, had hardened her.

"What exactly are you saying?" Celine asked.

"Helice and Septimus were meant to wait before they saw Trinas," Kimi said. "They were meant to take me with them."

Drake and Celine exchanged a glance, and it was Celine who voiced the question. "You're saying you were meant to be there when they were murdered?"

Kimi nodded.

"I think you'd better start from the beginning," Drake said.

Kimi sighed. "It started with Trinas killing two wardens, after which he fled to Leturn. There was evidence that linked Sabas to one of the murders, and you made the arrest, Drake. So, now Sabas is in prison, and Trinas is lightyears away, but for some reason he returned. Not sure why, but he was stupid enough to get spotted by Suns Watch officers, and he killed all three of them who went to arrest him.

"I looked into their deaths and there was nothing beyond the official report. And then suddenly someone turns up admitting to a whole bunch of murders and taking their own life, and now Sabas is free. Those Suns Watch were friends of mine. When you're around your guards all day every day, you bond with them. I lost people during my time in the OMC, good people who didn't deserve to die, and losing them hit me hard."

She took a shaky breath. "I found a link between Trinas and Sabas," Kimi said. "I think Trinas was Sabas' hitman. I think he killed the man who *confessed* to Sabas' crimes, and I think he helped Sabas cover up the deaths of the two Wardens."

"You believe that Sabas killed both Wardens?" Drake asked.

"Yes, I believe he alone ambushed them," Kimi said. "He's impulsive, sloppy. It's how you got him."

"You got any evidence?" Celine asked.

"Transcripts, data mines," Kimi said. "I can prove that Trinas and Sabas knew each other. I can prove that a large sum of money entered Trinas' account just before one dead confessor was found. I can prove that Trinas has involvements with several people who work for Sabas."

"That's more than a little suspicious," Celine said.

"It gets worse," Kimi continued. "We discovered that Trinas had quickly moved to Onnab to do security there for Sabas' father's company. A job he was ill suited to according to his arrest record. We knew we had to be careful contacting Trinas, otherwise Sabas would know. So, I made a few calls and got on an official inspection team for the planet. Unofficially, you understand. Sabas' name isn't on the company of

Expedited Systems, but that's who's working there, and it didn't take us long to find his hands all over it."

"What are Expedited Systems doing on Onnab?" Drake asked, remembering that Metan had mentioned the same thing.

"Digging up some old ruins," Kimi said. "We weren't allowed to actually see anything they'd recovered, but there were some pretty heavy-duty security personal there."

"And you spoke to Trinas?" Celine asked.

Kimi nodded. "Offered him a deal. You come testify against Sabas and everyone working for him who helped, and we make you vanish forever. New identity, new life. He jumped at the offer."

"New identity?" Drake asked. "That was part of the deal?"

Kimi looked over at him. "Yes, why?"

"Because Trinas was killed after being given a massive dose of chameleon," Drake said. "A drug that literally gave him a new identity."

"How long had Trinas been on Atharoth?" Celine asked.

"Few days at most," Kimi said. "He left with the inspectors and rode with them while they went to other worlds where corporations are doing work funded by the Council."

Things began to click in to place for Drake. "The Council are funding the Gossard's corporation and their dig into Onnab."

"Several councillors have ties to the organisation," Kimi said. "And with no Sabas officially involved, it probably didn't take long for a secure dig to be approved. The Council are always looking for old ruins, it's an easy way to make people impressed with them, and it gives the corporations the rights to the planet once they've finished the dig. And all for a small percentage of profits from the corporation involved. Everyone wins."

"So, what happened the night your friends died?" Celine asked.

"We arranged to meet Trinas," Kimi said. "Along with

Helice and Septimus. We were pretty sure that with his evidence we could go after those in the Council who were working with Sabas. Hopefully get some justice for the Wardens who were murdered. Obviously, it didn't work out that way."

"Someone set them up," Celine said. "They knew the trouble they'd get in for killing a member of the royal family, but the children of councillors are less worrisome. Who did you tell?"

"Hideo," Kimi said. "That's it."

Kimi sounded a hundred percent certain of that fact, and Drake believed her without hesitation. "Hideo would have told his husband. His husband would have told those his family work with."

"You think Caleus set them up?" Kimi asked. "He's a little cold and distant, but I can't see him wanting Helice and Septimus dead."

"He might not want anyone dead," Drake said. "But Caleus' father has long since been suspected of having ties to organised crime."

"Well, in that case, Caleus' father must be furious about Hideo," Kimi said.

"Why?" Celine asked.

"Hideo is running an investigation into several councillors who have been alleged to have ties with criminals on Leturn," Kimi said. "Caleus' father is one of them. And Hideo isn't shy in keeping that information to himself. He got into a shouting match with Caleus a few weeks ago, just after we returned from Ocrion. It was pretty intense."

"What was it about?" Celine asked.

"Caleus found out his father was being investigated," Kimi said. "He called Hideo a few names, and Hideo told him to stop being his father's stooge and think for himself for a change. It was pretty ugly."

Drake sat back in the chair and watched Kimi for a few seconds. "Did you know, Kimi, that when we were young you had a tell?"

"A what?" Kimi asked.

"I could tell when you were lying or keeping something to yourself. You did this thing where you looked past a person, over their shoulder. Like you've been doing when you've spoken to me."

"You think I'm lying?" Kimi asked, irritation steeped in every word.

Drake shook his head. "I think you're withholding something, and I'm curious as to what it is and why you're withholding it."

Kimi stared at Drake for several seconds. "I don't know you anymore, Drake. I knew the boy you were, and I have an inkling about the man you became, but I don't really know you. I don't know if I can share everything with you."

"The problem then becomes one of us not getting the whole picture," Celine said. "If you can't share what you know, we can't help. We'll be in the dark constantly."

Kimi nodded slightly. "I know."

"Okay, how about I ask you a question?" Drake said. "That sound okay?"

Kimi nodded.

"Why did you leave the OMC?"

Kimi smiled. "You figured out the OMC and why I'm here are linked?"

"Took a guess," Drake said, leaning back against the couch. "And my guess is that Sabas is involved in it somewhere. I heard your tone when you said his name. I get that you're angry about the Wardens agents, but there seemed to be more than just guilt at friends dying. Did you ask them to look into Sabas?"

Kimi gave a slight nod.

Drake stared at Kimi. "I just can't figure out what he could have done to make you hate him this much. And it is hate, isn't it?"

Kimi nodded again. "He killed Helice, isn't that enough?"

"Yes," Drake said, and for a moment he doubted himself. Was he right to push Kimi toward an answer she might not want to give? He wasn't sure he could push someone he thought of as the closest thing he had to a sibling when he was young. "Is there anything I can do to prove to you that you can trust me?"

"Why did you leave me and Hideo?" Kimi asked, almost immediately.

"I was scared that people would have gone through you two to get to me," Drake told her. "I didn't know how to handle that possibility. So I ran. It might have been a huge mistake, but it felt like the only option I had at the time."

"Are you going to kill the person who murdered Helice and Septimus?" Kimi asked. There was an anger in her eyes that Drake had never seen before.

"If it comes to that, yes," Drake said honestly, knowing that Celine would back him if it came down to it. "I'm hoping it doesn't come to that. I want answers, not more dead bodies."

"You ever heard of Glehova?" Kimi asked.

Celine shook her head, but Drake nodded.

"There are thousands of planets in Union space," Celine said.

"It's on the edge of Union space," Drake said. "A military planet. It has one city that's about sixty-million square miles in size, and takes up just over half of the surface of the entire planet." Drake looked over to Celine. "I remember reading about it a long time ago and thought it sounded interesting. They have huge ship and armament factories both on the surface and in orbit. Anything the Union needs when they're that far from here. Never been there."

"There's a large OMC base there," Kimi said. "Eleven million OMC. The planet has a population of just over four hundred million. Most of those work to ensure the synths don't break down. It's a strange place. Not exactly hospitable, but not unpleasant. There's just a constant feeling that you're just in the way."

"You were based there?" Celine asked.

Kimi nodded, settling back into the couch. "Nearly two years. It wasn't exactly fun, but we had a lot of time to relax and play war. Occasionally, a pirate ship or the like would attack one of the moons or planets in Union space, and we'd have to go track them down and show them the error of their ways, but sending a hundred thousand OMC after sixty pirates isn't exactly what you'd call sporting," Kimi said with a shrug.

"Anyway, after two years of this, everyone was feeling more than a little bored, and wondering if we'd been put there as some sort of punishment. Then Stradiasus happened."

"The planet?" Celine asked.

Kimi nodded. "We got a distress call from the government there. Stradiasus has three cities, each one several million square miles in size. In the centre of it are a large number of caves within a barren wasteland. It's an odd place, which is why we found it strange that there was any kind of distress call. Who attacks a planet with a hundred million people, and nothing to take?

"So, the higher-ups, put together a force of roughly two hundred thousand OMC to go find out. Five warships made their way to Stradiasus and found the enemy was in the system as we were told. Well, one warship and a frigate. That's it. We all had a good laugh about it. The warship was about the same size as the Union's but we have five of them, we'd have torn them to tiny pieces. Even so, the higher-ups decided it was as good a chance as any to get practise in. Two ships' worth of personnel were sent to the surface, leaving the warships in orbit. The other three returned to Glehova with tales of stupid pirates."

Drake wondered how long it took for everything to go to shit, but didn't want to break the flow of Kimi's story.

"So, we landed, took control of the government military, the usual," Kimi continued. "Imposed a curfew. Made sure everyone was ready for something that was never going to happen. The first we knew of something wrong was when one of our warships fell to the surface, having been torn apart somewhere above us. The second one landed on one of the three cities, obliterating a large part of it and killing approximately five-million people in the process when its rift drive exploded on impact.

"Refugees flooded into the other two cities, and of the OMC we were down to just under a quarter of our original size. In a way we were lucky. If the ship had hit one of the more populated areas, it could have been two or three times that number. We were still reeling when all communications off-planet were severed, and the enemy warship ship landed in the wastelands. We still had drones in the air, so we got a pretty good look at the ten thousand predator-armoured military who marched off that ship."

"Predator squads?" Celine asked. "I've never heard of them being used against us."

Predator-armour was designed to be worn a variety of species of all shapes and sizes, melding to the person wearing it. The majority of humans who wore it had undergone genetic augmentations as children, but even the smallest human would look bulky and menacing inside one. Drake had always found them to be imposing, even when doing nothing but stood still. Seeing them in battle, with the masks pulled over their heads, and guns blazing was something very few ever forgot, especially those who survived.

While those who wore it were amazing warriors, predator-armour took its toll on those non-augmented humans, and several non-human species were more suited to fighting without it. It was a useful but costly addition to any military. Each predator squad had a different name and colour scheme, although the names of which were usually only known to the military. Having a squad turn up calling themselves The Spirit Rippers was probably not going to help the morale of the people they were meant to save.

"Ten thousand predator-squad members against several times that number OMC?" Drake asked. "That's a hard fight for both sides."

"And we had the advantage of the city walls," Kimi said. "Two hundred feet high in some places, and a dozen feet thick. We were confident right up until we saw those other things come out of the landing frigate."

"Things?" Drake asked.

Kimi nodded. "We didn't have a name for them. Creatures. Monsters. All I know is that we fought on those walls against just the predator squads for a week, and we lost maybe twenty thousand people, both military and civilian. It took a thousand of those things two days to butcher over half a million people. And we were there for three months before one day they just all upped and left. Of the hundred thousand OMC that started, one hundred and eight of us lived. Over ten million people died in three months. Those things just tore through the population like they were nothing. They destroyed with impunity. And were seemingly immune to everything we threw at them. Only our aether worked to defeat them, and we didn't have enough Sage to make that a long-term strategy."

Drake and Celine left Kimi to her silence, waiting her out.

"I left the OMC soon after when it became apparent they put it down to a defeated insurgency. That's the official line. Millions dead and no justice. So, I looked into it. I found a dead predator soldier and hacked into their internal systems, discovered a moon that had a research station on it just outside of Union space. I went there with a few dozen of my OMC friends, none of whom wanted to leave this alone. Everyone who worked in that research station was dead. A creature was loose. Didn't take long to find out that it was one of the things we fought on Stradiasus. We killed it, but lost good people doing so. It was weaker than the others, smaller, but no less dangerous for it. I hacked the records of the station, and would you like to guess who was sponsoring the facility and its research?"

"Expedited Systems," Drake said.

Kimi nodded. "The bastards helped murder millions of

people, and I want to know why."

"We'll help," Celine said. "That's not something we can just walk away from. A biological weapon that can cause that kind of damage would be terrifying in the wrong hands. Or any hands for that matter. Trust me when I tell you, I've been on the receiving end of something like that."

"What was it?" Drake asked.

"Long time ago," Celine said. "Back when I was a Blackcoat. We made sure that nothing survived after. No data, no samples."

"You think they're linked?" Kimi asked.

"I hope not," Celine said. "However, like I said, we'll help you look into it."

"Good, because there's somewhere I'd like to go," Kimi said.

"Where?" Drake asked.

"The Wardens who were killed tracked Sabas to an old warehouse," Kimi said. "They were killed there but when the Blackcoats and Wardens arrived to investigate, everything in the warehouse had been removed, leaving no trace. Helice and I found out where they'd moved it all. That's why I came to see you today. I want you to come with me and find out what they're hiding."

CHAPTER SIXTEEN

Felix Drake

Celine stayed behind to deal with the aftermath of the two dead bodies in Drake's home, for which he was more than a little grateful. It left Kimi, Drake, and Dai'ix to travel to the warehouse. The journey took just long enough for Dai'ix to be filled in on what had been discussed.

"So," Dai'ix said once it was all explained. "You joined the OMC, got into a war with monsters, lost friends, left the service, looked into those monsters, found out about the Gossard company involvement, and came back to Atharoth. Once here, you started looking into the Gossards and discovered they, specifically Sabas, were up to all kinds of nasty shit. You had Wardens look into them, and they got murdered. You found out Trinas helped Sabas, so you tracked him down, offered him a new life, and it got him and two of your friends murdered."

"Pretty much," Kimi said.

"You've had a shitty few years then," Dai'ix said.

"That's an understatement," Kimi told him. They were both sat in the rear of the sky-skimmer, allowing Drake to fly the vehicle and ponder what he was going to do if he found evidence linking Sabas to the murders of Trinas, Septimus, and Helice. He'd hoped to be able to keep his temper in check long enough to not tear Sabas in half. He was about fifty percent sure he'd be able to do that, but the longer he thought about it, the lower those odds went.

It didn't take long to go from the skyblock to the warehouse district that sat next to the Cobalt River; a massive stretch of water that ran for hundreds of miles. The Spire was nothing but a small feature on the horizon, as if it were watching over all that surrounded it.

"Land over there," Kimi said, pointing to a port that sat atop the blue river.

"I always loved the colour of the water," Dai'ix said as the ship landed.

The three exited the skimmer, and walked up the dock, passing several workers who all ignored the newcomers.

"It's this way," Kimi said, leading Drake and Dai'ix past a multitude of warehouses, some of which were large enough to house an army.

Eventually, Kimi motioned for them to stop. She crept up to the edge of a warehouse and beckoned them closer.

Unsure of exactly what he was about to find, Drake peered around the corner. A warehouse sat at the end of a large alley that was wide enough to fly a shock-wing down it. The lights in front were out, bathing it all in an eerie darkness that didn't give Drake any good feelings about what lay inside. A bird-like machine perched above the entrance, looking below.

"Vulture drone," Drake whispered.

"That's a problem," Dai'ix said. "They pack a punch."

"That's why I haven't gone in myself," Kimi said. "If I break the drone and get in, I'm going to get arrested for a variety of crimes if it turns out there's nothing there."

"And you would have to destroy a vulture drone," Drake said. "Not exactly a fun task."

"You ever gone up against one before?" Kimi asked.

"Once," Dai'ix said. "It was a long day, and there were six of them." He nudged Drake with his elbow. "You remember that day, boss?"

Drake nodded. "It's not exactly a memory I like to be

continuously reminded of. It hurt."

"You think we can take one out?" Kimi asked.

Vulture drones had several inches of thick, triseriam-carbonate skin, the same material used to make warships. They stood three feet high, and weighed as much as a fully-grown man. Whoever had originally designed it to look like a bird had done a good job, although the green glowing eyes and finger-long, metal-fibre talons were probably unnecessary. They had a rapid-fire plasma cannon on each shoulder, and were made to track movement from high above the ground. Frankly, keeping one sat above the entrance of a warehouse was overkill.

"Do you have a plan?" Dai'ix asked.

Drake tapped a few things on his comm unit. "I do, as it happens. You reminding me of the last time we fought these things gave me an idea."

"And that is?" Kimi asked.

"I had Rosie install a piece of software that disables drones. You have to be within about thirty feet of them, and it's only for a few seconds but sometimes, that's all you need." Drake looked at Dai'ix. "You still a good shot with that coil rifle?"

Dai'ix smiled, and unslung the weapon from his back.

"You're going to shoot it with a coil rifle?" Kimi asked. "That's not going to get through the armour."

"You're right, it won't," Dai'ix said. "We have a special type of round that will."

Kimi waited for more information, and when none was forthcoming, looked irritated. "Well?"

"Fusion bolt rounds," Drake said.

"You use fusion rounds in a coil rifle?" Kimi asked, clearly less than impressed.

"They're specially designed," Dai'ix said, crouching to remove the magazine and heat coil from the rifle. He lay them on the ground beside him before taking a fusion-tipped round from a pouch on his hip and slotting it into the chamber.

"Normal coil-rifle rounds with a fusion tip. Not as good as pure fusion bolt rounds, especially over long distances, but good enough to punch through that armour."

"So, what's the downside?" Kimi asked.

"Two things," Drake said. "One, the round is slow. The vulture droid will easily shoot it out of the sky before it hits. And two, the rifle will need several minutes to cool down after one shot. That's why there's no heal coil inside the rifle. It'll explode."

"So," Kimi said slowly, "we need to distract a killing machine so we can get close enough for you to use your software, and in the process hope we don't die?"

"That's about the size of it, yes," Drake told her. "Aren't you glad you had us come along?"

Kimi didn't bother answering, and along with Drake they walked silently toward the warehouse. They were over thirty feet away when a voice sounded from the drone, "Identify yourselves."

"It's the creepy, monosyllabic tone I hate," Drake whispered before shouting, "I'm a Warden. Here to inspect the premises."

"You will not," the drone commanded, its voice never changing tone.

Drake glanced at the comm unit that displayed the software; the big red button still read inactive. He took a few steps closer, Kimi beside him.

"Move to the side of the alley," Drake whispered. "We need it to track us as separate entities."

Kimi took several steps to her side, until she was up against the wall.

"I told you to stop," the drone ordered.

"And I said that I'm a Warden," Drake replied, taking another step forward. "If you can scan my identification, you'll see I have every right to be here."

The drone let out an ear-piercing shriek. "This warehouse is off limits. You have ten seconds to remove yourselves."

Drake darted forward, and slammed his hand on the comm unit the second the software activated. He thought it had failed but the drone above let out an horrific screech of pain followed by an almighty bang as Dai'ix fired the fusion-tipped bolt. The round hit true, tearing the machine in half as it went through the body and out where it's spine would have been had it been alive.

The drone fell apart, the metal and synthetic contents of its insides spilling over the side of the warehouse to the ground below.

"That was oddly disgusting," Kimi said.

Dai'ix joined the pair, the coil rifle slung on his shoulder again. "Need to remember to replace the ammo and heat coil," he said. "Glad those fusion-tipped bolts worked out. Would have been embarrassing if I'd missed."

"For all concerned," Kimi assured him.

Drake examined the keypad at the warehouse's grey metal door. "Any chance you know the code?" he asked Kimi.

"One-six-four-one-one-seven," Kimi said. "Trinas told us Sabas uses the same code for all of his warehouses, so he doesn't forget it."

"Sabas is an idiot then," Dai'ix said.

"A psychotic, evil idiot is still dangerous," Drake replied. "Probably more so." He tapped in the number and heard the hiss as the locks disengaged. A few seconds later and the door slowly opened, the lights inside the warehouse automatically igniting.

Drake glanced through the open door before immediately walking inside as Kimi whispered for him to wait.

"You think Sabas is going to get an alert the second we opened that door?" Dai'ix asked. "Or when we broke his droid?"

"I don't know," Kimi said after she shared a look of concern with Drake. "Let's not dawdle."

"I think we're safe for the moment," Drake said, taking several steps into the warehouse as Kimi and Dai'ix followed him.

"What in the gods?" Kimi asked.

"I don't think this is what you were expecting," Dai'ix said.

The warehouse was devoid of anything except a few metal shelving units that sat along one wall, and several fake-wood pallets that littered the ground. The warehouse was big enough to fit six or seven shock-wings inside, and the emptiness caused every footstep and word to echo.

"I don't understand," Kimi said. "How can there be nothing here? This is where they moved everything, I was certain of it. And who would put a vulture drone outside an empty warehouse? That's just a massive amount of time and money that is completely pointless."

"I don't think it's empty," Drake said. He picked up an oval-shaped piece of fake wood that was about a foot in length, and tested it for weight before throwing it across the warehouse. The fake-wood spiralled through the air before vanishing from view. A second later, the sound of it hitting something pinged back.

"It's invisible?" Kimi asked.

"Some sort of light-based barrier," Dai'ix said.

Drake walked over to where the item he'd thrown had vanished and put his head through the invisible field. He swore loudly.

"What's wrong?" Kimi and Dai'ix said in unison, running over to Drake as he stepped through the field and used a working terminal to disengage it.

Kimi and Dai'ix stopped running almost the instant the field vanished.

"What in the name of the breach is that?" Dai'ix asked.

Kimi just stared, her mouth agape in horror.

The barrier had been hiding dozens of machines, all of which were connected to what looked like two large, albeit modified, regeneration chambers. The massive glass sphere contained a regenerative synthetic liquid that worked alongside a Sage's naturally increased ability to heal. Hideo had almost certainly been placed inside one after losing his arm.

Drake clicked a few things on the terminal and found several reports about the two large masses that floated vertically inside the chambers. The liquid was murky, something a normal regeneration chamber would never have, so it was hard to figure out exactly what was inside. "They've been in here for months," Drake said, finding information about when the chambers were switched on.

"Any idea what *they* are?" Dai'ix asked.

"Regeneration chambers can only be used for a day at a time," Kimi said. "Even the most powerful Sage would be unable to stay in one for more than a few days."

Drake clicked on a few more files, trying to bring up anything interesting, but most of it was password encrypted to a much higher degree that he was able to crack with just his comm unit.

"We need Rosie," Dai'ix said.

"Get in contact with Celine," Drake told him. "She's going to need a lot more than just Rosie here. Tell her we've found something really bad."

"You sure it's bad?" Dai'ix asked.

"Is anything ever good when it looks like this?" Drake asked, noticing Kimi had almost pressed her face up against one of the chambers. "You okay, Kimi?"

She nodded. "Whatever is in there is larger than either of us. Maybe as big as Dai'ix."

"Let's not let them out then," Dai'ix said as he walked back through warehouse.

Drake clicked on a few more files, until one of them opened. "Well, this isn't a surprise."

Kimi walked over to the screen. "Ramin," she said, reading the name of the person who had paid for the warehouse. "He's behind all of this? He's the one who had all of this hidden in the other warehouse?"

"Not sure," Drake said, feeling unconvinced. "My first question would be why would all of these files be encrypted with a level even the military would consider overkill, but not the one file with Ramin's name on it, and proof that he paid for this place?"

"You think someone's trying to set him up?"

Drake shrugged. "I think this is a lot more complicated than I originally thought. This is what you, Helice, and Septimus wanted Trinas to tell you about? You think these things are the monsters you faced on Stradiasus?"

Kimi nodded. "I figured it was Sabas financing them, but maybe it was Ramin."

"So, three people got murdered because you found out that someone in the Ramin network is funding monster research," Drake said after several seconds of silence. He clicked each of the dozen files that remained on the system, but none opened. Instead, he went back to the only file he could access, and read through the whole thing. "Genesis-Alpha," he said aloud. "Some kind of first birth? I'm not sure what it's meant to mean."

"Is that what these are?" Kimi asked. "Is that what the things that attacked us on Stradiasus were?"

"Not sure," Drake said, still reading. "There's a note here to say the Genesis-Alpha experiment was a success. That's it, no other information about them except that Ramin's name is on top of the file. Looks to be some sort of comm message."

One of the creatures inside the regeneration bumped against the glass, causing both Kimi and Drake to jump.

"Can we check their vitals?" Kimi asked.

Drake found a machine that was connected to both regeneration chambers, and woke it from sleep mode. "The one on the left is showing nothing," Drake said.

"And the one on the right?" Kimi asked. "That was the one that bumped the chamber."

"It appears to be alive but there's nothing here that..." Drake stopped talking when the creature bumped the tank for a second time before there was a flash inside the tank, and the life signs stopped.

"What was that?" Kimi asked.

Drake didn't have an answer. "Whatever it was, it killed it."

"Can we open these?" Kimi asked.

Drake continued to look at the chambers, an unpleasant feeling churning up his stomach. "That would be a bad idea."

"So, that's it?" Kimi asked. "We find that Ramin paid for this place, and these... *things,* but we can't actually find out why he did, or what they are?"

"Celine is on her way," Dai'ix said after re-entering the warehouse. "She wasn't thrilled."

"We'll wait for her to arrive, and then we'll go back to Ramin and find out what all of this is about," Drake said. He looked back at all of the equipment inside the warehouse. "Dai'ix, you got a visi-pad with you?"

The oreaf nodded.

"Good," Drake said. "Go take pictures and video feed of everything. I get the feeling I've heard the term Genesis-Alpha before, but I can't think of where or when."

Dai'ix left to retrieve his visi-screen, returning moments later and set about recording everything inside the warehouse.

"Maybe my father will have heard of Genesis-Alpha," Kimi suggested.

"It's worth a try," Drake agreed, the irritation of being unable to remember where the term Genesis-Alpha had come up in his life. It would annoy him for several hours unless he finally figured out exactly where it came from.

"If these things and the things you fought are one and the same," Drake said to Kimi, "Then we have a problem."

"Those tanks can fit a ten-foot tall being," Kimi said. "They're large enough to fit one of the things that murdered my people."

"Dai'ix, can you stay here with Kimi and wait for Celine to turn up?" Drake asked.

"Of course," Dai'ix said. "Why?"

"I'm going to go back to Metan Glornv and see if he knows anything about this," Drake told him. "Frankly, I'm not convinced he told us everything."

"Metan had a thing for Helice," Kimi said.

"Yeah, they used to be together when we were kids," Drake said.

Kimi shook her head. "No, he turned up at her home and told her to leave alone whatever she was looking into. He told her it was her one chance because of their previous relationship. She refused, and he said that she owed him, and he was calling in the debt. That she should leave Trinas where he was, and get me to back off. Said Trinas was a dangerous man, the kind of person to get people killed."

"He told me he hadn't seen Helice for years," Drake said, annoyed that he'd believed Metan's lies.

"He saw her at least three times in the last year," Kimi said. "At least that was what she told me. Septimus was pretty upset about it and wanted to go talk to Metan, but Helice told him not to. He went anyway, and I went with him. He threatened Metan, told him to back off. Metan laughed at him, and said the friendly warnings were done. He was just looking out for Helice, but if she was going to be stupid enough to stay with Septimus, she got what she deserved."

"Looks like Metan knew more about this than he was letting on," Dai'ix said.

Drake nodded, deeply irritated. "Then, I really do need to have a conversation with him."

The trio left the warehouse and walked back to the docks where the sky-skimmer remained. "Celine won't be long," Drake said. "She never is."

"Be careful around Metan," Kimi told him. "He's a snake."

Drake was about to say that he'll be fine when the night sky lit up across the river, and a few seconds later the sound of an explosion tore through the silence the flash of light had created.

"That's The Spire," Drake said.

"Ramin," Kimi whispered.

"I'll head right there," Drake told them.

Dai'ix climbed into the sky-skimmer while Kimi waited for Celine and the Wardens to turn up.

"If you have any trouble, get a hold of me," Drake told Kimi.

"I think I can take care of myself, Drake," Kimi said.

"Even those things in that warehouse?" he asked her.

Kimi thought for a moment. "No, if they wake up, I'm going to need help. And a lot more guns.

"And you thought those monsters made this more complicated," Dai'ix said as the ship's engine ignited, and the pair took to the air, heading toward the fire as it tore through the night sky.

CHAPTER SEVENTEEN

Bokk

Bokk had not had the best day. First, two Blackcoats had come to Drake's home, forcing Bokk to kill the pair and leaving them damaged in the process. Then Bokk had to steal a sky-skimmer, something they were pretty sure they weren't meant to be doing. And to top it all off, the damage done to them had been greater than they'd imagined, forcing them to land after only a few hours of flying so that they could break into a synth repair store and steal supplies, allowing Bokk to fix the problems they were having with their motor skills.

They'd hidden themselves in an abandoned building to conduct the repairs, leaving the sky-skimmer on the roof after disabling the remote positioning sensor so no one could track it.

Bokk hated having to take time to do this, but after the initial concern about Drake being in danger, they came to the logical conclusion that Drake would probably be safer with his Warden colleagues. Bokk was certain that anyone who could get through the entire group unscathed was still going to have difficulty going up against a Sage as powerful as Drake. Bokk knew that Drake didn't like to use his aether, didn't like to consider it a crutch should he ever be without it, but Bokk has seen Drake cut loose once, and knew that he was capable of more than defending himself should it come to it.

Even so, Drake needed to be informed about the two dead investigators, and Bokk was halfway to Ramin's location at The Spire when various systems had started to shut down, forcing them to land. A four-hour journey to The Spire, had turned into double that by the time Bokk found themselves back at the sky-skimmer, their internal sensors and cracked torso now fixed as best they could do by themself.

Bokk wasn't exactly a natural when it came to flying the sky-skimmer they'd stolen. The act of actually stealing the vehicle was easy, having only to interface with the on-board computer, reset it, and reboot it as a new user. It took seconds. They assumed in part because no one had ever worried that a synth might steal one. Bokk would have to check records when they had the time to see if there was ever a case of a synth stealing... well, anything.

They landed the sky-skimmer on a dock about three-quarters of the way up The Spire, below the private landing dock above. Bokk didn't want to have to deal with any hostility for landing there without authorisation, or the backing of law enforcement.

Bokk immediately noticed the two armed guards on the dock, who watched the small ship as it landed. The door opened, allowing Bokk to exit. The sky-skimmer had contained several items of clothing, including a long black coat with red padding inside. They'd found other items too, but Bokk was sure they were surplus to requirements; they'd only wanted the coat so they could hide a plasma blade and coil rifle, the latter of which hung against their back.

"Halt," one of the two guards said, raising his hand.

Bokk stopped. "I'm here to see Ramin."

The two guards glanced at one another. "You're a synth. You can't just demand to see people."

Bokk wasn't really sure what to say to that.

The second guard raised his rifle in Bokk's direction.

"My master has sent me here to speak to Ramin," Bokk

said, trying a new tactic. "My master is Felix Drake. He works for the Wardens."

"Synths can't lie," the second guard said.

"That's true," Bokk said with a slight nod. "I am incapable of lying. So, please allow me to continue on with the orders I was given."

"What if it's a trap?" the first guard asked. "We were told not to let the Wardens back in without notifying Ramin."

"Notify him then," Bokk said, hoping their tone didn't show any impatience, no matter how much they felt it. "I'm happy to make your lives easier."

The first guard went over to his small hut and Bokk watched as he contacted Ramin. Bokk tried to listen in, but the wind was too ferocious to allow them to pick up anything from this distance.

"He says to let the synth up," the first guard said after returning. "Anything to help the Warden."

Bokk took a step forward, and registered something in the guard's tone. "You're lying. He's not happy to see me at all, is he?"

The two men shared a glance, and the first guard shook his head. "No, but he still told me to let you up."

"Thank you," Bokk said, walking past the two men and into The Spire. They quickly found the elevator leading up toward Ramin residence and was soon watching the doors to the elevator open as several armed men and women were stood beyond them, all pointing weapons at Bokk.

"This isn't the reception I was expecting," Bokk said.

One of the men stepped into the elevator. "My name is Radner Puley. I will be taking you to see Mister Gossard."

"Why the armed welcome?" Bokk asked after exiting the elevator and walking down the hallway with Radner.

"Precaution. Synths don't usually just arrive and ask to speak to people," Radner said. "Also, there was trouble in one of the sky towers. A recon synth shot Hideo Wynn."

Bokk stopped walking. "I have not heard anything about

that. How is the prince?"

Radner stopped a few steps ahead and turned back to Bokk, studying him for a moment. "Alive according to our information."

Bokk realised he needed to show less personality, but part of him was now concerned for Drake, and the Prince. "You have people working for you inside the palace, I assume."

Radner smiled, but didn't reply. He opened the door, motioning for Bokk to enter.

Ramin stood next to a large desk, looking out of the windows and down on the city. "My son was released from prison just a few weeks ago, did you know that, synth?"

"Bokk," he corrected. "Not synth."

Ramin smiled. "A synth with a name?"

"We all have names Mister Gossard," Bokk pointed out. "Just very few ever bother to learn what they are."

Ramin studied Bokk for several heartbeats, allowing Bokk to do the same to him. Ramin appeared to be tired, as if his mask had slipped and he hadn't bothered to put it back on.

"Leave us, Radner," Ramin said.

Radner bowed his head and left the room.

"You belong to Drake?" Ramin asked Bokk when they were alone.

"He is... my friend," Bokk said slowly. "He told me that he trusts you. Or at least to a point. He believes that while you want to stop your son from doing anything damaging, you will also go to great lengths to ensure he is safe."

Ramin nodded sadly, as if he agreed with everything Bokk said, but he still didn't like it. "Did Drake tell you I didn't once try to get my son out of prison?"

Bokk remained silent for a moment while they ran through the responses to the question. "You contacted the prison seventeen times," they said eventually. "You did nothing to get him out, but you ensured he was safe."

Ramin laughed. "My son is many things, but I am still his father." His smile faded and he sighed.

"You are scared," Bokk said.

Ramin sighed again. "My son has become a changed man since being released from prison. I have discovered things about him that have… disappointed and upset me. I believe some of those things Drake should be aware of. I would like you to contact him and tell him I need to see him. Face to face, no comms."

Bokk scanned Ramin and found no trace of deception. "Of course. He's why I'm here."

Ramin turned away from the window and sat at his desk. "In what way?"

"Drake's home was attacked," Bokk said. "This was listed as his last place of visiting before I left his apartment."

"You think I hurt him?" Ramin's tone suggested he was amused, although his expression said otherwise.

"Yes," Bokk said. "Or I did before I met you. I believe you and Drake share a genuine friendship. Your tone suggests you would not want anything bad to happen to him. I do not know why."

"He never told you?" Ramin asked. "I knew his father. I was in the military during the civil war, and came here a few years before it ended. One day, Drake came to me at the age of sixteen and asked me to help him get off-planet. No questions. I did what he asked and never expected to hear from him again. Until a few years ago when one of his investigations led him to have to deal with my son. I asked him to take Sabas in without incident. Drake promised he would do all he could to achieve that, but if Sabas fought, he would have no choice. I set my son up, Bokk, because I knew he was going to end up dead. Drake kept his promise, although Sabas tried to stab him. He let my boy live, and for that, I will be forever grateful."

Bokk wasn't sure how to respond to what they'd just been told. "I just want to know where he went next. Someone is trying to kill him. It's my job to make sure that doesn't happen."

Ramin appeared like a weight had been removed from his

shoulders. "You're a security synth, not a bodyguard."

Bokk nodded, it was an act they were unsure was in the correct time, but they'd seen humans do it. "I'm a lot of things. Just like you are both a father and a criminal. We all wear a lot of different hats."

Ramin stared at Bokk and laughed. "That we do, Mister Bokk."

"Just Bokk is fine," they said. "I'm sorry about your son. He is… not a good man."

"I never wanted to admit this before, but I believe he's evil," Ramin said sadly. "Sabas was always mean, quick to anger, but as he reached his teenage years, he became cruel, nasty. He revelled in the viciousness of our profession more than he should. Despite that, he is still my son, and I love him. I told Drake that I would look into my son's business, and I'm sad to say I believe he was involved in what happened to Helice and Septimus."

"Yes, I saw on the news," Bokk said. "The Council gave a statement saying that their killers will be brought to justice."

"There was a third body," Ramin said. "His name was Trinas Brong. An ex-employee of mine who was less than happy at his dismissal. I've found evidence that he went to work for my son."

"Why did you fire him?" Bokk asked.

"He was friends with my son," Ramin said. "I thought him to be a bad influence, so I fired him. Unbeknownst to me, Sabas re-employed him. They killed those two Wardens together. And possibly several others. The information I've gathered should be enough to put my son away for a long time. Not even his most powerful friends will be able to help."

The conversation had not gone the way Bokk had been expecting. "Why are you telling me this?"

"Because I'm going to leave this planet and return home," Ramin said "I'm done with all this. I plan on retiring and leaving this role behind. Eventually, it'll come out that I've betrayed my son. He has many allies who will want revenge for that, probably ordered by Sabas himself."

Bokk thought that human relationships were far too complicated, but instead, said, "You're wilfully telling me to inform Drake of your son's involvement in these murders?"

Ramin nodded. "I don't know why, or how, but yes. Drake will never let it go until he finds the truth, and I cannot allow my son's behaviour to go without punishment. He killed Council family members. He's jeopardised everything I've worked for my whole life. He's jeopardised the neutrality of Leturn. Drake is his father's son, and his father was nothing if not stubborn."

Bokk had to repeat the words in his head for several seconds before it could come up with a suitable reply. "You never said how you knew Drake's father?"

"Evan Varlus was my general in the Rebellion," Ramin said, sounding sad about the memory. "I served Evan during the battle of Fendis VII, when he turned his back on the rebellion after so many years of fighting for them. So many of us felt betrayed by the Empire, forgotten about, left to fight rebels who were just trying to make a better life for themselves, that when we joined them, it felt right. Unfortunately, it wasn't. It was…they were…not what we had thought.

"After Fendis, I decided I needed to leave before things got worse, which it definitely did. As history shows, Evan was a dangerous man, but one I admired. I fled the Rebellion, re-invented myself, and came to Leturn to make a name, to make myself rich. I've done both of those things, but I can't forget Evan. Most who met him couldn't either. He was a force of nature in battle, a man we should all fear. And when the darkness came for him, when it tainted us all, it was only the will of him and his fellow generals who pushed it back and set us free from its grip."

The name Evan Varlus unlocked something inside of Bokk's head. They hadn't heard it in a long time. Bokk was confused at what was happening, but continued on anyway.

"What darkness? What grip?"

Ramin shook his head sadly. "I don't… I don't' remember."

Once again, Bokk found no readings to suggest that Ramin was being anything but honest. "So you want me to tell Drake that your son and Trinas worked together to kill the children of councillors?"

Ramin stood and straightened his dark blue shirt. "Yes. In the meantime, this is a farewell. It was a pleasure, Bokk."

Bokk still has so many questions, but it was clear that Ramin wasn't going to answer them. Still, one resided above all others. "You don't know where Drake is now, I take it?"

"Last I heard, he was at the palace," Ramin said. "I've left my data-pad unlocked and attached to its console. You're more than welcome to use it. Drake is too when he inevitably arrives. It'll prove everything I've told you."

"I do not understand humans," Bokk said. "I try to, but you are complex and… well, honestly, weird. I will do what you asked. If you are lying to me, I will come back."

Ramin laughed, and left the room.

Bokk glanced out of the window and wondered if Drake really was at the palace. They turned toward the data-pad, and took a step forward before the entire building shook, throwing Bokk across the room with considerable force. They knew the cause before they'd hit the ground – *explosion.*

A second explosion blasted out all of the windows in the office, and Bokk grabbed hold of the data-pad, tearing it free from its power supply and running toward the door. They burst through it, knocking the wood into splinters and placed the data-pad just outside the elevator doors.

Bokk punched through those metal doors and pulled them apart, looking down into what should have been a dark void below. Instead, heat rushed up the elevator shaft and Bokk dove aside as flame tore up toward them, pouring out of the opening and destroying the part of the hallway where they'd had been standing only moments earlier.

They grabbed the data-pad once again and ran back down

the hallway toward Ramin's office, continuing on through and out the other door without pausing. Fire alarms sounded all around, and Bokk wondered if Ramin had gotten safety. They needed to ensure Ramin was okay. If he was the target, finding Ramin was a good way to discover what was going on. On top of that, Bokk needed to find out what had actually happened to have caused such an horrific explosion. Their day wasn't getting any easier.

The room Bokk found themselves in was a massive open living area with sofas in the middle of the room, next to a visi-screen that was easily the size of a sky-skimmer. They opened the nearest door and found a small bedroom. The next one along was a well-stocked kitchen. All the windows led to a sheer drop into the nothingness. Bokk ran to the opposite end of the main living area and opened the three doors on that side, eventually finding a bedroom with a small window in one corner that overlooked a platform below. An emergency exit that led to a ladder stretching down to a platform fifty feet below. They were mandatory in all penthouses on the planet, and Bokk hoped the explosion hadn't moved anything out of alignment.

After kicking out the window, and their sensors showing the rush of air as it swept into the room, they crouched, and crawled through the ruined window. More sensors in Bokk's knees told them there was glass under their knees, each movement accompanied with an audible crunch. Thankfully, Bokk knew their body-shell was capable of withstanding cuts by even the most reinforced glass.

The outside ledge was protected from the majority of the elements by a large wrap-around wall, reducing wind shear. The ladder was encased by thick walls, so Bokk could descend without worry. It didn't take long to reach the path below, and follow it to an emergency door that was easy to break, and allowed them back inside The Spire.

Bokk ran to the end of the hallway, fire alarms blaring all around him as people rushed to the emergency elevators. Bokk didn't want to escape the building via the ground-level exit but to return to the penthouse dock and their sky-skimmer. Stolen or not, it was their best choice for escape.

People crowded into the elevators to the ground floor, and Bokk found one of the maintenance shafts to use. The ladder in each shaft only covered five floors at a time, then it was a short walk along a platform to the next ladder to repeat the process. Unlike the ladder Bokk had taken from the penthouse, those in the maintenance shafts were automated. All Bokk had to do was hold on and select the floor, then the ladder moved them.

Once at the top of the shaft, Bokk made his way to the exit, allowing them access to the floor below the penthouse dock. There were small fires in the hallway beyond, but nothing of a serious nature, and Bokk quickly made their way through the floor toward the stairs leading to the dock above. They opened the door and superheated air ripped out of the stairwell, forcing Bokk back, and setting off several alarm systems inside their body shell.

Thankfully, the force of the blast had re-closed the fire-resistant door, leaving Bokk laying on the ground wondering why they hadn't escaped. They didn't owe Ramin anything, and as far as they were concerned, Bokk was only interested in finding Drake. Bokk wasn't equipped to deal with the fire or the explosion's aftermath. They weren't even sure what had caused it, or just how much damage the building had sustained. Something told them to find out. They needed to ensure that Ramin was alive.

Bokk got back to their feet and tore the two feet square visi-pad in half, removing the tiny memory chip, placing it inside their coat. They'd be able to patch the memory into another console when they needed.

They then kicked the door and darted to the side, but no superheated air rushed back through. Bokk peered into the empty, charred stairwell and tentatively stepped inside. They were halfway up the stairs when they heard voices above and increased their speed.

Bokk reached the door to the dock; it was badly damaged and required more force to open than Bokk had anticipated. They took a step back and launched themselves at the door, removing it entirely and dumping them on the wet ground beyond.

Several small fires blazed on the dock, but most of it was now covered in foam from the helix—a massive, six-person utility vehicle—hovering above that was spraying the substance all over the dock. A sky-skimmer sat torn in half on one side of the dock; Bokk wondered if the sky-simmer they'd arrived in was still on the dock below. What had once been a shock-wing was now nothing more than scrap as the ruined hull had been ripped apart, presumably from the explosion.

Many people walked about the dock, moving pieces of scrap, and more than one person wearing a medical uniform was dealing with the large number of dead and injured that lay on the ground around them. Bokk made their way across the dock as a sky-skimmer landed. The helix stopped spraying foam, and they saw the remains of at least three people—charred beyond recognition—next to a huge piece of shrapnel from the shock-wing.

"Bokk?"

Bokk turned to find Drake running toward them, a confused expression on his face.

"Drake," Bokk said, glad to have found their friend.

"Why are you here?" Drake asked as he reached them.

Bokk looked back at the ruined penthouse of The Spire. Most of the exterior walls had been torn apart from the explosion; it was fortunate the blast hadn't occurred inside the building as it might well have ripped the entire top of the building free.

"It's long story," Bokk eventually said. "We need to talk."

CHAPTER EIGHTEEN

Jaysa Benezta

Jaysa was bored. It had been several hours since Ren and Takumi had left the estate. She'd gone to the second largest building on the grounds, where her room was, but found it devoid of anyone to talk to, so had gone back to the main building. With everyone else off in other parts of the massive complex, Jaysa had found herself just sitting on the comfortable couches, eating from the vast amounts of food servants had delivered.

Etamus had resorted to putting herself into a meditative state during those hours, and had been indisposed, so it was with a great fondness when Jaysa saw her friend leave the bedroom and pad across the floor, throwing herself on the large couch opposite.

"You feel better?" Jaysa asked.

"Alive," Etamus said with a smile. "I'd hoped that by the time I'd emerged from my room, we would be ready to move on. I assume that is not the case."

"I have no idea," Jaysa said. "I haven't seen anyone in hours. The visi-screen is doing endless stories about what happened to Prince Hideo, but no one seems to have one iota of information that's new or relevant, so they're just going around in circles."

Etamus glanced at the visi-screen. "So, essentially what

you're saying is that you're clawing at the walls to try and get out."

Jaysa smiled; her friend knew her well. "I'm not someone who enjoys being caged."

Etamus picked up a bowl of fruit and selected a large snowberry, taking a bite of the thumb-sized, pale-blue fruit, offering the bowl to Jaysa.

Jaysa took one and bit it in half. "Delicious," she said. "I've eaten about fifty of the things."

"They must get them imported from a planet several systems away," Etamus said. "They're not native to this world. Worth it though, as they can be used to make the most delicious snowberry crumble."

Jaysa raised an eyebrow in question. "And you know this how?"

Etamus popped another berry in her mouth. "Before I started to work for you, I used to go to this little cafe on Frocure, just outside of the Red Wall. It was peaceful there. Lots of trees and plants, and very few people to bother me."

The joy in Etamus' tone made Jaysa wonder what had happened for Etamus to end up on her ship. "You miss it?"

"I miss the woman I was seeing at the time," Etamus said with a broad grin. "I miss the cold mornings and the sound of birds singing in the evening as the sun began to set. I still want to be here. You're my captain."

Jaysa smiled. "What happened to the woman?"

Etamus shrugged. "We broke up. She wanted to see the stars and plot a trail for new discoveries, and I was settled. Turns out, I ended up in the stars anyway. What about you? When was the last time you even had a romantic interest?"

Jaysa let out a long breath. "Men and women aren't exactly beating down my door to get to me. And to be honest, I'm pretty happy with that at the moment. Relationships aren't something I excelled at. I know where my strengths lie, and usually it's in hurting someone, or finding someone, or generally just being angry at everyone."

Etamus placed a hand on Jaysa's shoulder. "Sounds like hard work."

"Sometimes it is, yes," Jaysa said with a nod. "And sometimes it's a security blanket I like to keep wrapped around me." Jaysa forced a smile as memories of her difficult childhood rose.

"You ever feel like going back to Benoran?" Etamus asked.

"No," Jaysa said immediately. "Once the military gained control it only took a few decades for the worst parts of the culture there to blossom. Power corrupts everyone eventually. Or at least, power corrupts those who allow it, and most allow it. Those who had been in power, lost it all and were relegated to a lower station, something not far off from slaves. Some say they deserve it," she said with a shrug. "After all, their ancestors were responsible for horrific crimes. I'm not sure that committing more horrific crimes cancels that out."

"It just piles on the pressure and resentment on both ends," Etamus said.

"Exactly. For all its faults, the Union actually treats everyone the same no matter what you look like. They only care about how much credit you have."

Etamus took another snowberry. "Wow, this is a depressing line of conversation."

Jaysa chuckled. "Do you see the kind of stuff we talk about when we're locked in a room for a few hours? It's not exactly a party."

Etamus looked around the large, lavish room. "So, where are Yanton and Kayos?"

"I haven't seen them since we arrived." Jaysa sighed again; her anxiety was rising. "There has to be a way to contact someone and find out what's actually happening. We're being treated like criminals despite having done nothing wrong."

"Have you spoken to the guards at the front gate?" Etamus asked.

Jaysa opened her mouth to speak, then wisely closed it.

Etamus suppressed a smile. "You've just been stewing in

annoyance and haven't gone out there to check, have you?"

"Well, no," Jaysa admitted.

Etamus got to her feet. "Right, let's go see what's happening."

They'd reached the door when Takumi stepped out of one of several hallways that lead away from the centre room. Ren followed a few seconds later, both wore the same clothes as earlier, although Takumi looked tired.

"You both okay?" Etamus asked.

"We're on lock down," Takumi said, irritated. "We were dealing with some Council stuff when the guard told us The Spire had exploded. Wardens are everywhere."

"And we've been forced to stay here," Ren finished, almost throwing herself onto the couch.

"We were about to see the guard out front and find out what's happening here," Etamus said.

"When did you last talk to a guard?" Jaysa asked the twins.

"Few hours," Takumi said. "The one who told us to stay put was maybe an hour ago. That was by comm, so actually we haven't *seen* any guards in some time."

"Is that weird?" Jaysa asked.

Ren sat up. "It is a bit, yes."

"Let's go see the guard out front," Etamus suggested.

"We'll stay here," Ren said. "Make sure no guard comes running through while you're out there."

Etamus and Jaysa headed out of the villa and into the front garden. Etamus walked barefoot, seemingly indifferent to the small, jagged stones that made up the pathway to the front gate.

"I wish the walls were a little shorter," Etamus said, staring at the thirty-foot high, pale brick monstrosity that encircled the villa. "It really does detract from how pleasant this place is."

Jaysa remained silent, wishing she still had her disrupter. The weight of it against her hip had been reassuring; without it, she felt more than a little defenceless, although she knew that wasn't true. Maybe she relied on it a little too much. Maybe not having it would do her some good.

Jaysa banged on the fifteen-foot high, dark wooden gates before taking a step back and waiting for them to open. Nothing. She repeated the action, although this time with more annoyance. The guard post was directly outside of the gates, it wasn't like the sound had far to reach.

"Are they just ignoring us on purpose now?" Jaysa asked and kicked the gate as hard as she could. It didn't budge, so she kicked it again. The second blow moved it a fraction of an inch.

"I don't think that's going to work," Etamus said, placing her hands against the gate to see how much give it had. "Maybe they've all gone for food or something."

"You don't sound convinced," Jaysa said.

Etamus pushed against the gate one last time. "I think we need to go find Yanton and Kayos."

Jaysa turned back to the villa. "I have no idea where they are." She turned toward Etamus who was kneeling in front of the gate, touching the earth near it. "What's wrong?"

"There's blood on the ground here. I can feel it in the earth. It's soaking in." Dreic could touch the earth with their bare skin and feel anything that wasn't meant to be there. They also had the ability to use a type of earth-sonar, showing them where living things were. It had been a power that had come in handy over the years, but it was something that took a lot out of Etamus.

"How much blood?" Jaysa asked.

Etamus stood, and wobbled slightly, resting one hand against the wall to steady herself. "Enough to have me worried. I don't feel anyone alive stood atop the ground."

Jaysa was immediately on edge. "We really do need to find Yanton and Kayos. Any idea where they might be?"

Etamus pushed herself away from the wall. "Ren will."

The pair made haste to the main building and found Ren and Takumi looking unhappy.

"The comms are down," Takumi said. "All of them."

Etamus explained what she'd discovered by the gate. "Is there another way out of here?"

"No," Ren said, still calm. "The whole point of this place was to be defensive should we need it. There's nowhere else to go, except to the sky."

"Something's wrong," Jaysa aid. "Where are the rest of my crew?"

"In their rooms," Takumi said. "Or they should be."

The group quickly left the main building and ran along the outside of it to the bedroom complex but found only Eronokos, who'd been stabbed in the back of the neck. Jaysa stopped, but there was no pulse.

"Damn it," Takumi said. "I liked him."

"We need to find my crew," Jaysa said, getting back to her feet.

"How about over there?" Etamus suggested, pointing to a building close to the landing pad. It was three-storeys high and detached from the rest of the property. "That looks like as good a place as any to check."

The four ran through the garden, and Jaysa pushed the door, which opened easily. "What is this place?"

"Offices, a small library," Ren said. "I keep a lot of confidential material here. It's usually locked up tight. Lots of guards too."

"You been in here since we arrived?" Etamus asked, as Jaysa took a step inside.

"Nope, you feel anything?" Jaysa asked.

Etamus shook her head.

"What does that mean?" Ren asked, still looking and sounding calm.

"It means the blocks used to build this property are thick enough to dull my senses," Etamus said. "Thicker than the main building."

The hallway in which they stood was a pale grey with no doors either side. It ended after a corner, revealing an elevator. Jaysa pressed the button, and it glowed a faint red.

"I really wish I had a weapon," Jaysa said.

"I wish I had a set of predator-armour," Takumi said.

The elevator arrived without noise, and the doors opened, revealing mirrored walls inside. The four stepped into the elevator and Jaysa turned toward the control panel. "There's an arrow going up, and one going down. No floor numbers. Where do you want to go?"

"Down," Etamus said. "Let's see if getting underground helps my senses. Maybe we'll find some clues as to what's going on."

"It's just empty rooms down there," Ren said.

Jaysa pressed the down button and the elevator doors closed, making Jaysa feel even less happy about being inside it. A second later, they re-opened into a hallway identical to the one on the floor above.

They all stepped out of the elevator, trying each of the doors they came to but finding the small rooms beyond were all empty except for a table and some chairs. It wasn't until the fifth door was opened that they found one of the guards slumped in the corner of the room, the front of his chest completely drenched in blood.

"He's dead," Jaysa said as Etamus rushed over to check.

"Throat was slit," Etamus said sadly. "One motion. Professional."

"They removed his armour and weapon," Ren said. "How long do you think he's been down here?"

"An hour at most," Etamus told her.

They checked the rest of the rooms, finding more dead guards in the last.

"Three dead here," Etamus said after examining the bodies as Takumi closed the door behind them. "All of them close-quarter blasts to the back."

"Who would do this?" Ren asked. "Attack my people? On the same day Hideo is hurt. Why would anyone do that?"

"Someone *really* doesn't like us," Takumi said.

Jaysa was about to say something when she heard

footsteps hurrying down the hallway. She shared a look of concern with Etamus before moving behind where the door would open—out of sight from anyone entering. Jaysa pulled the twins over to where she hid. Etamus sat on the floor in the middle of the room.

Jaysa knew what her friend wanted her to do, she just hoped that whoever was coming wouldn't open fire the second they saw Etamus. Jaysa held her breath as the figure appeared in the doorway.

"You weren't meant to leave the villa," the male voice said. "Where are the twins?"

Etamus shrugged. "Fancied a walk. You kill these guards?"

"Where are the twins?" the guard asked again.

"Back in the villa, I imagine. I only came in here because I was trying to find Yanton and Kayos," Etamus said. "I assume you have them too."

The man stepped into the room and Jaysa saw the tip of a gun barrel, but before she could reach out to grab it, the door was shoved toward her. Jaysa and the twins dodged aside, revealing themselves to their would-be attacker.

The man wore a black, armoured-jacket and trousers, and held a viper pistol. "You're coming with me," he said to Takumi.

Jaysa didn't see Etamus move until she was on the man, pushing the gun away and driving her forearm into his temple. He dropped to his knees, releasing the pistol, which Jaysa kicked across the room as Etamus smashed her knee into the man's face, knocking him to the ground.

Jaysa retrieved the pistol aiming it at the attacker. "Who are you? And where are my crew?"

The man stared at Jaysa for several seconds before laughing.

Ren removed a second pistol from a holster on the man's hip, and shot him through the knee, his laughter turning to screams.

"I'm not telling you…" the man began before Jaysa shot

him through the other knee.

"We're here to kill you and your crew," he stammered. "We… we took the villa this morning, k-killed the guards an hour ago."

"My crew," Jaysa demanded.

The killer closed his eyes, his face a mask of pain. Jaysa was about to kick him in the knee when he re-opened his eyes again. "Hurt, but they've barricaded themselves in a room on the second floor. We didn't want to use anything that would tip you off until… until we'd dealt with them. This was meant to be an easy job."

"Who do you work for?" Jaysa asked.

"I don't ask questions, just do what I'm told," the killer said, pale. "Kill you all and leave. That was our mission."

"How many of you are there?" Takumi demanded.

The killer was quiet for a moment, Etamus stamped down on one of his wounded knees and he cried out, the words spilling out of him, "Half a dozen. More are coming. We decided to just crush the whole place if we couldn't do it quietly. You're all dead, you just don't know it yet."

"And what a great job you did," Jaysa said and shot him through the eye. "Let's go find Yanton and Kayos."

"We're going to need more weapons," Takumi said.

"There's an armoury on site," Ren said.

Finally, some good news. "Right, that's our destination," Jaysa said, hoping the people sent to kill everyone hadn't gotten there first.

CHAPTER NINETEEN

Jaysa Benezta

They rode the elevator up again, and Jaysa turned the pistol over to check the reading on the side. Four shots left before the core would need to be ejected and replaced.

"That's not great," Takumi said, reading over Jaysa's shoulder.

"Yeah, let's hope we don't have to do much shooting," Jaysa replied.

"Shame that guy wasn't carrying more ammo," Ren said, checking the shot-count on her own pistol.

The elevator stopped and the doors slowly opened. Three men turned toward the sound; Jaysa shot two of them in the chest, and Ren shot the third in the head before any of them could fire their weapons. Jaysa dropped her pistol, taking a coil-rifle from one of the dead while Etamus grabbed a blast-gun, and Takumi removed two knives from one of the bodies.

"Now we're all armed," Takumi said, with more than a little anger. "Should make things easier."

They crept to the end of the hallway, and Jaysa peeked around the corner only to find it empty. Several doors sat open along both sides, while one door at the end remained closed. Jaysa and Etamus crept toward the end of the hallway, pausing to check each of the thankfully empty rooms.

"Yanton, you in there?" Jaysa asked. She was about to yell for a second time when she heard movement behind the door, and it was slowly opened to reveal a blood-drenched Yanton.

"I couldn't save him," Yanton said, his voice low and thick with emotion.

Jaysa stalked into the room and found Kayos sat up in one corner of what appeared to have been a supply room. Yanton had pulled down several metal shelving units to form a barricade while he'd tried in vain to keep his friend alive.

"What happened?" Etamus asked.

"They barged into where we were staying about an hour ago, killed Eronokos," Yanton said. "We managed to escape to here but that just made things worse. We had no way of contacting you, and Kayos had been hit when we ran. The blast nicked an artery. I'm sorry, I couldn't save him."

Jaysa looked over at Yanton while rage filled her. "They wanted to take out the guard before they came for Etamus and me."

"They knew Etamus was undergoing her monthly sleep, and figured you'd wait until last," Yanton said. "They thought I was the captain. I heard them talking about more people coming."

Jaysa placed a hand on Yanton's shoulder, squeezing slightly. "We're going to get out of here, and we're going to get vengeance for Kayos." She turned to Ren. "Where's the armoury?"

"Floor above here," Ren said.

"I heard these bastards talking about it," Yanton said.

"They should have killed me while I slept," Etamus said, her voice cold and hard. "Because that was their only chance."

Jaysa left the room and searched the dead hired killers, finding nothing of use.

"We need a comm-unit," Takumi said. "We need to find a way out of this before anyone else turns up."

When they reached the armoury, it had been all but ransacked. Murky light came from the one small window. Ren closed the door and tapped on a security panel. An alarm sounded a few seconds later. "Shit," she said. "Sorry, I don't know what they've done to the system, but it's not from here."

"Someone triggered an alarm somewhere else," Takumi said. "I think these people will want to finish their job quickly."

Jaysa stacked some crates atop one another and climbed up to the window, looking out at the villa. "There's a hut near the rear of the property, and several dozen people coming through the front gate. I think the reinforcements have arrived. Also a behemoth." She watched the twenty-foot-tall, armoured unit stroll across the compound, a plasma chain-cannon attached to one arm, a huge sword sheathed on its back. Jaysa couldn't see the organic person controlling it, but knew they were deep inside the mechanical beast, hooked up to one another to ensure optimal performance. She'd killed a few behemoths in her life, the screams of the mechanical beast as the human inside died wasn't something you soon forgot.

"Great, so what do we do now?" Yanton asked.

"Get geared up for war," Jaysa said and climbed down, discovering a partially hidden door, and opened it. Inside, were four large cupboards along one wall, each containing dozens of rifles and pistols of several types. Opposite the cupboards was another door, which held different kinds of armour.

Jaysa quickly changed into a set of black and grey recon armour and grabbed herself a force shield – a small device that clipped onto the shoulder of the armour giving the wearer an extra layer of protection against energy weapons.

"Etamus, you're going to want to see this," Jaysa shouted as she finished getting ready.

When Etamus entered the room, she smiled. "Predator-armour."

Jaysa returned to the first room and found Yanton working on the security panel. "I've hacked into the villa's network. The security here is dreadful. It's like they're not bothered about people getting into the system." He looked over to Ren. "No offense."

"None taken," Ren said. "This was never my main home. I just like to stay here when visiting family. I don't actually know much about the whole place."

"So, do you want good or bad news?" Yanton continued.

"Bad," Takumi said before anyone else could answer.

"I found some blueprints," Yanton said, confident now that he was in his element. "The walls are four-inch thick triseriam carbonate; they'd withstand a direct blast from a battleship."

"What about the floor and ceiling?" Jaysa asked.

"The ceiling is the same, it's completely protected. The floor... I don't know about the floor." He tapped a few things on the panel. "There's a trapdoor in the other room. It leads to a chute that goes straight down to the self-contained water system beneath the villa."

Jaysa looked at Ren who shrugged. "I had no idea it was there."

"Okay," Takumi said with a roll of his eyes. "What was the good news?"

"That small building you saw," Yanton said. "That's where all the communication equipment is. If we can get in there, we could get a message of help out of the villa."

"And you didn't know this?" Takumi asked Ren, his irritation finally bubbling over.

Ren shrugged again. "It wasn't like it was high on my list of priorities to know about."

"So, you hope the comm stuff is there, but you can't be sure," Jaysa said, ignoring the squabbling twins.

"Yeah, there's no guarantee about any of this," Yanton said.

Jaysa grabbed hold of an energy dagger and walked into the other room, cutting through the expensive carpet that covered the floor. She peeled back a large portion to reveal the trapdoor beneath. There was no handle, just a keyhole at one side.

A voice filtered through the room. "You have exactly ten

seconds to answer this before I allow my men to tear their way into here."

"You think this place will hold?" Jaysa asked.

Yanton nodded.

Jaysa walked over to the door and tapped on the security terminal screen, which flickered to life, showing a very angry-looking man with grey hair and dark skin stood outside the door. He wore burgundy and black power armour, and carried his helmet under one arm, a plasma rifle in his hand.

"Our employee has informed us that you're to be given the chance to surrender," he said. "You don't surrender, and I'll make sure you die real slow. Screaming."

"I've been reliably informed that these walls are made of triseriam carbonate, so unless you have something a lot more impressive than the plasma rifle you're holding, you're not getting in here," Jaysa pointed out.

A shadow fell across the room, and Jaysa looked out of the window as a helix came into view. They weren't fast or particularly well armoured, but they were more than capable of killing a bunch of troops on the ground and were usually equipped with detection and surveillance equipment. "We've got that," the mercenary said with a sadistic smirk.

"Everyone down," Jaysa said and ran at Yanton, shoving him against the far wall as the glass above them shattered, the plasma chain-gun destroying much of the room's contents.

"Etamus," Jaysa shouted, the smell of burning filling her nostrils. "Are you done preening yourself? We could really use a hand here."

Her second-in-command walked out of the room, green and black predator-armour gleaming. Etamus raised one fist toward the windows and a blast of energy smashed through the remaining glass and punched into the helix with incredible force.

"Keep them busy," Jaysa said, grabbing hold of the energy dagger and plunging it into the seam between the trapdoor and the rest of the floor. Eventually, she managed to cut through whatever locks were in place. There was a hiss of air and Yanton and Takumi joined Jaysa in pulling the hatch up and pushing it aside to reveal darkness beyond.

"We need to go," Jaysa said, grabbing a coil-rifle and handful of disposable lights from beside her. She activated one of the lights and dropped it through the hatch, hearing a satisfying splash as it hit the water below. She followed a moment later, riding the slide the dozens of feet in the darkness until she landed in waist-high water. It took her eyes a second to adjust to the meagre glow from the disposable light.

Yanton landed just as Jaysa had activated a second light and dragged herself over to a nearby ledge. The muffled sound of weapon-fire could be heard above, but it soon stopped and a few seconds later Etamus made a massive splash as she hit the water, followed quickly by Ren and Takumi, both of whom now carried energy pistols of one make or another.

"So, where to from here?" Etamus asked.

"This way," Yanton said, pointing into the darkness of the sewer. "The blueprints said there's a hatch up above, close to the hut."

"Isn't that where the behemoth is?" Takumi asked.

"It's that or we stay here and wait," Yanton said. "That hut is built to survive a direct orbital bombardment. We'll be safe in there."

"You hope," Ren said.

"The armour says the hatch is this way," Etamus told everyone. "All of the tunnels are mapped in the internal systems."

Everyone looked at Ren. "I have never seen that suit before in my entire life. It must have been commissioned by one of the guards here."

"Well, its directions are good enough for me," Jaysa said and followed Etamus down the tunnel.

They'd made it several hundred feet when Etamus stopped by a dark alcove. "Just here," she told Jaysa. "There's some kind of terminal here, I'll have to see if my suit can hack into it."

A laser blast smashed into the wall beside Jaysa's head, and she ducked into the alcove beside Takumi. "Hurry," Jaysa shouted to Etamus and fired back twice into the darkness beyond, only to have two more shots hit the wall nearby. "Hurry faster!"

Takumi fired into the darkness, and Jaysa grinned at the grunt of pain from the darkness. "Good shot," she said. "Hopefully we can get out of this damn water sooner rather than later."

Takumi didn't reply, and Jaysa hadn't really expected him to. She wanted out of the cold water she knelt in, and as she fired back at her unknown attackers, wished she'd grabbed some more tech, night vision goggles would have been helpful, or something that would make a large explosion.

More laser fire struck the wall, and she shot back twice more, thinking she heard someone fall in the tunnel. Hopefully, her shot hit a vital enough area that took the enemy out of the fight.

"If you come out now, we'll let you say your goodbyes," someone's voice boomed through the tunnel.

"You want to think about that, boss?" Yanton asked over his shoulder.

"No, I'm good," Jaysa said and fired down the tunnel again. "You done, Etamus?"

There was a scraping noise and a part of the ceiling above them moved aside, allowing a ladder to descend, and where a second hatch sat high above them.

Jaysa went last, and when she was far enough up, put two coil-rifle rounds into the control panel. The hatch closed below her feet, and her slight sense of relief was quickly extinguished when she spotted the behemoth in the distance.

The five of them sprinted to the small hut, with Etamus using her suit to get the door open, and they bundled inside.

"Do you have a plan?" Yanton asked Jaysa as he accessed

the communications systems and put out a general, high-alert call that they needed assistance from Marauders.

"We're sitting ducks here," Jaysa said. "Whether we're shielded or not, they'll eventually break in, so we need to leave."

"And once we leave, we're going to need cover," Takumi said. "There are no windows in here, so whatever's waiting for us out there won't be good."

Ren paced the small room. "If we can get over to the building on the far left of the compound, we can ignite the security protocols. So long as our would-be killers aren't already there."

"Wait, we've got a reply," Yanton said.

"What does it say?" Jaysa asked.

"*Are you in that little hut thing?*" Yanton said reading from the screen. He confirmed they were then read the next reply. "*Get down*."

All five hit the ground as it shook from the force of whatever was happening outside.

"There's another message," Yanton shouted over the sounds of a battle raging outside. "It says, '*I'm here to rescue you. Get your asses out of there*'."

The group raced out of the building as a second helix hovered above them, tearing the behemoth to shreds with its four plasma cannons, and avoiding any return fire with what appeared to be ease. As it lowered toward the ground, the plasma cannons never let up, destroying anything that looked even remotely threatening.

The rear of the helix lowered, revealing a young woman. "Name's Rosie, get in," she shouted, using the helix's external comm system to great effect.

Etamus, Yanton, Ren, Takumi, and Jaysa sprinted toward the helix as a second predator-armoured person—this one in black and grey—appeared, laying down covering fire. Jaysa took a blast to the arm from one of the mercenaries who got off a lucky shot, and she scrambled onto the helix, blood dripping freely onto the floor.

"How bad is it?" Rosie asked.

"Not bad enough to not kill me, but bad enough to hurt," Jaysa replied, turning to Etamus. "Anything in that suit able to stop me from bleeding all over the place?"

"It's not a medical suit," Etamus said, but tore a medi-box off the wall, ripping it open and removing various parts of it.

She passed it to Yanton, who knelt beside Jaysa. "I'm going to use this needle to numb the area, and then I'm going to pour foam over it and wrap it up. It's not going to feel good, but it'll stop the bleeding."

He removed Jaysa's hand then parted the skin around the wound, making Jaysa wince. "I think you nicked a vein. It's going to need treatment I can't do here, but this will have to suffice."

"Get it over with," Jaysa said and gritted her teeth as Yanton plunged the needle into the wound, injecting the numbing agent before pouring a liquid over it, which set as hard as stone within seconds, eliciting a grunt in pain. The last part of her treatment, the wrap, tightened itself around her arm until it was completely secure. It was sore and would feel worse when she got back to the ship and had it looked at properly, but that was later. Right now, she just needed to be able to have two working arms.

When Yanton was done, he helped back to her feet. "Try not to get shot again," he said with a smile.

The rear of the helix lifted up, the second predator-armour wearer riding it and continue to fire as they lifted off and flew away from the villa.

"Are you okay?" Rosie asked.

"Who are you people?" Jaysa asked.

"We're the Wardens," the predator-armour wearer said, removing the helmet to show the face of a handsome human beneath it. "Name's Rollos. You were lucky we were there. We're heading toward the palace. Should be able to patch you up. Who were those guys?" He looked at Ren and Takumi.

"Your Majesties."

Ren smiled, although it didn't reach her eyes, and Takumi hugged Rollos. "You, sir, are a beautiful person," he told him.

"I get that a lot," Rollos said. "You're safe now. Where we're going, you'll be fine. It's been a long night, so we're going to drop you off and then head back out."

Jaysa wanted to believe him, but she was pretty sure the highly-trained mercenaries weren't there for her. Which meant someone was trying to kill members of the royal family. And if that was the case, she wasn't sure that anywhere was going to be safe.

CHAPTER TWENTY

Felix Drake

"I know that Ramin is innocent," Drake told Bokk, as the rest of his team went about aiding the medical staff with the injured being helped from the penthouse. Drake had been listening to Bokk as the rest of his team arrived. Rosie, Rollos, and the rest of the Wardens had been on their way to The Spire when they were side-tracked by an attack on Ren's compound. There'd been several survivors, including Ren and Takumi, who'd been dropped off at the palace on their way to The Spire. Being surrounded by Suns Watch was probably the safest place for them at the moment.

Bokk explained to Drake what he'd seen and heard, and how Ramin knew his father. He left nothing out, and Drake remained silent until he'd finished.

"I knew that he and my father were acquaintances," Drake said. "I think Sabas was setting up his father to take the fall for all of this, I just don't know why. I need to talk to Ramin and find out what's actually going on."

Drake was about to say more when a commotion at the entrance to the penthouse took his attention as Ramin was removed from the building on a medical gurney that hovered a foot above the ground as it was pushed by med-staff into a waiting MES.

"Wait up," Drake shouted. "Bokk, with me." He didn't wait

for an answer, and ran over to the medical staff, ensuring himself a spot on the small, grey medical emergency shuttle after showing his badge. He waved over Rosie, who climbed inside, and they found Tuck sat waiting for them.

"I heard he'd been found," Tuck said as Ramin was taken to the far side of the two-room shuttle, separated by a blast-proof door. "I figured someone had better go with him."

"Good call," Drake said, taking a seat next to Rosie, with Bokk opposite him.

The synth removed a memory chip from his pocket and passed it to Rosie. "I took this from Ramin's personal system. He told me to give it to you."

Rosie took the chip and placed it inside a slot on her comm unit before she started tapping away.

"Anything we can do?" Rollos asked from the back of the ship, as he stopped the medical staff from taking off.

"Finish up here," Drake said. "When Sateri turns up, have her take charge. She's a better people person."

Rollos shrugged an agreement, and walked away to deal with the aftermath of the explosions.

"You think Sabas tried to blow up his own dad?" Tuck asked. "I think we're going to need a bit more than the word of a synth."

"We don't have proof of anything right now." Drake tried not to snap.

"Not to interrupt your annoyance, Drake, but I think I may have found some proof for you," Rosie said, looking up from her comm unit. She placed the portable device on the table and removed a small item from her pocket, tapping a switch and watching it unfold, revealing a full keyboard. "I prefer to type on these."

"What proof?" Drake asked. Kimi had told him everything, but without actual physical evidence, Sabas and his allies could get away with what they'd done.

"A few things actually," Rosie said, tapping some of the keys and causing a hologram to appear out of the comm unit.

"Bokk said the two investigators came to your home before you even got to see Ramin. The times match, Drake, there's no way those investigators appeared after we went to Ramin."

"Maybe it was a pre-emptive strike?" Drake asked, although he doubted that very much.

"Also, there's no contact from Ramin to any of the victims in the last few months," Rosie said. "And from the records Ramin left us, I can tell there are no payments to Trinas, no contact with anyone by that name. There's a lot of stuff here from Ramin making notes about how Sabas had been spending money on a project he'd been secretive about. Ramin got hold of documents to show payments from an account in the name of Genesis Enterprises. Something to do with Onnab."

Drake nodded. "There's a lot I haven't told you guys, mostly because The Spire exploded before I could. Ramin is innocent. Sabas is working with several councillors to do some kind of research on Onnab. They made a... thing."

"A thing?" Tuck asked.

"I don't know what it is," Drake said. "Kimi, Dai'ix, and I were at the docks. We found a... well, a thing called a Genesis-Alpha. Kimi, Septimus, and Helice, were all investigating together. Helice and Septimus found Trinas, who was working as Sabas' personal assassin, and convinced him to betray Sabas. My guess is, one of them spoke to Hideo about it."

"Ren told us on the flight over here that Jaysa worked for her," Rosie said. "Apparently she was looking for Trinas too."

"Why?" Drake asked.

Rosie shrugged. "No idea. Again, The Spire exploded."

"Looks like someone is trying to ensure no one knows about whatever this experiment was," Drake said. "Which does leave me with the question of why Metan told me about a problem with de-forestation that doesn't exist."

"Watching his own back?" Tuck suggested. "Maybe he thought you'd try to pin it on him."

"He did lie about seeing Helice," Drake said.

"It gets better," Rosie said. "You know you asked me to

check Hideo and his husband's comm use? Well, I did. And there's no contact from Caleus to anyone outside of the villa. However, I managed to hack the comm chip you took from the stealth-synth in the tower. It had contact with a blank number a dozen times in the hour before Hideo was shot."

"A blank number?" Drake asked.

"It's unregistered," Rosie clarified. "I found out just before you left to go back to your skyblock, and put a trace on it." A map appeared above the comm unit. "It'll take me a while to hack the location, but I think we can use that to find out who's trying to murder you, and trying to frame Ramin for three murders he didn't commit."

"Damn it," Drake said.

"Are you annoyed he's innocent, or that someone played us all?" Tuck asked.

"I never thought he was guilty," Drake admitted. "Ramin has been an informant for the Wardens for about five years."

Rosie and Tuck's expressions were both partially shock, and in Tuck's case, a little annoyed. "Seriously? A gangster of that level was working for us?" Tuck snapped.

"Well, me, technically," Drake said. "He helped put his son in prison. He monitored his son's movements, letting me know if something bad was going on. When I spoke to him earlier, he was worried that Sabas was going down a dark path. I think Metan tried to set him up."

"Why?" Tuck asked.

"That's a good question," Drake told him. "And one I'll deal with. Seeing how the whole team is busy and you already have the comms open, can you get hold of our boss and ask her very kindly to send another team to pick up Metan?"

"Will do," Rosie said and went back to her work.

One of the med-staff exited the area where Ramin was being attended. He had fresh blood-spatter on the light blue gown he'd wore over his uniform.

"Will he make it?" Drake asked.

"We don't know," the med-staff admitted. "The blast

gave him a bleed on the brain, fractured skull, damaged ribs, punctured lung, as well as serious damage to several organs. He was far enough away from the blast to not be instantly fatal, but close enough to be seriously hurt. He's lucky to be alive. We've stabilised him, but he's in a coma at present and won't be brought around until specialists have had a chance to look at him."

"Can you pump him full of something and wake him up?" Tuck asked.

The med-staff member's eyes narrowed in anger. "We can, but we won't. He needs a full mental and physical diagnosis before that happens. If we try to wake him at the moment, the shock might kill him. A dead suspect isn't going to be much help. We'll be landing at Paradise Hospital momentarily. We have enough security there to ensure his safety, should anyone try to finish the job."

"Thanks," Drake said, and the man returned to his patient.

"Wake him up from a coma?" Rosie asked Tuck. "Man, that's cold. Even for you."

Tuck shrugged. "We need answers, and he has them. I think it's pretty obvious his son wants him dead. Either Sabas figured out his daddy was a snitch, or he's trying to take over the business. We need to know which, because if it's the latter, there might be a lot more dead."

"We'll find out," Drake said, before a sudden jolt told him that the shuttle had landed. He'd been so preoccupied, he hadn't even felt it take off.

The Wardens left the shuttle as Ramin was rushed into the hospital.

"I'll go guard," Tuck said. "Just in case whatever security here isn't good enough to watch one dangerous criminal."

"Let us know where you are when you get there. I don't want to be given the run-around trying to find you," Drake said, and turned to Rosie. "Any luck with that location?"

Rosie looked up from her comm unit. She'd put the keyboard away the second they'd landed. "Nope. Whoever it is knows how to ping a comm device all over the place. It's literally going around the planet at this point. I'll get there though. Whoever it is, is *not* better than I am."

Drake smiled. "I have no doubt."

"What should I do?" Bokk asked, speaking for the first time since handing the chip to Rosie.

"We're going to go fill in a report about the attack at the apartment," Drake said. "And then we'll go from there."

"I am glad you're safe," Bokk said. "I was... worried."

Rosie studied Bokk as he walked into the hospital. "Your synth gets worried?"

"Yeah, he's a special case."

"That's one way of putting it," Rosie said cautiously. "I've heard of synths getting emotionally connected to their owners, but tracking them across a planet because they're worried is new. You want me to take a look at his programming? See if anything's been done to him?"

Drake shook his head. "No, he's fine as he is."

Rosie stared at Drake for a second. "You know that's not true. Synths don't hunt their owners down because someone tried to kill them. They stay and follow command structure. They inform the authorities and their owners, and then they wait. If they can't get hold of their owners, they sometimes get a bit messed up in the synapsis, but they don't do what they did. They certainly don't steal a sky-skimmer, take a coil rifle, and track them down. That's not even military-coded synth behaviour."

"I know," Drake admitted. "He's still fine. Maybe when we're done, I'll have him run a diagnostic and figure out what caused this to happen in the first place, for but now, he's good."

Rosie raised her hands in mock surrender. "Fine with me. Just keep an eye on him."

"What can you tell me about the hospital?" Drake asked.

Rosie grinned and tapped on her comm unit. "Largest in the area. Several thousand people can be brought here at any one time. Lots of private security as it's used by some councillors. Seems to be pretty exclusive. The kind of place Ramin would have instructions to bring him. You think maybe he has allies in here?"

"It's a possibility, and I don't want anyone trying to finish the job," Drake said. "Let's go see what's happening."

The pair walked into the hospital as Drake received a message on his comm unit from Tuck advising that he was in the forty-fourth section of the west wing, room 222.

"I doubt Ramin has any guards here yet," Drake told Rosie as they met up with Bokk, and all three got onto the moving walkway that ran the entire length of the hospital. There were two lanes, one that moved much faster than the other, and the two of them stood on the faster line.

"You know you can't use your aether here, right?" Rosie said. "Just in case someone does try to finish the job." She pointed to several panels on the walls as they passed by. "Security bots inside those panels. Anyone not authorized to use aether sets off an alarm, and... well, frankly, we get to play 'survive the attack of the killer bots'."

Drake smiled. "Let's hope everyone behaves then."

They found Tuck sat outside Ramin's room reading his comm unit, which he hastily put away upon seeing Drake.

"It's fine," Drake said. "You don't need to be on lookout, I counted six armed guards all trying to look very inconspicuous. I doubt very much that any of them are going to attack us." He looked through the glass window at the doctors working on Ramin with handheld regeneration devices.

"They decided a regeneration chamber might cause more problems," Tuck said. "I'm not a doctor though, so I sort of switched off then."

"We'll go find somewhere to set up," Drake said. "I want to have a command unit ready. Can you contact the head of security here and get them to come see me?"

Tuck nodded. "Already done it. She's waiting for you in the office at the end of the corridor." He pointed down the beige and grey corridor where dozens more hospital rooms sat on either side.

"What's she like?" Rosie asked.

"Seems okay," Tuck said with a shrug. "Her name is Delis. There's a small canteen just around the corner, Rosie can set up there if needs be."

"Sounds good," Rosie said and set off in the right direction, placing her comm unit in her pocket as she went.

"Bokk, go with Rosie," Drake said. "Just make sure no one bothers her."

"Will do," Bokk said and set off after Rosie.

"Why didn't she get augs so she could use the comm unit without having to pick it up?" Tuck asked.

"Her body rejected them," Drake said, aware that Rosie had no issues with people knowing. "She's got augs for other things and they're not compatible. She said she's fine with that."

"What other augs does she have?" Tuck asked in a whisper.

"That's for her to tell you, not me," Drake whispered back, trying not to show his irritation at the question show. In his mind, a person's augs were a private, and in some cases, personal decision. If someone wanted to know what they'd had done, they'd say so themselves.

Drake was about to walk down to see the head of security when one of the doctors left Ramin's room. "He wants to speak to you," she told Drake.

"I'll be back soon," Drake told Tuck, before entering the room.

Ramin was laid in bed, a dark blue sheet pulled up to his bare torso. A transparent mask covered his face, and he was hooked up to several machines that intermittently beeped. A small, hovering robot was performing a scan over his body, moving an inch at a time as it completed its task.

"You wanted to see me?" Drake asked.

"Two visits in one day?" Ramin asked. The mask issued

his voice through a set of speakers at the top of the bed, near his head, he sounded rough.

"Sabas had Helice and Septimus killed," Drake told him. "Trinas betrayed him, which I guess is why he's dead too. It's something to do with your company working on Onnab. Not sure what they actually knew that got them killed, but Kimi was meant to be with them. Thankfully not, or you'd have been looking at a scorched-earth policy on Leturn."

The small robot finished scanning and hovered out of the room. "I know," Ramin said. "I didn't know for certain until about an hour ago. I checked our company financials for any payments to Trinas. There's a lot of money being pumped into a dig that is officially not happening, has no employees and no results. Sabas tried to have me killed."

"Yeah, he did," Drake said. "I'm sorry."

"Me too," Ramin said, tears filling his eyes.

"I'm going to find out exactly what's going on," Drake said. "Seeing how Sabas really wants you dead right now, I'm also going to be staying here until you can leave under your own power."

"You're hoping he makes a second attempt?" Ramin asked.

"We both know he will," Drake said.

"He wants the business to himself," Ramin said. "Like I told your synth, he's a bad person I made excuses for. He was a monster. Is a monster. And he will try to finish the job."

Drake didn't feel sorry for Ramin, the man had always known what his son was. He just hadn't wanted to believe he was as bad as everyone else thought. "You think he knows you sent him to prison too?"

Ramin moved his head in an approximation of a shake, but he winced. "He'd have put two in my head if he had."

"He had experiments in a unit by the docks," Drake said. "Any idea what it is?"

"No, sorry," Ramin said. "I warned Sabas but he was too ambitious. Wanted power and infamy. That's all he's ever wanted. He has no self-control. He's... the worst of me. Took me a long time to realize that. No matter what he did, he was my son. I think you can understand that, yes?"

A slither of anger threatened to taint Drake's words, but he bit it down before he spoke. "Because of who my father was?"

"Yes. The history books have confined your father to the category of monster for what he did in the war. Is that how you remember him?" Ramin asked. "Your father was a great man. That's who remember."

"All I remember of my father was that he was good, and loved me and my mother very much," Drake said softly. "He was someone who believed in what he fought for. He sent us away before his betrayal of the Union Empire took root. I have a hard time equating the man I remember, with the stories of the war. Your son believes in nothing but himself. He thought of nothing but himself. He killed and hurt people because he thought it was fun. The history books might remember my father as a monster, but they will definitely remember Sabas as one. Because he is one."

Ramin closed his eyes and breathed slowly. "He's working with people in the Council though. I know that for a fact. Not sure who. When you find them, you find your link. Sabas needs to go back to prison. He's too dangerous out here. He *hates* you. You beat him, and he can't ever let that go."

"I know," Drake said. "He just wants to make sure everyone still fears him. It's a point-scoring exercise. Sabas can't be seen to have lost face. Once you're dead, he'll eventually come for me. You know what happens then, yes?"

Ramin nodded as he wept.

Drake left the room without another word. He walked down to the office where the head of security was waiting, and knocked on the door. It opened a second later, revealing a brightly lit room with a large window at the far end. A bald woman sat behind a large desk, tapping away on a data-pad that was linked to a large screen placed on one side of the desk.

"You must be Drake," Delis said, looking up from her data-pad. She glanced back down, tapped something, and the screen folded in on itself, before lowering into the desk.

Drake walked across the grey-carpeted floor, and offered Delis his hand. She stood, shook his hand, and sat back. "So, how much trouble are you causing in my hospital?" She motioned for him to take a seat.

Drake sat on one of the red chairs, and found it to be as comfortable as it looked. "Hopefully none."

The door to the office opened, and Drake turned to see Celine enter. "Felix Drake, I did wonder if you'd be here."

Drake got back to his feet. "Celine. I'm surprised to see you here."

"Don't be, I meet up with Delis once a week for a drink and chat. We go way back." She looked at Delis. "You want me to wait outside?"

Delis shook her head, and Drake began to think he was being ganged-up on. "You told me Drake was one of the best you have."

"That depends on what mood he's in," Celine said with a smile.

"Would you both like me to go?" Drake asked. "You can talk about me while I'm not there then."

Delis laughed. "I'm just messing with you. To be honest, I'm glad Wardens are here. Ramin isn't exactly the usual level of criminal we have under our care. The entire wing has been closed-off from the general public. Only guards and medical personal are permitted to enter. Ramin is as safe here as he is anywhere else."

"Yeah, that's the problem," Drake said. "I'm not entirely convinced that bringing him here hasn't put all of you in danger."

Delis smiled. "I was a Warden for ten years, I can deal with danger. You really needn't worry, we have great security here. We're paid to make sure we're the best. A lot of exceptionally important people consider this their hospital. We can't get that kind of reputation by being shoddy." Delis stood and walked around the desk. "I'll give you both a few minutes to chat. Gives me times to check on the people I have working here."

Celine thanked Delis, and watched her leave before turning back toward Drake. "So, it's Sabas then?"

"Yes," Drake said and explained everything he had discovered, leaving nothing out.

"We removed the bodies from the regeneration chambers," Celine said when Drake had finished. "Both dead. Both human on a genetic level." She showed Drake a picture on her comm unit of the two bodies. One resembled a squid, although with a human head, and the second looked like it had once been human but all of the parts were in the wrong place. As if someone had done a jigsaw and forced the pieces together."

"They're human?" Drake asked, feeling nothing but revulsion.

"Genetically, yes," Celine said, putting her comm unit away. "Except there was a huge amount of Aperture radiation. Similar to the aether used by Sage, but approximately a hundred times more potent. It was like they had been inside The Aperture without the protection of a space craft."

Drake stared in disbelief for a moment as his brain caught up with what he'd been told. "How is that possible?"

"No one knows." She paused, tilted her head, and looked over at the door. "Did you hear that?"

Drake got up from his chair, but wasn't quick enough to beat Celine, who was already opening the door when he reached her. The hallway beyond was dark; the lights sat in the ceiling, dead. Drake followed Celine out into the hallway as Tuck was thrown through the window to Ramin's room, landing awkwardly on the ground and rolling away as two armed men dressed as doctors—both wearing masks—left the room, with Ramin in front of them. They aimed their weapons at Celine and Drake, who both ducked back into Delis' office, avoiding the energy blasts.

Drake drew his viper pistol and turned back into the

hallway, firing twice at the two armed men. The first shot hit the closest enemy in the chest, knocking him back over a still prone Tuck, as the second man fired back and ran off to the side, pushing Ramin along.

Drake and Celine sprinted over to Tuck, helping him up. "Ramin," he whispered through gritted teeth.

Drake heard several shots ahead, and the two ran toward the sound. They found Delis slumped against the wall, a pool of ever-increasing blood under her. Celine was by her side in a second, feeling for a pulse. "Go find them," she told Drake, who set off in pursuit.

CHAPTER TWENTY-ONE

Felix Drake

Drake made his way through the hospital, pistol drawn, expecting an attack any moment. Occasionally, he passed a doctor or member of the medical staff who pointed the way that Ramin and the fake doctor had gone. He'd reached the automated walkway of earlier when he found the first body. A young man had been shot twice in the chest at close range.

The Warden comms were still blocked, so whoever had done this had some clout. Drake still couldn't contact Rosie or Bokk, and that didn't bode well.

He vaulted over the side of the walkway, next to a set of double-doors stained with a bloody handprint. Drake stood to the side of one door, and slowly pushed it open. The shots were instantaneous, forcing Drake to move farther away as both doors were torn apart by the weapon of unknown assailants.

After watching the door harmlessly torn to shreds, he heard the unmistakable sound of an overheating energy rifle. Drake stepped to the side and fired three times through the remains of the door, on his way to the opposite wall. He waited for a three count and glanced through the door, where one black-masked assailant was on their knees, hands clutched to their chest as thick blood pumped between their fingers.

Drake walked over and pulled off the mask, revealing a young, bearded man. "How many?" Drake asked.

The man continued to look down at the fresh blood leaking from his chest.

Drake was about to ask again when the man said, "Enough. Enough to do what we were sent to achieve." The man's voice was weak; he didn't have long.

Drake aimed his viper at the man's head. "And what was that?"

"This planet will burn," the man continued, never looking up. He sounded as though he were reading from a script. "All those unworthy, will die, their ashes becoming nothing more than a faded memory."

Drake wondered exactly what Sabas and his allies had involved themselves in. "How many times did you have to read that before you learned it by heart?"

"Don't you mock me," the man said, looking up at Drake for the first time, anger flashing over his rapidly paling face. "Ramin got free, grabbed my pistol. They left me here to die."

"Job done then," Drake said, and shot the man in the head. He checked the energy rifle, but the barrel had been warped by the heat. The man had been sent here to do a job, but hadn't been trained as well as expected. Drake continued on down the corridor until he came to another set of double doors. He slowly pushed them open, revealing a large reception area and yet another a set of double doors that lead out into a sizeable garden beyond. There were two more doors inside the reception area. Drake was about to check each of them when he spotted the dead man and woman behind the desk. Both had been shot in the head at close range.

Drake turned away from the bodies, and stepped to the side, narrowly avoiding a blast as it removed part of the desk. Drake threw himself forward, over the desk as the assailant walked toward him, firing the whole time.

Staying low, Drake moved until he was at the end of the desk. He peeked around. The man was about to look over it. Drake considered shooting him, but he needed answers. He took a breath, sprang up, and closed the distance between them as the man realised his mistake and raised his pistol. Drake got to him first. He pushed the pistol up, the blast tearing a hole in the ceiling, and tried wrench the gun free of the would-be-assassin.

The man punched Drake in the face, forcing him to take a step back. Drake wasn't done, and grabbed pulled the attacker off balance, throwing him over his shoulder and into the nearest wall. He dove for the closest viper pistol, but the attacker kicked it away. Drake put some distance between the two of them to avoid being kicked in the head.

"Felix Drake, yes?"

Drake nodded. "And you are?"

"Doesn't matter." He darted forward, kicking out at Drake's head.

While Drake dodged the attack, it left him open to a kick to the chest. He moved at the last second, and the blow hit the wall behind him. Drake brought his elbow down on the knee joint, before grabbing hold of the attacker's waist, taking him off his feet and dumping the man on his back on the cold, hard floor. Grabbing one of the attacker's arms, Drake locked it at the elbow, trying to break the joint, but the attacker rolled, removing much of the tension. When Drake refused to let go, the man punched him in the ribs hard enough for Drake's grip to relax, but the attacker had placed himself in a dangerous position. Drake smashed his knee into the man's temple and kicked him in the nose, which made an awful crunching noise beneath the mask. Drake rolled to his feet, his ribs were sore from the power of the punch, but he pushed the pain aside. He could hurt later.

"Where's Ramin?" Drake asked.

The man wore dark combat armour, and the mask was the same as the one Drake had seen on the assassin he'd killed earlier. A thin, dark mesh sat over one eye, hiding it from view, with the other eye visible. Judging from the ragged scratches across the eye hole, Drake assumed the assassin had lost the mesh in a fight.

"Where he needs to be," the attacker said as he got back to his feet. "You're almost as good as I heard. Shame you've got to die."

Drake motioned for the man to get on with it, and the assassin obliged by charging forward, throwing several punches, which Drake blocked or avoided. The assassin feinted with a punch to Drake's jaw, allowing him to get in a shot to Drake's kidney. Ignoring the pain, Drake kicked the assassin's leg, forcing him to one knee, then delivered another kick to the chest, sending him sprawling.

The assassin rolled back to his feet, his remaining hate-filled eye hardened behind the mask. He threw two small blades, each digging harmlessly into the sleeve of Drake's metal-fibre jacket. The distraction allowed the assassin to charge, lifting Drake off his feet and smashing him into a wall.

Drake's vision blurred for a second as the back of his head bounced off the tiled wall, giving the assassin enough time to throw Drake to the floor and put his hands around his throat. The man's strength was impressive, smashing Drake's head into the floor, hands wrapped around his throat. Drake's vision began to darken as the assassin sat on his chest, trying to choke the life out of him.

With desperate strength, Drake reached up and jammed his thumb into the assassin's eye socket, pushing deeper until the assassin screamed and released his grip. Drake refused to let up, and it was only moments before Drake felt the assassins' eye pop out. His would-be-killer rolled away as blood poured out of the open wound.

Coughing and spluttering, Drake used the wall to get back to his feet, where he realised he now held the assassin's eye. He tossed it aside. Every breath was like swallowing cut glass. Drake picked up one of the assassin's knives and walked over to the man, who was now on his knees, and noticed the second assassin arrive just in time to throw himself behind the remains of the desk as the blast tore through the wall.

Another energy blast ripped through the desk close to where Drake was, forcing him to roll to the side then back again toward the edge. The assassin fired twice more at where he believed Drake hid. The new man's hands shook slightly, his back to Drake; you just couldn't get good assassins these days.

A quick glance showed that the eye-less assassin was nowhere to be found. *One on one.*

It took seconds for Drake to be on the assassin and stab him three times in the throat, the last a cut across the flesh before pushing the dead body toward the desk.

"Don't move," a voice demanded from the reception's entrance.

Drake sighed as yet another masked man walked toward him with a blast-gun. "Is there some kind of place to rent you guys?"

Rosie appeared from behind the newcomer, wrenched the blast-gun up and back, smashing the stock into the attacker's face. She easily disarmed him and threw him up against the wall. A quick kick took out the assassin's knee, and she planted a second kick to his face as he fell forward, cracking the mask and driving his head back against the wall.

"Nice timing," Drake said.

Rosie removed the assassin's mask. "Do we need them alive?"

There was a rhythmic thud from nearby. The tiles on the wall cracked, and another assassin was thrown through it. Bokk followed the body through the hole, picking the man up from the floor and smashing him into the wall over and again, the sound of breaking bones filling the air.

"I think he's dead," Rosie said.

Bokk released the assassin, who slumped to the floor. They turned to Drake. "Are you good?"

Drake nodded. "Had a close call with someone who was

a lot more professional than this lot, but he escaped." He removed the medical kit on the nearby wall, popped the seal and took out a packet of med-gel, rubbing a fingertip-sized portion over his throat. It immediately felt better.

"We found Tuck," Rosie said. "He seems to be okay, but who knows, it's Tuck."

"Anything else?" Drake asked, grateful that his throat no longer hurt.

Rosie nodded. "Yeah, I've got my comm unit still running to find out where that call went to."

"And Delis?" Drake asked.

"We did not see her," Bokk said. "We left Tuck, and came to find you. We followed the sounds of fighting and there you were."

"Good call." Drake glanced out of the nearby door to the garden beyond. "I don't know who the assassin I fought was, but he has one less eye now, and he seemed to know me."

"Lot of effort to kidnap someone," Bokk said. "A lot of risk too."

Drake nodded. "Let's go find Tuck and Celine, and then we'll figure out what we're meant to do next."

The three of them headed back through the hospital, where several dozen security personal stopped them every dozen feet, forcing them to explain who they were several times before they reached Tuck, who was still sat outside of Ramin's room.

"Better late than never, eh?" Tuck asked, nodding toward the security people who were guarding the entrance to the wing of the hospital.

"I assume you're okay," Drake said. "You sound about as happy as ever."

"Well, I got thrown through a window, so there's that," Tuck said, tilting his head to show the cuts on his face.

"Did you bounce?" Rosie asked.

Tuck's eyes narrowed in mock anger.

Drake ached everywhere, but his job wasn't done. "Rosie,

you and Bokk go check on your decryption stuff."

Rosie smiled, gave a sarcastic salute, and walked off with Bokk.

"What happened in there?" Drake asked when he was alone with Tuck.

"I went in to check on Ramin," Tuck said. "A doctor wanted to see him. When I got in there, the doctor gave him something. An injection in the neck." Tuck got up and walked into Ramin's room, Drake following.

"Why is there a medical scanner on the bed?" Drake asked, pointing to the foot long device.

"I needed to check something, and no one was using this, so I borrowed it," Tuck told him. "I needed answers before the investigators or forensics turned up."

"Answers to what was in that injector?" Drake asked.

Tuck pushed a button on the side of the medical scanner, which opened up the glass top. The injector inside rose out of the scanner, waiting to be taken. Tuck placed the injector on the bed before tapping the screen on the front of the scanner.

"So, what did they pump him full of?" Drake asked.

"Chameleon," Tuck said. "A lot of it." He picked up the injector. "The amount in Helice and the Septimus was a hundredth the dose that's in here. At least in terms of potency. This is equal if not more than Trinas Brong, and he ended up dead in a bathtub."

Drake rubbed his face with one hand, feeling weary. "That can't possibly be good."

"That's a hell of an understatement," Tuck said. "It means we can't track Ramin, and it also means there's a good chance he's either going to have lost his mind, or is already dead."

Drake mentally ran through everything they knew. "Someone drugged him, kidnapped him, and presumably want to aim him at someone. From what Rosie told me about this stuff, Ramin is going to be incapable of rational thought."

"That about sums it up."

Drake rubbed his eyes in frustration. "Why isn't anything

ever simple in our job?"

"You got any idea what we're going to do next?" Tuck asked. "We've got Ramin out there, plus whoever tried to kill you and almost killed Prince Hideo. And then there's the whole point of the investigation – two dead councillor children, and the man responsible is Sabas, whose father was just kidnapped. I'm beginning to wish I hadn't bothered coming to work."

Drake couldn't argue with that.

"Oh shit," Tuck whispered.

Drake followed Tuck's gaze as he looked out of the room into the corridor beyond. "We have one very angry Celine coming this way. Go find Rosie and Bokk, fill them in. See if you can help them."

Tuck nodded. "Will do." He walked past Drake and whispered, "Good luck." He passed Celine with a nod.

"How's Delis?" Drake asked.

"Hurt bad," Celine said, looking around the mess of a hospital room. "She'll live, but she's got some way to go to recover. They used an energy shredder in the pistol. It tore up her insides pretty good. She's in a regen chamber."

"I'm glad she'll be okay," Drake said.

Celine nodded, as if unable to say anything else for fear that her anger would get the better of her. Drake knew the feeling well. He also knew it rarely worked as a long-term solution.

"If you have something to say, Celine, just say it," Drake told her. "Better here with me than on some guard who just happens to piss you off and you throw him through a wall."

Celine stared at Drake for several seconds, her gaze hard and unreadable. Then she sat on a nearby chair, and put her face in her hands. "This is all kinds of fucked," Celine said, removing her hands from her face and looking up at Drake. "Delis and I... we used to be together. My work got in the way of that because I was out at all hours, never really spending time with her. And when I did spend time with her, I'd be checking my comm every ten seconds because of the number of cases I was dealing with. I've been coming here to see where our relationship goes, and she gets hurt."

"She's not new at this," Drake said. "You can't blame yourself for whoever took Ramin. I fought one of them, almost died. At least some of them weren't fresh off the street. They had training."

Celine looked up at Drake and let out a long breath. "Doesn't make me feel a whole lot better."

Drake shrugged. "I can't make you feel blameless in all this. Only you can do that."

"You're not very good with the motivational speeches. Anyone ever told you that?"

Drake chuckled. "It has come up in the past, yes."

"You should know that a request was approved for you to have full authority to go after these people," Celine said. "Officially, it should go to the Blackcoats, but whoever these people are, they attacked a medical facility in a high-price part of this planet. Fuck them, they can deal with the Wardens instead. The judge didn't even blink before giving authorisation."

Drake felt like a weight had been lifted from his shoulders. "I can go anywhere?"

"Anywhere," Celine confirmed. "You have complete authority. Anyone tries to stop you is to be considered an enemy combatant and dealt with in whatever manner to see fit. I know you went to Hideo because you hoped he would put forward a petition to get you the jurisdiction increase, because you thought it would be quicker. I don't begrudge that at all. Turns out, almost killing the Prince of the Union has a similar effect. The King of Stars signed off on it himself."

Drake wasn't quite sure what to say to that. "That's not something he usually signs."

Celine nodded. "I know, but that was one of the provisos my boss attached when I asked her. She said, the King of Stars has to sign it. I think the fact that a lot of people now know who you are, or rather, who your father was, makes them nervous. The King signing off on it, makes it his problem if you try to... you know."

And the weight on his shoulders was back. "Overthrow the government?"

Celine nodded. "That or create an army and start a civil war."

"Well, that's my weekend screwed," Drake said, irritated that it had come to this.

"Don't joke about it," Celine said. "People are worried about you, Drake. You hid in plain sight for a long time."

"And at no point did I try to take over the world," Drake pointed out.

"Yes, well, people are also stupid."

"That I can't disagree with." Drake noticed Rosie waving to catch his attention, and he beckoned her over.

She soon had her comm unit set up on a small desk inside the hospital room.

"You know, you haven't said anything," Drake told her.

Rosie raised a finger meant to keep him quiet, and tapped on her keyboard. "Right, ready. I know who the call was to before the sniper hit Hideo." She moved her comm unit to show Drake and Celine a map of the area where the call was picked up.

Drake immediately knew who lived there. "Metan," he said, through gritted teeth.

"I had an investigator unit sent there to pick him up," Celine said. She left the room, and was already talking on her comm unit when she walked out of sight.

"I genuinely thought he cared about Helice," Drake said. "Guess he cares more about whoever employed him to do this."

"Sabas?" Rosie asked.

"Maybe," Drake replied.

Celine re-entered the room. "The investigators aren't responding to calls. On top of that, it sounds like the rest of your team just arrived."

"Rosie, you, Bokk and Tuck with me," Drake said, anger leaking from every word. "We've got an old acquaintance whose day I plan on ruining."

They took a few steps before another alarm went off, and Drake got comm notifications of an altercation at the rear of the hospital. The four of them raced through the building, stopping just before the doors that lead them to the rear of the hospital. They slowly crept outside, expecting a firefight, but instead found two dead bodies. The first was dressed like one of the people who had abducted Ramin. The man's throat had been ripped out, and he'd died on the spot. The second was Ramin. He was face down on the ground, a hole in the back of his skull. Rosie and Tuck rolled him over. There was blood around his face, but no exit wound from the blast to the back of the head.

Rosie checked the body as several hospital guards ran through the doors. "Ramin is dead," Rosie said. "Three shots to the chest, and one to the back of the head. Not powerful enough to be a through-and-through, but enough to kill and make sure he was dead."

"The chameleon kicked in," Tuck said.

"I assume Ramin killed his kidnapper," Bokk said. "And was executed for it."

"Looks like they hadn't expected him to be so violent so quickly," Drake surmised. "Damn it. He wasn't a bad guy. He just wanted to do the right thing."

"You need to see this," Rosie said, after checking the palms of Ramin hands.

Drake stared at them and felt a cold rage bubble up inside. One palm was blood splattered, but the other had words written on it. *Stop Sabas.* "I will, my friend," he said softly. "I will."

CHAPTER TWENTY-TWO

Felix Drake

Drake, Rosie, Tuck, and Bokk left the hospital and met up with the rest of the team. Sateri assured Drake that the explosion at Ramin's apartment was now under control, and Rosie showed everyone what she'd discovered about Metan.

"That's bad news," Sateri said as the group made their way back toward the helix they'd taken from Ramin's penthouse to the hospital. "Are you sure he's involved?"

"Yes," Rosie said. "Metan is at the very least involved in what happened at the hospital. I'd put credits on the idea of him also being involved in the murders of Helice, Septimus and Trinas. No idea why though."

Drake looked up at the sky; it was beginning to get dark. He let out a string of curse words. "He lied to me."

"You cared for Helice and Septimus," Rollos said. "He used that to point you in the wrong direction. I imagine we'll discover that Metan will no longer be at his residence."

"Well, we'd best go find out." Drake climbed into the helix, and a few moments later Luca was flying a ship full of Wardens toward Metan's home.

"This guy used to be a friend of yours," Dai'ix said to Drake.

"This guy used to be a friend of Helice's," Drake corrected. "Now he's at very least someone involved in attempted treason. He's smart, and augmented, so in a fight I have no idea what he's now capable of. We put him down, we do it fast and hard. I'd rather not get into a fight unless we have to."

"You think Metan is working for Sabas?" Rollos asked.

"How do you know he's working for someone else?" Dai'ix asked. "Metan could be the mastermind."

"Maybe," Drake said. "Something tells me he's for hire though. He must have known I would turn up at his door. Must have known that Helice and Septimus' murders would make me look at him. I genuinely never thought he'd have played a part in Helice's death."

"Everyone surprises us when money or power are involved," Dai'ix said. "And ex-lovers can quickly become bitter enemies when the heart is involved."

"You speaking from experience?" Rollos asked.

"An old love of mine was... unhappy I'd moved on," Dai'ix said. "They hired their new love to kill the female I had begun courting. I had to kill him. Oreafs can take a lot of damage before they die... even at the hands of another of my kind."

No one else spoke after that, and Dai'ix closed his eyes, a clear sign to leave him be.

They soon landed in a small, empty park only a short walk from Metan's home. After exiting the helix, Drake turned back to the still-seated team. "Rosie, can you keep Bokk company? I don't want them involved in a Warden operation if it can be helped."

Rosie nodded. "We'll be here, I want to see if I can figure out what Metan is up to. Bokk can help."

"It would be a pleasure to help," Bokk said.

Rosie raised an eyebrow in Drake's direction, and he knew she wanted to ask why his synth sound very un-synth-like.

Drake shrugged slightly. "Look, I know I promised

explanations about who I am and everything, but right now we've just discovered that Metan is behind a lot of what has happened. Definitely Hideo's attack, most probably the three murders, along with Sabas."

"Explanations can wait," Dai'ix said and left the helix.

"Like the big man said," Rollos agreed, following Dai'ix out.

"Tuck, Sateri, I want you both to go around from the opposite side of the building and get into the garden," Drake told them. "If we flush him out, he might come your way. Luca, I need you to stay here, keep this helix ready to go."

Drake, Rollos, and Dai'ix raced toward their target, keeping off the main street, and using the network of alleyways to try and stay out of sight. Rollos continued to wear the predator-armour suit he'd put on after finding it in the last helix. A blast-gun sat over his shoulder, while Dai'ix had disposed of the coil rifle from earlier, and taken to carry a fusion rifle around with him. The large rifle appeared almost normal sized against the oreaf's massive frame. All three wore headsets allowing them to communicate.

They reached the end of an alleyway and stopped.

"So, are we bringing Metan in then?" Dai'ix asked, his voice a low rumble.

"So long as he'll come quietly, yes," Drake said.

"And if he doesn't?" Rollos asked.

Drake had considered his options on the ride over. "Then we make him." He tapped his headset. "Sateri, you there?"

"Ready as we'll ever be," she said. "Let's get this done."

"We've dealt with more dangerous people than Metan," Rollos said.

The three of them moved toward the house.

"Sateri, Tuck, you both in position?" Drake asked.

"We're here," Sateri said. "Garden is empty. We'll keep out of sight."

"Be careful, if you need to move, move slowly," Drake whispered into the headset. "I have no idea if Metan put traps anywhere."

"Will do," Tuck said.

"Stay safe," Drake told them and pushed at the front door, which opened slowly. The three Wardens stepped inside, closing the door behind them.

The house was dark but the lights from their headsets illuminated their surroundings. Nothing looked different from the last time Drake had been inside the building. They moved room by room through the right-hand side of the building, returning to the front door when the sweep was completed.

They continued on upstairs, searching in the same manner as they had below, until they reached the last room, where they found two dead men and a dead woman. The man and woman were middle-aged and the second man much younger. All had been killed from blasts to the head at short range.

"The actual owners of the building, I assume," Rollos whispered.

Drake looked around the room. Anything even slightly personal had been removed from wherever it had sat and then been dumped in what had at one point been a bedroom.

"Metan cleared out the house after he took it over," Drake said, picking up a photo that changed showing all three of the occupants. He put the photo back on the pile, as anger bubbled up inside of him.

The three Wardens left the bedroom and returned to the foyer. "Only the left side to check," Rollos said.

Dai'ix took point and they left the main foyer, walking into the room adjacent – a large office. A visi-screen on the wall flickered to life, showing Metan sat in an armchair in front of a grey wall. Three dead men lay on the floor in front of the screen.

"Drake, you came, so good to see you alive. Well, not good, but… something." Metan moved toward the camera on his end. "Get your two friends there to leave the room, and we'll talk.

They probably want to find the bomb I planted."

All three shared a look of concern.

"I assume you've seen what a shock-wing core can do to a building, you were at The Spire, yes?" Metan said. "Well, they have two cores. Want to guess what I did with the second one? Hint, it's in the street." He raised his hand showing a detonator. "They can go find it, and get rid of it, or I blow it to tiny pieces. Once I click this, you have sixty seconds."

"Go," Drake said. "Find the bomb."

"It's down the road, behind number one-eight-nine-four," Metan told them. "They have three young children. It would be a shame if the number of pieces those kids were in multiplied."

Rollos and Dai'ix ran out of the room and Metan placed the detonator on a table beside him. "You're meant to be dead."

"You're meant to not be a murderous bastard, but here we are." Drake found a chair behind the desk and sat. "So, is this where you gloat a bit and tell me your grand scheme?"

Metan laughed. "I did plan on doing a little gloating. You know, you're the only person who knew me when we were growing up. You're the only person who understands why I would kill Helice."

"So Septimus and Trinas were just in the wrong place at the wrong time?"

"Oh, you misunderstand," Metan said with a wide smile. "All three were my targets. All three needed to die. Kimi too. Unfortunately, she wasn't there when I arrived, and it's been hell trying to get to her. I just got a level of pleasure from Helice's death that the other two couldn't match. I didn't kill Septimus and Trinas myself, of course. I was too busy with Helice to do them all. No, you met their killer. You removed his eye. He's not very happy about that."

"I'll take the rest of the head next time," Drake said. "Why kill any of them?"

"My employer wanted them dead," Metan said. "The why is irrelevant."

"Bullshit," Drake snapped.

Metan laughed. "I do like that word. It's just so old fashioned." Metan's expression flickered to serious in an instant. "I had to kill her, Drake. Had to. Whether it was for this or something else, doesn't matter. I've been planning Helice's murder since the day I left prison and found she'd moved on."

"You planned a murder for over twenty-years because you got your heart broken?" Drake wondered at the level of pettiness and spite that would have to live inside someone to maintain a hate for that long.

"I lost *everything* because of her," Metan snapped. "I took the fall for *her* crime. She told me she'd take care of me when I got out, that we'd be together. Instead, I catch her fucking some other guy."

"We were sixteen years old," Drake said. "You can't possibly hold a grudge for that long. That's insanity."

"Then I guess I'm insane because that grudge kept me warm at night," Metan said. "I wanted the murder to be right, so I planned it a hundred ways but in reality, it never went like I wanted it. She was surprised to see me, even more surprised to see Trinas' body in the bathtub. And then when my companion killed Septimus first, well... she went into meltdown. Lots of begging, lots of pleading, saying sorry for all she'd done. She didn't mean it. She died because it was my job to kill her, but that didn't mean I wasn't going to enjoy myself."

"Septimus was just a job then?" Drake asked, hoping his team had found the bomb.

"Something like that," Metan said. "I had no specific problems with him. The targets were all four of them. Septimus was like a puppy, always following Helice around, doing whatever she asked. If he hadn't gone with Kimi and Helice to find Trinas, he'd still be alive."

"Trinas and Sabas killed three Wardens together to keep their little Genesis-Alpha experiments secret," Drake said, trying to make sure he kept Metan talking. "Sabas got involved with some heavy hitters, and they started using the Expedited Systems as a cover to let someone create these monsters. Monsters that were used on a planet where the OMC had answered a distress call. Your employer helped murder millions of people for an experiment, and then Sabas decided he was now in the big leagues and wanted to off his dad. Some Wardens started sniffing around on Kimi's request, but Sabas found out, and he had Trinas murder help him murder them.

"Sabas got caught because his dad found out what had happened, told me, and I went to arrest the little shit. In the meantime, Sabas sent Trinas as far away from here as possible. I'm guessing your employer isn't Sabas, it's whoever is backing Sabas. They're having you clean up Sabas' mess. Killing Helice, Trinas, Septimus, and wanting to kill Kimi because she figured out what was going on and managed to get Trinas to betray Sabas. Did you also go after Ren, Takumi, and Hideo today too?"

"Very good," Metan said with a slow clap. "Ren had been looking into the deaths of some Suns Watch members Trinas killed when he stupidly came back to the planet a few months ago. He said he needed to make amends for having run, and he was going to kill Kimi. I'd spoken to him while he was on Onnab, and then my employer went there, and found out that he'd run back here, killed three Suns Watch, and ran off to Leturn. More trouble than he was worth."

Metan sighed. "On top of all that, Ren hired a Tracker to find the moron. Apparently, one of the Suns Watch was on her protection detail. The Tracker went to Onnab too. The whole thing was becoming a clusterfuck. Couldn't risk anyone looking into those deaths as it might link back to my employer. They couldn't be sure, but better safe than sorry. My employer couldn't have anyone figure out exactly who knew what, so everyone involved had to die. That synth was waiting for Hideo for hours, and then you arrived, the order was given to kill you both. You first though. Couldn't believe the little Prince jumped in front of the round meant for you."

"You tried to kill me because I was on to you?" Drake asked, forcing himself to stay calm.

Metan laughed. "No, because you're a lot more dangerous than you're letting on. I know where you went after you left here as a teenager. I told my employer, and they were most insistent that you die."

"I'm going to find you, Metan," Drake said, finally allowing his anger to rise. "You're going to tell me exactly who you're working for, and then I'm going to kill you."

Metan paused and sat back in his chair. "I always liked you, Drake. It was why I didn't kill you when you came over the first time. I genuinely hadn't wanted to kill you, but my boss really was insistent. I'm glad you lived though. I was angry with you for a long time after you ran away, after you vanished, but I was also happy to hear you were still alive, and a Warden to boot. Exceptionally impressive. I'm actually sort of glad you figured out I was involved too. I really hoped you'd think it was Ramin behind it all, but damn I did not expect that you and he were working together. To bring down his own son, too. Sabas was livid. He obviously blames you for his father's betrayal. We know it wasn't like that, don't we?"

Drake nodded.

"Sabas wanted Ramin's death to mean something," Metan continued. "Pump him full of chameleon and send him off to murder as many people as possible. He wanted his father sent to the Warden offices. Lots of dead there. Ramin dies in the fighting, and Sabas gets his revenge on his dad, and his revenge on you."

Images of Ramin's dead body flashed into Drake's mind. "That didn't work out so well."

"Yeah, well, you know all about fathers not living up to expectations," Metan said.

"Go fuck yourself," Drake snapped.

"Your dad was a bad guy too," Metan continued. "I mean, was it your birth that turned him to a life of fighting the Union? Did he just hate being a father that much? Shame he ended up going all noble right at the end and getting himself and his allies killed. That's not part of the public story though, is it? Your daddy being evil and attacking us, sure, but not that his turning back to the Union actually saved everyone. They were losing until he did that. Before then? Wow, he was a nasty bastard. Killing, destroying cities, just all kinds of awful stuff. People feared him. People *respected* him. I wonder if he'd be happy that you went to work for the people he tried to overthrow."

Drake wanted to lash out, but kept his mouth shut.

"No, you know what? I think he'd be okay with it," Metan continued. "You went your own way. You know people say he was tainted by the darkness. Have you heard that before? That he fought back and pushed it away? Do you know what the darkness is? I always thought it a metaphor for, you know, life. I figured you might have more insight into it."

"Sorry, can't help," Drake said through clenched teeth.

Metan appeared to be genuinely upset about it. "Ah, shame. You'll find out soon enough if you don't get killed. Your dad was big news for years, that whole Rebellion was fascinating. Did you know no one really knows exactly who was behind it? Really interesting stuff."

"I'll take your word for it." Drake wondered how Rollos and Dai'ix were getting on, and whether or not he needed to stall for even more time. "You used chameleon on Trinas to give him what he wanted, yes?"

Metan clapped. "You figured that out? Yeah, that was a beautiful bit of thinking on my part. If I'm honest, I wasn't expecting you to turn up. I certainly wasn't expecting anyone to figure out my involvement. And then you arrived here, and things sort of spiralled."

"I'm going to find you, Metan."

"You're angry, aren't you?" Metan stared at Drake for several seconds. "You were angry with your friends being murdered, angry with a lot of things I imagine. Helice messaged you while she was tied up. She wasn't exactly subtle, and I figured once you knew what was happening, you'd never stop until you learned the truth. She wanted to make amends with you. Why?"

Drake saw no reason to lie. "When I was fifteen, I used my aether to kill people who were trying to kill Kimi and Hideo. It all came out who I was, and several of the old group, including Helice, blamed me for making their lives more difficult because they were friends with the son of a notorious traitor."

"That was selfish of them," Metan said with a knowing smile.

"Yes, it was," Drake admitted. "We were fifteen or sixteen, I can't really stay mad at people who did something stupid as children. Anyway, when I joined the Wardens, she was one of the group I ended up working to protect on one of her trips away. She was mad at me that I'd run from Atharoth. She said that Novia got hooked on a lifestyle she never would have found if I'd stayed, which we both knew was bullshit. After that, we barely spoke, and I left one of my team in charge so as not to jeopardise anything. She had a lot of pent up resentment and anger she'd never dealt with, and I was the one she aimed it at. Apparently, she felt bad."

Metan laughed. "Too little, too late."

"I didn't hate her, Metan," Drake told him. "I felt sorry for her."

"Liar," Metan snapped.

"There are very few people in my life I've hated," Drake said, welcoming the calm inside of him. "Helice wasn't one of them. You're getting pretty close though."

"I thought we were forming a bond, you and I," Metan said, irritated that his attempt at angering Drake wasn't working. "I thought you'd be able to see why I might have wanted to kill Helice after what she did to me. You don't, and you never will."

"Why don't you hand yourself in, get a chance to say your piece on record?" Drake asked, knowing full-well that Metan would never do such a thing. "Get a chance to right a few wrongs."

Metan laughed so hard, he started to cough and walked

out of shot, coming back with a glass of water in one hand. "My word, that was an impressive attempt at making yourself look like a puppet of the Union. Good job."

"How many years have you been a hitman, Metan?"

"Oh, wow, must be eleven years now. I've killed several thousand people at this point, although not all with my own hands, obviously. I blew up a cruiser about four years ago, which was impressive. Just to get to one person. A platoon of people dead because one person angered the wrong group. I get paid a lot of credits for what I do. It looks like you're no longer on my list, though. My boss doesn't seem to want me to try to kill you again, although I assume if you keep annoying them that might change."

Drake's comm unit flashed with a message. He glanced down to see it was from Rollos with the word *defused*. "I'm going to find out who they are, Metan. I'm going to find you too. You're going to be punished for all you've done. And after you've watched me take apart your life, I'm going to kill you."

"Not arrest me like a good little Warden?" Metan mocked.

"No," Drake said, his eyes never leaving Metan's face. "You don't get to live after this."

Metan stood, grabbing the detonator off the table. "I guess I'll be seeing you then. Just so you know, Sabas is going to be coming for you sooner or later. It might be wise to find him before he finds you. And in the meantime." He pushed the button on top of the detonator and the screen went blank.

Drake rushed out of the house, sprinting down the road, past the helix and the large group of people in the street, toward Dai'ix, Rollos, Tuck, and Sateri.

"Where is it?" Drake asked.

"We dragged it to the lake, threw it in," Dai'ix said. "It weighed a lot, more than enough to let it sink to the bottom of the lake."

"The shock-wing core wasn't rigged to go off if it was moved, but we evacuated those houses closest to the bomb." Rollos looked over at the people huddled together. "I don't think Metan specifically wanted these people to die, I just think they were a good way of keeping us busy."

The explosion was muffled by the amount of water covering it, but was no less impressive as part of the lake tore into the sky, covering the street in water. People screamed and tried to hide behind whatever was nearby, to avoid being hit with anything more dangerous, but apart from being drenched, there was nothing to worry about.

Dai'ix exhaled. "That would have taken out half the houses at the end of the street. Metan wasn't messing about."

"We'll find him," Drake said. "And whoever his boss is."

Rollos' comm unit activated and he took a call, walking away for several seconds before returning. "Rosie. We're needed back at the palace. She didn't say, but it's apparently important. Celine contacted her. She said the boss didn't sound happy."

Drake looked over at the house where Metan had lived. "Get the Blackcoats here. Metan murdered the people who lived in that house and then tried to blow up another few houses so he could escape. They're going to want to look into it. Once we've got this place secured, we'll head back to the palace and see what Celine wants."

"You know it's not going to be good," Dai'ix said.

Drake chuckled, although there was no humour in it. "After the last few days, I'm pretty much certain of that fact."

CHAPTER TWENTY-THREE

Jaysa Benezta

After being dropped off at the docks, and placed into the charge of the head of the Wardens, Jaysa, Yanton, Etamus, Ren, and Takumi were all ferried to the palace with enough bodyguards to defend a space station.

Once at the palace, they were passed to several Suns Watch who put them in what was apparently protective custody. In reality, this meant a small room with a view of the ocean and as far as Jaysa was concerned, a blasted prison.

Fortunately, they were only there for a few hours before Ren arrived, sashaying into the room as if she owned the place, which Jaysa assumed she actually might do one day. Ren now wore a long black dress, and her hair had changed to match, although it had deep red highlights throughout. A thin rapier hung from her hip.

"So, we've all had a very shit day," she said as soon as she sat on the comfortable but small sofa that was close to the door.

"Most people start with hello," Takumi said as he closed the door and nodded to the crew.

Ren sighed. "Fine, Takumi. Hello everyone, it's a pleasure

to be here." Sarcasm dripped from every word.

Takumi had changed into an expensive looking suit in various shades of blue and grey. He carried a sword-cane in one hand.

Ren followed Jaysa's stare down at the rapier. "It's for show," she said. "Apparently, you have to dress up for these ridiculous meetings."

"What meeting?" Jaysa asked.

Takumi gave a world-weary sigh. "The Council are getting together to discuss what inept thing they're going to do to stop people from trying to kill anymore members of the royal household. You're going to be joining us."

"I'd rather not," Jaysa said. "I just lost a crew member."

Ren scowled while Takumi's grin could have almost split his face. "I did say it wouldn't be the best timing," he said cheerfully.

"I don't care about timing," Ren snapped. "Look, you three are the only ones—along with Takumi and me—who saw what happened back at the compound. You can bet the Council wants to see you. They want to know what happened. And I need you to sell it like you were terrified."

"I was terrified," Etamus said. "We all were. They were trying to kill us."

"That's the stuff," Takumi said. "Look, Ren isn't very good with people. Or anything that has a heart, but essentially, we need you to tell them what happened. We need them to do something about these bastards before it gets a whole lot worse than it currently is. We don't even know who they are or where they came from, let alone what they actually want."

"Us dead," Yanton said with a grimace.

"And it's the Council's job to make sure that doesn't happen," Ren said. "I'm not going to let anything happen to any of you."

"Why didn't you use your aether?" Jaysa asked. It had been something that had bothered her. "Back at the compound?"

"We couldn't," Takumi said. "All royal residents have anti-aether security in them. Someone had activated it before we reached you. We were, essentially, as helpless as anyone else in our situation."

"So," Yanton started. "You want us to agree to help the Council hunt down those who tried to kill us. And the only reason they tried to kill us was because we happened to be there at your compound."

"We think there's a bit more to it than that," Takumi said. "It sounds like someone is trying to kill anyone involved with Trinas. Seems he was involved in something much worse than we first thought."

Ren sighed. "Just be ready to come with me to the Council chambers. You've got about an hour."

"Any chance we can get some air then?" Jaysa said, pointing at the beach.

Ren appeared to think about it for several seconds before answering, "So long as you don't do anything stupid, yes." She walked over to a door leading to the outside, and used her palm print to unlock it. "I'll be back in an hour."

Jaysa pushed open the door and walked toward the water where she remained for several minutes, her eyes closed, feeling the breeze on her face and the sand beneath her feet. It was the most relaxed she'd been in weeks.

"You alone for any particular reason?" Etamus asked.

Jaysa opened her eyes, and watched Etamus pick up and throw several stones into the clear water of the Pancin Ocean. "I just needed to do some thinking," Jaysa said, not really wanting to discuss her thoughts.

"How are you holding up after what happened?" Etamus asked. "I mean everything, not just the last day."

"Lost two crew. One who was a traitorous piece of scum, and one a friend. Not used to having my people die on me." Jaysa lowered herself to the sand. "I'm fine. Tired, but fine. I'm looking forward to getting as far from here as possible, as soon as possible."

"Really? I like it here." Etamus glanced out over the ocean.

"It's calming."

Jaysa looked over at her first mate. "So long as you ignore the people trying to kill you, or use you in their political games, yes, it's very calming."

"Not the last few days, just this bit right here." Etamus picked up another pebble and threw it across the water, watching it skip the surface four times before it stopped. "Maybe I should find myself a little home somewhere quiet, by a lake and just relax."

"Give up being a Tracker?" Jaysa asked.

"Sure, why not?" Etamus said with a shrug. "We can't do this forever."

That wasn't something Jaysa wanted to think about. "You'd get bored."

"Of course," Etamus said and smiled. "And that's why you'd be living with me. So I'd always be entertained."

Jaysa turned toward Etamus and raised an eyebrow. "I'm your entertainment?"

"Well, after we've drunk all the wine my house will have, we'll need to find something to do," Etamus said. "I assume you can juggle, or something."

Jaysa took a pebble and skimmed it over the water. "Not a lot of call for a juggling Tracker."

"No, I don't suppose there is," Etamus agreed. "Shame, but you'll have to come up with something."

"Buy a pet," Jaysa said. "They'd keep you entertained."

"I don't think allowing me to look after a living thing is a good idea," Etamus countered. "And rocks don't make the most fun pets."

"I don't think I'd let you look after a rock," Jaysa said with a chuckle.

"I'm pretty certain you're not meant to say things like that to your second-in-command," Etamus said. "Aren't you meant to be nice to me, so I don't mutiny?"

"I'm pretty certain a mutiny requires an effort to complete," Jaysa told her. "Do you have that effort?"

Etamus thought about it for a moment. "No, probably not. It seems like a lot of hard work running a ship for anything longer than a few days at a time. I don't think I've got the patience to deal with stupid people either."

Jaysa laughed. "Which is why you never go to collect our money from people I don't want pissed off."

"Probably for the best," Etamus agreed.

Jaysa glanced around and spotted Ren walking toward them. "Oh, why can't she just go away."

Etamus followed the glance. "I think after this, we need to work on our arrangement with her."

Jaysa couldn't agree more.

"I have a favour to ask you both," Ren said as she reached them.

"And that would be?" Jaysa asked as she got to her feet.

"One last job, then I'll pay you both enough credits to go live on a planet far away from everything."

Jaysa liked the sound of that. "A job that'll get us killed?"

"I wouldn't have thought so," Ren said. "The Council are going to suggest that Felix Drake and his Wardens track down where Sabas might have fled. Sabas is the person behind what's happening here. He seems to be working with some awful people, and we'd like that stopped. I want you to go with them."

"There are so many questions I have about that," Jaysa began. "First of all, how do you know they'll ask that? Second, who is Felix Drake? And third, why?"

Ren paused, and for a moment Jaysa thought that she was going to say that she'd given them an order and the whys didn't matter. "Answers in no particular order to your questions, I need you to go there because I trust you, and I think Drake is going to need people on his side. We have intel that suggests Sabas has fled to Onnab. I want to know what was so important on Onnab that Sabas moved his operation there, and hid Trinas there too. I know the Council will request it because I want them to suggest it and I'm working to make sure that happens. Drake is… a complication."

"That's not an answer," Etamus said.

"Felix Drake is the son of Evan Varlus," Ren said.

"The Rebel General?" Etamus almost shouted.

"Yes," Ren said softly. "The one and the same, and I'm pretty sure that now everyone knows he's back here, they're going to want to get rid of him again."

"Drake being here scares people?" Jaysa asked. She'd only been young when the Rebellion had taken place, and had been sheltered from most of what had happened, but she'd been aware of the fighting happening, of the fear in people's eyes as they discussed how badly the Union was doing. She remembered her mother's anger at the loss of friends. It had been the time that allowed her to escape with her father, so to Jaysa the Rebellion had saved her from a life she'd wanted no part of.

"Drake being *alive* scares people," Ren said. "His father fought against both the Union and then against Rebels. No one knows why. They're afraid that if the son ever turned out to be like his father, that a lot of people would rally behind him if he asked them to. His father had an ability to make people want to fight for him. From what I've seen, Drake has that same ability. Ten million diamond credits for the job. As per our last agreement, half up front."

Jaysa couldn't believe what she'd just heard.

"I know it's a lot," Ren said. "You've been helpful to me, and I want to reward you for saving my life back at my compound. I might not be the most charismatic or emotional person in the world, but I value loyalty and competence. And you and your crew have shown both more than once."

"We'll do it," Jaysa said. "We'll help Drake and his Wardens get to Onnab, and then we'll leave them to their work."

"Excellent," Ren said with genuine pleasure. "That's a weight off my mind."

"One question," Etamus asked.

"Of course," Ren said, although Jaysa noticed the slight irritation in her voice.

"Will the Council send their own people on this job?"

Ren nodded to Etamus. "It's highly likely, and the one part I can't influence. There's no way of knowing who they'll pick, but I'm going to guess it'll be an up-and-coming councillor, or an aide who wants to better themselves. Whoever it is, they'll be the Council's eyes and ears, so they'll need to be watched."

"You don't trust the Council?" Jaysa asked.

Ren's smile didn't reach her eyes. "I trust very few people. Being in line for the throne means there are many who want my influence to help them, or want my head to do the same thing. I try to stay away from both groups if I can, and there are plenty of each in the Council." Ren removed a comm unit from her pocket. "You're now five million diamond credits richer. Don't spend it all at once." She turned and walked away, stopping to look back at the pair for a moment before vanishing from view as she entered the palace.

"You know this sounds like a lot more hassle than we normally look for," Etamus said.

"Of course."

"So, why agree to the job?"

"Ten million diamond reasons for a start," Jaysa said. "Also, I want to know what's so important that she wants us there to tell her about it. There's more to Onnab than people searching ruins. Something there was important enough to send Trinas, and I didn't like the feeling I got the last time I was there. It was utterly devoid of anything humanoid. There were crates with Sabas' company name on them. Ren is hiding something, and I want to know what it is. I'm not retiring to a life of luxury and leaving her to finish whatever plans she has. I can't look back on this in a year's time and wish I'd done something. I *need* to know what she's up to."

Etamus placed a hand on Jaysa's shoulder. "Glad to see you've finally decided to stop ignoring everything about her that feels wrong."

The words stung, but Jaysa knew they were accurate. "Yeah, well, I've been constantly on the move for a long time.

I want to be able to settle down after this is done, and I don't want Ren deciding she'll just let slip to my mother where I am. I'm not living my life looking over my shoulder. I need to know what Ren is up to."

A sly grin spread across Etamus' face. "You want to know who we can trust? Because you don't trust any of these pampered arseholes."

Jaysa looked at Etamus and smiled. She'd enjoyed working with the dreic over several years, and she couldn't think of a single person she'd rather entrust with her life. Etamus was the one person Jaysa could be completely honest with. "The thought has crossed my mind, yes."

"Excellent," Etamus said with a smile.

CHAPTER TWENTY-FOUR

Felix Drake

When Drake and the rest of the Wardens landed back at the palace, he was immediately ordered to the Council chamber. He was on his way when he spied Hideo following him in a hover-chair, which moved slowly about a meter above the ground.

"You're up already?" Drake asked as his old friend reached him. "It's too soon. You only lost your arm yesterday."

"Spent the night in one of the regeneration chambers," Hideo said. "The skin and flesh are all healed. They let me out of the tube for a few hours so I can get some fresh air. Apparently, the body can't stay in one of those things for longer than twenty-four hours before it starts driving the occupant crazy."

"I've always hated them," Drake told him. He hated the fact that while you felt no pain during the stay in the chamber, you were conscious of everything going on around you, even if you were meant to be asleep. He'd been in one twice, and hadn't wanted to repeat the experience.

Hideo raised his hand, showing a bare forearm. "And I don't get my magnus bracer back until I'm healed, I feel naked without it."

Hideo caught Drake staring at the bandages that covered the stump where his arm used to be. "They had to remove it from the shoulder," Hideo said. "And before you say anything, please don't apologise."

Drake wasn't sure what to say. Sorry didn't seem to be a good enough word. He decided that a change of conversation was probably for the best. "You're getting a new arm?"

"Top of the range synthetic," Hideo said. "I'm going to have the hand transform into a cannon. They can do that, right?"

"I have no idea," Drake said with a smile. "Make it a small cannon though, you don't want to accidentally put holes all through your house."

Hideo chuckled, and then winced. "That would be embarrassing."

"Still some pain?" Drake asked, concerned.

"Only when I laugh," Hideo said. "I want to scratch my hand too. I woke up this morning and went to reach for a glass of water. Took me thirty seconds to figure out why it wasn't working."

"And how are my two favourite people?" a woman asked.

Drake looked up, and Hideo moved his chair to get a better view of Kimi walking toward them. "Kimi," Drake said and hugged her. "It's been a few hours. How's things?"

"Celine told you about what we found at the warehouse?" she asked.

Drake nodded, feeling suddenly tired. It had been a long few days, and there was no sign of it being done soon.

"I heard about the Genesis-Alpha thing in the tank," Hideo said. "Not something I've heard of before. Do you know who's behind my shooting?"

Drake shook his head. "Not totally. Metan arranged it, but I don't know who he's working for. He had Helice, Septimus, and Trinas killed to clean up Sabas' mess. Was meant to have Kimi killed too, but she wasn't there, and I assume after the failed attempt on your life, and that of Ren and Takumi, they put a hold on trying to murder members of the royal family to flee the planet instead. We'll find Sabas, and then we'll get the answers we need as to who Metan's working with, and how to find them."

"So, I *was* meant to die back in that apartment?" Kimi asked.

Drake nodded. "Helice didn't wear her magnus bracer though. Not sure why."

"She didn't like to wear it in that district," Kimi said. "Too many glances her way when they saw it. Custom magnus bracers aren't exactly common, and she couldn't just wear some off-the-shelf model, it would have been worse than useless."

"She couldn't use her aether without it," Hideo said. "I told her not to go anywhere until we'd looked into everything."

"She told you?" Drake asked him.

Hideo nodded. "Kimi, Helice, and Septimus came to me. They'd gone to Ren and Takumi too."

"What did they talk to you about?" Drake asked.

"Mostly how to find Trinas after he was shipped off world," Hideo said.

Drake shook his head. "Whoever Metan is working for, they're removing anyone who knew about these Genesis-Alpha experiments. You should have gone to the king."

"We had no proof," Kimi said. "He would have told us to leave it to the professionals."

Drake didn't see the point in telling them the king was right. It wasn't going to make things better by making them feel worse. "We'll find him eventually. Sabas is too stupid to stay hidden for long."

"I hope so," Kimi said with a slight sigh. "So, how is the next in line to the throne?"

"Sore," Hideo said. "And enough with that, we were both chosen as successors, I have just as much chance as you, probably less, considering several of the Council are unhappy with the fact that I won't be providing them with a steady stream of children anytime soon."

"I'm going to have a walk, why don't you both join me?" Kimi suggested. "The Council hasn't convened yet. You have a while before they need you."

The three took a stroll around the property, reminiscing and discussing their youth.

"I missed you," Kimi told Drake at one point. "I didn't tell you that earlier, as it wasn't exactly the time, but you vanished and no one knew where you were. No one knew if you were dead or alive. You were as close to me as my brother when we were growing up, I needed my big brothers. And one of you was gone. I almost found god."

"Almost?" Drake asked.

"I was upset, not stupid," she said with a laugh. "Being a part of The Serenity doesn't really suit me."

Drake chuckled. The Serenity were people with a lot of power on Atharoth, and throughout Union-controlled space. They believed that several dozen deities all came out of The Aperture and that every time someone went through it, they were essentially communicating with one god or another. Some of them had actually managed to take themselves into The Aperture, never to be seen again. Drake doubted very much there were any gods within, and if there were, that they gave even a glimmer of thought to anything done outside of it. He firmly believed that it wasn't up to him to tell people their beliefs were the stuff of a crazed imagination. Life was hard enough already; he didn't need to take people's faith away from them if it helped them deal with reality.

"I'm sorry I never contacted either of you," Drake said. "It was becoming more and more obvious at the time that once people knew who my father was, they were more than willing to tar me with the same brush."

"I get why you did it," Kimi said, "but that doesn't mean I wasn't mad at you when I found out you'd hidden from us." She raised her arm showing off her magnus bracer. "Why aren't you wearing your bracer? That I don't understand."

"I don't need it," Drake admitted. "Wearing one shorts-out my aether. Means I have trouble using it or, depending on the amount of power the bracer is designed to allow, it means I blow up a lot of things around me."

"And if you'd been practising with it," Kimi said, "you could have used your aether to turn you and the synth that attacked Hideo into a cube."

"I wanted to keep it in once piece, which I guess didn't really work out very well for me," Drake said. "It's time for me to head back and see the Council."

They made their way back to the palace and entered through the doors closest to the hall where Council meetings were held when conducted at the palace. Drake noticed several aides and personnel that didn't work for the King of Stars. Considering the stares, and occasional glare, they probably worked for people who really weren't happy with his re-emergence.

They reached the outer doors of the chamber, which was barred by two large, human Suns Watch officers. "You'll have to wait," the first said.

There was no point in arguing, so Drake headed into a nearby waiting room and took a seat on a comfortable bench while he waited for his summons. "You two don't have to wait with me," he told them.

"I don't have anywhere else I need to be," Kimi said.

"Me neither," Hideo assured him.

Drake was grateful for the company. He'd wondered what kinds of people Hideo and Kimi had grown into, and hoped that the political nightmare that ruled Atharoth hadn't changed them too much. He was pleased to see they hadn't become tainted by the Council's unpleasantness.

"Well, look who it is," a large man said as he walked down the hallway, another similar-looking man beside him. His tone suggested he was unhappy. "It's the two delightful favourite children, and the rotten one. The latter of whom should have had the sense to stay dead."

Drake sighed. Ryota and Norio were the eldest children of the King of Stars, and ones who had resented every other child that came after them. Despite not being related to the King of Stars in any way, Drake had unfortunately been lumped into the same category. Ryota Kong, as the eldest, was fifteen years Drake's senior, although like all Sage looked much younger. Norio was only ten years older, but took after his older brother in personality if not in looks.

Ryota had the nickname of Ryota the Handsome, which Drake was pretty certain he'd given himself and then paid people to use until it caught on. His long silver hair had been dyed since he was a teenager, and his eyes were cyan. Drake had to admit that at a good foot taller and considerably wider than him, Ryota cut an imposing figure.

Despite having different mothers, Norio could have been Ryota's twin if not for his dark hair and much darker blue eyes. The two had been inseparable for as long as Drake could remember. They were bullies, but smart ones, and had won over a large portion of the population by being likeable in front of a camera. Drake liked them both about as much as being bitten by a snake. Of all of the King of Stars eight children, Hideo and Kimi were Drake's favourites, and Ryota and Norio were as polar opposite as was possible.

"Oh, good, it's those two," Drake said.

"Do you have a problem with our being here?" Ryota asked, closing the door behind him.

"Is that meant to be intimidating?" Drake asked. "Because I'm pretty certain I'm not a child anymore, and I've met a lot scarier people than either of you."

"He should be in chains, not free to walk about," Norio snapped. "Can't risk having the son of a traitor walking around. Our father always was blind to what needed to be done when it came to Drake."

"Do you have any idea how stupid you sound?" Hideo asked.

"Says the man who got shot trying to save the traitor-in-training," Ryota said with a laugh. "Shame it didn't go a few inches to the right, it would have taken off your head, saved everyone a lot of bother of pretending you were important."

"Fuck off," Kimi said, anger leaking into her voice. "Seriously, just both of you fuck off."

"Little Kimi want to play with the big boys?" Ryota asked and took a step toward her.

"What are you going to do, Ryota?" Kimi asked. "Pick a fight? We both know you're not. You're not that stupid. So just leave us be, and go back to whatever it is you two do to keep yourselves occupied."

"Got a mouth on you," Norio said, venom in his voice.

Of the two, Drake noticed that Norio had always been the one who disliked his sisters more. He appeared to have a serious issue with any woman at his level or higher. Rumours had raged that a few of his companions had disappeared over the years, but nothing was proven and the gossip soon died away. When they were younger, Norio was always the one who had trouble keeping himself in check, always the more overly dangerous.

"Oh look, Norio, it's Takumi and Ren. Isn't it good? It's almost a full family reunion," Ryota said, voice dripping with sarcasm as the twins walked into the room.

"What are you both playing at?" Ren asked. "Shouldn't you be off breaking rocks with your heads or something more suited to your abilities?"

Norio stalked toward his younger sister. "Are you saying I'm stupid?"

"I'm pretty certain that was implied, yes," Ren said, almost sounding bored.

"It's not nice to call someone stupid," Norio told her, as he continued to make his way across the room.

"It's not nice to be such a colossal dick either, yet you manage it quite well," Ren told him.

Norio stopped only a foot away from his smaller sister.

"Maybe I should teach you some manners."

Ren smiled beautifully. "Maybe you should put your hand on me, so I can take it off and stuff it up your arse. Wouldn't that be a fun time for us all?"

Norio's hands curled into fists, and Takumi walked by him without a second glance. He continued on to Drake, completely ignoring his older brothers. "Good to see you're alive. I had a sleepless night worrying about you."

"A whole night?" Drake said with a slight laugh. "Must have been awful."

"It was a little," Takumi said, feigning all seriousness. "My skin was dry for days after. I believe that's as close as I've ever been to mourning someone." He turned back to his sister. "Ren, either kill him or walk away, but please do stop playing. You know how sensitive Norio is about being a colossal dick."

Everyone in the room who wasn't Norio or Ryota, laughed. Norio turned to look at the larger group, his face red with anger. He turned and stormed toward everyone, with even Ryota stepping out of the way.

Drake watched as the royal sibling's trajectory put him on a line with Kimi, and he stepped between them. "Now is hardly the time or place for your childish idiocy."

"I can defend myself, Drake," Kimi said from behind him.

Drake turned to Kimi. "I know, I was trying to stop it from getting that far, not trying to protect you. I'm a Warden, and that means I investigate crimes committed against and by members of the royal family."

As Drake turned back, someone shouted something just in time for him to avoid the punch Norio had thrown. Drake pushed the arm away and stepped toward the bigger man, landing several jabs to his side as he avoided another powerful punch. Drake replied with a kick to Norio's chest that contained enough power to force him back.

Norio's expression was one of pure shock that quickly turned to outrage, and he charged at Drake, who used the older man's momentum to throw him over his shoulder and into the wall behind them, narrowly missing Hideo.

"Get him out of here," Ren shouted at Ryota, who stood frozen in shock.

"Norio," Drake said as the larger man got back to his feet. "This isn't like the time I was ten and you decided to change a sparring match into a fight, or the time I was fifteen and you knocked me out. This is about now, and if you stand and throw another punch, I'm going to hurt you very badly. And it will be completely within my right to do so."

Norio's hands were balled into fists as he took a step toward Drake. "I will kill you for this."

Drake made sure to stay locked to Norio's gaze. "Not even on your best day."

Norio's head shot forward, but Drake had read the attack and moved aside, bringing up the side of his hand into Norio's exposed throat. Norio stopped moving and began to choke. Drake spun and drove his foot into the man's stomach, dropping him to his knees as he tried to suck in air through a painful throat. Before anyone could stop him, Drake smashed his knee into Norio's head, snapping it to one side with incredible force as the larger man toppled to the ground unconscious.

"He can stay here if you'd prefer," Drake told Ryota as the door opened and a young man entered the room.

"The Council is waiting for you, Drake," the man said without so much as a glance toward the still prone Norio.

Drake nodded and took a step only to find his hand held tight by Kimi. "Be careful," she told him.

"After that, I don't think it's Norio we need to worry about," Hideo said and Drake smiled, although it felt forced.

"Brute had it coming," Ren told him with a slight smirk. "Think nothing of it."

"Let's go see what they have to say," Drake said with a sigh.

"If all else fails," Takumi said as Drake was near the door. "Just tell them you have information on their after-work activities. Always seems to make them forget what they were going to argue about."

Drake exited and almost collided with Rosie. "Hey, you okay?" he asked.

"You're going to the Council chamber, yes?" she asked.

Drake nodded. "What's wrong?"

Rosie tapped a few things on her comm unit. "You need to see this."

CHAPTER TWENTY-FIVE

Felix Drake

The Council chamber was created to be as intimidating as possible to anyone using the front entrance. Whether this was purely accidental or by purposeful design, Drake wasn't really sure. Oval in shape, councillors sat on the chambers' sides, which sloped up toward the ceiling. The more important the member, the closer they sat to the front, but even those on the bottom seats were higher than Drake's head.

To make things worse, every councillor wore face masks in a variety of colours and designs, making identification next to impossible. The King of Stars and his wife sat at the far end of the room on matching thrones atop a staircase, looking down on everyone else.

"Son of a traitor," one councillor shouted out, showing Drake exactly the type of evening he was about to have.

The King of Stars stood, irritation etched on his face. "I will not have outbursts such as that," he said, his voice booming around the chamber. "Felix Drake is a member of the Wardens. He has shown bravery and loyalty to the Union and those who would serve her. If anyone suggests otherwise, you're more than welcome to come find me in my private chambers after this meeting so that we can discuss it further."

No one spoke. Drake knew that while members of the Council would be quite happy to play their little political games and move their little pieces around outside of the chambers, no one would be stupid enough to stand up to the king inside. The King of Stars wasn't the all-powerful tyrant the position had been in the past, but he wasn't someone to be crossed lightly.

"For those of who don't know," Drake started. "My name is Felix Drake. My father was Evan Varlus, the man who helped lead the Rebellion against the Union. The man who ended up fighting both Union and Rebellion forces until his death. So, yes, I am the son of a traitor. However, I am not a traitor myself. I wonder if everyone here today can say the same."

Drake noticed the slight smile on the King of Stars' lips as the chamber broke out in a chorus of boos and jeers, which eventually dissipated.

"As some of you know," The King of Stars began, "Drake has been looking into the murders of Helice and Septimus. I believe the Council would like an update."

Apart from the strangeness of the request—Wardens didn't usually give status updates on crimes to the whole Council—Drake nodded and explained what he'd discovered so far, taking care to look around the chamber, spotting anyone who appeared to be uncomfortable. It was hard to do when everyone was masked, but there was more to a person's body language than just their facial expression. When Drake got to the part about the attack on Hideo's mansion, several of the councillors fidgeted.

After a few minutes, Drake was done and nodded toward the King of Stars.

"Thank you for that," the king said. "As you can tell, the investigation is still on-going, but will now be handled by a secondary Warden unit here on Atharoth."

Drake was taken aback by the words. This was *his*

investigation... he stopped before his irritation showed. Maybe it was for the best. He clearly had a personal stake in finding Metan and bringing him to justice. Maybe it was time to allow someone else to continue lest it become all-consuming in his hunt.

"I have asked Drake here for another reason," the King of Stars began, to murmurs of the Council. "All of you will be aware of the murders of Helice, and Septimus, and the attacks on Ren, Takumi, Hideo, and Drake here on Atharoth. It is time for us to unmask those perpetrators who have aided these attacks, and have them brought before us begging for mercy."

Drake wondered whether the King of Stars had used the phrase 'unmask' as a way to worry any councillors working with Sabas and Metan, although Drake had no way of knowing if any of them were. Drake smiled to himself and wondered if the information Rosie had given him was going to make it look like the King of Stars had known their identity in advance.

The king glanced around the room before continuing on. "To that end, Drake will be given full authority to travel wherever he deems fit to find those responsible and bring them to justice."

The noise in the chamber suggested the Council approved. Drake assumed because if the son of a traitor wasn't on Atharoth he was no longer their problem to deal with. Or maybe some of them hoped he'd be killed while there and they could forget he ever darkened their door. Drake took a slight breath; he was letting his paranoia get the best of him.

The king waited for the murmuring to die down before speaking again. "As is befitting a Warden member who will be leaving Atharoth, Drake will be given a total jurisdiction overhaul, allowing him and his team to go wherever they wish. They may talk to whoever they wish, and administer whatever justice they deem appropriate. This also means that any actions they carry out in the name of the Union will be completely and utterly within the law."

It took a few seconds for everyone to understand what the

king had just proposed, but once it sank in, the chamber was in uproar.

"You're giving that traitor the means to arrest and interrogate anyone he wishes?" one of the councillors almost screamed.

"And execute," a second councillor shouted.

Drake glanced over at Ren, and saw her stood next to a sarcian female he hadn't met before. Ren was smiling; she hadn't bothered to wear a mask, she never did. She was completely at ease with anyone's opinions of her. Drake had always found that admirable.

"Are you all quite done?" the King of Stars boomed once again, taking advantage of the small amplifier that sat on his lapel.

The silence that followed was uncomfortable, and Drake wondered how many of those in the chamber were wishing to leave as quickly as possible to lodge protest after protest about what had been had proposed.

Drake looked around the chamber; why had the king wanted to do this in public? How did it benefit him or the Union to have Drake come before the Council and make them all as angry as possible? While he knew Celine had told him he had jurisdiction to leave the planet and hunt down those responsible for the attack at the hospital, the king had ensured that Drake now had the law behind him to literally go anywhere and do anything. That was unprecedented for a Warden, and even more so for one whose father was as infamous as his. Drake stared at his foster-uncle and tried to figure out why, but the king's expression was blank.

"You are wondering why I have done this," the King of Stars began. "Primarily because I trust Drake to find these Marauders, wherever they might be and whoever they might be allied to, and deal with them. Drake is not his father, and those of you who are so blinded by your anger for his father would do well to remember that. Several of you had connections—both private and public—with members of the

Rebellion. If you wish, I could air those connections here today?"

The King of Stars waited in the silence. "No? Are you sure? It would be a simple matter. About as simple as revealing which of you was working to try and kill Drake and my children only a short time ago." The King of Star's voice was cold and hard. "Drake will do this because he is the best man for the job. It's that simple."

"It needs to be voted on," one of the councillors said.

"No it doesn't," the king replied without any trace of annoyance.

"If Drake is as powerful as his father, he could become a threat with that kind of backing," another councillor said. "We need to make sure that doesn't happen."

"I have a proposal," Drake said.

Everyone in the chamber turned to look at Drake.

"Go on," the King of Stars said.

"I was coming here because I was asked to," Drake started. "The King of Stars wants to keep things open and honest. He wants you all to understand that I am not my father. And no matter your anger toward him, your anger is misplaced when it is aimed at me. A short time ago, someone ordered a recon synth to occupy a skyblock and kill everyone working there. After which, he was ordered to kill Hideo Wynn upon his return home. At first, I had considered that his husband, Caleus Wynn, had been involved." Drake looked over at Caleus and Hideo, the former of which was red with anger. "And for that I apologise. Caleus was not involved in the attempt on Hideo's life, nor the attempt on mine. He hates me, always has, but I allowed the knowledge of that hate to cloud my own judgement."

"You admit to having a personal issue with my son," Caleus' father shouted, removing his mask, and throwing it across the chambers toward Drake, who sidestepped it easily.

"Lewei Winter," Drake said. "Good of you to unmask yourself."

"I demand reparations," Lewei bellowed.

Drake tapped a few things on his comm unit. "May I have access to the screen over the chamber door?" Drake asked the King of Stars, who nodded despite looking slightly confused.

Drake connected his comm unit to the screen. "What you can see are the calls made between a synth and an untraceable comm unit that occurred today. The synth was the same one responsible for Hideo's wounding. It was there to kill him." Drake found a message that gave the synth instructions to kill Hideo Wynn when the target showed himself. "We had some difficulty tracing the comm unit that sent the message as it was encrypted. Someone went to a lot of effort to hide it from us. Unfortunately for them, I have someone on my team who really likes a challenge."

Drake tapped his comm unit and the screen changed to a map, pinpointing the exact location from where all of the calls were made. "This is the Winter residence," Drake said.

There were gasps in the chamber, followed quickly by Lewei Winter being escorted onto the floor by two large Wardens.

"How dare you," Lewei said. "I was not involved in such a thing!"

Drake showed screen after screen of bank records for Lewei, who had received several million diamond credits in deposits over the last few weeks.

Lewei scoffed. "I make money. That is not a crime."

"True," Drake admitted. "These amounts were placed in your account by one Metan Glornv. The same one who also arranged for Helice and Septimus' murders. The same one who admitted as much to me." Drake played back the video he'd recorded from Metan when they'd last spoke.

"Doesn't prove anything," Lewei said dismissively.

"Last chance to admit it," Drake whispered. "Maybe they'll go lenient on you."

"Prove I did it," Lewei replied.

Drake sighed. "He tapped a few things on the comm unit

and the comm number that called the synth rang."

Everyone looked at Lewei as his comm unit began to beep.

"You going to answer that?" Drake asked.

Lewei lunged at Drake, who pushed the older man to the ground, where he was taken by two more Wardens.

"I hate you," Lewei screamed. "Always hated you. Hate your whole damn family. My son would have gone up in rank, he would have been showered with power after Hideo died."

The Wardens dragged Lewei away, and Drake noticed that Caleus and Hideo were still watching in disbelief. "I didn't want to do that in front of you all," Drake said, taking a momentary pause to let everyone focus back on him. "I do, however, want you all to know something. If any more of you are involved in this, I will find you. I will ensure you lose everything you hold dear. I care little for your titles or your power. I care that any of you who believe you are above the laws of this land will be proven wrong. And I will find everyone responsible for the murders and attempted murders that happened on this land, and I will bring them to justice."

There were whispers throughout the chamber.

"This is adjourned," the King of Stars said. "The details will be settled. Drake, I'd like to see you in my chambers."

Drake nodded, and followed the king into a nearby private room.

The office wasn't large, and consisted of a small desk, table, green sofa, and several chairs. It looked over the ocean, and Drake knew this was where several high-profile judgments had been made before being taken to Council for approval.

"You didn't need to do that," the King of Stars said.

Drake nodded. "I did. I placed our laws above them. Above even my own best interests. It had to be shown."

"And also, you enjoyed it," Hideo said from the doorway.

"There's that too," Drake admitted.

"My husband assures me he knew nothing," Hideo said. "I believe him."

"As do I," Drake said.

Kimi entered the room. "You should have done that in private, but I won't lie, I got some enjoyment from seeing him taken down a peg or two."

"I did it in public because I want his accomplices to panic," Drake said. "And they will. That's the funny thing about people like Lewei. They run from that sinking ship as fast as they can once they get a sniff of flame. You'll see some of those councillors doing a lot to distance themselves from Lewei. You're going to want to run checks on them."

"You've left us with work," the King of Stars said.

"And Caleus will hate you even more now," Hideo said.

"No offense, Hideo, but I really don't care if he hates me," Drake said. "He hated me just for falling in love with his sister when we were teenagers. Once this all came out, he was always going to hate me more."

"Your team will be ready for you at a custom-built ship," the King of Stars said, changing the subject.

"We get a new ship?" Drake asked.

"It's a corsair-class interceptor named *Sunstorm*," the king said. "Lots of speed, lots of firepower; vastly more than is needed for a ship that's only designed to house twenty people at most."

Interceptors were designed to fly both in deep space and also within the gravity of a planet. They were usually equipped with a lot of powerful weaponry and used as a run-and-gun ship.

"Twenty?" Drake asked.

The King of Stars nodded. "Your team, a few people Ren was working with who saw the attack, and whoever the Council pick."

"So a lot less than twenty?" Drake said, hoping for some clarification.

"You only need about five to actually run the ship," the King of stars said. "I figured having a bigger ship meant more space just in case you needed to get away from everyone."

"Anything else?" Drake asked.

The king pressed a button on his terminal. "Can you send Rosie in, please?"

Rosie entered the room a moment later, and took a seat next to Kimi. "This is weird."

"You get used to it," Hideo said.

"Officially, you're no longer searching for Metan," the King of Stars said. "Unofficially, I've given Rosie unfiltered access to the comm network. She's currently trying to hack Metan's messages on the comm units we found at his house."

"You found anything?" Drake asked.

Rosie shook her head. "He's vanished. It'll take a lot of work to try and track him down. Sabas, however, well that's interesting. He left Atharoth and went back to Leturn, we know this because he used his comm unit there. And once on Leturn, he hired a private ship with a flight plan to Onnab."

"Why would he go there?" Drake asked. "And so blatantly?"

"No idea," Rosie said. "We should probably go find out. He sent Trinas there for two years, and his company spent a lot of money on a mining operation there, so maybe he had Trinas hide something? Or maybe he's just running?"

"It's worth looking into," Drake said. He turned back to the King of Stars. "Thanks for doing this."

"Please, we both know you were going to keep looking into Sabas and Metan anyway."

Drake shrugged and smiled.

"One last thing. Be careful." The King of Stars hugged Drake. "Come back in one piece."

"I'll make sure we don't do anything stupid," Drake said. "Mostly not stupid."

"Take care on your trip," Kimi said. "I'm sure I can talk to Celine about looking into other members of the Council. We got on pretty well."

"Don't stay away for so long this time," Hideo said.

"I'll see you later," Rosie said. "I want to get a few hours of sleep on the new ship. Can't rest otherwise."

Drake left the chamber, mind racing with possibilities of the mission that lay before him. He paid little attention to his surroundings until he found himself in the palace gardens.

"So, how'd it go?" Ren asked from where she leant against a marble railing, surveying the land before her.

"Could have been worse."

"Are you coming back, Drake?" she asked. "This time, I mean?"

Drake nodded. "I hope so; I don't plan on dying out there, or running off again."

Ren hugged him in a rare display of affection. "Take care of yourself."

"You too, Ren. Your father could do a lot worse than give you the Kingship. Maybe it's time for a change."

Ren's smile was forced. "The first female King of Stars in two hundred years? It's a nice dream, but I doubt it'll happen."

Drake said his goodbyes and made his way back into the palace and through the corridors. He stepped past an open door, and was immediately blinded by a flash of light. Drake staggered forward, trying to figure out what had happened when he was struck in the side of the head with a metal bat, and fell to the floor.

"Did you think what you did would go unpunished?" Norio asked and used the bat to hit Drake in the ribs hard enough to break them. "Did you think I'd just let you leave after humiliating me?"

Norio dragged Drake into the room before hitting him again. Drake reached out with his aether in an effort to stop the beating, but was hit in the face before he was able to use it. "Can't have you throwing aether around now, can we?" Norio asked, and hit Drake twice more, before stamping on his elbow, breaking it.

Drake roared in pain, making Norio laugh, a sound that had rage explode inside Drake. He pushed the pain aside and rolled away. He was still unable to see past the black dots covering his vision, but he saw the mass that was Norio. He exploded upward, running at Norio, who threw him into the wall. Drake hit the floor as pain wracked his body, and all he could do was watch as Norio walked toward him and hit him in the head once again.

For a moment he wasn't certain where he was, but that moment was enough for Norio to grasp the back of Drake's hair, and repeatedly punch him in the face, splitting open his lips and breaking his nose.

"I'm not going to kill you," Norio said, holding Drake by his bloody hair. "I'm just going to make you wish I had."

Drake was semi-conscious by the time Norio had finished his relentless attack, one of his eyes was swollen shut and he had no way of knowing just how badly his internal organs had been damaged.

Norio slapped Drake around the face. "Don't pass out, we're not done yet."

Drake's one good eye focused on the gun barrel that suddenly rested against Norio's temple.

"Let him go. Now," a sarcian woman said as she stepped around to the side of Norio. Drake didn't recognise the voice.

"You'll regret this, you whore," Norio seethed.

The woman laughed. "Do you really think name calling is going to do you any good?"

"And what do you think is going to happen when you try to get Drake out of here? You'll have to lower your gun and then you're mine." Norio smiled.

"Good point," the woman said.

Drake watched as she shot Norio in the head with a disruptor before holstering it and kneeling beside Drake. "Let's get you to a doctor."

The last thing Drake thought before passing out, was how grateful he was that whoever the sarcian was it was a good thing she was on his side.

CHAPTER TWENTY-SIX

Felix Drake

D rake woke in a strange cabin. He sat up and immediately wished he hadn't. His head was sore, and he felt like he'd been kicked by one of the massive waterhorns that lived in the swamps of Benoran.

He propped himself up on the many pillows at his back, and rubbed his temples before managing to shift himself out of the bed and stand, his back cracking with the movement. Norio had really done a job on him. Drake was pissed that he'd been blindsided, and then beaten before he could defend himself. He should have known Norio would have tried something, but his mind had been elsewhere. He'd been lucky for the sarcian's intervention.

Drake looked out of the window at the purple light that sped past. They were in The Aperture. Aperture-drive technology had been around for thousands of years, making travelling between systems—or from one part of a system to another—something that could be measured in hours or days instead of years and lifetimes. No one knew who invented it; they just liked the fact it had been invented.

An aperture-drive allowed space to be torn open—a

breach—and for a ship to travel into The Aperture itself. Once there, huge distances could be travelled in relatively short periods of time. There were always tales of ships being attacked once inside, and others never making out, but most were seen as urban superstitions or old tales passed down over the generations to scare children and the gullible in equal measure. The majority considered Aperture-jumping to be a completely safe and, more importantly, a wholly necessary part of life.

Once inside, the ship was essentially automated. A destination had to be loaded into the aperture-drive before the ship entered, and once the destination had been reached, the drive would open another breach into normal space. While in The Aperture itself, the course couldn't be altered, although they still had access to their speed, weapons, and shields.

Drake pushed the comm button on the panel beside the bed. "Any chance someone could tell me how long I've been asleep?"

"Someone will be with you shortly," Tuck said. "Glad to hear you're awake."

As much as the idea of lying back down and just waiting appealed to Drake, he knew that if he went that route, it would be even harder for him to get back up again. Instead, he did a few stretches before having a shower, using the hottest water setting his body could manage. He still ached, still would have rather gone back to bed, but at least he felt vaguely alive.

There was a knock on the door as he pulled on some underwear, and was about to call out that he wasn't exactly dressed when the door slid open and a female sarcian walked in.

"How are you feeling?" she asked.

"Close to naked," Drake told her. "Any chance of telling me where my clothes are in this room?"

"You'll find something in the cupboard," she told him and tapped a button beside her, which let the cupboard door slide open revealing several rows of clothing. "My name's Jaysa

Benezta. You were lucky I walked past when you were getting your arse handed to you."

"Thanks," Drake grabbed a set of tan-coloured recon armour, some boots and under garments. He placed all of the clothing on the bed and turned around as he pulled on the recon-armour trousers.

"Lots of scars on your back," Jaysa said.

"I spent a lot of time on Terentus as a teenager," Drake explained. "They're not exactly a fan of the *soft and nice* approach to helping you get used to your abilities."

"Why not get them removed?"

"Do you often ask personal questions of people you just met?" Drake asked, turning to face her.

Jaysa shrugged.

"Because they remind me what happened, and what I went through to get them." He pulled a black tunic over his head before applying the armour. "Thank you for saving me from a worse beating. And for getting me here. How long was I out?"

"A few days. Yanton wanted you out for a while," Jaysa told him. "Said he wanted to make sure there wasn't any swelling on your brain. He was worried your body would go insane if you were awake."

"Yanton?" Drake asked.

"My doctor."

"You have your own doctor?"

"I'm a Tracker," Jaysa said. "Yanton is the crew's medical specialist. Our teams have been mingling, and seem to get on quite well."

"Did they send a Council representative along with us?" Drake asked, knowing he wasn't going to be happy with the answer.

"Unfortunately," Jaysa said. "We left quickly after your attack, but not quick enough for our guests to arrive."

Drake wasn't exactly surprised by that news. Although he wasn't about to complain. "So, what happened to Norio? I saw you shoot him. Is he dead?"

"I shot him with a low-level disrupter blast, so he won't die," Jaysa said. "Won't feel good about it either. It was decided to get you off-world before he woke up and tried again. The King of Stars didn't look very impressed with what had happened. He's not a man to cross, is he?"

Drake shook his head and was grateful it didn't hurt. "No, he certainly isn't."

"He also told me to tell you that there's a present under the bunk."

Drake reached under the bed and pulled out a large box. Inside sat a sheathed, obsidian-fibre spearhead, about a foot in length. A two-foot pole protruded from the bottom, which had an obsidian-fibre pommel on the end, sharpened to a point. He removed the black and silver sheath and placed it on the bed. The pole itself was made of a fibre Drake couldn't identify, but the red and black colour surely signified that the King of Stars had a hand in its creation. Drake lifted it out of the box and stood, pushing the button just below the blade. The pole extended to its five-foot length in an instant, and a red ring signified where the extension was joined to the rest of the haft.

"That's nice workmanship," Jaysa said.

Drake looked at the ring and tested its strength. "This was made by an obsidian artisan," he said. "The King of Stars has two on retainer. This isn't a new blade. They take months to create." He pushed the button again and the pole extension vanished. "Genuinely impressive." Drake picked up the sheath and placed it over the blade before noticing a scabbard in the box that would allow him to wear the spear like a sword.

"He thought of everything," Jaysa said.

"Looks that way, doesn't it?" Drake removed the scabbard, which was the same colour as the spear, and put it on. "Been a while since I wore a weapon like this."

"Well, it's nice to know that you're able to defend yourself when the need arises," Jaysa said. "I actually came here to talk to you about our plans. My job is to help you get to... actually,

I'm not real clear on that. Ren wanted me with you, so here I am."

"The King of Stars mentioned something about you being present when they attacked Ren's compound."

Jaysa nodded. "It wasn't one of the most fun things ever. I lost someone in that attack."

"I'm sorry," Drake said. "What did you do for Ren?"

"Didn't even know I was working for Ren until a few days ago," Jaysa said. "I was hired to find Trinas, but he'd already gone by the time I arrived. I went to Leturn, where I was betrayed, and the man ended up dead for it. Ren found me, introduced herself as my employer. Doesn't look like it worked out well for anyone."

A knock on the door stopped Drake from asking anything else. "Come in," he said.

Rollos entered the cabin and nodded toward Drake. "Good to see you up and about. The King of Stars gave me predator-armour to keep. Can't complain about that. Figured I'd come see how you were doing, and let you know there's a certain synth who wants to see you."

"Bokk is here?" Drake smiled. He was glad to hear they'd be on-board.

Rollos smiled. "They wouldn't take no for an answer. I get the feeling they would have tracked you across the galaxy if you'd gone off-world. They've been waiting for you to get up, and watching the councillor and other synth like a fire-hawk."

"A synth?" Drake hadn't expected that, although it made sense. A synth would work to the word of the law, it wouldn't care about outside influences if he did anything wrong. It would just execute its plan. "What kind of synth do they have with them?"

"Some sort of battle-synth variation," Rollos said. "Looks formidable enough, but it's not exactly chatty. Apparently, their version got rid of anything they deemed to be a bug, like a personality."

Drake took a deep breath and let it out slowly. "Okay,

where are they?"

"Mess room, along with Luca, Sateri and pretty much everyone else," Rollos said. "We want to know what's going on. Also, you promised to go through exactly why you've been lying to us."

"I did, yes." Drake got the feeling it was going to be another long day.

He followed Rollos and Jaysa to the mess room, stopping every now and again to get his bearings on the maze of corridors that snaked through the ship. It wasn't even that big, relatively speaking, but all of the corridors looked identical and it took him a few minutes to notice the little colour-coded arrows on the ceiling pointing toward various parts of the ship.

Once at the mess room, Drake discovered that everyone from his team was there, including Bokk, who appeared to have been repaired from the damage he'd received from The Spire explosion.

"I have a few things to explain," Drake said, taking a seat at one of the tables. "First, I need to thank Yanton."

"It's my job," a young man said.

"Either way, glad to have you on the team," Drake said.

"Is that man carrying a weapon?" a voice asked from the other side of the room.

Drake discovered the speaker was tall for a sarcian male, at just over five-seven. His skin was a pale blue, with patches of darker blue around his hands and face. He'd shaved off his hair, revealing the smooth skull beneath. He was thin, and wore an expensive suit that Drake was certain would be armour-lined. A pistol of unknown make sat on his hip.

"A bald sarcian," Drake whispered to Jaysa. "That's unusual."

"I do it to ensure people do not know my feelings, Mr Drake," the sarcian said. "And it's rude to talk about people to someone else. And you still appear to be wearing a weapon. Remove it."

Drake walked over. "I'm entitled to wear a weapon. I'm not a criminal here, I'm a member of the Wardens. If you have a problem with that, you're welcome to shove it up whatever cavity you find most appealing."

The sarcian didn't look impressed to be told he wasn't going to be getting his way.

Drake took a moment to glance over at the synth. It was just over six feet tall, with a silver and blue paint scheme over its entire body, which was broad shouldered but not as much as a battle synth. The synth's head was almost human in nature, although its eyes were on a railing that allowed them to swivel all around its skull. Its face was impassive, and apart from the blue eyes, showed no signs of being able to have any sort of expression. It wore a coil rifle across its back and an energy pistol on its hip.

"It's the latest model," the sarcian said proudly. "We're calling it an infiltration synth, capable of both recon and battle synth properties. And it will kill you if you step out of line."

"Do you and your synth have names?" Drake asked.

"You can call me councillor," he told Drake.

"No, I won't be doing that," Drake said in as nice of a tone as he could manage. "Your name, please."

The sarcian appeared ruffled for the second time in as many minutes. "My full name is Gusin Yann. Obviously, as a male of low birth, I do not get a third and fourth name as I have no clan and no rank within it."

"Gusin," Drake said. "Let's try to make this as pleasant as possible."

"If you behave, you will have no problems with me," Gusin snapped.

"Excellent," Drake said and flashed his warmest smile. "Does your synth have a name?"

Gusin looked back at the synth. "He is XE4485-N5D0."

"Xendo it is," Drake said and turned to the synth. "Do you have any objections with being named?"

The eyes on the synth moved to both focus on Drake. "No,

but you will still be executed should I be ordered to do so."

"Fair enough," Drake said. "Crew meet, Xendo. Xendo, meet the crew."

A few people said hello, but it was quickly obvious that Xendo had no intention of responding.

"How long before we reach Onnab?" Drake asked.

"Four or five days," Tuck said. "We've been in The Aperture for a while now."

"Okay, first things first," Drake said, not relishing the following conversation. "Yes, I am the son of Evan Varlus. Yes, I hid that detail from you all. Yes, I'm sorry about that. No, I'm not insane or planning on overthrowing the Union. If anyone here has any problems with that, let me know."

No one appeared to, although Tuck's expression turned hard.

"Problem, Tuck?" Drake asked.

"Your father killed a lot of Union soldiers," he said. "Good men and women."

"That he did," Drake admitted. "I'm not him. The sooner the Council recognises that, the better."

"The Council has reserved judgment," Gusin said.

"We both know that's not what's going on here," Drake said. "They can't punish my father, so they're going to let their petty stupidity dictate that they need to punish me instead. It's why I left Atharoth in the first place, it's possibly why I should have stayed away. Frankly, I don't care if you believe I'm about to try and conquer the Union. Believe what you like, I'm just here to do my job. To track down Sabas and bring him to justice."

No one else had anything to say.

Gusin stood. "I want it on record that I am completely against giving you the power that has been bestowed upon you and your team."

"That's great," Drake said. "I don't care. You're free to go pout somewhere until this is over. This is my operation, my ship and my team."

"Jaysa, Etamus and Yanton aren't under your team's remit," Gusin said.

"You three are now members of the Wardens until further notice," Sateri said. "You don't get a badge, try not to kill anyone, and we meet the first of every month to eat cookies. Welcome to the club."

Gusin's skin turned a darker shade of blue. "You'll be hearing from the Council about this."

Not until we've left The Aperture, Luca said to Drake, and from the sounds of chuckling from his team, several other people.

Gusin stormed from the mess room, Xendo following close behind.

"So, do you actually have a plan?" Sateri asked Drake.

"We get to Onnab and try to find out where Sabas is," Drake said.

"You really think he went there?" Rollos asked. "Could have been a fake destination."

"Could have been, but something strikes me as being off about that place," Drake said. "Expedited Systems were working with someone to get these experiments to work. That someone is Metan's boss. Metan has vanished, but I'm guessing Sabas paid a lot of money to Metan's employer for a reason. We should figure out what it is."

"It feels like someone is pulling strings," Jaysa said. "I don't like that one bit."

Drake looked over at Etamus, who'd been staring at him since the moment he'd entered the room, and tried to ignore it. "Okay then people, let's get moving."

Everyone left the mess room, leaving Drake alone with Etamus. "Is there a problem?" he asked.

"I'm not sure I trust you," she said slowly. "I can sense the darkness, the corruption inside of you. I have sensed it in others over the years. I sense it in you."

Drake took a deep breath. "I'm not sure how many times I need to say I'm not my father, but—"

"Nothing to do with that," Etamus interrupted. "You genuinely don't feel it? That's unusual."

Etamus got up and sat opposite Drake, rubbing the back of her neck with her hand. "You are an unknown entity, Drake. I don't like unknown things. They make my skin itch."

"I have no idea how to respond to that," Drake admitted.

"Don't get Jaysa hurt," Etamus said, voice quiet, tone hard. "Or anyone else for that matter, but especially her. She's done a lot for me and Yanton. She's lost a lot too. I'd rather not see her repaid with something unpleasant."

"I don't want her to get hurt. Her or anyone else," Drake said. "What did she do for you?"

"Helped me find a path," Etamus said. "I was an assassin. Work for hire. I did bad things to bad people, and she was on my list of names to remove. She convinced me to join her and help people instead of killing for money. Although, as it turned out, since we're Trackers, we still kill for money. We're just more selective about it, get paid less, and I don't have to feel guilty about those deaths I've caused. We hunt bad people."

Drake stayed silent for a few seconds. "Then we do the same thing."

"I can talk for myself," Jaysa said from the doorway.

"Sorry," Etamus said. She got to her feet and walked over to Jaysa. "I just wanted to make sure he understood."

"Yanton likes you," Jaysa said to Drake after patting Etamus on the shoulder and watching the dreic leave the mess room. "He appears to have made friends with Rollos, Luca and Dai'ix. I am not sure how much corruption they'll lead him down."

"A moderate amount," Drake said, happy people were on board he trusted. "They're good people."

"So, I see," Jaysa said. "It's nice to see you work with a variety of species. I met a human Wardens member who refused to work with anyone but humans."

Drake had met and disliked people who believed that way. "They were an idiot then. I work with the best. Not much else matters."

"I noticed you have another sarcian as a member of your team."

Drake wondered if there was going to be a problem. "Sateri has worked with me for years now. Is there an issue?"

"You ever been to Benoran?" Jaysa asked.

"Once," Drake said, wondering where this was going. "It wasn't exactly a fun trip. Everyone was very stand-offish and while not outright hostile, I got the impression that it could go that way at any moment. I'd brought a female high-ranking sarcian with me, and they spoke to her most of the time. I was tolerated, but wasn't well thought of."

"Yep, that's Benoran in a nutshell," Jaysa told him. "You were a non-sarcian male, so you'd have been allowed to speak and not obey everything the females asked of you. A lot of what happens there is kept secret, behind closed doors. Back when I was thirteen, we'd been living on Leturn for a few years, and there was a human neighbour by the name of Tarsell, or Trasel, something like that. Anyway, she was at least ten years older than me with a husband and young boy. The husband doted on the boy like he was the next King of Stars, but I started to notice things were strange with the mother. She wouldn't venture out very often, and when she did it was for short periods, and she'd wear extra concealing clothing. If you asked her something and the husband was around, she'd also look over at him before answering, to check it was okay that she spoke. That's sort of like how Benoran society is. Everything is behind closed doors, and while the people around them know something bad is happening, no one wants to get involved, no one wants to be the person who stands up and says, 'hey, this is wrong', because people are either scared of what will happen to them, or they think it's none of their concern. That if they bury their head in enough sand, they can pretend it isn't happening. Except on this occasion, the neighbour is an entire planet, and everyone around them, is *everyone*."

Drake picked up his glass of water and drank it, still unsure of exactly what Jaysa was getting at. He stood and stretched, aware of Sateri watching him from the entrance. "What happens when you meet more female sarcians who didn't leave?"

"Usually it's okay until they want our names," Jaysa said. "Then it can get a little dicey. We're not well liked by those who rule the home world. And Yanton is downright hated. My mother's family are still on Benoran, last I heard anyway. I'm pretty certain they'd like me dead. What I'm saying is, you can't pick the family you were born into. Like me, Sateri seems to have picked a family who matters to her. Where our levels sat back on Benoran doesn't matter, because out here we make our own family. The family we were born into isn't as important as the one you choose. I think you know that."

"You can be whoever you want," Drake said, understanding what Jaysa was getting at, and wishing she wasn't so keen to beat around the bush to get there. "You just need to be able to look yourself in the mirror every day and be happy with what you see. The day that no longer happens is the day you do something about it. I'm many things, but I'm not my father. Something you may have heard me say once or twice."

"Your father terrified the entire Union," Jaysa said. "People remember stuff like that."

"Yeah, I've noticed," Drake replied, feeling a little irritated at his father being brought up so much since his parentage was discovered.

"Must be frustrating, people considering you to be the son of a monster," Jaysa said.

Drake wasn't really sure how to respond to that. "I never saw him like that, but then I never delved into that side of it much, maybe I never wanted to know just how bad he was. We were sent away when I was young. The war had just started, or was just about to, I can't quite remember. I know he betrayed the Union, and then betrayed the Rebels. No one seems to know why."

"Maybe you should find out," Jaysa said.

Drake chuckled. "I'll add it to the ever-growing list of things to do."

CHAPTER TWENTY-SEVEN

Jaysa Benezta

After several days of boredom, they were finally leaving The Aperture. Jaysa headed toward the bridge, wanting to see Onnab for herself, and met up with Drake on the way.

"Good of you to show up," Rollos said to Drake when they arrived.

The bridge was considerably larger than that of Jaysa's old ship, which she was beginning to miss. It was large enough to seat everyone for one thing, although besides Drake and herself, only five people were actually present – Rollos, Tuck, Etamus, Sateri and Yanton, the latter of whom had managed to form bonds with the Wardens, which Jaysa had found both surprising and warming. She'd told herself she wasn't going to mingle with the Wardens because she didn't want to form attachments, but maybe she'd been wrong about that.

The colours of The Aperture suddenly vanished and Onnab materialised on the viewer beside her. "It's one of the strangest places I've ever been," she said.

"How so?" Drake asked.

"There's just something… *wrong* with it," she said, unable

to put a finger on exactly what the *wrong* was.

"Do you remember the darkness I saw in you?" Etamus asked Drake.

"Yes," he said, clearly unhappy about the memory.

"Well, that planet feels just like that," Etamus said. "And only that. As if pure darkness spread out over it. The creatures there are twisted, monstrous. They attack people on sight, something I've never seen before. Humans, sarcians, oreaf, it doesn't matter, it's almost as if the entire planet hates them."

"Sounds lovely," Rollos said. "I, for one, am looking forward to relaxing on the planet of death."

"I've scanned the ground and there's nothing resembling a crew of people down there. No human life signs, so no Sabas," Sateri said.

"So either he's not here, or he's hiding himself from scans," Drake said.

"Might as well go look," Jaysa told him. She'd remained quiet as the Wardens had talked amongst themselves, not entirely sure where she fit in. As a Tracker with her own ship, she wasn't used to being lower in the pecking order. It was unnerving. "You ready?"

Drake nodded. "Like you wouldn't believe." He turned to Sateri. "The ship is all yours. Anything shows up to cause trouble, please feel free to blast it out of the sky."

Sateri smiled, and there was an unnerving twinkle in her eyes. "With pleasure."

Drake and Jaysa walked through the ship to the cargo hold, where a shuttle waited alongside Gusin and Xendo. The councillor marched up and down beside the ship, appearing to be less than pleased, while the synth sat cleaning its rifle.

"You're finally here, it's about time," Gusin snapped. "I don't know if you're aware, but I actually don't want to spend my entire life watching you. I would rather we get this finished so that you can apprehend Sabas and his criminal companions, and I can go back home."

"You got someone to go home to?" Jaysa asked. "They're

probably welcoming the break."

Gusin's expression darkened. "I'd advise you to not mock my family."

Jaysa considered her biting reply and decided against it, instead walking up the ramp to the shuttle and finding a seat next to Bokk. Etamus took the pilot's controls and Gusin sat opposite Drake. Xendo was last on board, and he sat next to Etamus. Jaysa presumed so the synth could monitor Etamus' flying and ensure they weren't going anywhere that might lead the councillor into a trap. Or maybe the synth just really liked sitting up front. Synths were hard to get a handle on.

Etamus went through a pre-flight check, then the cargo doors opened, and the shuttle dropped into the void of darkness beyond. Jaysa always loved that first moment of leaving a ship's artificial gravity, the initial nothingness until the shuttle's thrusters were engaged. It was a peaceful moment, and she watched with a smile on her face as the planet got bigger and bigger.

"Why are you smiling?" Gusin asked.

Jaysa shrugged, she felt no need to share her thoughts with him, so she closed her eyes and concentrated on her breathing, slowing her heartrate, and keeping herself perfectly calm.

"Do you know how much my family suffered because of your father?" Gusin asked Drake, regaining Jaysa's attention. She noticed Drake also had his eyes closed, and hadn't bothered opening them to respond to the councillor.

"It's weird," Drake said without opening his eyes. "The rich always want to tell you how much they suffered. How it all affected them, as if somehow it should be more important that *they* went through something awful. As if the universe now owes them because of their mistreatment."

"Are you trying to say that their suffering was irrelevant compared to those who have nothing?" Gusin snapped.

"Not at all, it's just that they moan about it more." Drake opened his eyes. "Please, do go on, regale us all with tales of how my father personally made your life awful."

"My father was in favour of trade with the Rebellion," Gusin began. "He was in favour of peace; he'd donated his own time and money into ensuring that there would be peace between us. Once your father ended that dream, it broke him. Broke the family too, we lost millions of credits, prestige, power, and everything that went with them. I've had to claw my way back into the good graces of everyone in the Council."

"I'm sorry," Drake said softly. "If hating me helps, then I hope you find closure."

Gusin's face turned purple with rage. "Sorry? Sorry? Is that what you have to say? Fuck your sorry. Your father was a selfish, nasty, evil, prick of a human. He killed countless in your war, and hurt millions more. And you're sorry. Burn for your sorry."

"Not my war," Drake began. "I keep telling people this. I'm not him. I get it. I look like him a bit, and he's long dead, so all of that deep-seated anger can't be directed at him. However, what you all seem to keep glossing over is: I'm. Not. Him."

"I'm finding it strange," Bokk said, "that anyone would want to suggest that a man innocent of something should be forced to pay for the mistakes of his parent."

Jaysa ignored the continued argument and went back to looking out of the window. "We're going to land close to a mountain range. The landing site is next to a waterfall, and is about three hundred feet above a lake. Several minutes' walk outside of the town."

Gusin folded his arms and looked away as the shuttle slowed and Etamus engaged the landing protocol. The shuttle had touched down on the surface of the mountain, and moments later, the sealed locks for the door disengaged. Drake was the first to walk out, to witness the devastation. Jaysa walked around to the front of the shuttle and saw the destroyed forest.

"I don't know what Sabas' people were looking for, but they sure were thorough," Drake said. "Was it like this when you were here?"

Jaysa shook her head. "What the fuck happened?"

"It's even worse than when I was last here. They tore the land asunder," Etamus said, clearly saddened. "What was so important that they needed to rip this place apart to find it?"

"This has the hallmarks of an orbital bombardment," Drake said.

"You think we're safe here?" Gusin asked, clearly nervous at the ruination of Onnab.

While they were a few minutes away from the town, most of the buildings had been turned into rubble.

Jaysa looked over at the mountain pass. "That used to be a darolf spider nest. It's all burned away. There's nothing left, even the rock was destroyed. We'll be fine here. Expedient Systems were thorough in removing all traces that they were ever here."

"There were temporary buildings here," Etamus said, pointing off to the distance. "Scientific, I think, although they were completely cleaned out. They burned them before leaving."

"Someone came back here after you visited," Drake said to Etamus and Jaysa. "They made sure there was no evidence. Just in case."

Jaysa set off down the pathway, constantly keeping an eye out for any life, with the rest of the group just behind her. She relaxed for a moment as she reached the outskirts of the buildings Etamus had pointed out. The two-storey houses had, just as she'd seen, collapsed in on themselves as fire had eaten at them, leaving only the occasional wall and rubble remaining. Scorch marks littered everything, and there was still a stink of burning in the air. She continued down what used to be a street, stopping to climb over a wall and walk through the remains of a house.

It took the group close to forty minutes to navigate their way toward the town square. Having to climb over rubble made Jaysa lose her bearings once or twice, but eventually she skirted a small wall and found herself in a large open space. A massive chasm had been created in the centre, and Jaysa took cautious steps as she made her way toward it. She noticed a faint orange glow from within the chasm, and as she neared, saw catacombs far beneath her feet. Jaysa tread lightly, less she be introduced first-hand with the catacombs.

"Maybe there's more to this than just clearing out," Drake said. "I get the feeling something very strange happened here. Sabas and his people came here for a reason. It could be those catacombs."

"Why would they want them?" Jaysa asked.

"Why would anyone want to dig up what looks like old houses?" Bokk asked.

"Let's see if they found a safer way inside, and maybe we can figure it out," Etamus said.

"Let's split up and cover more ground," Drake suggested. "Comms are spotty, so we'll meet up in here in an hour."

Bokk and Drake headed off together, refusing to take Gusin or Xendo with them, forcing the synth and councillor to join Etamus and Jaysa. After an hour of searching and finding nothing, the group returned to the shuttle.

"Do you have to do that?" Jaysa asked Gusin as he whistled to himself.

"It calms me," the councillor told her, and resumed his musical distraction.

"Well, I don't feel very calm here," Jaysa told him.

"I care very little for what you feel, *Tracker*," Gusin sneered.

"You say *Tracker* like someone would say *whore*," Jaysa said, her eyes narrowing in anger. "And I really don't like the latter of those two words."

"You're not dissimilar," Gusin said with a dismissive wave of his hand. "You're both paid based on how well you perform."

"Actually, I get paid to perform well, not to just lay there and have some rich arsehole do what he likes," Jaysa snapped before she could stop herself.

Gusin shrugged. "I still see very little difference, except in a whore's case it's for the act of sex while yours is one of violence."

Jaysa tensed. "If you say that word to me again, I'm going to show you how we compare, and just how much violence my job entails."

The synth, Xendo, looked up from his weapon cleaning. "I will go discover how Drake is doing."

"Excuse me, *synth*," Gusin said. "You don't get to do anything without my order. You're not human, you're specifically created to not make your own decisions."

"Actually, I can make my own decisions without any problems," Xendo said. "Synths of my calibre are programmed with human thought patterns, allowing us to make judgment calls. Too many fleshy things have died because their master could not order them to help. If you'd wanted someone who stands there like a statue until you speak, you shouldn't have picked a top-of-the-range protection model. And you certainly shouldn't have picked a model still in the testing phase."

Gusin's mouth dropped open as Xendo walked off.

"Bet they haven't done that before," Jaysa said with a laugh.

"It's meant to do as it's told," Gusin said. "It's not meant to make decisions about its duties!"

Jaysa noticed the whine in the Gusin's voice and tried to ignore the need to punch him in the face.

"Maybe your brilliant personality unlocked their hidden disobedience chip," Etamus said with a laugh.

"It's not funny," Gusin snapped. "It could be defective."

"Or you could be," Jaysa said. "Stop pouting, we'll get Rosie and Rollos to check them out when we get back to the ship. Maybe the dust and crap down here got into their system. I'm sure they're fine."

There was an uncomfortable silence between them for several moments until Gusin said, "I'm sorry for my attitude toward you. It was unbecoming of me, and I apologize."

Jaysa shrugged. "I'll soon have ten-million reasons why I don't give two shits about your attitude, but thank you for the apology."

"The Union makes everyone's lives better," Gusin said suddenly. "They provide stability and the assurance that no matter what happens, no matter who our enemies are, we will stand united against them."

Jaysa stared at Gusin for several seconds. "Wow, you actually believe that shit, don't you?"

Gusin puffed out his chest with pride. "Of course. Without the Union there is only chaos. The old world proved that when the King of Stars ruled all, wars were commonplace. Sage were the same when they believed themselves to be gods."

"I don't ever remember them believing themselves to be gods," Jaysa said. "They were powerful, sure, and numerous, but not gods. Most of the old history I've read described them as statesmen, peace makers, and protectors of the people. Doesn't sound like murderous despot material to me."

Gusin waved away her comment. "Yes, well, that hardly matters now, enough of them wanted power that they brought about a war for it. Just like Drake's father."

There it is. Jaysa shook her head; Gusin's delusions of what the Sage were had nothing to do with her. She turned and walked back around to the opposite side of the shuttle, making her way to the edge of the mountain, and looking down at the lake far below. She wondered if even the life inside it were spared from the attack, but she had little interest in getting close enough to find out, and quickly stepped back from the edge.

"You hungry?" she called out, but received no reply. "Don't be a petulant idiot, you can't get upset every time someone pisses on your Union bonfire." She walked around the shuttle and paused when she saw the man stood behind Gusin with a blade to his throat. A second man held his blade against Etamus' throat, the dreic's expression was one of irritation rather than Gusin's total fear.

Jaysa's disrupter was out of its holster a second later, aimed at the strangers head. The man wore state-of-the-art combat armour, and small patches of burned armour sat around the man's chest – he'd been in a firefight recently.

"Camo-suits," Jaysa said. "They cost a pretty credit."

"That it does, Jaysa," the man behind Gusin said. "Now ease that shooter of yours onto the floor before I slit this little sarcian's throat." To emphasise his point, he pulled back on the knife, drawing a thin bead of blood on Gusin's neck.

She continued to aim at the head of the stranger. "You don't know me very well if you think I'm going to give up my weapon to save him."

Jaysa never even knew there was a shot coming until it smashed into her armour, tearing through it, and punching into her ribs with enough force to take her off her feet. She tried to remember how to breathe and frantically tore at her armour to stop the blood loss.

"Don't bother, it didn't break the skin," the stranger said without emotion. "Armour shredders. Not designed to pierce flesh. Hurt like the fires of The Aperture though, don't they?"

"Fuck..." Jaysa managed before pain overrode her need to tell him exactly what she thought of his words.

"Concentrate on your breathing," he said and removed the knife from Gusin's throat, smashing the pommel into the back of the councillor's head, knocking him unconscious.

The stranger walked over to Jaysa and knelt beside her. "Just breathe in and out in slow, steady motions, the pain will go after a few minutes. We've been waiting for you for a few days now. You're probably thinking you hadn't scanned us, that's because of the camo-sheet we have over the ship, masks us from anything but an isolated scan. It's usually enough."

"Who are you?" Jaysa managed in one quick breath, before going back to dealing with her pain.

"Name is Radner Puley," he said. "I wish we'd met under nicer circumstances."

"I hope you die," Jaysa said and tried to crawl back to her

knees.

Radner placed the tip of the blade against her neck. "Don't. I have no quarrel with you, but my employer does, and I don't want to hurt you more than I've already had to." He turned back to Etamus, who was prone on the ground, the man behind her aiming a coil rifle at the back of her head. "I can have him kill your friend if you like."

"Who do you work for?" Jaysa managed while Radner placed a pair of metal-fibre cuffs on her wrists.

"Don't struggle. There's no getting them off without the key, and I'm not likely to give that to you," Radner told her. "As for your question, I want what everyone wants – to get rich and die surrounded by a bevy of beautiful souls. Whether I get that or not is very much dependent on whether I perform to my boss's satisfaction, so why don't you just lie there and behave for a few minutes before he turns up. I'd rather not have our sniper friend put another round farther up your torso. Let's not bruise that skin any more than it already is."

Radner gathered her disruptor from the ground. "Lovely weapon," he said. "Odd to see a disruptor with so many settings, normally it's fire and your opponent drops to the ground." He flicked the gun to level five and fired a shot at a nearby rock, basting through it. "Wow, you've had it modified so that you can fire a lethal round should you want to." For the first time, there was emotion in Radner's voice. "That's pretty impressive. Pretty unpleasant too when you think about it. Must hurt a lot to be hit with a killing round."

"Shoot yourself and find out," Jaysa managed. It hurt to speak, but she didn't want Radner to know that.

Radner chuckled. "Maybe some other time. I read your file, you know, your military one. You were quite the little warrior. Sorry, that sounds patronising when I really didn't mean it to be, I was genuinely impressed."

"Excellent, my life now has meaning," Jaysa said and spat on the ground.

"Oh, come on, I know you're cuffed and hurt, but you can

still be nice," Radner said, "You know, I really thought you were going to shoot that councillor."

Jaysa took a deep breath and let it out slowly, trying to calm herself. "Like I said, you don't know me at all."

"But I do, don't I, Jaysa," a man's voice said from somewhere behind her.

She was facing away from the path but knew exactly who it was, and a shiver went up her spine.

"Ah, you know who I am?" he asked and kicked her onto her back as Radner passed him Jaysa's disruptor.

Jaysa stared up into the face of Sabas Gossard as he studied her weapon. "Yeah, I've read all about you. Never met though. I'd have remembered that punchable face. And just so you know, I'm going to get that back."

Sabas placed his large, booted foot on her chest and pushed down, aiming her own disruptor at her head.

Jaysa couldn't breathe, and panic set in for a split second until he removed his weight, and stepped away.

"I'm going to kill you slowly over the span of the next few hours. I'm going to record your screams so I can listen to them when I get nostalgic." Sabas pulled Jaysa to her feet and threw her against the shuttle. He pulled his arm back to punch her.

"Maybe beating her senseless right now is a bad idea," Etamus said.

Radner looked back at the dreic. "I would remain silent if I were you. Doing otherwise would only make it worse for your friend."

Sabas paused and removed as one of his thugs walked over. "Boss, we found the other one?"

Other one? Oh shit, Drake.

"You're going to regret ever coming back here," Sabas said. "Bring Drake here, he's worth a lot more alive than this one. And he's caused me a lot more trouble than this one too." He turned to Jaysa and bared his teeth in a snarl. "I'm going to enjoy this, and you're going to suffer for ever getting in my way."

Jaysa spat in his face. For a second, she thought she was a dead woman, and then Sabas laughed. "Oh, I'm going to enjoy breaking you. Enjoy it a great deal."

CHAPTER TWENTY-EIGHT

Felix Drake

Drake had no idea how long he'd walked through the ruin of the town of Onnab, Bokk at his side. Eventually they both sat beside a group of large rocks edging another huge chasm that showed part of the catacombs underneath the town.

"The synth has decided to join us," Bokk said, sounding less than happy about the situation.

Drake turned to find Xendo walking toward them.

"I did not mean to disturb you," Xendo said, raising his hands to show he meant no threat, an odd action for a synth to perform.

Drake got to his feet and brushed his knees clean. "That's okay, I probably needed to head back anyway."

Xendo didn't stop walking until he reached Drake and then looked down at the ground. "A lot of people died there?"

Drake nodded.

"I am sorry," Xendo said. "Which disturbs me."

"You're disturbed because you're sorry people died?" Drake asked.

"Yes," Xendo said softly. "I should not be. I was designed to have no emotional reverence to the deaths of anything fleshy and mortal. I should not care, it's in my programming. So why do I?"

Drake shrugged. "Is your programming faulty?"

"I'm a prototype, there are only four more like me. We were all designed to be completely reliant on human orders, without being able to empathise with them in any way." Xendo paused. "I can. Why can I? My programming appears correct. I ran a diagnostic and there's nothing wrong with it nor my memory. Yet, I am developing a personality, one which was rude to Gusin."

Drake smiled. "I think that's a normal way to behave towards him."

"Not for me," Xendo explained, his tone no longer neutral. "I should be respectful, but he annoyed me. I shouldn't even know what being annoyed feels like, I should have no concept of it, but I do."

"Why are you telling me this?" Drake asked.

"I do not know," Xendo said and stared at Drake for a second. "I have no knowledge of why I should care, but for some reason my circuits are drawn to speak to you. Maybe because I am to execute you should my mission need it. Maybe I want to know more about you because of that. Something is wrong."

"He sounds…" Drake whispered.

"Scared," Bokk replied.

"I know," Xendo said, having heard them speak. "I am exactly three weeks, two days, four hours and thirty… four minutes old. This is the first time I've experienced anything like it."

"Are you designed differently from other synths? Drake asked. "Maybe something has shorted out."

"Maybe I can have a look when I get back to the ship," Bokk said. "That way you don't have to trust yourself to anyone but another synth."

Xendo turned to Bokk. "Are you able to do it?" There

was something in the tone of the of the synth that sounded disturbingly like... hope.

"Yes, I can," Bokk assured the synth. "I'm working with Drake, do you not consider me to be the bad guy? Would you want me to do it?"

"I do not know. A lot is confusing to me. Please look now." Xendo knelt on the ground and placed a finger to what would have been his temple. The fingertip opened and a thin needle extended and entered a tiny slot. A second later, the top of Xendo's head opened, exposing the various parts of the synth that made up his core personality and memory.

Drake glanced inside. The stuff in Xendo's head was so far removed from what he was used to seeing in the older model synths, that he supposed Xendo was technically a separate species.

He was about to tell Xendo to close his head when he noticed that the memory and personality relays had fused together. They'd been placed next to one another, a design that, as it turned out, was a pretty bad flaw. It could account for why Xendo's personality was developing... quirks. Drake didn't understand why anyone would do that. Most synths had those two parts completely separate to ensure that a personality or memory could be erased so as to re-build should the need arise. It also kept any problems from jumping between the two main aspects of the synth. A personality could be rebuilt from the memory, but if they fused and something happened then they stayed like that or you started from scratch.

Bokk closed the top of Xendo's head, which clicked as both parts locked together.

Xendo stood. "Did you see the problem?"

"Maybe," Bokk said. "I think Luca or Rosie need to take a look. Both know more about that sort of stuff than I do. I know I'm a synth, but my technology is several degrees older than yours."

"Then I shall have them perform an analysis when we return." Xendo walked to the edge of the chasm and looked down into it. "We should leave."

Drake turned as the shot hit Xendo in the head, sending him tumbling into the darkness of the chasm. Drake reacted as quickly as possible but not quickly enough to dodge the second shot that smashed into his chest, tearing through the armour but not puncturing the skin. *Armour shredders.* Pain tore through his body, and he concentrated on the place in his mind that could take him to where the pain was a distant ache. He knew that no matter where his mind went, he couldn't calm the outrage at having been attacked where so many had died.

"Bokk, you need to run," Drake shouted. "Get away from here. You're going to be our only hope of escape."

The synth didn't need to be told twice, and leapt into the chasm, vanishing from view as a second shot rang out; one that would have smashed into their skull.

The next thing Drake knew, five men and three women sauntered out of the ruined town, weapons drawn, all pointed at him. A shot hit Drake in the chest, and a bolt of electricity coursed through his body, sending him into spasms. Drake rolled to his side and tried to speak, but nothing came out except guttural grunts. One of the men shot him again, knocking him onto his back once more. There was little Drake could do as his wrists were shackled, and he was dragged away without comment.

He remained conscious for the entire trip where he was dropped at Jaysa's feet.

"Nice reunion," she said.

Drake glanced up and gave a half-hearted smile, noticing the cut just above her eye. The bleeding had stopped, but not before it had run down the side of her face.

"Which one did that?" he asked.

"The one who doesn't realise he's dead yet," she told him and shifted her legs so that Drake could roll onto his knees and sit beside her.

Drake nodded toward Etamus. "You okay?"

"Fine," she snapped. "I'm sorry, but your close presence on

this planet makes me uncomfortable."

Drake shared a look with Jaysa, who just shrugged.

It had gotten dark since he'd been grabbed, and a cold wind was setting in. He wondered how long they were going to be made to sit outside while their captors were all warm and comfortable in the dozen tents that littered the mountainside. A large shuttle sat farther away, accompanied by three stalkers; single-seat fighters used for surface- or low-orbit combat. They were fast and deadly. Much more manoeuvrable than the shock-wing, but with barely half the firepower.

"How are you feeling?" Jaysa asked.

"Great, thanks," Drake said. "I've been having a fun time with my new friends. They took my weapons."

"Any chance you can use your aether and get us out of here?" Jaysa asked, although she didn't sound hopeful.

Drake raised his foot, his trouser leg pulling back to reveal the bracelet around his ankle. "Can't. See that little thing?" The silver device was in such a position as to be impossible to remove without taking off his foot. "It limits my aether. No idea how it works, the technology is ancient, no one has ever been able to figure it out. It's what they keep trying to incorporate into bracers, but they never quite work."

"It looks new," Etamus said.

"They don't rust or break or anything, and there are loads of the little bastard things all over the universe," Drake said with barely suppressed irritation. "Best guess is they were designed during the Sage Wars. They don't quite stop the use of aether, but I probably have one use and that's it. I'd rather save it for a special occasion, seeing how I have no idea just how much aether I'll be able to use."

"Can I just break it off?" Jaysa asked.

"Not unless you want me to receive a massive dose of poison that will kill me in seconds," Drake hid the bracelet again. "So, how's your day been?"

"Not exactly brilliant," Jaysa said. "Been told I'm going to die a lot, which is beginning to lose its power."

"You know, I've been threatened so much in my life, it's sort of lost all meaning," Drake said and looked around at the group keeping them prisoner. "I guess we're not here for some sort of party... at least not the kind I like to be invited to."

Drake and Jaysa shut up as a man with a shadow rifle strapped to his back, brought Gusin back to them. He wore green and brown camo gear and a black half-mask, that sat over his eyes, leaving his nose and mouth uncovered. Shadow rifles were essentially coil rifles with an extra-long barrel, used primarily for long distance shooting. They used modified rounds designed for longer flight, with some truly terrifying power once they hit whatever they were aiming at. He shoved Gusin to the ground and then knelt in front of Drake. He smelled of grease and sweat, his smile just a little bit off. "I just wanna say, was a pleasure to shoot you. Both of you. Real pleasure."

Drake wasn't really sure how to sure how to respond. Headbutting was his first choice, but that would probably not end well.

"I mean," the sniper continued. "I got to shoot a woman who the boss is extremely angry at, and the famous Felix Drake. Do you know who this is?"

"Yes," Jaysa said. "Son of a traitor, etcetera, etcetera. We've met."

"Do you know what his father did before he decided to fight the Union and Rebels at the same time?" the man asked.

"Crochet?" Drake replied.

The man's smile faltered. "Murdered a lot. A whole lot. Wiped out towns, military posts, anyone who got in his way. Your dad was part of the Sworn. He betrayed them."

"Who the hell are you?" Drake asked, voice hard, leaving no doubt as to what would happen if he wasn't cuffed.

"Just a soldier who saw him strike down his sworn brother," the sniper said. "I was on Yenrithal, I know what happened. As I can't kill your father, it was an utter pleasure to put a round in your chest. It might not have killed you, but it was a lot of fun nonetheless." The sniper grabbed Drake's hair and bent his head back. "Your father murdered my general; he murdered the man a lot of people would follow through The Aperture with nothing but our weapons. And now I'm going to make sure you're delivered to our lord so he can tear you inside out." He released Drake and stood up, removing his mask. It was the same man who'd kidnapped Ramin from the hospital. The one who had lost an eye to Drake.

He placed a finger to his eye and pulled it out. "I had to have a replacement. It's cybernetic." The man popped his eye back into its socket.

"Hey, will you look at that," Drake said. "I get another chance to kill you. Looks like it's my lucky day after all."

The assassin smiled. "I'm going to pay you back for the eye."

Drake winked. "Good luck with that." He watched the sniper walk away without uttering a word. "We need to get out of here."

"Good plan, but how?" Gusin asked. "I tried to reason with them, to tell them that if they let me go, they would be handsomely paid by the Union Council. They laughed."

Jaysa stared. "You tried to negotiate your own release?"

"Of course," Gusin replied, as if anything else wasn't even worthy of thought. "You're a Tracker, and he's a Warden. Neither of you are important in the scheme of things."

"Remind me to beat the shit out of your cowardly ass when we get back to the ship," Jaysa said.

"You have a friend," Drake told Jaysa when he saw a Radner walking toward them.

"He's on my list of people to kill too," she told him. "I'm going to be busy for a long time."

Radner knelt in front of Jaysa.

"Who told you we'd be here?" she asked him.

"Oh, you don't know?" Radner smiled. "Looks like there are more people on Atharoth who want you dead than you'd expected. Maybe Ren did it."

Drake didn't believe it. "She's always been a little full of herself, and has done some shady things over the years, but selling us out to Sabas isn't one of them."

Radner laughed. "No, she didn't sell you out to Sabas."

"Come on, you may as well tell us if we're all going to die," Drake said. "I want to know who to be mad at."

"Alastia Sark," Radner said.

Drake shrugged. "Who the fuck is that?"

"She got Metan to make sure he left a trail to here," Radner said. "She's who we'll be handing you over to. She's Sabas' boss. I was the one who put her in touch with Sabas to start doing those Genesis experiments. It was her idea to use them on Stradiasus. She was *really* excited when it turned out that OMC would be there. She hired Metan to remove all of you from the gene pool so that no one could point fingers his way, and thus trace him to her."

"She tried to kill Ren and Takumi," Jaysa said.

Radner nodded. "They were meant to kill you all, but then you actually managed to escape. She was pretty angry about Kimi not being there when Helice, Septimus, and Trinas were killed. And she was *really* angry when Hideo's father-in-law changed the target of the synth to kill Drake too."

"Why are you telling us this?" Jaysa asked.

"Because I want you all to understand just how unbelievably screwed you all are," Radner said. "Alastia has plans, and none of you are in them. And, if I'm completely honest, the looks on your faces are priceless."

Sabas walked over, looked down at Drake, radiating hatred, and kicked him in the chest. Drake coughed and spluttered as he hit the ground, but waited until Sabas and Radner had walked far enough away before sitting himself back up.

"They will not kill me. They would be foolish to." Gusin sounded so sure of himself, that for the briefest of heartbeats, Drake actually felt sorry for the man's ignorance of the situation.

Drake shook his head. "They will hand you over to this Alastia, whoever she is, who'll pay much better than the Union ever would. Unless we can get out of here, I'd prepare your life for a short time of torture before an agonizing death."

"They wouldn't dare," Gusin snapped, looking between Drake and Jaysa. "Would they?"

"Union councillor would be quite the catch," Drake said. He looked over at Jaysa. "Where's Etamus?"

"I don't know," Jaysa said slowly, as if noticing her friend was gone for the first time.

"We need to get away," Drake said.

"Good job I have the key then, isn't it?" Etamus whispered from behind a nearby boulder. She tossed the key toward Drake, who moved slightly to scoop it up before anyone saw.

"We were just talking about you," Jaysa said.

"I heard," Etamus said softly. "Sorry it took so long."

"You brought a key, all is forgiven." Drake unlocked his shackles, dropping them to the ground. He unlocked Jaysa's next, keeping an eye out for anyone looking their way.

"Now me," Gusin demanded.

"You were going to negotiate yourself off this planet," Jaysa said. "You can sit here and wait to be given to whoever, for all I care."

"You take me with you or Drake dies," he snapped. "Xendo will kill him."

Drake sighed. "It would be easier to not add to the number of people trying to kill me."

"Can we chat later?" Etamus asked. "Preferably after we escape."

"Fine," Drake said. "We're not far from the cliff, we're going to have to scale down it."

"How far down?" Gusin asked.

"Few hundred feet."

"There has to be another way," Gusin complained, his complexion now pale.

"There's nothing between us and the forest but several

hundred feet of ruined, open space, and it doesn't matter because we'll get about ten feet to it before they spot us," Drake explained. "Running in any direction is going to just result in our deaths, I don't fancy our odds."

The four of them made their way to the edge of the cliff and looked down at lake far below. In the darkness, the distance was distorted; it didn't look quite as bad as it might have otherwise.

Drake knelt and found his footing. "Follow me, exactly," he said, wishing he had climbing gear. "If you slip, you die, so don't slip."

"Great pep talk," Jaysa said.

"Let's go, slow and steady," Drake said and began his descent.

The climb was relatively straightforward, the rock was solid and the handholds plentiful. Thankfully, the cliff face also had a slight angle to it, and was much wider at the bottom than the top. Drake was grateful there were no difficult points where he had to swing from one spot to another, or something equally unpleasant in the dark.

They were about halfway down when the first shot came from high above them, destroying parts of the cliff as the energy rifles slammed into the rock. Drake managed to move across as a round from a coil rifle slammed into the rock beside him, showering him with tiny, razor-sharp pieces of rock.

"We need to jump," Drake shouted.

"We're too high," Etamus said as she lost a hand hold when a second coil round went through the rock nearby.

Gusin slipped and fell, clawing at the rock face, but found nothing but air until he collided with Drake, who grabbed his arm and dragged him back to the rock. "We're all going to jump, I'm going to get us to safety, but you have to trust me. You all need to hold onto me like there's no tomorrow." Because if they didn't, there wouldn't be.

Gusin, as the smallest and lightest, climbed awkwardly onto Drake's back, holding on as tightly as possible.

As the closest to Drake, Etamus grabbed hold of his arm. "I hope you know what you're doing."

Drake reached out a hand, bringing it back when another coil round slammed into the rock an inch next to it. Jaysa launched herself at Drake, who managed to catch her as he kicked off the rock face.

The four held on to one another as they plummeted toward the shark-infested lake beneath them. Drake knew that if it were light, they'd see the fins, the shadows of the massive creatures that swam underwater. Thankfully, if his plan failed, they'd probably all be dead before they got eaten. It wasn't exactly a comfort.

Gusin screamed in Drake's ear the entire way down, as he tried to concentrate, tried to make his aether do what he wanted. Something that was difficult with that damned anklet restricting his power.

They were fifty feet above the water when Drake's eyes burned purple. Light surrounded the four of them and in an instant, they went from being a solid mass to vanishing from view.

The teleportation portal opened a hundred feet up the bank, near the ruined forest that Drake had walked through with a gun aimed at him, and what felt like a lifetime ago. They crashed onto the soft sand and cartwheeled until they separated, each of them thrown into the forest where they finally stopped.

Drake had impacted with the remains of a large tree, tearing through it as if it were paper, and slamming into the ground behind it. His body burned with pain, and he cried out as he tried to figure out what damage he'd managed to do to himself. Nothing was broken, which was a good start, although he was bleeding badly from a cut across his forearm. He clamped his hand on it, and ignored the pain as he got to his feet. His head spun, so he quickly dropped back to his knees.

"Are you okay?" a voice asked, which Drake quickly discovered was Gusin. He walked with a severe limp, and had a cut across his forehead, but otherwise appeared okay.

Drake nodded slightly. "A lot of power to use while I have that anklet on. A lot of power that anklet really doesn't want me to use. I was slowly building it up when we started to scale down the cliff, just in case. Hadn't contemplated using it while falling from the cliff through. I'll be okay in a few minutes."

"We might not have that," Etamus said as she walked into the clearing. "Can you hear them?"

Drake forced his brain to focus until he heard the yells of those hunting them. "We need to find shelter."

"Ummm... any chance one of you can help with this?" Jaysa asked and raised her top slightly to show the piece of tree protruding from her right side. "Hurts like hell."

Etamus studied the branch. "It's not far in, but if I pull it out it's going to bleed. Can you move?"

"If I have to," Jaysa said.

Drake raised a finger to let them know to give him a second, before he forced himself back to his feet. His head was a little better, he was less dizzy, less fuzzy. "We need to leave. We'll get it out when we're somewhere a little safer."

"Got anywhere in mind?" Jaysa asked.

Etamus crouched, her hands buried in the top of the soil. "That way," she said, and pointed off in the distance. "It's not too far a walk, you think you can make it?"

"I'll be fine," Jaysa assured her.

"I'll be okay too, thanks for asking," Gusin said, sounding annoyed.

Drake ignored him.

"How'd you manage to stop us slamming into the ground at the same speed as we were falling?" Jaysa asked, slinging an arm around Drake's shoulder to help take her weight.

"I can control the velocity we exit the teleport," Drake said once they began walking. "This thing they put on my leg didn't give me the control or power I needed to be able to do a good job. Hence, the fact we still slammed into the ground, just slightly less than hard enough to kill us all outright."

They walked in silence for a few minutes, the sounds of the hunt somewhere behind them filling the night sky. Eventually, they reached a series of boulders that sat in front of a massive cliff face.

"We're here," Etamus said.

"I don't think I can climb that," Jaysa told her.

"I know I can't," Gusin agreed.

"Don't have to," Etamus told them both and walked around to the side of the boulder.

The group quickly followed and squeezed behind the boulder to find themselves in a much larger area than they'd expected. Etamus stood in front of a door built into the cliff face; the boulder used to block it from the view of anyone except those had taken the effort to look behind it.

"What is it?" Gusin asked.

"It's the entrance to some old ruins," Etamus told them.

"Can you get it open?" Drake asked.

"Not sure." She placed her shoulder against the door and pushed slightly.

The door opened, and all four of them to scrambled inside before Drake and Etamus pushed it closed again. Dozens of lights around the ground came to life, illuminating the room inside, showcasing the dozens of ornate carvings on the stone.

"How old is this place?" Jaysa asked.

"Thousands of years," Etamus replied. "At least."

The group moved through the room, the lights igniting with every step, showing the way forward.

"So, what are we meant to do now?" Gusin asked.

"First, we need to make sure Jaysa is okay," Etamus said.

"Then we need to find Xendo and Bokk," Drake added.

"We'll get you a new synth," Gusin said.

Drake was at Gusin in a second, grabbing the sarcian around the throat and slamming him into the wall behind him. "Bokk is my friend. They are a synth, but they're more courageous than you could ever possibly comprehend. And if you ever speak about Bokk in such a dismissive way again, I will be happy to die knowing I've crushed the life out of you. Do you understand?"

Gusin nodded repeatedly and Drake released him.

Drake turned back to Jaysa and Etamus. "Once we've done that, we're going to find Sabas."

"And kill him," Jaysa finished, her tone making it clear it wasn't up for discussion.

CHAPTER TWENTY-NINE

Bokk

The fall through the chasm to find Xendo was one of the stupider things Bokk had decided to do. At first, they figured they'd land, find the other synth, and then go help Drake and his people from whoever had decided to attack them, but that plan was quickly discarded when they realized it wasn't going to be that easy.

Bokk hit the ground hard, their sensors automatically registering the impact and pushing out the force to all parts of their body in an effort to keep their legs in one piece. Apart from a few systems going offline, Bokk found they were still able to function at seventy-percent capacity. Well, at least it was above acceptable perimeters for maintaining a useful function.

They glanced up at the chasm-lip high above, and wondered how they were going to get back out. Scanning the surrounding area, they discovered they were in the middle of some old ruins. It took a few seconds to realise that they stood in what used to be a street. The stone walls around them used to be part of a building... a *really* old building. They needed to find Xendo.

They scanned again, looking for signs of synth life, until they found a faint sign close by. They climbed up the stone wall and into the gap above the building, pulling themselves along before the roof gave way and they crashed through what used to be the ceiling, landing with a thud that made the floor shake.

Bokk got back to their feet and discovered their function had dropped to under seventy percent. They were going to need to see Rosie or Luca when everything was over.

It didn't take them long to find Xendo. The synth was on a mound of soft earth, which Bokk deduced they must have landed on after crashing through the roof. Bokk glanced up and found a second hole in the roof above, and a quick calculation told them that Xendo had bounced off one of the jagged rocks on the way down, sending him away from where Bokk had landed.

They crouched beside Xendo and tried to perform a scan, but there were no signs that the synth was even capable of booting-up let alone being able to do anything close to operational. Bokk traced their finger around the bullet hole in what would have been the synth's head. The armour shredder had probably jumbled up a bunch of Xendo's primary processors.

Bokk knew that if they opened Xendo's head and their internal components had been torn to pieces, it would mean the end for being able to put Xendo back together. They looked around the building, trying to find something they could use to make a stretcher. They could carry Xendo without one, but as they had no weapons, doing so would mean they would be at a considerable disadvantage should those who shot the synth decided to find them and finish the job.

In the end, the decision was made for them as the sound of voices echoed throughout the catacombs. Bokk slowly moved toward the wall facing the street outside and tried to figure out the direction. They were unable to perform a full scan of the area outside, and the second they tried to force it through, error messages flashed up all over their body. Apparently, they were more damaged than the sixty-seven-percent function suggested.

Sixty-four. Sixty-two.

Bokk thought of every curse word they'd ever heard and mentally went through them. Something inside them was leaking power, and taking with it their ability to function. They ran a self-diagnostic, shutting down anything non-essential, which stopped the fall in numbers at fifty-seven percent. It would have to do.

They went back to Xendo, and covered the synth in pieces of dirt and stone, hoping that at the very least, it would make it difficult for anyone to see them from the outside. Once Bokk was sure Xendo was safe, they crept back toward the front wall just as two men walked past. Both carried blast-guns, and wore some kind of combat armour.

"Why do we have to look for this synth?" one of the two men asked.

"Because we were told to," his friend said.

"It's just a synth," the first one said with impatience.

"The boss thinks the synth was sent to The Spire to plant the bomb that exploded," Man Two said. "So, we find the synth and we disable him so that Sabas can tear it apart with his bare hands."

Man One whistled, the sound echoing around the catacombs. "You know what, I always thought Ramin was too soft, but Sabas... he's got a head full of hate for these people."

Bokk heard a noise like someone kicking a rock.

"He wants that Warden dead, but he's not allowed to," Man Two said. "Has to hand him over to that Metan guy. He gives me the creeps."

Bokk climbed up onto the wall, remaining silent and hidden in the darkness. They spotted the two armed men, checked there were no others in the vicinity, and then lowed themself onto the street, keeping the men in their vision as they darted around another wall and into a second building.

"What about the other synth?" Man One asked.

"The one the sniper hit?" Man Two replied.

"That sniper is really creepy," Man One said in a whisper, as though he was concerned the sniper might hear him. "Don't know where the boss found him, but I wish they'd left him there."

"He works for Metan," Man Two said. "That's all you need to know about him."

Bokk had been making their way through the building until they were right behind the would-be attackers. They climbed out of the ruins and moved behind the men, grabbing the first around the neck and crushing his throat before punching the second in the chest.

The first man dropped to his knees as the second rolled to his feet—his armour having absorbed the blow—and levelled the blast-gun at Bokk, who picked up the dying thug and used him as a shield against the blast. Bokk threw the now dead thug at his partner, sprinting toward the one they'd punched to try and stop him before they had another shot.

The thug moved aside quickly and shot through his dead friend's legs as his body tumbled through the air, tearing both limbs to ribbons. Alarms screamed through Bokk's software as the blast-gun shot him in the upper torso, destroying part of his shoulder and left arm. Bokk put the messages aside, and tackled the thug to the ground, smashing his forearm into the side of his head.

Bokk yanked the blast-gun free, aiming it at the thug's head, but it was coded to the prone man's handprint, and refused to work. They placed one foot on the man's neck and pushed down until they heard a crunch.

They stepped away, tossing the blast-gun to the side, and ran a quick diagnostic of their internal systems. Forty-six percent functional. Their left arm was badly damaged, and would be utterly useless in whatever battles lay ahead.

Voices nearby suggested more thugs were coming their way, so Bokk ran deeper into the maze of streets and partially-destroyed buildings. They stopped after arriving at a large building, the front of which had long since collapsed, revealing dozens of destroyed rooms inside.

Part of the brick exploded from a rifle-shot, forcing Bokk's hand, and they ran into the ruins, trying to find a place where they could stage an ambush and give themselves some sort of hope for survival.

They reached a corridor and heard shouts from behind them. Those tracking Bokk would soon catch up, and they were running out of options. They turned a corner and noticed a glow of light behind a nearby door.

Inside, Bokk discovered several terminals lit up along one wall in what was otherwise a room filled with nothing but more dirt and dust. They walked toward the terminal and placed their hand to the screen, which flickered.

"And you are?" a voice beside Bokk asked.

Bokk felt no living thing on his sensors, but they turned to look at the apparition hovering beside him. "I am Bokk. I am a synth. There are people trying to destroy me, and frankly, I'd rather that didn't happen. Are you here to hurt or help me?"

"Does it have to just be those two options?" The image stopped flickering and a young human female appeared. She wore a black tunic, long grey skirt, and her feet were bare. Her hair was shoulder length and dark, and she had a deep-green tattoo on her right cheek. "My name is Quinon. I was a Sage here many thousands of years ago."

Bokk looked around the room. "You made the terminals light up?"

Quinon nodded. "I wished to speak to you. You are injured, and you killed several humans. We had synths in our time, but they were not as... free with their behaviour as you appear to be. The terminals can respond to the echo of the power we once wielded. The terminal won't be sustained for long, but it was enough to make sure that you noticed it."

Bokk wondered how much time he had. "If you don't help me, this particular synth isn't going to be free for much longer."

"What would you have us do?" Quinon asked in a light, airy tone.

"I don't know," Bokk said, wishing he was able to sound agitated. "I've never conversed with the spirit world before."

One of Sabas' men rushed into the room, firing wildly. Bokk avoided the blast, diving to the side and toward the man, grabbing him around the top of his armoured vest and throwing him into the far wall. He landed with a jolt, and Bokk stalked toward the prone man, ready to finish what they'd started.

Quinon floated in front of Bokk, looking down at the injured man. She flickered once, before vanishing from view.

"This is a strange experience," Quinon's voice said from the man's mouth as his body sat up. "I believe I can help you, Bokk." The man stood and retrieved his energy rifle. "It's been a while since I've used one. You stay here, and I'll go deal with your problem."

"How do you know I'm the good guy here?" Bokk asked, wishing his programming would just let him not ask the questions he might not want answers to.

"I wasn't going to do anything until I saw this man's life ebb away," Quinon said. "It's a new talent for me, I didn't realize it could be done. Interesting. Anyway, he's fully aware of the kinds of crimes those he works with have participated in. This will not be a problem."

Quinon left the room and soon after the sounds of battle were all that could be heard. Bokk ran another diagnostic. They'd dropped to twenty-eight percent, and non-essential parts would begin shutting down soon. They searched behind the terminal and removed one of the coils that plugged into their back. It was out-dated technology, and might blow out most of the sensors in their body, but it was better than nothing. Besides, they just had to wait for Quinon to return and then they could tell her their plan and she could hopefully help enough to make sure they had continued power, or at least go find Drake. If she could talk to Bokk, there was no reason she couldn't talk to anyone else. Maybe she could keep one of the thugs outside and possess them like she had the meat sack she currently wore, using them as a sort of marionette.

A multitude of screams and shouts reached Bokk's sensors, but it didn't take long for them to whittle down to only a few, which sounded much farther away. After several seconds of silence, Bokk thought Quinon had been victorious. That thought was quashed when Radner Puley walked through the entrance to the room, an energy pistol in his hand, which was aimed at Bokk's head.

"I know you," Radner snapped. His face was coated in dirt and blood, and Bokk wasn't convinced the later only belonged to him. "You were there when The Spire exploded."

"Yes, I was," Bokk said. "It was you, wasn't it?"

Radnar looked almost impressed. "How'd you figure that out?"

"You were there," Bokk said. "You had opportunity, and clearly the motive."

Radner smiled. "I was made an offer. Join Sabas or die with Ramin. Easy decision to make."

"And you're okay with Sabas' methods?" Bokk said, as alarms went off inside his body. He would start shutting down soon. "Your men spoke about his plans. Who's bankrolling him?"

"Everyone with Jaysa dies," Radner said. "So long as that Drake is handed over to Metan, whatever happens to the others doesn't matter."

"You're being used," Bokk said. "The person who arranged this will kill you all too. They can't have anyone out there knowing they exist."

Radner nodded. "I know. I don't want to be here. I don't want to hunt people in this place. I never wanted to hurt anyone, I'm a lawyer not an assassin."

"Then don't," Bokk said. "Help me escape. Help all of us get off this planet. Help us bring Sabas, Metan, and whoever he's working for to justice."

"Sabas is a monster, did you know that?" Radner didn't give Bokk time to reply. "He murdered, and tortured, and hurt people for fun. He's working for Alastia, and she doesn't care one bit about this. She cares about results. And she has people in her pocket all over Union space."

"We can stop this," Bokk assured him. "We can make sure no one else has to die."

Radner shook his head. "I have to do what Sabas wants. I can't go against Alastia and Metan. I can't have them hand me over to Sabas to dispose of me as he sees fit."

Radner fired twice.

Bokk wasn't fast enough to evade both shots, and the second hit their chest. Alarms signalled in their internal sensors, and they ignored them, grabbing hold of Radner's arm before they could fire for a third time. Bokk snapped the limb at the elbow and pushed him back toward the entrance.

Twelve percent.

Bokk looked down and saw the fist-sized hole where their heart would have been had they been human. They collapsed beside the terminal, tossing the energy pistol to one side.

Radner remained on his knees, weeping, as Quinon walked up behind him, and placed the barrel of a gun against the back of his head.

Radner looked at Bokk. "I'm sorry."

"Me too," Bokk said.

Quinon pulled the trigger twice, killing Radner instantly. The body she occupied was different to the one she'd originally taken, although it was considerably beat up. Several holes littered the new body's chest and what had once been a dark grey suit, was now covered in blood.

"This one wore no armour," Quinon said. "I don't think they expected a war today."

"They expected easy pickings. Their arrogance will be their downfall," Bokk said. "I need to be connected to the terminal. I need the power to keep me alive."

"I can stay here with you," Quinon said, helping Bokk move to the corner of the room, where it was easier to pull the plug from the back of the terminal.

Quinon opened Bokk's power port on the back of their neck and placed the plug inside, locking it in place with the clamps that would normally have moved automatically.

Three percent.

"My friends will find me." Bokk said, and felt fear. They did not want to die alone.

"I'll make sure of it," Quinon said as she left the body she possessed, allowing it to fall to the floor. "It was a pleasure." She stepped into the terminal, which glowed.

One percent.

Bokk's world became one of darkness, they only hoped that Drake would find them before there was any permanent damage done to their memory chips.

CHAPTER THIRTY

Felix Drake

"You've rested as much as we can allow, we need to move," Etamus said to Jaysa.

Etamus' had removed the spike from Jaysa's side and patched her up as best as possible, but Drake could see the pain in the sarcian's face as she slowly got to her feet.

"I don't think we're going to be going anywhere in a hurry," Gusin said, his ankle had swollen and was probably broken, although there was little anyone could do about that until they got back to the ship.

The group continued on, moving deeper into the ruins until they came to the partially-collapsed remains of a large building.

"You find that strange?" Drake asked, noticing lights flickering inside the building.

Etamus and Jaysa stood beside him. "Some sort of old power supply," the former said.

"Let's go take a look," Jaysa said. "Maybe there's something there that can tell us where we are."

The group headed into the old building and along a dark, crumbling corridor, the lights appeared to retreat from them with every step, guiding them into the unknown, until they entered a large room. Along one side were a bank of terminals that hummed with power. Blue and yellow lights shone from them, lighting the otherwise mostly-dark room.

Two dead bodies were on the floor, both looked like recent kills. Drake rolled one onto his back, and discovered that it had been the man who'd worked for Sabas, Radner. The lawyer.

Drake stepped around the bodies, toward the closest terminal, reading what was on the screen. "This says that a lot of people died here. There was some kind of war." He went to touch the panel and noticed that there was a synth crouched in the corner of the room. He walked over and found Bokk. They'd sustained serious damage to their outer shell, and had connected themselves to the terminal, which was presumably what had ignited the power source. Drake pushed down the thought of losing Bokk, the rage that bubbled up at the idea of someone having hurt them. Now was not the time. He checked it was safe to do so, and then disconnected the cable keeping Bokk tethered to the terminal.

The lights from the terminals dimmed to nothing. "You'll be okay," Drake said as he knelt beside Bokk, saying it more for himself than his friend. He began removing the rear of the synth's head plate.

"We need to hurry" Etamus said to Drake. "Sabas won't take long to figure out we're in the catacombs below the city."

Drake ignored her and removed the memory chip from Bokk's head, pocketing it before he stood.

Etamus took a step and stopped. "There are things here that don't feel like something we need to be messing about with."

"What does that mean?" Gusin asked.

Etamus held Drake's stare. "*You* know what I mean, don't you?"

Drake nodded; he'd felt the hum of power the second he'd stepped into the catacombs. He'd felt it once before on a battlefield where a lot of aether had been used, where a lot of Sage had died. "There wasn't just a war here, it was a war of the Sage. A huge number of ancient Sage died here."

Etamus nodded. "If that's the case, the spirits might well

be drawn to the corruption inside of you."

"Does anyone want to explain what you're talking about?" Gusin said.

"Not really," Drake told him. "Just be careful and don't touch anything."

They left the room, and followed the corridor, finding several of Sabas' men dead. Drake was certain Bokk had dealt with them before trying to preserve himself by plugging into an ancient terminal. He hoped his friend would be okay once plugged into a new body, but only time would tell.

Eventually, the group found the exit, feeding them into an old street, and Drake was relieved at being out of whatever the old building had once been. He looked back as part of it collapsed behind him. Maybe it was luck, or maybe there really were things down there that didn't like them being present.

"She's fun to be around," Gusin said when there was enough distance between Etamus and him that he hoped she couldn't hear.

"At least try not to piss off everyone you work with," Drake said, and moved swiftly to catch up.

They kept a quick pace as they walked down old streets, past houses that had remained standing, and several that had fallen apart.

"What happened here?" Gusin asked after several miles of silence.

"War happened," Drake said, feeling the power all around him. "The Sage Wars destroyed this place. Over time, the earth covered up who had lived here, buried it deep beneath the ground, and everyone forgot it ever existed. Doesn't explain why Sabas, Ren, or Metan wanted it uncovered."

"So this whole place became a warzone?" Gusin asked, looking around. "These houses look like they're made of the same materials we use back on Atharoth. The metal, brick and wood look identical. The Sage Wars were thousands of years ago."

"Some things don't go out of date," Etamus said. "I'm

sure yours is updated, but the idea that people were using it four-thousand years ago shows how advanced they were. How much the Sage Wars destroyed."

"I'd love to be able to come back and search though it all," Gusin said, his eyes lighting up.

"I wouldn't advise it," Etamus told him as the group walked around a crack in the ground. "There are things here that would take offence to items being removed."

"You mean the spirits?" Gusin said with a chuckle. "Look, I know there's a lot of weird stuff in the universe, and I know my share of people who have seen old Sage spirits, or spirits from beings of power, but they're just an echo. They can't actually do anything."

"You sound quite sure of yourself," Etamus said as an explosion ripped through the air far behind them. "Sabas is trying to get into the ruins. We should hurry."

They picked up the pace, any notion of discussing the ruins around them, long gone. Until Etamus stopped and placed a hand to the soil. "We need to go this way," she said pointing away from their current heading.

"Why?" Drake asked.

"The way to the chasm is no longer viable," Etamus explained. "Rocks have caved in the path. Dreic and the earth have a mutually beneficial relationship. I can tell where things are for several miles around me. I cannot see down there. Something blocks me."

"Yet, you want us to go down there?" Gusin asked. "Anyone else think we're being set up?"

"If I wished you dead, I would merely take a knife and do it myself," Etamus told him.

The group made their way down, and the glow from the handheld lights dimmed considerably, although they didn't extinguish.

"Felix Drake," a voice cried out from somewhere in the distance. "Come alone."

"Are you kidding me?" Gusin asked, his voice nasally and

full of fear. "You want us to stand here and wait?"

"What is it?" Drake asked Etamus, ignoring the sarcian.

"That's for you to discover," she told him. "We'll wait here. Either it will allow us to take this path, or it will kill you and we'll have to find another way."

Jaysa placed a hand on Drake's arm. "Be careful, something doesn't feel right here. And frankly, I'd rather not go back to your ship and tell your team we lost their captain the first time we left."

"Back soon... I hope." Drake turned and took a few more steps, but when he turned back toward the group, he was alone in the darkness.

"Follow the light," a voice boomed all around him.

"That's a little cliché, isn't it?" Drake said as he walked toward the blue light, which never seemed to grow in size.

Whatever was there didn't respond.

Drake continued on, and eventually the light grew, slowly at first, but then in a massive explosion that enveloped him, forcing him to shade his eyes.

"Where the fuck...?" he stopped mid-sentence as he lowered his hand and looked around. He stood on a field with short-cut grass the colour of rust. Huge, snow-capped mountains sat in the distance and a small stream weaved around the side of the field, vanishing behind the long, wooden building couched at the edge of the field. Woodland acted as a fence for the area, encircling it, making it feel cut off from the rest of reality.

Drake turned and saw the sky-skimmer sat in the distance. It was yellow and blue, standing out against the surroundings as if the grass had given bloom to it. He couldn't see the landing port, nor the small town it served. He knew they were there, knew what awaited his return from the hut.

He set off toward the building, noticing that it was considerably larger than he'd first anticipated. The white wood was stained red at the base from where the grass had grown up along the sides, but otherwise, it was just a wooden hut in the middle of a field. Nothing anyone in their right mind would be interested in.

He ascended the building's few steps, before knocking on the flimsy door. *How does it keep the rain and snow out?* Drake shook his head and stepped back to the ground. "I'm not going to play your games."

"You'll do as we say," a voice told him.

"Blow it out of whatever holes Sage spirits have," Drake said. "You want to talk to me, talk to me."

"We want to know why you did it, why you went back on it," the voice said. "How you managed to fight through the darkness to destroy it. You are corrupt, yet it is only a shadow of the darkness, an echo of what should be. Too many Sage here were lost to its grip."

"I have no idea what you're talking about," Drake said, perplexed about everything.

The silence lasted for several seconds. "Interesting."

"Is that why you destroyed the people here?" Drake asked. "You thought them corrupt?"

"The darkness had to be contained."

Drake looked all around him. "Show yourself. I don't want to be talking to air."

The world grew dark until Drake appeared to be stood on an Onnab street, but it wasn't like the Onnab he knew. The houses were different, and looked more like those he'd seen in the ruins except not covered in years of dirt and grime.

"What are you showing me?" Drake glanced down and saw hundreds and hundreds of dead that littered the streets. Soldiers, civilians, children, all joined together in death. "What is this?" Drake demanded.

"The city you call Onnab once had another name – Solea," the voice said. "Solea was the largest city on the planet of Akaton, which was a jewel under the control of the Union. A place of riches and peaceful living. Until the Sage Wars."

The air beside Drake shimmered and a young human male appeared. Dressed in a blue tunic, black trousers, and boots, his long, light-brown hair was tied back, and several scars radiated around his right eye.

"My name is Aquas," he said.

"You're responsible for what's happening right now?"

"One of many Sage spirits here," Aquas said softly "Originally, we were angry. You were corrupt and walking through our ruins. We thought you were here to hurt us."

"How could I hurt you? You're spirits."

Aquas gave a slight chuckle. "Given enough time and incentive anyone can be hurt, even those of us who no longer live in your world."

"What do you want from me?" Drake asked.

"Answers," Aquas told him. "Like we said, but I want to show you this. I want to explain what happened to Akaton over four-thousand years ago."

Drake thought that was obvious. "Everyone died."

Aquas nodded. "The hut you were stood outside of just now, have you ever seen anything like it before?"

"No, thankfully." Drake avoided saying that he'd have destroyed it, and done so with a smile in his heart. There was something more than a little wrong about it. Drake wasn't one to use the word evil often, but it was the closest word he could find.

"There was once many places like it. Hidden places, shrouded in secret," Aquas said. "Shrouded in darkness. It's rumoured that one of those huts started the Sage Wars, but that was never proven. I won't bother asking if you remember what was in that hut you visited. Everyone remembers."

"What hut? I've never been in a hut," Drake said. "I told you, I've never seen anything like it before. I have no idea what you're talking about."

"Darkness," Aquas muttered. "A darkness that consumes and twists. A darkness that turns friend against friend, brother against sister. A darkness few who feel it wish its destruction. Too many revelled in it, fell in love with the power it gave."

Fear crept up inside Drake. "What happened on Akaton?"

"The darkness you let into your heart and soul," Aquas said, seemingly ignoring Drake. "It spread, didn't it?"

"I let no darkness into my heart," Drake snapped, increasingly impatient with whatever was going on. "I don't know who, or what, you think I am, but I really have no idea what you're talking about."

"The darkness spread like wildfire," Aquas said, once again ignoring Drake. "And soon we all found ourselves in its clutches. We took difficult measures too. I was the one who walked into that cave. It was inviting, filled with interesting things that constantly caught my eye. I only went because a man in town had been arrested for murdering his best friend. He'd told us about the cave before tearing out his own tongue. Maybe we were already infected before I entered, but I don't think so. I think he was just broken and sent on his way to get our attention.

"I went willingly. And I found the keeper. I remember asking him about the murderer, about what he said about the cave. The keeper just sat there smiling. He appeared to be human, it's my guess that they often appear as whatever they need to be."

The view changed to the inside of a cavern, a huge expanse where shadows appeared to move of their own accord. In the centre, a hooded man bent low over a fire.

"I don't remember what he looked like beyond being able to state that he was human, and that he smiled," Aquas said. "No one does. I assume the person you met was the same."

"I. Didn't. Meet. Anyone," Drake snapped.

Aquas stared at Drake for several seconds. "I can feel the power inside of you. I can feel The Aperture."

"I'd really like it if you could give me some actual answers," Drake said with a sigh.

"You never submitted to this, did you?" Aquas asked, his tone now curious.

Although Drake thought the question rhetorical, he shook

his head. "I've never done anything like this."

"Your parents." Aquas' mouth dropped open. "You're born of The Aperture. You are not Sworn."

"I've heard that word before," Drake said. "That sniper above used it. I have no idea what that means but I'm beginning to sense that's the theme for this talk."

"The man in the cave offered me the chance to save the planet," Aquas explained. "He told me the war was coming. That he could give Sage on the planet a chance to save it. Could give me a way to make me more powerful. To make us all more powerful. To make me Aperture-touched.

"I agreed to his terms. I don't remember why I forgot about the murderer, but he was no longer important. I don't remember the trial he put me though, he rendered me asleep for it. I do remember the nightmares though, the horrific scenes of violence, and when I woke, I was at home in bed. I felt no different... no, I felt better."

"What happened to the city?" Drake asked, wishing to hurry it on before Sabas and his people arrived.

"The Union arrived first," Aquas said. "On the other side of the planet, they initially said they were there to protect us all. Their enemy came soon after, they called themselves Sworn. They believed Sage should rule over all others, that nothing was as important as a Sage's right to do as they wished. That all non-Sage should bow down to them as gods. They also wanted to execute all cai, they called them an affront to the sanctity of aether. Throughout the war, horrific acts were perpetrated against the cai, no matter their sex, race or age."

"What's a cai?" Drake's frustration grew as the number of questions increased with every second and remained unanswered.

The scene changed again to one of a battle – two massive armies bearing down on one another over a huge landscape churned up and destroyed during the fighting. Dead littered the ground as weapons of all shapes and sizes were used against one another. Drake instinctively stepped aside and looked behind him to see a plasma bolt heading his way.

Aquas moved his hands and the scene played out around them. The death and destruction was total, Sage and non-Sage alike died in the carnage, while huge behemoths and tanks —both appearing very different than the modern-day variety —fired a constant stream of unstoppable death upon the opposing side.

The scene paused again. "This waged on for a month. Hundreds of thousands died here. Why Akaton was picked, I do not know. Maybe it was just chance. Both armies slowly moved across the planet, fighting all the way, destroying all in their path. Cities vanished in days, the civilian casualties numbered in the tens of thousands. And the soldiers kept coming. We knew Solea would be soon in their path. The mountains protect us here, but eventually the fighting would spill into the city, maybe an errant bomb or a crashed battlecruiser from the battle going on high above the clouds. We had to do something. Had to stop it.

"Akaton was home to a research station that looked into ways of fighting with airborne viruses. It was near the centre of the two, next to what would now be the library. Officially, it was a hospital, but the underground bunker contained more sinister things. It was decided that we'd unleash a particularly horrific plague against the incoming armies. If we could kill them, we'd be spared. We just had to make it appear that one side did it to the other."

"You unleashed a plague on them?" Drake asked. There was no criticism in his tone, no judging what had happened, just a genuine question.

"We unleashed a plague the likes of which I hope was never seen again," Aquas said. "It's waterborne and renders the victim unconscious in less than thirty minutes, even Sage. We infected the lake, the source of the water they were drinking. It had the unseen side effects of transforming the sharks into the monsters that currently inhabit it, but it worked. One of the armies drank the water; it was the only clean source for miles, and they fell, comatose. Not all of them, but enough for them to state their enemies were responsible. The resulting battle was short-lived, and when it was done, the Sworn were victorious."

"You killed the wrong army," Drake said.

"No," Aquas snapped. "After I went through the trials, I encouraged others to do the same. A few weeks later the leader of the Sworn arrived in town, he told us all that if we joined them, we'd be spared. We'd be able to live our lives in peace, but that we'd also have the full backing of the Sworn once they won the war. I'm ashamed to say, we agreed. We poisoned the water the Union army drank, killing most of them. The Sworn then set up hidden camps on the planet, and waited for the inevitable Union re-enforcements. We would lead them to ambushes, wiping them out. During the months that followed, everyone in town began to change, strangers would vanish almost as soon as they arrived, members of the Union military who came to town were murdered in horrific ways, their screams shattering the air. No one thought what we were doing was anything other than protecting our own."

"You became monsters," Drake said, finally feeling like he understood at least some of what he was being told.

"Literally," Aquas said sadly. "We became the Sworn. The darkness spread through the population, forcing a change on us. For some… we changed physically. Others became more violent, less controlled. A few of us recognised what was happening, we knew we needed to do something before the spread of whatever it was, tainted us changed us all for good. It took us three months, but we managed to turn the plague we'd created into something even worse. We made it airborne and released it onto the populous of the city. Eight thousand, four hundred and eighteen people were affected. That left the twenty-two Sage who worked in the laboratory."

The horror of what had been done, sent a cold shiver up Drake's back. "What did you do to kill them all?"

"You've probably heard that obsidian-fibre is the only way

to truly kill a Sage," Aquas said. "However, that's not entirely true. Do enough damage and they will die."

The view vanished again, replaced with one of the same street, except now it was covered in thick ash, burying the people who were unaware of their fate. Drake glanced off to the side and saw that the mountain was on fire, spewing fiery death across the city.

"You made the volcano erupt," Drake said.

Aquas nodded. "It was a simple case of the right amount of explosives with the right ingredients at the right time. Several Sage helped with its explosion, and all of us stood at the foot of the mountain and waited for death. When it came, I was so scared, so utterly terrified of what would happen to us. Even so, it needed to be done. We needed to stop the spread."

"So, why are you here?" Drake asked after several seconds of considering his next words carefully.

"I don't know," Aquas said. "All twenty-two of us exist as spirits here. Our hypothesis is that in going through the trial, and subsequent realisation of what we needed to do to stop its spread across the planet, across the system should we ever leave, we designated ourselves spirits of this city."

"I've come across spirits who died in defence of a city before," Drake said. "People who just couldn't bear to be parted from it, people who felt they needed to watch over its people. Spirits have a tendency to corrupt through. They need to be careful."

"That was why we needed to see you," Aquas explained. "We needed to find out whether you were, in fact, still corrupt or if you were clear."

"You don't appear to have been listening to me," Drake said. "I'm not corrupt. I'm not one of the Sworn."

"No," Aquas said. "At least one of your parents was though."

"I don't understand," Drake said. "My parents weren't monsters."

"Are you sure?" Aquas asked.

Drake wasn't sure of anything at that moment. "People say that my father committed horrific acts against those who stood against him, but that he managed to defeat the darkness and change his path."

Aquas stared at Drake before saying, "Your father must be incredibly powerful to have defeated the darkness inside of him."

"He died over thirty years ago. I don't really understand what happened to him," Drake said. "Why do you think I have darkness in me? What are the cai?"

"Lots of questions," Aquas said. "The Aperture is a place that no one should venture into unprepared. Once there, time and space are different to what we have now. Any Sage going into The Aperture without the protection of a ship can increase the power of their aether to great and terrifying levels. Any non-Sage who is exposed to the power inside is able to transform their bodies into creatures of incredible might, but more often than not, also incredible evil. They're called Aperture-cursed.

"The cai were a group of people who were able to touch the aether, but unlike Sage, weren't able to bend that power to their will. They could do a variety of things; nullify a Sage's power, detect a Sage, increase someone's power, heal... the list was vast. I assume the fact you don't know who they are means they're extinct in your time. Or people hide their true power.

"If a Sage who has taken power directly from being inside The Aperture has a child, part of that power transfers to the child. It means they have access to great power, but also a great darkness that the creatures in The Aperture will sense if ever given the chance. We called these children Aperture-onset."

Drake frowned. "Is that what I am? An Aperture-onset?"

"I sense the darkness inside of you," Aquas said. "The corruption of The Aperture, the power it placed in you. Should you ever discover how to tap into that power, you could be a force of great good... or great evil."

"What if I don't want to tap into it?" Drake asked, none too happy about this sudden revelation.

"Then you will go through life never living up to your potential," Aquas said. "I'm sorry you never discovered this earlier in your life."

"I don't want something evil inside of me," Drake said. "I have a hard enough time trying to convince people I'm not about to destroy the Union without having to deal with that too. Without having to control a desire to do evil."

Aquas shrugged. "Maybe you should control it by embracing it, not fearing it."

"And what if it makes me want to seek out a cave in some far reaches of the universe?" Drake asked. "If I begin to think that the best way of achieving my goals is to allow that darkness inside of me to corrupt me, what happens then?"

"That's why you surround yourself with people you care for," Aquas explained. "You need not succumb to the call."

"I've lived my life without even knowing it was there," Drake said. "Maybe it's dormant."

"For now," Aquas said. "However, these things have a tendency to never stay dormant forever. Eventually, a Sage who has been in The Aperture itself will find you, and that could be the key to what is dormant becoming very much active."

Drake looked down at his hands, half expecting to find talons where his fingers were. "I won't let it consume me. Whatever it is." Drake sighed. "At least I have more information than I started with. This is why Sabas, Metan, and their employers were excavating here. They wanted to find this cave. The source of darkness."

"That is probable. We will allow you to go back to your friends," Aquas told Drake. "We thank you for being honest with us. It saved your life."

"Thanks for revealing the secrets of this place," Drake said. "I hope you can all find some peace."

"We promised that this land would never see the type of bloodshed we visited upon it, but we have no power above the ground, this is where we died, and this is where we shall remain," Aquas said. "Good luck to you, Felix Drake, I hope *you* find peace."

Drake turned to leave and paused. "One last question, what was the room we found ourselves in with the ornate carvings? The one behind the boulder?"

"It was an old shelter," Aquas said. "There's a hidden staircase that leads down into a bunker big enough to house everyone in the city. We built it when the Sage Wars started in case we needed protection. I guess we were the ones others needed protecting against."

The images vanished, along with Aquas, and Drake found himself stood in the remains of a ruined building. He managed to get out, but had no way of knowing where his comrades were.

"Follow the light," a voice whispered, and Drake saw the small blue light that hovered a few feet in front of him.

He walked after it, down winding roads until it vanished just as he reached Jaysa, Gusin and Etamus, the latter of whom appeared very surprised to see him.

"Yes, I'm alive," Drake said.

"How?" Gusin asked, his voice revealing the obvious concern at his ability to still breath.

Drake gave a short recap, finishing with, "They were happy that I wasn't a threat to them and let me go. Now we need to leave this place and get off Onnab."

"We need to stop those hunting us," Jaysa said. "We need to get word to the ship."

"How?" Gusin asked. He sat beside the broken Xendo.

"You found your synth?" Drake asked.

"They were buried under some rubble," Jaysa said. "It looked someone tried to hide them."

"Bokk," Drake said, and wished that both synths would have been around to help them with the coming fight.

"The comms aren't working," Etamus said.

"Actually, I think Sabas is the one responsible for that,"

Jaysa said. "They must have a way to stay in contact with whatever ship brought them. And they certainly wouldn't want us contacting anyone above."

"I hope the rest of my team are okay," Drake said.

"Sabas and his people will have to die," Etamus said to Jaysa. "He will never stop hunting you."

"So, Drake, is your plan to kill Sabas and his people?" Jaysa asked. "Because I'd rather be safe than sorry."

Drake nodded. There was no choice in the matter. "Any objections?"

"Not a single one," Jaysa said with a cruel smile.

CHAPTER THIRTY-ONE

Felix Drake

When he was young, Drake had been told that spirits were strange things, prone to asking for favours... and they always collect. Owing a debt to a spirit was a pretty good way of making your life very miserable, very quickly, or at the very least never going back to that planet ever. As if he needed more convincing to leave Onnab and never return, Drake's encounter with the spirits in the catacombs of the city solidified that thought.

As the group made their way under the chasm and looked up at the night sky high above, Gusin tripped and landed on his knees. He'd been dragging Xendo behind him, and kicked the synth in frustration. "This whole place is a death trap."

They continued on for a short time until they found a set of stairs that lead up to the battered land above.

"The Sage, screwing around with stuff even after they're dead," Gusin grumbled, and with Drake's help, they carried Xendo up the stairs.

"When everyone is up top, find a place to stay that isn't out in the open," Drake told the councillor.

Etamus stepped close. "While you were off talking to the

spirits, I meditated and linked myself to this ground. There are no living things for at least a mile in all directions," she said, with more than a hint of smugness in her voice.

"The sniper who shot Xendo wouldn't be all that concerned about a mile," Drake said.

Etamus didn't argue, but Drake knew she wasn't happy at being second guessed. Either way, she and Jaysa made her way around to the rear of a building that was all but destroyed.

"Do you have a plan?" Jaysa asked Drake.

"Gusin is going to take the synth and hide in whatever remains of one of these buildings," Drake said. "I'm going to find whoever is up by the camp and kill them. I assume you'll want to go after Sabas."

Everyone spoke at once.

"Look, you can all argue with me as much as you like," Drake said. "The fact remains, we need to get rid of the unwanted guests who have managed to infest this place. The likelihood is, there are more of Sabas' people with him than back at the camp. Etamus should go with Jaysa, and hopefully remove Sabas as a problem. Gusin, you'll stay here and make sure you don't get in the way. I'm going to go to the camp and deal with whoever is there."

"You're not going without me," Gusin said. "I won't have you from my sight."

"You can fight then, can you?" Drake asked.

"I've been trained my whole life in various forms of combat," he said with more than a hint of pride.

"And how often have you used that training?" Drake asked.

Gusin glared. "That's not the point."

"It sort of is," Jaysa told him.

Drake sighed. "Look, no one can leave this planet until we contact the ship. And before we can do that, we need to get that camp cleared. We need to see what they've done to fuck up the comms on the surface."

"How do you know there won't be a large group left at the

camp?" Etamus asked.

"Sabas wants me for Alastia, and Jaysa for himself," Drake said. "That sniper had all of us dead to rights when we were climbing down the cliff, and at no point did he kill us. He missed with every single shot. Because he was told to. He wants us alive, because the thought of anyone else killing you isn't going to work in his mind."

No one spoke for a moment.

"Sabas will have numbers, pure grunt muscle at his disposal," Drake continued. "They'll be trying to follow us into the catacombs, and eventually he'll realise that we'll have gone through the town to escape. So he's going to follow us here and wait, or he's going to follow us here and send people down to hunt us. Either way, he's coming here. For all I know, he may already have people on the way, which means we need to hurry."

"I don't trust you," Gusin said.

"I really don't care," Drake told him.

Gusin's breathed out slowly. "I'll let it go. For now."

"Excellent," Drake said, throwing plenty of sarcasm into the word. "Stay here, don't die."

Jaysa and Etamus left without another word. Drake watched them walk off, keeping low behind the row of destroyed buildings as they made their way down toward the ruin entrance.

"So, I'm staying here then?" Gusin said, sounding incredibly unhappy about the situation.

Drake didn't much care. The councillor had no actual combat experience, and all the training in the world meant nothing in a real-life fight. Drake had seen highly-trained people falter at the first sign of actual combat, and he couldn't risk his own life on the gamble of someone else not screwing up.

"Yes, just stay out of sight." Drake left the councillor behind a stack of rubble, and crept around the back of what had once been a town hall. Drake hugged the ruined buildings, keeping his head down in case the sniper was watching for anyone coming toward the camp. He reached the end of the row of buildings in fairly quick time when the shouting and weapon fire began in the distance. Seemed Jaysa had gotten to Sabas and his gang. He was certain she'd be okay; she was more than capable of taking care of herself, and she packed a hell of a punch. He would have pitied Sabas if it weren't for the fact the man wanted Drake's people dead, and thus clearly deserved whatever horror befell him.

Drake peeked around the corner and saw his first sentry – a thin, wiry sarcian male who wore furs and appeared more interested in searching through the badly burned chest he probably found in the house, than actually taking note of what was going on around him. Drake reached out with his arm, using his ionic aether to manipulate the space around the guard's head, crushing his skull in seconds with an awful sound. There was a sudden feedback of pain up Drake's leg, causing him to lose the link to his aether. The anklet wasn't about to let him use it without consequences. He would need to get that damn thing off him before it got him killed.

He rolled the dead sarcian onto his back; the skull was grossly misshapen. He'd caught the guard unaware, and was lucky. If the guard had known what was happening and reacted in time, he might have gotten away before the space around his head had done its job. Drake searched the sentry and found an eight-inch, black-bladed dagger. Drake pushed the blade against a nearby piece of unburned wood, and found it cut straight through. *Triseriam carbonate after all. Must have cost him a small fortune.* The plasma rifle was coded to the sarcian's handprint, so Drake tossed it aside. No point taking something he couldn't use.

He was about to stand when a second sentry walked around the corner. The human opened his mouth to speak when Drake threw the dagger into his throat. The sentry fell to his knees, and pitched forward to the ground. Drake removed the dagger, wiping it on the first sentry's furs. He searched the second sentry, but only found some vapour-sticks, and a coil rifle – the same one Xendo had carried before he'd been shot.

Drake checked the feed and found it was already loaded with a magazine of small projectiles, each one with a tiny explosive charge inside it. He slung the rifle over his shoulder and made for the end of the row of rubble. Drake had two options. He could either carry on in this direction, which would take him through what used to be a forest and toward the mountain camp from the side, or he could double-back and make his way through the town's remains to go straight to the camp.

He ran toward the forest, ensuring he was in the open for as little time as possible. A large part of the forest had been burned to ash, any trees remaining upright out of pure stubbornness. There wasn't a lot of cover if anyone spotted him, but the trees meant he had a better chance of remaining undetected than he did running through the centre of Onnab.

The darkness helped, but it also meant he couldn't properly see where he was going. He wished he'd taken some of the lights from the ruins with him, but then that would defeat the objective of staying hidden. It took him a while to make his way through the forest, stopping occasionally to hear fighting in the distance. Jaysa was certainly making Sabas and his people earn their money.

Drake pushed them from his mind—there was little he could do to help no matter how much he wanted—and set about his mission once more. After a long walk, he came to a series of large rock formations, and knew he was at the darolf spider nests Jaysa had mentioned. He couldn't imagine they'd have survived the bombardment, but the little bastards were notorious for surviving situations most creatures wouldn't. Moonlight illuminated the entrances to the dozens of nests, but Drake saw no movement. He took a moment and stopped, using his aether to feel all around him for life-forms. It was a difficult talent to master, as the wielder had to push his consciousness over a wide area, leaving them open to attack.

Coupled with the minimal aether Drake could use, made it even more difficult.

The anklet stopped the aether after only a few seconds, and Drake inwardly cursed it. He purposely hadn't used his aether in the open for years, but now, when he needed it most, his own power was too limited for it to be useful on a regular basis. Damn those bastards for putting it on him.

In the few seconds Drake had managed to check around him, he'd felt nothing alive. He couldn't be certain he hadn't missed anything, but he took a few steps, knowing that if any darolf spiders were in their underground nests, they'd feel the vibration. Drake waited, not knowing whether his next step would bring a herd of the evil monsters his way.

He paused before taking another step. Paused once again. If any spiders were alive in their nests, Drake would have met them almost immediately. Patience was not one of their prime abilities.

Drake took a few more steps when the rock beside him exploded, showering him in tiny shards of sharp fragments, cutting open his hands and arms as he raised them to protect his head. He darted behind the nearest rock as a second shot destroyed a blackened tree. He slung the coil rifle off his shoulder and, while kneeling, peered around the side of the rock, looking through the scope, and switching the view to try and pick up a heat signature.

Nothing.

Drake quickly ducked back just as a second shot slammed into the side of the rock. The shooter was wearing a camo-suit, a good one if it were capable of completely masking a heat signature from a scope as good as the one on the coil rifle.

A third shot caused the rock behind Drake to tremble, and pieces of stone and dust rained down on Drake's head. He was stuck, and there was little chance the shooter was going to let Drake get to a better position to shoot back. He lay prone and placed the rifle as high up as he could before another shot cracked through the rock, exactly where his head would be if he'd been sat there aiming the rifle. The rock collapsed on one side, and Drake quickly pulled the rifle back. He used the scope, looking through the rubble, and waited to see just how confident his adversary was that he'd made a kill shot.

It didn't take long.

There was soon movement at the top of the path. The digital readout on the scope said two-thousand-eight-hundred feet away, an impressive shot. The shooter's camo-suit hid his heat signature, but it couldn't hide his movement. Drake rested the barrel of the rifle on the remains of the rock, and breathed out slowly as he squeezed the trigger.

Drake watched as the round smashed into whoever, or whatever, was moving, throwing it back. Camo-suits weren't designed to stop an explosive round from a coil rifle, and there was no way to wear it over armour. There was a good chance that whoever had been hit by that round was, at the very least, missing a sizeable chunk of their body.

He waited several seconds before slowly moving around the rock, keeping the rifle high, his finger on the trigger guard, ready to move to fire another shot should the need arise. It was an uncomfortable, and nerve inducing walk, but he made it as quickly as he could, stopping every few feet to ensure he was still alone.

When he reached the clearing above, the shooter was on his back, the camo-suit flickering from the damage. The shadow rifle was several feet away. Considering the size of the piece missing from the shooters chest, there was very little chance the man was getting back up.

Drake knelt beside the body, and pulled the hood up, needing to know if the man he'd killed had been the sniper who had shot him and Jaysa when they'd arrived in Onnab. As the mask reached the man's nose, Drake paused when a cold blade was pressed against the side of his throat.

"Not me in there," the sniper said from behind Drake's shoulder, standing out of reach from any possible defence.

Without moving his head in anyway, Drake glanced down

at the blade. "That's my spear."

"Yes, it's very nice," the sniper said without looking down at it. "I'm going to skewer you with it and watch you bleed out all over this shit-heap of a planet."

"Ah, you should come back when its summer," Drake said. "I hear it's beautiful."

"You seem to be under the impression that you're not currently on your knees, about to have your throat slit by your own spear," the sniper said. "It's obsidian-fibre, yes? I very much doubt you'll be surviving that wound."

"So, you were on Yenrithal, then?" Drake asked. "How'd you survive?"

"Managed to hide, wait for your father and his people to leave," the sniper told him. "Your father murdered his own."

"People really need to give me a list of things my father did, so I can read up on them," Drake snapped.

"Your father stabbed my master through the heart," the sniper said. "He cut his head off in front of those who worshiped him like a god."

Drake rolled his shoulders a little. "Sounds like a productive day."

The sniper ignored the jab. "And then he had his people destroy us."

"I remember reading about Yenrithal," Drake said. "The people who died there butchered their way across an entire system. I didn't realise my father was the one to stop you. I guess the removal of history is something the Union still likes to do. I wonder, how many died at your hands? Five, ten million people? Even more? If I remember correctly, you and your *people* rendered whole planets into burning ruins. All because they wouldn't surrender."

"Your father was no better," the sniper snapped. "He killed those who refused to surrender, who crossed his path. He hunted those who had tried to escape his clutches."

"Yes, so people have told me," Drake said, fed up with the conversation. "It's strange, I lived my whole life not knowing much about the man at all. The information available, even to Wardens, is limited, and few wanted to talk to me about him. Your master was Patrog Vaile, yes? He didn't believe he'd done anything wrong, but he was a murderer and a criminal. The news I read said he begged for death in the end."

"Lies! He was kiretan! He did not beg. He knew what he was doing. We all did. We revelled in the deaths we caused against those who would have wronged us. Who stood against us and our glorious Lord!" The sniper walked around so that he was facing Drake. "I want you to see your death. I watched through the scope as your aether kept stopping; you don't have a lot of charge in there, do you? Probably wishing you had enough to stop me."

"Who's the dead man?" Drake asked. "I think it's nice to know the people you kill."

"Just one of Sabas' servants," the sniper said dismissively. "No one important. Gave him my spare camo-suit and told him to fire off a few shots in your direction. He was a good shot, almost got you once. I wanted an up-close-and-personal kill though. Couldn't really have you dying and not watching the life ebb from your eyes. Where would the fun be in that?"

"You know the problem with people like you?"

"Like me?" The sniper chuckled.

"Yeah, arrogant bastards who think they're something special because they hold a blade to your throat," Drake told him. "People like *you*."

The sniper's eyes narrowed in anger but Drake knew the man wouldn't kill him, not until he'd made Drake beg for forgiveness, or whatever he was after. Just killing Drake wouldn't be enough; the sniper wanted him to be humiliated.

"Well, the problem is you had a chance to kill me," Drake continued. "You should have worn your camo-suit, hidden somewhere and put a round through my brain; you should have done that instead of this gloating and complaining about things that happened in the past."

The sniper smiled. "I'm going to cut pieces off you."

"Not today." With lightning speed, Drake used the dagger he'd taken to push away the obsidian-fibre spear. He launched himself back, putting several feet between him and the sniper, who responded by twirling the spear between his hands.

"You can twirl it, congratulations," Drake said. "Let's see if you can fight with it."

The sniper jumped over his dead comrade, holding onto the end of the spear as he brought it down over his head before switching his stance and swiping the spear toward Drake, who managed to move back far enough for it not to be a concern. The sniper darted forward, pushing the spear toward Drake, who blocked the blade with his dagger, before moving in closer and forcing the sniper to dart back.

Drake piled on the pressure, driving the sniper to use the spear's shaft to block several swipes, thus avoiding injury. A missed kick from Drake, and the sniper took full advantage, thrusting the blade forward. Drake grabbed the shaft and pulled the spear toward him, launching himself up toward the sniper, catching the wrong-footed man on the jaw with a vicious kick.

Keeping hold of the spear, Drake swiped the dagger at the sniper's hands, forcing him to relinquish or lose fingers. Once he had his property back, Drake spun, swung the spear around until he was holding the pommel, and the blade bit through the side of the sniper, who stifled a cry of pain. Drake kept moving, never once losing his momentum as he spun closer, until he moved his hands up the spear's shaft, and drove the spear into the man's stomach.

Blood poured from the sniper's mouth and Drake twisted the spear, before dragging it out, leaving a large wound. The sniper placed his hands over his gut in a desperate attempt to keep his insides inside.

Drake pressed the button on the shaft, retracting the spear. He stood in front of the sniper, who'd fallen back, a look of panic on his face as blood seeped from between his fingers.

"Should have shot me when you had the chance," Drake

told him. "Should have run away to be honest."

"Your father should have died instead of my master," the sniper seethed, his voice full of hate despite how weak it was becoming. "My master should have killed him."

"Probably, but he didn't, and here we are," Drake said. "You don't work for Sabas. Who do you work for?"

He tried to shrug, but it caused him obvious pain. "Alastia really wants you dead. I was told to come here and kill you. The pay didn't matter as much as seeing you in pain."

"Why does a woman I've never heard of or even met, want me dead?"

"Ask her when you see her," the sniper said with a chuckle that quickly turned into a grunt of pain.

Drake crouched just out of the sniper's reach, and showed him his forearm. "I think I may have cut my arm when the bullet hit those rocks. It really stings."

"You mock me?" the sniper shouted. "After all of this, you think you can mock me?"

Drake stood and extended the spear. "The comms unit. How is it being jammed?"

"Localized array," he said and coughed up blood. "It's in the camp. I hope my master finds you and guts you like a fish."

"You first," Drake said and raised the spear to punch through his head when a blast-gun shot hit Drake in the chest, sending him sprawling. He rolled to the side behind a boulder as another of Sabas' guards came into view. He stood beside the sniper and fired off a second shot, which partially destroyed the boulder.

"I've got a plan to end you," the sniper said, getting to his feet and limping away.

Another blast-gun shot showered Drake with tiny pieces of shrapnel, and he was grateful for the armour he wore. He knew that eventually he'd have to move, despite not really wanting to. Drake feinted as if to throw the spear at the blast-gun wielder, causing another shot to smash into the boulder, but Drake was already moving around the other side. He threw the dagger with as much force as he dared. The man used his blast-gun to bat the dagger aside, giving Drake the opening he needed to dart forward, whipping the spear up toward the blast-gun. The blade cut through the combat armour around the man's forearm as if it wasn't even there.

The man screamed as his arm fell away, taking his only weapon with it. Drake spun the spear around and drove it up into the attacker's skull, killing him instantly. With a twist of the spear, Drake removed it, flicking the remains off the blade before shortening it and returning it to its holster.

He looked across the barren land toward where he saw the sniper climb into one of the three stalkers—a light, fixed-wing, one-person ship used for quick manoeuvres within gravity—at the base camp. He took off after his prey at a sprint, arriving just as the other ship lifted into the air. Drake was in his own stalker, strapping himself in as he activated the ship's power as the sniper flew away from the base camp. Apparently, running away was the method he'd decided on for living through the rest of the day.

Drake's stalker lifted vertically off the ground, and he turned the engines before speeding off in pursuit. Nothing was going to get in his way. He paused once, spotting the array. It needed to be destroyed more than the sniper needed hunting. Drake used the forward cannons to destroy the array that blocked the comms then changed the frequency of the comm unit until he heard chatter from someone he recognised. "You okay up there?" he asked.

"Little busy," Sateri said. "You've been dealing with Sabas, I assume."

"Jaysa's off killing him and his people as we speak," Drake said. "I thought I'd make sure all was okay before I went to deal with my own problem."

"We're going to be a while," Sateri told him. "Sabas brought a battlecruiser. It's not an issue anymore, but long-range comms are out, and we're going to need to land. Is it safe?"

Drake looked around him. "Will be soon enough. Feel free to land when you like." He disabled the comms unit, looking up at the stars above him and hoping his team were okay.

In the distance, he spotted the sniper's stalker flying toward him. Drake smiled. Looked like he wasn't going to have to hunt after all.

CHAPTER THIRTY-TWO

Jaysa Benezta

Jaysa wanted to find Sabas and hurt him very badly before finally killing him. Anyone who got in the way of that happening was going to have a world of pain for the short remainder of their lives. It wasn't just that he'd ambushed her, beat her, spoken badly to her. It wasn't even that since he'd come into her life, she'd fallen from a cliff, just missed being eaten by sharks, been stabbed by part of a tree, and had to walk through dirty ruins. All of those things annoyed her. It was the fact that Sabas had her disruptor. She really didn't like anyone else touching it, so the fact that big piece of shit had actually threatened her with it enraged her more and more.

Jaysa took a coil rifle and dagger from a dead thug, and after discovering the former wasn't handprint activated, decided to keep it for herself. It would do until she got her disruptor back. Etamus had taken an identical rifle from a second thug, and sat beside her as they both aimed down the hill toward where she assumed Sabas and his people would come. They didn't have to wait long.

Three of his gang arrived – two human men and a sarcian woman. Jaysa put two shots in the sarcian, both mid-chest range, while Etamus put a round through the head of each of the men.

"Show off," Jaysa said with a smirk.

Two more gang members, who spotted their dead comrades, both received a bullet through the back of the head when they turned to flee. And two more died before they could even register what they were seeing.

"They will stop coming that way now," Etamus said. "They'll find a way to flank us."

"Good, this is boring." Jaysa looked at the overheat gauge on the rifle to see how many shots she had left before she needed to vent the extreme build-up inside the barrel. "Four shots. You?"

"Three," Etamus told her. "That's a problem because are more than seven members of the gang left."

Jaysa had to agree. "How many gang members?"

Etamus paused for a moment. "We've killed eight, depending on how many Sabas left behind. From what I remember back at the camp, anywhere up to another ten."

"Ten?" Jaysa almost shouted. "I remember being told as a child about tales where people defended cities with less personnel than that."

"Military-trained are considerably more impressive than those who would stab you with a bottle in a dark alley so they don't have to get into a fight."

"You're dead either way," Jaysa pointed out.

Etamus looked through her scope. "I don't see any movement. My guess is, they've made their way around the beach to try and get behind us. This will be a fight to remember."

"Any chance you can ask the earth real nicely if it wouldn't mind killing a few for us."

Etamus looked offended. "My link to the ground does not include asking it to murder for me. That isn't how my gift works."

Jaysa sighed. "Yeah, I know, but I thought maybe on this

occasion it would be worth asking. Let's see if we can thin the herd a little bit." Jaysa took off at a sprint, occasionally stopping to look through her scope. When she reached the end of the row of ravaged buildings, and with nothing but open, burned ground in front of her, she waited for Etamus to catch her up.

"A little warning," the dreic said.

"Why?" Jaysa asked with a grin.

Etamus shook her head, a smirk of her own on her lips. "Sabas will have left guards at the entrance to the ruins. At least three."

"Let's go say hello then," Jaysa said. "When you see them, you'll know what to do."

Jaysa passed Etamus the rifle and stepped out around the rubble, her hands raised in surrender. She set off at a steady pace down the hill, ignoring the bodies she'd put there only a few moments ago. It took her until she'd almost reached the bottom of the hill before someone from Sabas' gang saw her. He was a middle-aged kiretan who carried a blast-gun, which Jaysa was certain she wanted no part of.

Etamus had been right about the guard, but wrong about the number, as three others—one human female, a kiretan male, and a synth—stepped out from behind the boulder that obscured the entrance to the ruins.

"Where's the dreic?" one of the two women asked.

"Who?" Jaysa replied. "Oh, isn't she with you?"

Everyone appeared confused for a split second until three shots, one for each of the women and synth, all found their homes. The kiretan appeared shocked for just a moment. Taking his eyes off Jaysa, she darted forward to drive the dagger up into his throat, but he saw it coming and dodged back, trying to aim the blast-gun. Jaysa grabbed the barrel and hoisted it into the air with one hand while stabbing the kiretan in the stomach with the dagger. The kiretan roared in defiance and kicked Jaysa square in the chest, sending her flying back.

"Wants you alive, but fuck it," the kiretan said as he

walked toward her, and readied his blast-gun.

Jaysa was up on her feet in a second, sprinting toward the larger opponent and pushing the gun aside, stabbing him repeatedly in the stomach and side. The kiretan's rage boiled over and he dropped the gun, taking powerful swings at Jaysa's head, which she managed to dodge before grabbing the blast-gun and with only the barest of aim, fired it into the kiretan's chest. Both the dead kiretan and Jaysa flew apart. She hadn't braced for the kick of the massive gun, and found herself on her back wishing she'd thought of a better way. She wasn't seriously injured, although she knew she'd feel sore in the morning. Whatever Etamus had done to stop the bleeding of the wound in her side, had opened, and she felt the trickle of blood run down her stomach.

She rolled over onto her front and got gingerly back to her feet, ignoring the blast-gun and grabbing a plasma pistol instead.

Jaysa trudged back up the hill but found Etamus missing, replaced with two more dead gang members, each with stab wounds to their throats. Both Jaysa's and Etamus' coil rifles sat on the ground, their remaining rounds ejected.

"Jaysa," Sabas shouted. "I saw you go back there! We know you're alive. Come out or this one gets a lovely hole in her pretty head."

She cringed. Never should one man exist more who shouldn't use the words lovely or pretty. Jaysa edged around the side of the building to find Sabas standing behind a kneeling Etamus, holding Jaysa's disruptor to the dreic's head. A further eight men were stood behind them, all catcalling and shouting insults at Jaysa. She blocked them out; they were nothing but white noise to her. All she cared about was making sure Etamus was okay, killing Sabas... and retrieving her disruptor.

"You've lost a lot of people," Jaysa called out. Sabas was a little over twenty feet away, too far for her to get to him before he killed her... or Etamus, she quickly reminded herself.

"Maybe you should give this up as a bad job and just fuck off."

"Not until your head is above my mantle," Sabas snapped. "I'm going to show it off to my friends. Drop the pistol. Now."

Jaysa did as she was commanded. "I'd put yours above mine, but you're too ugly for that shit."

Sabas bristled from the insult. "You think you're such a clever girl, don't you? Don't worry; I'll manage to beat that out of you. I'm going to kill you; I'm going to do it slowly. I'm going to hear you scream."

She wondered why people like Sabas had to gloat so damn much. "I guess it's good to have a goal, even one that's never going to happen. Besides, you're not man enough to make me scream."

Sabas' gun shot up toward Jaysa, who smiled.

Still kneeling in the dirt, Etamus placed her hands on the ground and muttered something. Sabas' reactions were too slow, and his gang too busy shouting abuse to make any difference as the ground between Etamus and Sabas exploded upward, forming a thick wall between the two.

Etamus was up and sprinting in a heartbeat, joined by Jaysa as they ran down the hill toward the ruins.

"Did you have a plan, beyond angering him?" Etamus asked.

Jaysa decided honesty was the best policy. "Nope, that was pretty much it, worked though."

They rounded the boulder in front of the ruins entrance and stopped to take a breath. Shouting followed them down as Sabas and his people finally managed to get their heads around what had happened.

"So, do we have any weapons, or did they take everything?" Jaysa asked.

"Took everything."

If there were deities in the universe, they didn't like Jaysa at all. "We'll have to get some back then. Into the ruins seems the best bet."

Etamus nodded, and they re-entered the ruins.

"Leave the door open, we want them to come get us," Jaysa said.

Etamus paused for a moment. "You think they will?"

Jaysa's smile didn't hide the cruel thoughts in her head. "I think Sabas can't resist. His men will do what he tells them."

The pair ran into the ruins and hid inside one of the houses halfway down the first street.

"Any chance those spirits are still here?" Jaysa asked.

Etamus closed her eyes. "Yes, the earth suggests they still patrol this place. I do not believe I can contact them though. I'm not sure they would be of any assistance even if I could."

"That's okay; I just wanted to make sure they'd stay out of this," Jaysa said. "I don't want them uppity because more blood got spilled on their ruins."

Raised voices echoed throughout the ruins as the six surviving members of Sabas' gang strode up the street, with the big man himself behind them barking orders. "Every single building! Do you understand me?"

Jaysa and Etamus ducked back into the darkness of the house but continued watching as the gang members spilt off to search the buildings.

"They should have stayed together," Etamus whispered.

"They're nervous," Jaysa said, keeping her own voice low and quiet. "Sabas wants results. They don't want his anger aimed at them. They're going in twos. We need them dead quickly and quietly. We need their weapons, not a beacon for everyone else to come running our way."

"I've done this before," Etamus reminded her.

They pair waited in silence for several minutes until the sound of boots on old timber resounded through the house.

"I don't see why this bitch is so worthwhile," a woman said.

"Don't let the boss hear you say that," a male replied. "He's already furious that he didn't bring more people with him."

Jaysa stayed in the shadows under a partially destroyed staircase as the two gang members walked past. Neither used a torch or any sort of night-vision. They were ill-prepared to search in darkness, just doing what their boss told them so he wouldn't be angry.

She motioned for Etamus to go after the male, who had walked farther into the building, splitting up from his partner. Etamus nodded and moved silently after her prey while Jaysa followed the female who headed toward the rear of the building.

The gang member began kicking dirt around, presumably in an effort to sound busy, and her obvious distraction was a boon as Jaysa moved quickly, wrapping her arms around the woman's neck in an effort to snap it before she could alert her comrades. Unfortunately, the woman moved at the last second, resulting in Jaysa striking her in the side of the neck instead. The gang member jumped forward and turned toward Jaysa, who was already dealing with her failure by kicking the woman in the stomach. The gang member doubled over, coughing and spluttering as the air was driven out of her. Jaysa drove her knee into the woman's exposed throat, which dropped her silently. Jaysa couldn't risk leaving the woman alive, so she placed a knee between her shoulders, grabbed hold of her neck and snapped it.

Jaysa got back to her feet, grabbing an energy pistol and another dagger. She walked back through the house and saw Etamus with blood on her legs.

"He's dead," she told Jaysa, as she checked the ammo on her newly acquired coil rifle.

Jaysa nodded. "Mine too."

"I assume you have another part to your plan?"

"I want you to start shooting at the rest of the gang," Jaysa told her. "I'm going to Sabas."

"Works for me." Etamus made herself comfortable by the front of the building, ensuring she was still shrouded in darkness before looking through her scope.

Two shots, followed immediately by screams and shouts.

"Not got all day," Etamus said without looking up.

Jaysa left the house and ran at Sabas who was busy wiping the blood of his lackeys from his face. Etamus had shot the one closest to Sabas through the throat, splattering the boss with blood. He stared at Jaysa, saw his dead employees, turned, and ran. Sabas tripped over some rocks and dropped the disruptor. He ignored it, clambering back to his feet and sprinting out of the ruins as fast as he cold.

Two more shots sounded behind Jaysa as she picked up her disruptor, set it to the fifth setting, and re-holstered it. She would clean Sabas' stink of it before using it. Jaysa gathered a coil rifle from the ground and set off after her target.

She tracked Sabas down to the beach, running along a bridge-like rock formation that jutted out over the lake. It allowed someone to travel to the opposite side without having to go all the way around the city of Onnab. Jaysa raised her rifle and took a shot, which smashed into the pale rock by Sabas' feet.

The crime boss stopped and turned toward Jaysa as she ambled toward him. She was in no hurry and if he moved, she could put a round through his leg.

"How about we call it quits?" Sabas shouted as Jaysa stepped up the smooth ramp to the bridge.

Jaysa shook her head slightly. "You don't get to walk away from this."

Sabas raised his hands in surrender. "I can pay you."

A stalker flew at low altitude above her head, but she ignored it. "Fuck your money," she shouted over the noise of the ship's engines.

"You're just going to shoot me then?" Sabas snapped, as though bluster might save him.

"Thought about it," Jaysa said. "Then I thought, how can I possibly cause him the right amount of pain he deserves? You know what I came up with?" She shot him through the leg. Sabas dropped with a scream, blood pumping freely from the large hole.

"I switched off the explosive charge," Jaysa said as she

walked toward him. She stood far enough back from Sabas and glanced over the edge of the rock into the lake where large fins broke the surface of the water. "Looks like your blood has caused a bit of a stir."

Sabas understood in an instant what Jaysa had planned. "Kill me," he begged. "Please."

Jaysa shot him through the shoulder then the other leg. "You were going to torture me to death. You were going have your fun, and then you were going to murder me. There's zero chance you deserve a good death." She kicked Sabas in the face, breaking his nose. Jaysa tapped the panel on the stock of the coil rifle, reinstating the explosive charge. She moved to the edge of the bridge as Sabas crawled along the rock. Jaysa fired a shot into the rock itself. A second, third and fourth shot.

The bridge crumbled.

Sabas screamed as the rock gave way and he plunged into the cold water.

She watched from the bank as he tried to swim, tried to get away from the dorsal fins that rose out of the water nearby. Sabas screamed again as he was dragged under the water, immediately bobbing back up.

"Kill me," he shouted.

Jaysa raised her rifle and looked through the scope as a huge dorsal fin broke the surface. A moment later, a massive shark sunk dagger-length teeth into Sabas' arm, biting it free from the rest of him.

A second huge shark closed its giant maw over Sabas' chest and the crime boss screamed one last time. He begged wordlessly for a second until he was torn apart. She lowered her rifle; he hadn't been worth the waste of a round.

"You done?" Etamus asked when Jaysa walked past the ruins' entrance. "I figured you wanted to do this alone."

Jaysa was thankful for that. "Yeah, let's go back to the ship."

They were silent during the walk back toward the Onnab town square, and twenty minutes later they found Gusin still sat with the synth.

"I heard shooting," the councillor said.

"It's done now," Jaysa told him and walked off before he could ask anything else.

CHAPTER THIRTY-THREE

Felix Drake

The sniper-piloted stalker banked hard at the last moment, avoiding Drake's barrage of chain-gun fire. Drake still hadn't strapped himself into the cockpit when he'd seen the ship fly toward him, low and menacing.

With a few seconds of respite, Drake activated the cockpit's safety measures, and the seat moulded itself to his body, the straps appearing from the side, and fastening around him, keeping him in place as he planted his feet on the pedals in front of him. He pushed with his right foot and the stalker accelerated after the sniper. Drake used the pad on either side of the seat to move the craft, tapping the buttons to fire the chain-gun when the sniper's ship was close enough. The control panel allowed him to change the weapons selected, as well as adjust the shields, and allow the ship to take full control of flight or weapon duties. Unfortunately, Drake liked neither as he'd always found the computer to be too conservative in their approach to either flying or shooting.

He pushed the throttle, and banked hard to the left, tracking the sniper's ship but keeping an eye on the number in the top left of the panel. He'd reset it once when getting into the stalker, and it showed how far from the lift-off point he was. The number continued increasing as Drake stayed with the sniper, taking shots as needed, and trying to cause the enemy stalker to turn back toward the camp.

Just before the distance hit four miles, the enemy ship banked to the left again, and pulled up, flying higher and higher into the dense cloud coverage. Drake activated the ship's shields, and the canopy was encased in a thin, metal-fibre sheet. From then on, Drake had to use the built in mask that allowed him to use the ships sensors to fly the ship.

With his view now superimposed with a green hue, Drake flew into the clouds, and immediately banked to the right as chain-gun fire tried to intercept him. Drake dropped the ship out of the clouds, and raced toward the ground while the stalker's alarm warned of enemy fire.

"I know there's enemy fire," Drake shouted. "That's why I'm flying away from it." It didn't do anything to stop the alarm, but it made him feel marginally better.

Missiles exploded to the left of his stalker, forcing Drake to push forward on the throttle, before immediately shoving it to the right, almost spinning the ship as it turned toward the camp. Drake dropped the stalker's countermeasures – tiny, explosive shrapnel that would misdirect any missiles, with the added effect of damaging the sniper's craft should he fly through them.

As Drake flew over the camp, he slammed the thrusters into reverse, a move that would have killed him were it not for the ship absorbing the impact of such a sudden shift in acceleration and trajectory. The sniper was clearly unprepared for such a maneuverer. It flew by, allowing Drake to fire several missiles, all of which detonated harmlessly in the countermeasures the sniper deployed. When Drake was certain the shrapnel had vanished, he fired his last missile, which streaked through the air, smashing into the stalker's right engine, spinning it around toward Drake's ship.

The sniper fired the chain-gun, and Drake immediately

pulled up on the throttle, but only in time to avoid the energy blasts from the chain-gun tearing apart the cockpit. Instead, they ripped into the belly of Drake's stalker, causing even more alarms to sound and various readouts to vanish.

Drake kept the ship heading vertically as he assessed the damage. The shields had stopped most of the shots but they were weakened and would be unable to take much more damage. He dropped the stalker forward, down toward the sniper's ship, which was billowing black smoke from one of its three engines. Drake opened fire with the chain-gun but the sniper activated the shields, and Drake was moving too fast to get another shot off before he'd flown past the damaged enemy ship.

He banked hard to the right before diverting as much power as he could to the weapons, hoping the extra energy would punch straight through the shield and end the fight. As he neared, something smashed into the side of the stalker, causing the alarms to sound once again. Drake performed a scan of the ground below, and found someone with a rifle inside the remains of a building. A second shot went through the shield over the right wing, tearing through the casing around it. Drake glanced over at the sniper's stalker, and it exploded just as the sniper ejected. At least he wasn't a threat anymore.

Drake pushed the throttle, and turned his attention to the attacker inside the ruined house. He opened fire, the chain-gun making short work of the building's remains where the attacker was hidden before he flew past at high speed. He slowed the engines and turned the ship, performing another scan as he went, but found no traces of life inside the rubble.

He flew back toward the camp, hoping to land the stalker somewhere in the area, and hunt for the sniper before the man managed to flee. As he got within a half mile of the camp, he was met with the third stalker. It hovered above the campsite, as if awaiting Drake's return.

"You didn't think you could get rid of me that easily, did

you?" the sniper said through the communication channel, his words punctuated with a grunt of pain.

Drake cursed himself; he should have destroyed the third stalker before engaging in combat, but he hadn't considered the possibility the sniper would simply eject from one ship to get into the other.

When Drake opened fire, the stalker didn't move, allowing the energy rounds to collide with the shield before unleashing a barrage of missiles, all of which exploded between Drake and the sniper, bathing the whole area in sparking blue and green mist. Drake knew a partial missile when he saw it. He tried the same trick as before—to slam the throttle into full reverse—but the ship refused, throwing up alarms all across the control panel. Drake had no choice but to fly into the particle cloud.

The instant the stalker touched the cloud, all internal instruments stopped working. The shields vanished, removing the metal-fibre from above the cockpit, bathing Drake in light that made him blink. The ship continued on the same trajectory, only now it was racing toward the ground at high speed, and with no power, there was no way to eject safety.

Chain-gun fire tore through the side of the stalker's hull as the sniper chased after Drake, trying to ensure he didn't survive the upcoming crash.

Drake had no choice but to brace for impact and hope for the best, but when he saw how close he was going to crash to the river, the flicker of a plan emerged. Particle missiles didn't work in space or in water, which meant if he could reach the river, the water would wash away the particles. The ship was waterproof, and hopefully from there he'd be able to restart the engines and escape. Or he'd slowly suffocate as his air supply ran out. Neither were great choices, but he had to work with what he had.

He reached around to the side of the seat until he found the handle he was looking for. From previous experience, stalkers had a problem with heat. Putting three powerful engines in a combat craft the size of a stalker was asking for trouble, and if they ever took fire, there was genuine probability the engine would start to build up heat until exploding. In the event of a heavy landing, the crafts had a tendency to vent that heat all around the ship. People had died because they'd gotten too close to crashed stalkers before they'd vented.

To combat this, the designers installed a manual vent mechanism. There was a way to use it through the control panel, but that was currently fried, so the manual release was all Drake had. He had only one chance to do this as venting would shove the stalker forward several dozen feet from the sheer force of the expulsion.

Drake waited, the world almost moving in slow motion around him as the stalker dropped closer and closer to the ground. More chain-gun fire tore into the left wing, but without the control panel, Drake was helpless to know exactly what damage had been done.

He grabbed the straps that held him in place and braced for impact. Drake kept his eyes open as the ship slammed into the ground, his body jerking violently. His head crashed into the back of the seat. For a second his vision darkened, and he forgot what he was meant to do. How he wished he had access to his aether, although if he had, he'd have never needed to get into a stalker in the first place.

He dropped his hand to the side of the chair, found the lever and pulled, dumping vast amounts of heat from the rear of the ship as it skidded along the ground. The force blasted the stalker several feet into the air, taking it over the edge of the cliff, where it spiralled down into the dark river below.

The ship sank deeper and deeper into the darkness, quickly consuming it. Something huge moved past the window, just outside of visible range. He'd seen the shark fins when he'd escaped from Sabas' camp. Knew how dangerous the creatures could be, and hoped the lack of external movement on the part of the stalker meant they'd ignore it. It had been a long day, and having to fight off sharks was not going to be a good way to end it.

He engaged the power to the ship, and the control panel flashed on for a second before falling back into silence. Without power, there were no lights on the ship, which was probably for the best. Something bumped into the ship, moving it slightly, but by the time Drake had turned to look, whatever had done it was already gone.

Drake breathed out slowly, trying to remain calm as the ship continued to sink. He had no idea just how deep the river ran, but hoped the ship would fire to life before they reached the bottom. Getting out of the water was one thing, landing on rocks and mud, possibly damaging the ship further… well, that was something else entirely.

He flicked the power on again, and once more the control panel came to life. Instruments and readings flashed up all around the cockpit. Systems activated one after the other, including the external lights, which Drake really wished hadn't happened when he saw the ten-foot shark swim past. A second followed, equally as large, but darted away when the light touched it. Drake spotted half a dozen more sharks, all cruising around the ship, mostly ignoring him, or swimming away if the light stayed on them for too long.

The engine spluttered to life, keeping the ship from sinking further, just as the head of a gigantic shark came into view. It dwarfed the stalker, and must have been about forty feet in length as it swam through the depths. It neared the stalker, and Drake thumbed the chain-gun in case it decided to get a little too interested in the smaller ship, but it soon changed direction and disappeared into the darkness.

Drake ran a diagnostic and discovered there were damaged readings all over the ship. Part of the wing and belly were destroyed, and Drake didn't think the ship could handle any more dogfighting once out of the water. He needed a plan, and fast. He routed all non-essential power to the scanners, and moved the thrusters to lift the ship slowly through the water.

Eventually, it was high enough in the river that the scanners could break the surface. Drake got readings for another stalker hovering above the river. Presumably, the sniper was waiting for Drake to emerge, or he was gloating at his death. Either way, Drake planned to punish that mistake.

He moved the thrusters so the ship's nose pointed toward the surface. Drake's plan was probably not what one would call safe, or wise, or… well, Bokk would probably not give him good odds. The image of his friend, broken and crumpled, reignited Drake's anger and defiance. He wasn't about to be beaten by some two-bit murderer with ideas about his station. He was Felix Drake. Warden. Atoned. His father was one of the greatest generals the Union ever produced. His mother a high-ranking member of the military before the war, a warrior without equal. Drake rested his foot on the throttle, and prepared to carry out his plan.

The large shark swam into view just over head, and Drake once again thumbed the chain-gun. The creature was a complication he hadn't considered, and he was loath to hurt something just for doing what came naturally, but he needed a clear shot to the surface, and several tons of shark would make that difficult.

Drake checked the available weapons on the stalker and saw there were still several shrapnel deployments available. He put a timer on them before dumping them from the rear of the ship. They tumbled down into the river until softly detonating a few seconds later. The vibration had the desired effect, and the great shark shot down past the stalker to investigate. Drake pushed the throttle as high as it would go, and thumbed off the drive lock.

The effect was immediate and spectacular.

Drake's stalker shot up toward the surface like a bullet, breaking the calm of the water, and speeded into the air toward the second stalker, which hovered a short distance ahead.

Drake launched all of the particle missiles he had on board, bathing the sniper's ship in the cloud of blue.

It dropped from the sky like a stone.

Straight into Drake's path.

He held the ship as long as he dared before releasing the ejector seat. Drake was thrown out of the stalker at a horizontal angle, and the resulting explosion as the two stalkers impacted, caused a shockwave that drove Drake farther back. He almost laughed when he landed up on the cliff where he'd been kept captive not that long ago. The seat kept him from serious harm as it tore through the ground, and eventually, he came to a stop and sighed in relief. He unfastened the seat's harness, and rolled out onto the ground.

"So, that *was* you," a welcomed voice said.

Drake looked up at Jaysa, who offered him her hand. He took it, and she helped him to his feet as Gusin and Etamus joined them.

"Everyone dead?" Jaysa asked.

Drake nodded. "They are on my end. You?"

"Sabas was eaten by a shark," Etamus said. "A really big shark."

"I think I saw it," Drake told her. He couldn't feel much sympathy for a man who'd brought as much pain and suffering to as many people as Sabas and his allies had over the years.

Jaysa looked at the blood on his arms and clothing. "Had fun?"

Drake shook his head. "Not a whole lot, no. You?"

Jaysa shrugged. "Killed a lot of bad people, and I can't say I'm going to feel all that unhappy about their deaths."

"There's a problem with the ship," Drake told her.

"What problem?" Jaysa asked, her tone making it very clear that angering her any further than had already been done was probably a bad idea.

"Sounds like Sabas brought some friends," Drake said. "The crew are coming down once they've dealt with the matter."

"Sabas is dead," Etamus said. "This Alastia sent him to kill us."

Drake nodded. "I get the feeling we're far from done here."

The clouds above them parted as the *Sunstorm* slowly lowered out of the sky. It landed close to where Sabas and his people had, and Drake noticed the damage sustained across the ship's hull.

The external door opened, and the ramp from the *Sunstorm* descended. Sateri was the first one out of the ship, followed closely by the rest of the crew.

"Everyone okay?" Drake asked.

"Sabas left some people for us to fight," Sateri said. "Other than that, we're good."

"Nice of him," Drake replied.

"We thought so," Rollos said, sporting a nasty looking bump to the head that Yanton was trying unsuccessfully to look at.

"Let the doctor do his job," Drake told him.

Rollos rolled his eyes, but did as he was told.

Sateri smiled. "We have a few superficial injuries, and the ship took a bit of damage, but nothing too serious."

"How much damage?" Jaysa asked.

"A few days repair," Rosie said. "I need to run a full diagnostic, but we should be good to go soon enough."

"Okay, everyone gets a few days to rest and to help fix stuff," Drake said. "Rosie, can you come with me. Luca too." The three of them walked off to find Xendo, who had been placed nearby.

"I don't know," she said. "Where's Bokk?"

Drake removed Bokk's memory from his pocket. "They didn't make it. Their body is still in the catacombs below. I don't want it left there."

It took a short time for Luca to go with Drake and help him find Bokk's body, the pair of them carrying it back up to where Rosie remained beside Xendo.

"You okay?" Rosie asked, placing her hand on his shoulder

as Drake placed his friend on the ground, and remained crouched beside Bokk.

Drake shook his head, unable to put into words what he was feeling. "Can you fix them?"

Rosie stared at the prototype synth, scanning them with her comm unit, before doing the same to Bokk.

We'll sure try, Luca said.

Rosie finished scanning. "We'll do everything we can, I promise."

"The ship takes priority," Drake said, hating himself for saying it.

Bokk and Xendo were quickly loaded on-board the ship, and people found things to do. Drake had spent a few hours repairing one of the damaged landing gear, and was getting some water when Rollos and Sateri turned up.

"So, some mystery woman set us all up?" Rollos asked, sporting a line of medical gel on his forehead to stop the bleeding.

"Yes," Drake said. "I'm unsure how to find her, or figure out who she even is."

"Question is, what do we do about her?" Sateri asked.

"Nothing right now," Drake said. "We find Metan. Then we use him to find her. And after that, we nail them both and let the law deal with their remains. First, we go home. We go back to Atharoth and inform the King of Stars that we tracked down one of the people responsible for the murders of Helice, Septimus, and Trinas, and we tell him we need to find Metan. And then we go hunting again, but not until we know exactly where Metan is. I'm not going to be blindsided for a second time."

Drake walked off with Sateri, leaving the rest of the group to talk, and found Rosie crouched under the interceptor.

"You come to help, or get away from everyone else?" Rosie asked without looking over at them.

"Just wanted to see how you were doing," Drake said. "It's been a few hours since you arrived, and I thought you might want some assistance."

"You can pass me that," Rosie said, pointing to a nearby tool that Drake couldn't identify.

"How long?" Sateri asked, passing the tool to Rosie before Drake could pick it up.

"An hour or two. The blast you managed to dodge so... *effectively*, knocked a few things out of alignment."

"Is that sarcasm I hear?" Sateri asked with a smile on her face.

"Not me, no boss," Rosie said.

"I'll leave you to it," Sateri told Rosie, and looked over at Drake. "You okay?"

Drake nodded. "I need to go talk to Jaysa. She handed herself well. And I think we're all in the same boat here."

"She walked back off toward the ruins," Rosie said. "I think she had some things to deal with."

"You're in charge, Sateri," Drake told her.

"Always," Sateri said with a smile.

Drake grinned back, and headed off to look for Jaysa. He found her some distance from the rest of the group, and sat on the remains of a wall beside her. "You okay for company?"

Jaysa nodded.

"You did a good job keeping people alive down here," Drake said. "Even Gusin, who is actually helping out and not pretending he needs to lie down."

"No problem," Jaysa said without emotion. "You have a good team."

"A team you're now a member of, whether you like it or not," Drake said. "Whoever this Alastia is, she set us all up, Jaysa. I don't think she'll be thrilled about her plans falling apart. We'll get to her, I promise. I'd like to work with you on this, not have you run off looking for vengeance."

"Never thought about it," Jaysa said, not looking at Drake.

"Liar," he said with a smirk.

Jaysa stared at Drake for a few seconds. "Okay, I did think about it. I'm angry."

"Me too," Drake said. "First, we need long-range comms, and Rosie tells me she can't fix those with the parts available. Which means the plan hasn't changed. Back to Atharoth. I want you to consider joining the team full-time." He offered her his hand.

Jaysa looked at it. "Do I have to take orders from you?"

"Yes, but I'm not really much of a give-orders kind of person," Drake said. "I just expect people to do their jobs."

Jaysa stood and took Drake's hand. "I'm in. Let's go make sure Onnab doesn't happen anywhere else."

CHAPTER THIRTY-FOUR

Felix Drake

Three months later.

Despite Drake being outed as the son of a traitor, his entire team received a hero's welcome when they arrived back on Atharoth a week after the battle on Onnab. A few days later, work returned to normal. Or whatever passed for normal when Wardens were concerned. A few more councillors were implicated over the coming weeks, and charges were brought against them, while several others resigned their commissions and left the planet.

Drake found himself sat on the roof of his skyblock with his entire team, looking over the city's nightscape.

"How's Bokk?" Sateri asked, raising a glass of beer to Drake.

"They've been placed inside an upgraded body, so they're pretty happy," Drake said. "I think they like the recon shell more than their old one." Bokk was in a state-of-the-art recon-synth shell, courtesy of the King of Stars wanting to do something as a reward for everyone who had taken part.

What about Jaysa and Etamus? Luca asked.

"They couldn't come tonight," Rollos said.

"I came though," Yanton said with a smile. The doctor had really come into his own since arriving on Atharoth, and had been more than helpful in several cases since they'd returned.

"Any luck finding Metan?" Tuck asked.

"None," Rosie said. "He has officially vanished."

The roof of the skyblock was bug free, it was why Drake only allowed talk of Metan up here. Even so, Rosie had activated the jamming systems on everyone's comm units.

"We'll find Metan and everyone working with him," Celine said. "I've ensured you keep your status to go anywhere in Union space for your jobs. And I'd quite like this Alastia person nailed to a wall."

"Ren hugged me," Sateri said after several minutes of less work-orientated conversation. "It was weird."

Drake laughed. "She's not much for showing emotion."

The door to the roof opened and Etamus and Jaysa appeared, both carrying large bags of food and drink. "We decided to be social," Jaysa said and held the door open for Kimi.

Drake raised his glass to them all, and got to his feet. "I'm sorry Metan got away, I hope what we achieved with Sabas helps with the loss of your Suns Watch friends."

Kimi smiled. "It does, thank you."

The conversations flitted between work and as normal a social-life as Wardens and princesses ever have, until Rosie said, "Actually, I think I have something about Metan. I didn't want to say anything until I was sure."

"Is it a big map with an X on it?" Dai'ix asked. "Because that would help."

"I've been looking into anything Expedited Systems was working with," Rosie said, ignoring Dai'ix. "It's hidden under several layers of shit, but there're at least another six research stations with a link to them. Unfortunately, they also seem to be decommissioned, so I've been going through each one in turn to find any evidence of life there. It's not a fast process, but

I'm hoping if Metan was involved in what happened with that Genesis-Alpha stuff, he was involved in other projects with Sabas' fingerprints on them."

"So, we're getting a step closer," Sateri said.

Hopefully, anyway, Luca said, as Sateri kissed him on the lips.

"You sicken me," Rollos said with a playful laugh.

"We go about everything as normal," Drake said. "We've been doing it for three months, and we're getting ever closer. It won't be long before we have concrete information on them."

"And in the meantime," Jaysa said, raising a bottle of something Drake wasn't sure of. "This is meant to be a joyous occasion, and celebration of another case cleared. So, can we all please drink our troubles away like adults are meant to?"

After several hours, Drake found himself alone on the opposite side of the roof, out of sight of the festivities when Sateri appeared next to him. "You still feel bad for your friends?"

"Helice wanted to make amends," Drake said. "I just wish she'd sent that message and maybe she'd have confided in me."

"And you'd be dead," Sateri pointed out. When Drake didn't reply, she said, "You ever think it's weird that apart from being held up as heroes, we're not actually seen differently from when we left? We're still Wardens. We're still led by the son of a traitor, and some in the Council still seem poised for you to try and overthrow them."

"I've noticed it too, I just don't care anymore," Drake said, exhausted by the whole thing. "Gusin knows what happened, and I actually think he might be on our side. Hey, whatever happened to Xendo?"

"Taken to some secure military facility and no one has seen him since," Sateri said. "No one has even mentioned what happened on Onnab since we returned. It's like they either want to forget or hope everyone else does."

"The Council quite possibly has more traitors in their midst, and they're blind to it," Drake said softly.

"We'll just have to open their eyes then," Rollos said as he walked over. "I wondered where you'd gone."

Drake took the beer Rollos offered, and took a swig. He looked behind him as the rest of the team arrived carrying a lot more food. They'd gone for a supply run.

"Speech," Jaysa shouted. "Make it a good one."

But not a long one, Luca said, making everyone laugh. He'd managed to connect with the new members of the team quite well, and after the initial headaches everyone suffered from his telepathic connection, they were now used to it.

"I wish to agree with Jaysa," Bokk said, having joined the group while Drake was by himself.

Drake still found it strange to see them in their new body, looking just like the synth that had tried to kill him back at the skyblock. It was good to see them back. Drake had been scared Bokk would never be alive again, and been tearful when told their personality and memory chips were comparable.

"Okay," Drake said, raising his bottle. "We've got more bad guys to find, and a way of life to protect. We *will* find those responsible, and we *will* stop them. This is just the beginning. And anyone who hopes to hurt the people we love and protect, are going to find out just how bad we can make their lives."

"Stirring speech," Celine said.

Drake looked up at the sky. Wherever Metan was, Drake hoped he was living his life to the best of his ability because soon enough, Drake would find him, and destroy whatever plans he and his allies had concocted. He would make sure of it.

ACKNOWLEDGEMENTS

Atoned is the first part of my new Science Fiction series that I started work on many years ago. It had gone through many different versions until it reached one I was happy enough to actually get published.

As always, a huge thank you to my wife, Vanessa, and our three daughters, Keira, Faith, and Harley. They're a large part of the reason I write, and why I started writing so many years ago.

To my agent Paul Lucas for being supportive, helpful, and just all around awesome.

To Amanda J Spedding, my editor, who helped turn my words into something readable. It's never anything less than a pleasure to work with you.

A massive thanks to Jamie Nobel, for his amazing cover. I look forward to working with you in the future.

To my friends and family, and everyone who has been behind me the whole way, thank you.

To all of my Patreon members, you guys helped get this book published, and your continued support is always appreciated. And a special thank you to members Charles Burkett, Paul Boobyer, Lydia A. Dean, Vicky Hayward, and Yair Mayer.

ABOUT THE AUTHOR

Steve Mchugh

Steve is a bestselling author of Urban Fantasy and Science Fiction books. His novel, Scorched Shadows, was shortlisted for a Gemmell Award for best novel. He was born in Mexborough, South Yorkshire, but now lives with his wife and three young daughters in Southampton.

Amazon UK https://amzn.to/2KqGrys
Amazon USA https://amzn.to/34The9s
Twitter https://twitter.com/StevejMchugh
Facebook https://www.facebook.com/hellequinchronicles/
Instagram https://www.instagram.com/stevem

Printed in Great Britain
by Amazon